ROAR OF THE SKY

INFINARA DRAGONS 1

CALLA ZAE

PROSE & CONCEPTS

Roar of the Sky

Copyright © 2025 by Calla Zae

Cover Art Copyright: Calla Zae

Character Art Copyright: Zelly Ink

All Other Interior Art: Calla Zae

Editor: Anna Nesbitt

Copy Editor: Lindsay York at LY Publishing

Proofreader: Violet Rae

Prose & Concepts LLC

210 Park Avenue, Suite #280

Worcester, MA 01609

www.proseandconcepts.com

Email: info@proseandconcepts.com

Library of Congress Cataloging-in-Publication Data

Library of Congress Control Number: 2025937656

First edition Ebook ISBN: 978-1-952820-64-9

First edition Paperback ISBN: 978-1-952820-65-6

Hardcover ISBN: 978-1-952820-66-3

Special Edition Hardcover ISBN: 978-1-952820-67-0

For those who feel the roar in their hearts.

"Wherever you go, go with all your heart."
— Confucius

·

·

"The truth is not always beautiful, nor beautiful words the truth."
— Lao Tzu

Aldabaran O
Northern Empire
The Great Nasu
Western Empire
The Nasu Channel
Shelleeta Ocean
Bay of Sighs
N
W
E
S

Chanti
Funan
Sokara Sea
Eastern
Empire
tral
pire
Southern
Empire
Lin Din Ni
Tealock Sea
Wan
Formalhalt
Ocean
aeda Sea
The Infinara Dragon World
Map Design by Calla Zae

Central
Empire
Rebel Territory
Central Border
Emerald
Song
Valley
Western
Empire
Persimmon
City
Western Border
Ming
Shan
Dai
Shan
Sun Wheat
Village
N
Orchaeda Sea
W
E
S

Southern
Empire
Southern Border
Green
Fog
Lake
Green Fog River
Market
Square
Jade
Junction
Tealock Sea
Lotus Crane
Harbor
Lin Din Ni
Map Design by Calla Zae

PRONUNCIATION & GLOSSARY

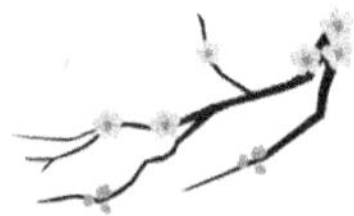

Locations:
  Lin Din Ni: Lynn Din Nie
  Luklum: Look-lum - Capital City

Characters:
  Wen Hung: When Hung
  Zhao Mei Su: Jow May Sue
  Mẹ: Meh (Mom/Mother)
  Ba: Bah (Dad/Father)
  Zhou Ren: Jow Ren
  Shen Luzi: Shen Loo-Zee
  Tang Li Wei: Tahng Lee Way
  Jayaatu Yeeva: Jai-ah-too Yee-vah
  Ru Malik: Roo Mah-Leek
  Huang Yunxi: Hwang Yoon-cee
  Keiya: Kay-ya
  Chun Kai: Choon Kai
  Li Tao: Lee Tow
  Gong: Goong
  Churan: Chew-Ran

Items:
> **Dudou**: Doo-Dough - undergarment
> **Ingot**: Ing-Get - oblong piece of metal used as currency
> **Pipa**: Pee-Pah - pear-shaped instrument with strings

PROLOGUE
SU

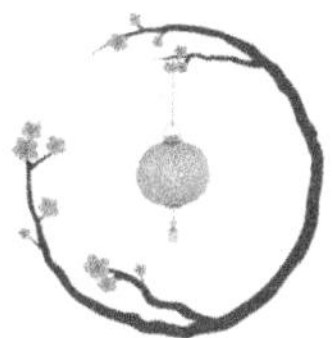

WITH MY HEART drumming in my chest, I snuck down the dirt path that led into the lush forest where I practiced my kung fu in secret. I had an hour to myself before I needed to return to the City Apothecary to treat patients. I shouldn't have felt guilty about learning something that interested me, but teachers, artisans, court officials, and women my age insisted that a woman was better suited to more delicate hobbies.

Who made up that rule? And why should one rule apply to everyone? People were allowed to have different interests and views. I didn't like eating chili peppers or lemongrass, but that didn't mean something was wrong with me, right? Having a different preference didn't make me an incapable healer, artisan, or whatever I wanted to be.

A bird cawed somewhere in the distance as though it agreed with me. Leaving the path and heading into the woods, I rushed to my usual spot with my instructional kung fu pamphlet safely tucked into my tunic. I'd purchased it from an old bookstore.

The clearing was still the same as ever, surrounded by trees, flowers, bushes, rocks, and moss. I hadn't been here in a while, but nothing seemed out of place. I constantly feared someone might have discovered my hidden sanctuary, and I'd need to find another space to practice.

"Hello there." I smiled at the moss, sat on the ground, ran my fingers into its softness, and felt its healing energy. The vibrant green brightened everything else around it. The energy here thrummed with vitality compared to the moss growing closer to the city.

Fully aware of my limited time, I took out the pamphlet and placed it beside me. I straightened my spine and squared my shoulders, preparing to drop into myself. I had to do this each time before reading the pamphlet. It cleared my head so I could understand the lessons and diagrams better.

Having a teacher would help even more. There were certain parts of the book I didn't understand. For all I knew, I could be interpreting the illustrations all wrong. But where would I find a teacher willing to teach a twenty-two-year-old woman? I wouldn't enroll in a school either—I'd be the biggest kid in a beginner's class. They wouldn't accept me anyway. The school only taught boys. I rolled my eyes at how few options girls had to pursue their dreams. Painting, poetry, cooking, or jewelry classes didn't interest me. But those classes taught all genders. So why limit martial arts to only boys?

If I had a daughter or a little sister, I'd demand they change the rules. But I had neither, so I didn't have an excuse.

Take a breather. Change takes time, Su.

I had to be careful how I conducted myself. I didn't want my actions to affect where I worked and lived at the City Apothecary. Everyone there worked hard to serve the community on a sliding scale basis. People paid what they could. If they couldn't, it was free. But most clients always paid and came bearing gifts and food for the staff.

You're here for kung fu. Focus.

I straightened my posture and concentrated on my breathwork. Breathing was a vital action that most people had forgotten how to do properly. When stressed, people held their breath, suffocating their energy flow. But I needed all the energy I could muster to tap into my essa, a higher frequency life force comprised of pure energy.

I took a deep breath, letting the energy fill my lungs. The fresh air in the forest heightened all sensation around and within me. I closed my eyes and breathed in and out until my body relaxed. Practicing in my bedroom was useful during inclement weather, but immersing myself in nature was a hundred times better. Everything was made of energy, and learning how to channel it was the first step in becoming a warrior.

Yes. A warrior.

The desire to be a skilled fighter zipped through me. I could be a warrior and a healer, couldn't I? Who said I had to choose one or the other? Who said I had to choose anything at all?

Stay focused.

Tingles rose on my skin as my mind cleared of responsibilities. All the irritation from the difficult patients slid away, leaving me in stillness. For a moment, it felt like I'd stepped into another world with completely distinct energy.

A sound echoed around me, and I honed in on it. *Birds?* No. The sounds jumbled together as though several people were whispering.

"There are six of them," said a female voice.

An electrical current raced along my spine as she continued to speak.

"How do you even know that?" asked an adorable voice that sounded like a little kid. *"They're still inside you."*

"I just know." She laughed, and I didn't know how, but I could sense the joy in her. *"They're growing fast."*

I opened my eyes and looked around me. No one was in this sacred space. Why was I hearing this conversation? I waited a beat, but the talking stopped. When I closed my eyes, it started again.

"Does anyone know you're pregnant?" asked the cute voice. It sounded like a boy. Was that her son?

"*Not yet. But they will soon. It's inevitable.*"

"*When will they hatch?*" he asked. "*I can't wait to meet them.*"

"*Soon. I'm going to need your help. The timing has to be right.*"

Who were these people? Were they raising chickens? Were they talking about chicken eggs? I remembered holding baby chicks in my hands when I was a child. They were so precious.

"*Okay. But when is that?*" the boy asked.

"*They're waiting for the spark. Have you forgotten that timing is everything, little one? They have to connect to the perfect essa.*"

Just like me trying to hone my essa through my kung fu practice.

"*Timing is everything and nothing at all,*" said the little boy.

Right now, he sounded too wise to be little.

"*Keep speaking in riddles, and you'll confuse yourself.*"

"*Not riddles, but secrets of the universe. You taught me that, remember?*" He paused and continued, "*Clash of Thunder is thinking of you.*"

"*As am I of him. We'll see each other soon.*"

"*Yes, you will. How are you feeling?*"

"*Happy and tired,*" she said. "*The Cosmos is changing, and we all have to contribute to maintain the balance.*"

"*But at what cost?*" asked the adorable voice.

"*Whatever it takes,*" she said.

An image of a feral eye flashed before my vision, startling me. I opened my eyes, and the image disappeared. Curious, I shut my eyes again, and the image reappeared. The single eye belonged to some creature, and its iris appeared like a dark night, twinkling with moving stars and mysteries. The image zoomed out, allowing me to see two powerful eyes staring at me. I couldn't see the face they belonged to. But the skin texture around the eyes had a rough and intricate pattern. The more we stared at each other, the more my skin heated.

"*Who's the intruder?*" asked the cute voice.

Was he referring to me? It wasn't intentional. It wasn't like I barged into a room where two people were talking.

Maybe *they* had intruded on *my* meditation!

The eye flashed again, looking right at me. For a moment, the irises shifted, and the starry night disappeared, replaced with a blue sky with floating clouds. Lines crinkled around the eye as though the creature were smiling. Or getting ready to attack its prey.

I wasn't listening to a conversation between a woman and her son but a creature and her child.

The scar on my arm flared like hot metal touching my skin.

"There you are," said the creature.

A powerful roar erupted, and the sound vibrated my entire being. Fear pierced the magical bubble, and I instinctively opened my eyes. The ground appeared unaffected, but my body thrummed from the roar. It carried an energy that swished through me like it was sweeping things out of me. My muscles contracted, and my organs shifted. I inhaled a breath and blew it out as I tried to balance my energy.

I must've achieved a deep meditation today. Digging into my silk satchel, I glanced at the clock made from jade and wood. *Fire-hell!* How had I meditated for forty minutes? Or had I tapped into something I wasn't supposed to?

I'd heard wild stories of people who could tap into fantastical worlds during meditation. I loved listening to those stories, even though they seemed farfetched. But right now, I couldn't help but wonder if I had just done that.

The heat in my body intensified as the scar on my forearm illuminated.

"I've been searching for you."

CHAPTER ONE

SU

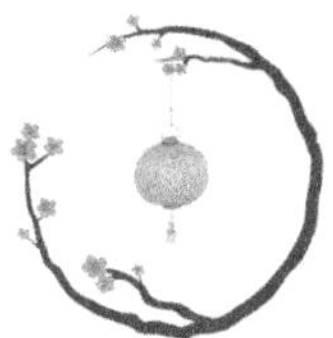

NERVES TUMBLED inside me as I pressed my ear to the door, ensuring no one was walking outside in the courtyard in front of my bedroom. They shouldn't be at this late hour, but I didn't want to risk it. I threw on a set of gray men's clothing I'd gotten from a thrift store, tied my hair into a bun, and covered it with a scholar hat tall enough to hide the bun. Grabbing the small porcelain jar, I dabbed my cheek with an indigo paste made from the indigo plant.

I looked in the mirror at the fake birthmark and bushy eyebrows gracing my face. Not bad at all. My disguise as a man would suffice tonight. No one would recognize me as Zhao Mei Su, a healer at the City Apothecary.

Satisfied with my look, I opened my bedroom door and peered out, glancing around. Though the weather had been stormy lately, the moon glowed like a pearl in the sky tonight. I took that as a good omen for what I was about to do. I waited for a beat, listening for incoming footsteps. Nothing sounded as I surveyed the area. The lanterns hanging from the wooden beams cast a soft glow to the corridor surrounding the courtyard.

My gaze slid to the window that belonged to Healer Churan's bedroom. As the owner of the City Apothecary, she often worked late. But no candlelight shone through the window tonight. All the healers had their bedrooms in the courtyard, at the back of the apothecary. We all got free room and board for working here.

I didn't see any candlelight in Yunxi's room. Relief settled in me as I stepped out, closed the door quietly, and exited the courtyard through the back door.

Outside, I looked up at the sky and saw strips of wispy clouds cutting through the moon.

Storms, please stay away.

We'd had enough rain, lightning, and thunder to last us for months. The herb garden could use some sunlight. So could all of Luklum, for that matter.

Too many deaths had occurred in our city recently. Everyone was stressed about it, including me. Sick people had come to the apothecary for help, but I couldn't help them. Their symptoms escalated too fast, and the medicine we had didn't help. Most had died before my eyes. I hated feeling hopeless.

What kind of illness had invaded Luklum? The bustling city had flourished, drawing merchants from neighboring towns and distant empires eager to trade. But lately, the number of merchants had dwindled. I didn't blame them. No one wanted to risk sickness or death to sell wares. A strange illness had entered this city, and I had to know what it was. Tonight, I'd get answers.

Straightening my posture, I tried my best to walk like a man. I made my way down the dark street with only a few lanterns dangling from the roofs of homes and businesses. I passed the time announcer, an older man with long white hair wearing a brown cotton tunic and pants. He nodded at me as he hit the gong three times with his stick, announcing the rat hour, the time between eleven at night and one in the morning. Normal people would be asleep right now, especially given the mysterious illness. Not to mention the missing people that had perplexed the authorities.

We'd never had anyone go missing until Uncle Shen reported his brother and family missing two weeks ago. Aunt Mai bought herbal remedies and body soap only months ago. I remembered her adorable and well-behaved children, Luzi and Bao. I'd given them dried dates to eat while they sat on the bench waiting for their mother to shop. Some kids ran around the store, touching things they shouldn't. Luzi and Bao had manners. What had happened to the Shen family? No bodies had been found.

Stay focused, Su. You can worry about them later.

I rushed to Samo's Meat Shop, hoping to see the butcher, Samo. He was supposed to meet his friends tonight for some secret gathering related to the illnesses. At least, that was what I'd overheard three days ago when shopping in the Market Square.

I walked up to the vendor stand, but didn't see Samo. Voices sounded from the back. I made my way toward the commotion, staying in the shadows so no one would notice me.

"What took you so long?" Samo asked. "We can't be late for this."

I didn't recognize the other two men, though the tall man looked familiar. Perhaps he'd been to the apothecary for treatment before. All the men carried oil lanterns.

"Urgent matter. Diarrhea, man!" said a short man with a round belly wearing a cotton top and bottom.

"Peng." The taller man in an embroidered satin tunic slapped a playful hand on his shoulder. "Stop eating, and you won't have that issue."

"Shut up, Jie," Peng retorted.

"How come we didn't get a notice this time?" Jie asked.

Samo shrugged. "Maybe he wanted to save time and sent out only one notice. They asked me to inform the others. Here, look." He showed them a piece of paper.

After a glance, the three men walked off. I stayed as far behind as I could without losing sight of them. Though the men whispered, I had no trouble hearing their conversation.

"They're paying us one thousand in gold ingots!" Samo said excitedly. "I could open another shop on the border of Lin Din Ni and the Central Empire. More stores mean more money."

"There are many merchant festivals for us to make money," said Jie.

"We could buy properties around there to make traveling easier too." Peng kicked something on the ground and cursed.

Jie frowned. "But I heard several rebel groups are wreaking havoc at the border."

"I thought the soldiers from the Central Empire had chased them out of the region," Peng said. "Since we're helping the Bloodshade Bandits, maybe they can help protect us."

"With gold, you can buy protection from anyone, Peng." Samo slapped his friend on the back. "Even adept warriors."

"He has a new job for us?" Jie paused in his steps and lifted his hand, carrying the lantern. "Do you know what it is?"

The lantern illuminated his face. I recognized him now—Jie Chen. He was from a noble family and had often visited the City Apothecary with his wife.

"That's what the notice said." Samo shrugged.

"If it's another poison, I want the antidote," Peng said. "I don't want to get sick like those people who drank from the wells. I had to keep reminding my family not to use the public ones."

"I'm sure he'll provide that," Jie replied.

"How can we continue to help him if we're dead?" Samo asked with a laugh.

The other two men laughed, and I wanted to pick up the rock at my foot and whip it into one of their faces.

They were making people sick by infecting the well water— and they were laughing about it. My fingers curled as anger coursed inside me. How could they do this? Innocent people had been coming into the apothecary in droves because of these crimi- nals! They deserved death! I had to report them to the Military Pavilion tomorrow.

It would be easier to just kill these men. If my parents were still alive, they'd be disappointed in me right now.

I was a healer who had sworn to help people, not kill them. I shouldn't harbor violent thoughts.

But I was human, not a monk or a nun. I was prone to all kinds of human emotions, especially when I saw an injustice like this.

Despite my feelings, I suspected something bigger was at play here. Who hired these men? What was their agenda? More importantly, where was the antidote? This could save so many lives.

The men turned down a street and entered an abandoned temple.

"Are you sure this is it?" Peng glanced around at the overgrown bushes. "The last time we met them at a tavern. Ru Malik reserved an entire room and treated us to a delicious meal."

Were they referring to the leader of the ruthless Bloodshade Bandits?

Samo shrugged. "Maybe he wants to be discreet this time."

"More people are getting sick," Jie walked around, using his lantern to survey the area. "He probably doesn't want anyone suspecting anything."

One of the temple walls had completely fallen. I watched, crouching behind a large, toppled column resting on a stone figurine of a tiger with tall grass growing around it.

The men walked to the center of the barely intact room with a rotting roof. They looked at the dais with two long tables. Three chairs with broken legs sat farther back on the raised platform. A statue of a goddess covered with spider webs sat on a large slab of stone with a counter. Several candles flickered on the counter, making the atmosphere eerie. Smoke streamed out of a small iron cauldron on the other end of the counter. A tray of small porcelain cups sat near the cauldron. Who had prepared the candles, cauldron, and cups?

My stomach twisted, signifying something bad was about to happen. I should go, but I couldn't make my feet move. These men had access to the antidote needed to cure the sick people. I couldn't leave without answers.

Their conversation hinted that Ru Malik was meeting them here tonight. If that was true, I needed to know what this evil man looked like. Rumors of his malice had spread all over Lin Din Ni, making people fearful of traveling near the Central Empire. These bandits had taken over an area that belonged to Lin Din Ni and called it Rebel Territory. I wasn't sure why the Imperial Army hadn't fought them to reclaim it. But I assumed it had to do with the wild beasts that existed in that region.

Samo looked around. "Where is he?"

"What's the rush?" asked a deep voice.

A man wearing a black mask that resembled a snake's head stepped out from the shadows. How long had he been standing in the shadows? Had he seen me? Fear skipped down my spine.

A black cape billowed behind him as he moved closer to the dais's edge. Was he Ru Malik? Power, malice, and mystery emanated from him as he stood tall and proud, looking at those below him.

"No rush." Samo offered a sly smile. "We just want to make sure we have the correct time. Don't want to have you waiting."

Two guards stepped out from the shadows at the back of the dais. They wore demonic masks and dark clothing with swords and other weapons slung on their belts.

Ru Malik reached into the pocket of his top and pulled out a packet. "Put this into the four major drinking wells around Luklum. Do this tonight, and there will be extra compensation for your cooperation." He gestured to the reward bags in the guards' hands.

One guard opened a bag, revealing pearls and gems.

The men's eyes lit up, and greedy smiles stretched across their faces.

"More poison?" Samo asked.

"Does it matter?" Ru Malik cocked his head. "You're being paid to complete a task, not to ask questions."

Samo bowed his head. "Understood."

Fury ignited in me. I wished I had the skills to kill Ru Malik, his men, and these traitors. Right now, Ru Malik could kill me easily. I wouldn't get close to him before he whipped his daggers straight into my heart. The apothecary still needed a healthy, dedicated healer to continue treating the citizens.

I had to report this to General Wen immediately. He could take his army and capture Ru Malik and his faction.

One guard walked over to the counter, picked up the tray of cups, and brought it over to Ru Malik.

"Let's seal the deal with a toast of rare wine." Ru Malik grabbed a wine cup and lifted it to the slit on his mask.

The guard brought the tray of cups to the men while the other guard gave them each a bag of ingots and a bag of jewelry.

The men grinned, took the bags, and grabbed the cups.

"To more business ventures!" they cheered.

The guard gave them a packet of powder after they drank. "Do this tonight."

His voice was also deep. It was difficult to tell Ru Malik from his guard. Maybe all evil people sounded alike.

A rat raced across my foot, startling me. I shrieked, but immediately clamped a hand over my mouth. *Shit.*

"Show yourself!" Ru Malik demanded.

I rushed away from the temple, running as quickly as I could in the unfamiliar clothes.

"Get him!" I heard Ru Malik bellow at his men.

Footsteps pounded behind me, but they sounded distant. I hurried behind a shed hidden by overgrown bushes. The dark night hid it well from view. Footsteps soon arrived and paused.

"Ru Malik said to let him go," said a guard. "He won't survive long anyway."

What did he mean by that? Why wouldn't I survive?

Their footfalls faded into the distance. A wolf howled from the woods behind me as a chill rushed through me, followed by a sliver of heat. I couldn't tell if that sensation was my body's reaction from fear of being a wolf's dinner or something else.

I debated rushing toward the Military Pavilion to inform General Wen of my findings. Would he believe me? He seemed like a serious man who didn't like people. How would he react to someone waking him up in the middle of the night?

I glanced down at my attire. How would I explain my disguise to him? Would he believe what I had to say or arrest and interrogate me?

Shit. Firehell.

A slew of curses escaped my mouth. I hadn't expected this predicament. I didn't want my clandestine activities to stain the apothecary's pristine reputation.

Ideas bounced around in my head. The sick residents of Luklum couldn't wait until tomorrow.

I ran to the Military Pavilion, and my heart sank at the closed doors. Lanterns glowed along the poles, illuminating the platform. The guards were probably asleep inside. But I had to try. I climbed up the steps and banged on the wide metal door. I glanced into the dark street behind me, but no one had followed me.

When the door didn't open, I clenched a fist and pounded with all my might. Finally, the door creaked open.

"Do you know what time it is?" a soldier asked, but he was dressed in his Imperial Army navy uniform with a red belt.

"Sorry to wake you. But I overheard Ru Malik telling three men to poison our wells. They were in the abandoned temple. You should ask General Wen to go there now! Is he here?" I looked behind into the pavilion.

"No, he's not here. He's probably at home sleeping right now. I'll send some guards to check out the temple." He studied me. "The wells would be examined tomorrow in daylight. Why are you out so late, sir?"

Oh no. "I haven't been sleeping well," I lied. "I was hoping the fresh air would help me relax."

He nodded, but I could tell he wasn't buying the whole story. I pretended to yawn before he could ask me more questions.

"I'll be back tomorrow to follow up," I said, walking down the steps.

As I headed home, chills and heat battled inside me.

CHAPTER TWO

HUNG

A KNOCK SOUNDED on my door, and I covered the map I'd been examining with a document regarding war strategy. I didn't need unnecessary questions thrown my way, and I certainly didn't want to explain about the map.

"Come in," I said.

Ren Zhou smiled, strode in, closed the door, and turned around to greet me with a fist to his chest. "Prime General. Lina wanted me to drop off some egg tarts for you."

Lina was his younger sister. She was like a sister to me too. Four years younger than me, Ren had no interest in following his father's military footsteps. He preferred the pen over a sword. We had played together as children when my parents were alive.

Rising from my seat, I returned the respectful greeting and walked around my desk, gesturing to the round conference table Emperor Tang had gifted me years ago when I defeated the Horned Rebels. The table was made from wood and the rare blue fulgurite stone, which was only found in Luklum. It held the power of lightning and only activated when it resonated with the person's energy. The table didn't glow or radiate when I touched it, but it was still a beautiful piece of furniture.

"Have a seat," I said. "Please thank Lina for me."

"You can thank her yourself," he said.

Ren wore a red scholar's hat, different from his father, General Zhou, who protected the Southern Border of Lin Din Ni. Even though he reported to me, I admired and respected him as if he were my father.

"Why so formal today?" Ren placed the bag of pastries on the table and sat down. "I would've come sooner, but there was a fight in the street. Two boys were bullying a younger one. I had to stop it. See?" He pointed to the stain on the silk tunic most scholars wore.

I looked at my friend, no longer the little boy who had been the victim of bullies. A bitter memory intruded on the moment.

"It's fine—I don't need it back," says Ren as he rubs his black eye.

"That's your jade tiger talisman your mom gave you!" I fume. "You should cherish it."

Ren's mom died from an illness years ago, but his father had since remarried.

Guilt splashes onto my friend's face. I'm protective of Ren as if he were my younger brother.

"We'll get it back," I seethe. "Stupid bullies."

I know exactly where Moo, Quack, and Oink hang out. It's not a secret. They're known bullies, firstborn sons of noble families. They irritate me, and I don't care who they are. If they pick on my family, they'll pay for it.

I punched Moo once and bruised his arm for ruining my book. My father had a talk with his father, and the two men forced us to apologize to each other. These boys think they rule the school. They're my age, and that makes it worse that they're picking on Ren.

Unlike these lazy asses, I spend my time learning martial arts with my father's soldiers. I love learning all the styles of self-defense. Hopefully, I can help him soon so he doesn't need to work so much and be home more.

Ren drags his feet behind me, obviously nervous about confronting the bullies.

I pause so he can catch up. "Don't be afraid. I'm here with you." I place a gentle hand on his shoulders as I glare at his swollen eye. "You need to go to the healer for your eye and chin."

He holds a hand to his bruised face. "My father's going to be angry . . ."

"It's not your fault." He meets my eyes, and I see fear in his. "Those assholes gave you a black eye, bruised your chin, and took your talisman for no reason. They're troublemakers, and someone needs to stop them! You're not the only victim," I snarl. "I'll give them what they deserve."

Nodding, he looks away. "But I don't want you to get hurt."

"Don't worry about me." I snort. "I've gotten so many scars from climbing trees and being reckless that my mom expects them. She's got a lot of healing balm. Want to stop by my house after?"

"No, it's okay. I'll go home."

He probably feels ashamed.

Unlike my father, who makes time to teach me martial arts and war strategies, General Zhou is usually busy and has a short temper. So, I understand why Ren feels lonely.

"You should learn kung fu with me and the soldiers. Come with me next time."

He shrugs. "I'm not coordinated like you."

"You can take your time." I sling an arm around his shoulders. "Learn it so you can defend yourself."

"I'll think about it."

We make our way down an alley where Moo, Quack, and Oink love to gather. I spot them sitting around a table, looking at talismans, marbles, fans, and miscellaneous items. Are those all stolen?

"Farm boys!" I yell, knowing they hate that name.

They look down on anyone who doesn't measure up to their family's wealth. My family isn't wealthy like theirs, but my father is the General of the Luklum Army. Without him protecting the *capital city, rebels would create a lot of trouble. The idiots should thank my family.*

"What are you doing here?" Quack barks as though I fear him. He has short hair and a narrow face with big lips.

The other two boys rise from the bench and flank Quack. Moo narrows his small eyes and smirks while Oink snarls, shifting his big belly. I try my best not to address him as Piggy.

I point to the tiger talisman. "That doesn't belong to you. Give it back now." I hold out my hand.

"No." Moo smirks. "We're going to sell it."

Oink glares at Ren. "You can't fight us, so you went to get your friend? Stupid idiot." He takes the tiger talisman and whips it to the ground, smashing it.

Ren screams in horror, and the bullies laugh.

Fury bursts through me, and I charge at them. Something changes in Ren's demeanor as he helps me.

It doesn't take long for Moo, Quack, and Oink to run away with split lips and bruised eyes. As they rush away, they promise retaliation.

"I'll be ready for you, assholes!" I pick up a rock and whip it at them, but the rock doesn't make it far.

I grab the pile of stolen items and shove them into the bag on the table.

We drop off the stolen goods at the Imperial Court and tell the officials what happened before Ren and I head home. When I get close to my house, I see Uncle Seeto standing outside. He's my father's assistant and has been with my family since I was born.

He spots me and rushes over. "Where have you been? What happened to you?" He grips my chin, looking at the scratches and blood. The scratches sting, but the other boys are worse off.

"I got into a fight. I need to tell my dad about—"

Tears well in his eyes.

My heart thuds in trepidation. "What happened?"

"Your parents are dead."

From that day on, I retreated into myself and dwelled in darkness. The world got darker when I entered the battlefield, seeing my men die while defending their country. But I always remembered those who had helped me along the way.

Ren's friendship helped me overcome a difficult phase in my life.

"Didn't sleep well?" He studied me. "You look like shit."

No one dared to speak to me that way except close friends.

"As always, the words that come out of your mouth are poetically shitty."

"That's why I'm the best scholar in Lin Din Ni." He laughed. "And the reason the Emperor assigned me to lead the Imperial Poetry School."

"I'll need to ask him to reconsider his choice." Shaking my head, I sat across from him and poured some tea into a cup for him, then one for me. "A lot going on in Luklum lately."

"Thank you." He took the teacup, sipped, and placed it down. "How's the investigation going? According to the City Apothecary, more people are falling ill."

"It's still ongoing," I said. "What brings you to the Military Pavilion this early in the morning?"

"People are saying Ru Malik is behind the sickness spreading in Luklum. Is that true?"

I arched an eyebrow at the news. "Where did you hear this?"

The soldiers notified me this morning about an incident last night at the abandoned temple. I'd already sent my men to take samples of the well water for testing.

"Everyone's talking about it in the Market Square. Someone claims he saw the ruthless leader."

Intrigue sparked in me. "Who?"

"I don't know." He shrugged. "They said a man saw Ru Malik last night. Others claimed it wasn't him but another rebel."

Rumor had a way of spawning wild stories, so I had to examine everything that came into my office closely. However, an anonymous letter was delivered to me this morning, giving me three names to investigate. Who was this man who had seen the incident last night? I needed to ask him more questions. But he didn't leave his name or where I could reach him. How could I trust he was a citizen of Luklum and not a rebel trying to steer me in a different direction?

"Do you think the Bloodshade Bandits are here?" A crease formed between his eyebrows. "Are you prepared to capture them?"

"For someone who wasn't interested in crime, you seem invested in the bandits."

"Who isn't? They're ruthless. I don't want them here!"

I twirled the teacup between my fingers, watching the jasmine leaves move around in the liquid. "They've infiltrated the city by buying people off. A plan is already in motion. I'll catch them soon."

Relief settled onto his face. "Want to share the details with me?"

"No." I placed the teacup down. "It's best that you don't know. Focus on your poetry and students. Let me handle this. If anyone asks, tell them we're increasing soldiers around Luklum."

Sometimes, too much information wasn't beneficial to anyone. I didn't want him to inadvertently do or say something that could give away my careful scheme. The Bloodshade Bandits had killed too many people, instilling fear in merchants who wanted to enter Luklum to conduct business. I didn't want my people to live in fear.

Years ago, I'd fought Ru Malik, but he'd escaped, and it had been difficult to locate him since. Stories about the vicious leader had spread like wildfire. Some said he took over the rebel faction after an enemy killed his father. Others said he created the group himself. His rebellion had spread into regions bordering Lin Din Ni and the Central Empire. The dangerous terrain and wild beasts in the Rebel Territory made it difficult to destroy the Bloodshade Bandits.

If I hadn't been occupied with battles in other regions, I would have my army focused on destroying Ru Malik. Now that his people were in Luklum, I had to be extra cautious.

Why were the Bloodshade Bandits in Luklum? The Imperial military was based nearby. They should fear we could catch them. I didn't dismiss the idea they could target Emperor Tang Li Wei and Empress Jayaatu Yeeva.

"I've got to head back to prepare for class." Ren rose from his seat. "Keep me posted on the investigation, will you?"

"Absolutely." I got up from my seat. "I have a few things I need to take care of in the Market Square. I'll come with you."

The Market Square was a business section of the city and wasn't far from the Military Pavilion. I usually walked there, but I hadn't been sleeping lately, and Ren was a man accustomed to the noble treatment. I rode in Ren's horse-drawn carriage, which had the Zhou family seal of a tiger attached to the side windows. A guard sat on the front, urging the horse to move. It didn't take long for the horse to arrive at the Market Square.

"Thanks for the lift," I said, hopping off.

He held the curtain aside, looked at something, smiled, and hopped off the carriage.

"I thought you had a class to prepare for."

"I do." He grinned. "But I'm in the mood for more pastries now. There's someone I want to say hello to. Do you want any pork buns? My treat."

"I won't ever say no to pork buns," I said, even though I had a bag of egg tarts from Lina in my office. I was intrigued by who had captured his interest. The look on his face told me it was a woman.

Ren had always been popular with the ladies, even when we were younger. He had charm, something I lacked. But who had time for those kinds of things?

"Who is she?" I asked, studying the group of patrons around the Jade Sun Bakery. "Or is it a man?"

He elbowed me. "Nothing wrong with that, but I favor women, my friend. Maybe if you loosen up a bit and smile more, they'll come for you."

I didn't have trouble getting women. But I didn't want to bring up my private life. I stared at him, trying to process his comment. Was I uptight? I didn't think so.

Why would I smile if there was no reason to smile?

"What's wrong with you?" I asked.

"Nothing." Laughing, he waved me off. "A man who appreciates literature understands beauty more than *men* of war," he emphasized while looking at me. "You need love and a beautiful woman to show you the way."

"Unlike you, I'm not lost." I snorted. "I thought General Zhou gave you a stack of military books to read. But now I know his son prefers reading romance—"

"Don't start a rumor." His eyes widened. "My dad would kill me."

I winked at him. "Now *that* made me smile."

"You're an ass," Ren said, then his eyes sparked when he spotted a woman standing with her back facing me. "Su!"

She turned around, smiled at Ren, and gave her head a slight bow. "How are you?"

Su had a beautiful smile that made my chest flutter. The reaction surprised me, and I dismissed it as my body simply needing rest.

I recognized her as a healer at the City Apothecary. She'd treated my men and delivered healing balms and tonics to the Military Pavilion several times. She had an unforgettable face—a lot younger than mine.

I could see why Ren was attracted to her.

"Better." Ren smiled like a fool. "Your cold remedy is unmatched."

"Thank you," Su said and turned to me, offering a nod. "General Wen."

Why didn't she smile at me? I blinked at the strange thought sneaking into my head like a criminal trying to incriminate me. Why did I care if a woman smiled at me?

An unusual energy stirred between us that made me fully

aware of my body. A tingle coursed through me, forcing me to straighten my spine and square my shoulders. She looked at me as though she sensed it too. But neither of us said anything.

This could all be my imagination, of course. I hadn't slept well in days, and an unbalanced body yielded an unbalanced mind. However, the imminent danger in my city demanded my full attention. Sleep could wait.

Shaking off the odd sensation, I returned the nod. "Has the number of patients decreased?"

"A few came in this morning, but it wasn't like the last few weeks." Pretty brown eyes stared at me with curiosity. "Is it true that the Bloodshade Bandits are responsible for the illnesses?"

"See?" Ren turned to me. "I told you. Everyone's talking about it."

"A public announcement will be posted on the market bulletin soon."

I knew any news about the Bloodshade Bandits would travel fast, but this was quicker than I expected. Who had started it?

"Okay. Thanks." She nodded.

I could tell she wanted to say something else but stopped when Ren interrupted.

"Can you make me three more of the cold concoctions?" he asked, standing a bit too close to her.

An unfamiliar emotion came to the surface, surprising me. I immediately shoved it away. Jealousy made no sense right now. I didn't know this woman. Besides, my best friend liked her. What the fuck was wrong with me today?

"Oh. Are you sick again?"

"No. I have some students suffering from a cold. Don't want to catch it again. I'll stop by the apothecary later to pick them up."

"We can do that," she said and shivered, looking paler than before. "Yunxi and I have to get back to the apothecary now."

Standing beside Su, Yunxi smiled and bowed to me and Ren. We returned a nod.

"You should rest up." Yunxi placed a hand on Su's forehead.

"Are you not well?" Ren studied her.

"Just a minor cold," Su said. "I'll be taking those concoctions I made for you."

"If you're sick, don't rush on my order."

"Yunxi or Healer Churan can prepare them for you. See you soon." Su and Yunxi bowed and walked away.

"Of all the noble daughters swarming you, you've chosen a healer."

He sighed. "Unfortunately, she's not the woman swarming around me."

"Maybe she's with someone."

"She's not," he blurted out.

I looked at my friend, intrigued by this unfamiliar side of him. "I didn't know you were a stalker and a hopeless romantic."

He rolled his eyes. "That's because I'm not spending my days discussing war strategies or fighting criminals. Wait until you encounter a stunning woman you can't forget. Then you'll understand what I'm going through."

"Stop reading romance novels, and you'll be fine."

"Maybe I'll buy you a novel and send it to your office." His lips tilted. "I've got to go. Let me know if you have updates on the Bloodshade Bandits."

When Ren's carriage left the Market Square, I strode to the Bronze Barracks, one of two training camps in Luklum. This smaller camp was near an open field with an obstacle course to train recruits. I strode into the camp and walked up to the guards.

"General Wen," said the two guards dressed in the navy uniform. They placed fists on their chests and bowed their heads to greet me.

"Is Gong here?"

"Yes, sir." The two guards gestured to the training field.

I walked to the field and watched Gong holding a spear, demonstrating his martial arts to a group of new soldiers. When he finished the spear, he chose a sword from the weapons rack and showed them defensive moves. The soldiers mimicked his animalistic fighting style as best they could, but no one performed it better than Gong.

Gong wore all black, looking like a swift, powerful panther. The purple cloak he always wore was draped over a nearby chair. He spotted me and offered a nod.

Returning the gesture, I strode to the platform's edge overlooking the open field.

"Excellent form. Keep it up," I told my men as Gong walked up the steps to the resting table and chairs. I pulled out a chair and sat down.

"How's the investigation going?" Gong asked, sitting across from me.

Fifteen years older than me, he was a remarkable warrior. His hair was tied with a leather strap. He had sharp brown eyes, a straight nose, and a scar that zigzagged from his cheek to his neck. This warrior had been in more battles than I had. I respected him like an uncle. Gong and I were part of the Emperor's Council, which consisted of five trusted members.

"As planned. We'll catch Ru Malik." I flicked him an inquisitive look. "Any updates on the missing people?"

"Nothing yet." Gong shook his head.

I'd been concentrating on the rise in illnesses while Gong assisted with the investigation of the missing citizens. The Shen family was the most recent disappearance.

"I'll assist as soon as I catch Ru Malik."

"You think he'll show up?"

"Maybe." I shrugged. "But he'll know we're aware of his intentions. We have more guards monitoring Luklum."

"It's been one thing after another. Are you doing okay?"

I supposed my fatigue was obvious if everyone kept asking me about it.

"I'll be fine." I looked out at the training field. "Thanks for showing my men your skills."

He waved a hand and rose from his seat. "A powerful army makes a powerful empire." He grabbed the purple cloak from the chair and put it on. "I have a meeting with the Emperor. Something's on his mind."

"Besides the Bloodshade Bandits and the missing citizens?"

Gong sighed and nodded.

What else could the Emperor be worried about? We had kept rebels away for so many years. Had he heard something that hadn't been shared with his council?

I had a meeting scheduled with him next week. Perhaps he'd inform me then.

I looked up at the clouds with sunlight sneaking through. The storms from the past few months had destroyed a lot of crops. "The farmers are struggling. Let's hope for more sunshine."

Something odd stirred in the air, but I didn't know what it was. I couldn't trust my intuition right now. The tingle I'd felt standing next to Su still lingered in my body. The sensation wasn't the usual attraction I sensed when I was close to a beautiful woman. I'd been with women, and this wasn't it. This was something else.

"Something wrong?" Gong asked, studying me.

Fucking hell. Since when had my mind wandered because of a woman?

I scrubbed a hand over my face, stretching my neck from side to side. "Just tired."

"Catching criminals is an urgent matter." Gong stepped up to me, placing a hand on my shoulder. "But your wellness is even more crucial, Hung. We need a fully functional general to battle the storms."

"I know."

"The weather hasn't been kind to Lin Din Ni." Gong pointed to the grass. "Rain is good, but too much of a good thing spoils its effect. Empress Jayaatu has been struggling with her gardens too. We all know she's a master of plants." He patted my back. "Get some rest, General."

"I'll do my best," I said, silently promising myself a good night's sleep.

Kai and Tao could update me on Ru Malik when they returned from their assignments.

After instructing the guards to survey the city for anyone suspicious, I made my way back to the Prime General's Villa. I desperately needed a bath and a bed.

A man stumbled in front of me, struggling to walk. When I approached, I realized it was the meat vendor, Samo. He bumped into patrons but didn't apologize. Looking pale, he clutched his stomach, wincing with every step.

I'd been investigating Samo and his associates for a while now. He and his friend were named in the anonymous letter I received this morning. Complaints about him cheating customers had increased over the years. But somehow, those complaints had been miraculously withdrawn. I knew he'd paid those people off. I left these complaints in the hands of the court representatives, but I still received updates to see if anything stood out to me.

My job was to ensure my soldiers were well-prepared for battle. Protecting the country was my top priority, and that included crimes from within as well as those instigated by outside enemies. Criminals often left clues, and it was up to me to see and connect them.

"Get out of my way!" Samo barked at a woman walking with her little son.

"You don't own the street!" the mother replied, wrapping an arm around her son protectively. "What's wrong with you?" She gestured a finger at him. "I won't be shopping at your meat market ever again!"

"Why is he so mean, *Me*?" asked the boy, holding a candy stick.

"I don't know." She ruffled his hair. "Maybe he's having a bad day. Come on, let's go home. *Ba* is waiting for us."

My chest constricted as I watched the mother and son stride away, reminding me of my childhood. It had been filled with love until my parents died, making me an orphan at twelve years old.

I shouldn't envy the little boy for having something I lacked.

What was wrong with me today? My emotions were in chaos. I was feeling things I shouldn't be feeling at all.

After experiencing so many shades of darkness, I couldn't look at life the same way. I prayed the child would be protected from what had hardened me. My job as Prime General was to ensure that all children in Lin Din Ni were safe.

A flash in the sky caught my eye. I glanced up at the dark cloud, and lightning flashed again. What was going on with the strange weather? The sun made it through a gray cloud, shining bright not too far from where I stood.

"Stop being a jerk!" a patron scolded Samo, yanking me back to the present moment.

Samo growled at the man and walked over to Jie Chen, who also looked sick. His father, Lord Chen, served at the Imperial Court.

"I was careful not to touch the powder." Jie gripped his stomach. "He said there's no more antidote for the poison."

Powder? Poison?

"Fuck! It's their poison! They should have the antidote."

"Have you heard from Peng?" Jie asked.

The two of them whispered amongst themselves as they continued walking.

My plan to go home and rest changed immediately as I followed them.

CHAPTER THREE

SU

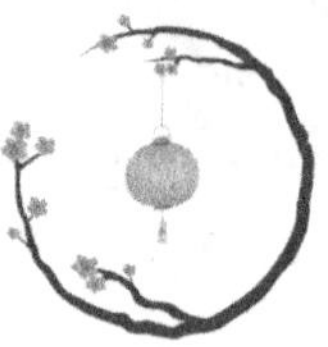

"YOU SHOULD'VE COME to me, Su," Healer Churan huffed, making me feel guilty for worrying her. She sighed as she pierced the acupuncture needles into my ears, wrists, and ankles.

Healer Churan had taken care of me after my parents died. Skilled and smart, her graceful beauty stood out from the noble ladies who came into our store to shop. Like always, she wore minimal makeup and had a floral accessory in her braided hair. My eyes slid to the precious jade earrings she never took off. Simple and eye-catching at the same time.

Unlike her, I didn't spend money on precious earrings and only wore affordable accessories. My money would go toward a worthy sword or dagger. But first, I had to learn the skill to use these weapons. I had still a long way to go.

Healer Churan added heat to the needles with incense to invigorate the points on my body. "How did you get poisoned, anyway?"

If *Me* were still alive, she'd be the same age as Healer Churan.

"I'm not sure," I lied. "It's been chaotic at the apothecary with people coming in and out. I could've caught something. Or touched a toxic plant while collecting herbs in the woods."

Healer Churan didn't need to know where I'd been or what

I'd been investigating. Maybe it had been a bad idea to follow Samo and his friends. But if I hadn't, I wouldn't have known the Bloodshade Bandits were behind the illnesses and that their leader, Ru Malik, was already in the city.

I replayed what had occurred last night in my head, trying to figure out how I'd gotten poisoned. Maybe I touched a poisonous plant at the abandoned temple? Symptoms had begun last night. The chill and heat had warred inside me, keeping me up most of the night.

"Your pulse is erratic." Her eyebrows furrowed. "But your blood flow seems stable. Take this herbal pill to stabilize your heart rate. It's a temporary remedy. I'll need time to determine an antidote."

Sitting up, I popped the herbal pill and drank a warm tea to help it go down. "Do you know what kind of poisoning it is?"

She tapped under my ear and sighed. "Three red dots with swelling around them. That's a signature of the toxic red thorn plant." Her perfect eyebrows furrowed. "You need to monitor your essa. Let me know if your energy level drops."

Firehell.

I rose from the chair, grabbed the handheld mirror from the table, and walked over to the hanging mirror on the wall. Three red dots forming a triangle sat behind my ear. Swelling surrounded the dots.

"I saw this years ago, but the patient died within days. His heart rate rose quickly, and his eyes were glazed with prominent red veins." She looked into my eyes. "Yours look healthy."

"Other than the increased heart rate and the random heat, I feel fine."

She gave me a pouch of pills. "Keep this with you in case the poison flares up. If you feel abnormal, the pill will help balance your essa."

"Thank you," I said, honing into my body's essa. It seemed normal.

"Help us!" someone shouted from out front.

"You rest." Healer Churan pointed to the bed in the exam room.

"I'm okay. Really," I said. "The medicine helped. It'll be good for me to work."

We went to the front to see Samo and Jie hunched over in pain. The veins in their eyes looked like they were on fire.

Yunxi carried over a basket of supplies and placed them on the desk beside the chairs. "Take a seat. What are your symptoms?"

"I'm cold." Samo shivered and winced. "Pain in my stomach. Too weak to do anything. I'm nauseated too."

"Same as him," Jie said, sounding out of breath as he leaned back in the chair.

My heart raced when I saw the red dots and swelling near their ears. But they had more than three dots, and the color appeared brighter. I whipped a glance at Healer Churan, and a silent understanding passed between us—we were all poisoned by the same thing. But somehow, they appeared worse.

"You can help with those." She gestured for me to go over to the counter to sort the tray of dried herbs.

"I just saw you a few days ago." Healer Churan checked Samo's pulse with her fingers. "You didn't look sick then." She looked over at Jie. "Both of you got poisoned at the same time? What happened?"

At that moment, General Wen walked through the door, bringing a new energy into the apothecary. Like always, my body immediately reacted to his presence. But this wasn't passing him in the Market Square with a delicate fluttering in my stomach. This was the same powerful sensation I'd felt yesterday standing next to him. His gaze fixed on the men. Then, as though he sensed my eyes on him, he turned to me.

The muscles in my stomach trembled. I placed a hand on my abdomen, rubbing it. This stupid poison wasn't helping with my body's reaction to him. Everything became more heightened.

General Wen strode over to the counter. "What happened to them?"

This would be a great opportunity to alert him of what I'd heard. But then he'd ask me how I knew, and I didn't want him to know about my spying.

"Not sure. Do you think it has anything to do with Ru Malik?"

His brown eyes landed on mine, and my heart jolted. Up close, he was more handsome, and I couldn't stop myself from studying his features. High cheekbones reminded me of the sturdy mountains watching over the land like imposing warriors. Inviting lips that fascinated me, making me wonder about too many things. What would those firm lips do to his face if they shifted into a smile? His chiseled jaw completed a strong-boned face with brown eyes that held strategies and secrets. They reminded me of smoldering wood that became more intense over time. I'd love to see the world through his eyes.

"What do *you* think?" he asked.

Heat shot to my core. I shouldn't be feeling these sensations when poison was stirring in my blood. But somehow, I couldn't help it. It was as though the poison didn't matter when it came to General Wen. He had the power to take over my body.

"I'm not the one investigating him. But at a glance, I think Ru Malik is attacking Luklum."

Amusement gleamed in his eyes. "Seems like you're following the investigation well."

"It's hard not to when we get sick patients in all the time," I said. "But today, the symptoms are different. They don't resemble the illnesses from weeks ago."

While I studied him, he also studied me. My heart rate increased, and I wondered if I should take another pill from Healer Churan. But I didn't think her pill could subdue my attraction to him.

He was an experienced man who had seen more of life than I had. Though he was twelve years older, I couldn't stop this attraction. Now I understood why women in the Market Square giggled and whispered whenever he browsed the streets.

"He's the most handsome bachelor," one woman had said.

"*Why isn't he married?*" asked another.

"*I heard General Zhou's daughter fancies him.*"

"*She's pretty but too snooty.*"

"Can you elaborate?" General Wen's voice broke my trance.

What was wrong with me? The city was in crisis, and all my thoughts were on a man instead of treating patients.

"Those men have red dots with swelling, whereas the other patients had extreme nausea, high fever, and diarrhea. They couldn't keep food or medicine down."

"What exactly did you hear about the Bloodshade Bandits?" His eyes stayed on mine. "Who did you hear it from? When did you hear this?"

The situation sounded like an interrogation. I had to choose my words carefully.

"People in the market were all talking this morning. A man said he overheard someone saying the bandits had poisoned the wells in Luklum. You should check them out."

"He said the wells were poisoned?" He lifted a dark eyebrow.

But I couldn't tell if my reply surprised or satisfied him.

I nodded. "You should get samples of the well water to test. That explains why so many people got sick so fast." I looked over at Samo and Jie, moaning in pain. Maybe these new symptoms were an escalation from the previous weeks. Or maybe it was a new type of poison.

"Did you see the man?"

Nerves spiraled. "No. I overheard men talking about him."

"You should be an investigator," he said. "Your mind works like one."

Was that a compliment, or was it another form of interrogation?

"Thanks. But I prefer to stick to healing. It's what I'm good at."

I took out the prepackaged anti-inflammatory herbs and started the brew. "I hope there's a cure for them."

He crossed his arms and leaned against the counter. "Would you heal them if you knew they weren't good men?"

The question caught me off guard. I knew the answer logically —I was a healer. I healed people. But I'd heard what Samo, Jie, and Peng had discussed with Ru Malik last night. It had made my blood boil.

"That's a hard question to answer," I said. "But I can tell you this. If anyone comes into the apothecary during work hours, I'd be objective and treat him or her." I paused and inhaled, preparing to say something that could tarnish his view of me. "But if I encountered an injured person outside of work and knew he'd done evil things, I'd walk away wishing he suffered before his death."

That was the truth. I didn't want to lie to seem like some compassionate woman. I'd seen too much pain and suffering to know that some people deserved punishment. Like those bandits who killed my parents or husbands who abused their wives and children.

His eyebrows rose slowly as he stared at me. I thought the corners of his lips tilted for a moment, but then they pursed with a question. "So your moral compass depends on the individual and not some vow you've made as a healer to treat everyone equally?"

"What's *your* moral compass, General? Are you the mighty hero who only does admirable things? Someone who could do no wrong?"

His eyes bore into mine, and I could tell he didn't want to answer that question. But I didn't want to talk about my moral compass anymore. So I helped us both and said, "Sometimes I let the universe decide."

Though he nodded, his gaze was still on me, and the muscles in my inner thighs flexed.

Two customers carrying a container entered the apothecary: Aunt Red Bean and her husband, Uncle Soy. They met my eyes, smiled, and rushed over; they had more energy and color to their faces. Three days ago, they'd been sick like others in Luklum.

General Wen stepped over to the display of soaps and essential oils, making room at the counter.

"We're feeling better," said Aunt Red Bean with eyes that had more vitality in them today. "No more fatigue, diarrhea, or fever."

"It's a miracle!" Uncle Soy beamed, lifting an arm to demonstrate his improved health.

The couple owned a restaurant that was forced to close because of their illnesses.

"That's fantastic news. What did you do differently?"

Uncle Soy shrugged. "A group of soldiers went around offering soup and water to everyone. I asked him what was in the soup, and he said it was egg soup with cilantro. Nothing special."

I looked over at General Wen, who was eyeing Samo and Jie. He knew more than what he had told me about those men.

Having the military hand out food to the citizens wasn't odd. The Military Pavilion had a larger kitchen and more staff to produce large quantities of food. Did General Wen order his men to distribute the soup? What was in it? Something told me there was more to this mystery.

"Su, can you please start the anti-inflammatory brew?" Healer Churan asked.

"I'll do it now." I pulled out a drawer and retrieved a packet of herbs. Opening it, I placed the herbs in the small pot on the stone stove beside the counter and added wooden sticks to feed the fire.

I put the lid on and returned to Aunt Red Bean. "Sorry, I needed to get the brew going."

"No worries." Aunt Red Bean smiled. "The neighbors on my street are also better now. I know you're busy, so I brought food to thank you and everyone here. You've been working hard keeping people safe."

Uncle Soy placed the food container on the counter. "Dumplings, red bean buns, and tofu dessert for all of you. Enjoy!"

"Thank you." I moved the container to the back counter.

Samo shrieked and startled Aunt Red Bean and Uncle Soy.

"We'll head out now," Uncle Soy said. "Don't want to get sick again."

When the brew was done, I poured the anti-inflammatory concoction into two cups and brought them to Healer Churan. Perhaps the brew would help. I placed a finger under my ear, trying to feel the swelling. Mine felt minimal compared to the large lumps that had grown since they entered the apothecary.

I'd be lying if I said I didn't fear the same would happen to me.

General Wen approached to stand beside me, studying Samo and Jie who were now lying on the cots, wheezing. Their feet were also swollen, and the red dots had spread over their faces.

Yunxi dabbed the sweat beading their foreheads.

I knew what Samo and Jie had done, and I tried my best to remain neutral. Like I said to General Wen, I was working as a healer right now, and that was my responsibility. Nothing more. Still, frustration warred inside me. These criminals had poisoned the town and knew who was behind it. Would they tell the truth if I asked them now? They'd probably fear General Wen more than me.

Despite how much I despised these men, a more dangerous criminal had used them. I looked at General Wen, who wore an impassive expression. He had to know these men were bad. Was he using them to lure out Ru Malik?

"What's your analysis?" General Wen asked Healer Churan.

"They've been poisoned." She helped Samo drink the concoction.

"Red thorn poison . . ." Samo muttered. "Need antidote . . ."

Jie moaned between sips as Yunxi assisted him with his medicine.

"How do you know it's red thorn poison?" General Wen looked at Samo. "What do you know about it?"

"Nothing," Samo replied, looking away quickly to examine his swollen fingers. "I don't think the medicine is working."

"It's a concoction to reduce the inflammation, not the antidote. How were you infected with red thorn poison?" I asked. "Do you know where to find the antidote?"

"Ru Malik has . . . the antidote," Jie said between moans. "Waiting for his reply . . . but I don't think he's . . . giving it to us."

"What do you mean?" General Wen asked. "You contacted him? Why are you in contact with him?"

"Jie!" Samo barked and winced as pain splashed across his face.

"Ru Malik . . . won't help us, Samo. He used us . . . Just tell the general the truth . . . so our families won't be incriminated."

"No," Samo growled. "He'll give us the antidote soon."

"If he wanted . . . to give us the antidote, he would've . . . done it already." Jie winced. "We're no longer useful . . . to him." He looked at General Wen. "Please . . . keep my family out of this. They have nothing . . . to do . . . with my crimes. Ru Malik paid us . . . to poison the city wells. We did it last night but . . . woke up sick this morning."

"Your nose!" Samo pointed to his friend. "It's bleeding."

Yunxi grabbed a towel for him, but Jie used his sleeve to wipe the blood from his nose. Then Samo's nose started bleeding too.

The red dots on Jie's face and body burst, and blood splattered everywhere. Yunxi leaped out of the way as Jie screamed in pain, grabbing his chest and gasping for breath. He collapsed onto the cot.

Terror splashed onto Samo's face as the swollen dots on his body erupted. Seconds later, he died.

Healer Churan placed a comforting hand on Yunxi, who looked sad. As healers, we never wanted to see our patients die, especially in this painful way.

"I'll have my men remove them." General Wen took one step closer to look at the corpses.

"Precautions need to be taken," said Healer Churan. "Their bodies need to be burned, not buried."

CHAPTER FOUR

HUNG

INSIDE THE OFFICE of the Imperial morgue, I waited for the ashes that belonged to Samo, Jie, and Peng. Peng had stumbled into the apothecary and died a few minutes after his friends. These cruel men had cheated people out of their money and poisoned total strangers. They deserved their demise.

After the cremation, Samo's, Jie's, and Peng's ashes were placed in urns and delivered to their families. These men had committed treason by working with the Bloodshade Bandits to harm our people. A part of me struggled to give their family closure. What about the families of those who died at their hands? Where was their closure?

But I reined in my anger and offered closure where I could. I'd learned a long time ago that justice was a strange thing. It wasn't as black and white as it should be.

"Deliver these urns to their families so they can have an appropriate burial," I told the two guards. "Be discreet about it."

"Yes, General." The guards nodded and left the morgue.

My goal was to find out what the Bloodshade Bandits' agenda was. Did they want to destabilize the capital city so they could carry out an attack? I would never let that happen. I'd defend this land until the day I die.

If you don't get some rest, you'll die before your enemies can even get to you.

I heard Uncle Seeto's voice reprimanding me. He'd worked for my parents for a long time and became my guardian after they died. The Deathcap Clan had raided our home and slashed their throats. There must have been a lot of them because my father was an experienced warrior. He would've fought back. Poisonous mushrooms had been found scattered around the house, probably dropped by the clan when they'd searched the home for gems. This clan used deadly mushroom poison. My vendetta against these ruthless rebel groups was both personal and professional. The Bloodshade Bandits were no different from the Deathcap Clan.

"*Don't be so angry, Hung. Let it go. Shrug off the weight.*"

A warmth bloomed on my shoulder as though it remembered Uncle Seeto's hand, trying to comfort me in moments of despair.

I tried to let things go, but it wasn't easy. Every time I saw or heard about the bandits killing another person, my blood boiled. They had to be stopped. Dismissing their heinous acts was like agreeing to them.

Uncle Seeto had passed away two years ago from an illness that took his vision and ability to walk. I hadn't made time to visit his grave. Being too busy wasn't a valid excuse, and I hated myself for that.

How could I face him when I hadn't achieved the very thing he asked of me before his death? He wanted me to forgive any wrongdoings and live in peace.

"*You'll be happier and safer.*"

I wasn't a monk and certainly not a god.

Did he know I was the Prime General of Lin Din Ni? That responsibility came with so many worries. My goal—and that of generals before me, including my father—was to achieve peace. I didn't know if peace was possible when there was so much darkness in the world.

Thoughts swirled in my head as I headed out of the morgue,

making my way toward the Harmony Well outside of the Market Square. It was artificial, engineered by Three-Eyes, an advisor to the Emperor. As a prophet, he could see and sense things most couldn't. He discovered a source of water that ran beneath the land and designed an innovative irrigation system to benefit Luklum. This tributary was connected to the Green Fog River by the Misty Mountains.

The water was pure and carried healing light energy, confirmed by Empress Jayaatu, who had a unique ability to see essa—a higher vibration of life force. Energy existed in everything, and the strongest concentrations could be harnessed as essa. This took time and practice, and most warriors spent their lifetimes cultivating their essas.

The well water needed to be cleared of contamination before the public could use it again. The water in the other wells came from natural springs, but their energy wasn't as pure as the Harmony Well's. I needed to take a trip to the Green Fog River to ensure it wasn't contaminated either.

"General!" Kai approached and placed a fist on his chest.

As an Elite Guard to the Prime General, he wore a navy uniform with gray accents with a sword slung over his back. His hair was tied back with a leather band. I didn't like the anxious look on his face. His brother-in-arms, Li Tao, was the second Elite Guard, and together, they were an irreplaceable team that helped me with countless tasks.

"Bad news?" I asked, making my way back to my pavilion. The visit to Harmony Well had to wait.

I needed to know what Kai discovered. I sent him to Sun Wheat Village late last night to investigate. The village was known for its longevity noodles, but within the last few months, there had been a shortage of those noodles entering the Market Square.

"Hopefully, Tao will have better news for you, General." Kai fell into step with me.

"Let's talk in my office," I said. "How many times have I told you to address me as Hung?"

His lips curved. "Do you want the public to shame me for disrespecting their Prime General?"

"The public will think what they will regardless," I said. "You should do as I say."

Despite that, I understood his reason. People were more open to our questions during investigations if they trusted us, and respect often came with trust.

"I'll address you as Hung in private. But to be honest, I'm used to calling you General after all these years."

When we arrived at my office, I closed the door, sat at my desk, and asked, "What did you discover in Sun Wheat Village?"

"You were right." Kai took the seat in front of me and slammed a hand on the table. "The Bloodshade Bandits have taken over that area, setting up a camp. They took the villagers' jewels and slaughtered several of them. I escorted some survivors to nearby villages for safety. They said many people had gone missing before the raid."

"Fucking hell! They'll pay for this." My fingers curled into a fist. "If they think they can barge into our territory, killing our people without repercussions, they're wrong."

"They've set up traps around the village."

Despite how much I wanted to take my army there to fight them, I had to be careful. I needed to step back and look at the scenario from different angles. Mistakes could cost lives, and too many lives have been destroyed lately.

"I have a feeling the missing people from Sun Wheat Village are connected to those missing from Luklum."

"Looks like it." Kai crossed his arms, leaning back in the chair.

"Why didn't anyone report this to us?" I asked. "Where's the mayor?"

A mayor monitored a region of Lin Din Ni to help Emperor Tang oversee his country.

"The mayor and his family may be dead, General," Kai said. "According to those I spoke to, no one has seen him in months. They thought he had a meeting at the palace."

The more I investigated these Bloodshade Bandits, the more I wondered who was backing them.

"Do you want me to send our men to retaliate? Give me the order, and I'll do it."

I'd want nothing more than to kill those bandits, but something more dire was happening. I only had one piece of the puzzle and needed more information before any battle could take place. What if my snap decision only caused more destruction?

"Let's wait," I said. "They could have attacked our villages years ago. Why now? What gives them the courage? Who's supporting them?"

"You think they're working with someone? Who?"

"Time will tell. Meanwhile, let's monitor them. Have more guards stationed around the Market Square, looking for anything suspicious."

A knock sounded on the door.

"Come in."

Tao greeted us with a fist to his chest. Like Kai, he wore a blue uniform with gray accents and a belt decked with a sword and other weapons. Unlike Kai's slim physique, Tao had broader shoulders and thicker muscles. Usually, his long hair was neatly secured at the back with a metal accessory. But today, it looked disheveled.

"Great timing." I gestured to the chair next to Kai. "Have a seat."

"What happened to your hair?" Kai pointed to the loose strands hanging on either side of Tao's face and laughed. "Need me to comb it for you?"

Tao tossed him an annoyed look. "You don't want to know." He walked over to the wooden table and set down a fabric-covered box. Placing his sword on the table, he dropped into the seat, looking distracted. Between my two Elite Guards, Tao was calmer and not easily perturbed.

"But I do," Kai retorted. "You look like you had an unforgettable adventure. What did you escape from?" He tried to fix Tao's hair.

Tao shoved his arm away. "I don't want to discuss this right now."

"Then why are you here?" Kai asked. "We both went on assignments, and I just reported my findings. What are yours?"

Tao slid a look at Kai before turning back to me. "Next time, you can have Kai investigate the Green Fog River."

Kai widened his eyes. "Now I really want to know. Don't you, Hung? Just look at our friend here." He smirked. "Something has unraveled him."

"If I weren't too tired, I'd kick your ass right now."

"I'd like to see you try."

Despite the tease and taunt, there was love and respect between these men.

Laughing, Kai poured a cup of tea and offered it to his comrade. "What's bothering you, brother?"

"*You*," Tao said, but took the teacup, sipped it, and placed the cup on the table. "Kai's more suitable to scout the Green Fog River." He flicked what looked like a dried river weed off his sleeve.

"Why?" I asked.

"A group of women attacked me," he blurted out.

"What?" Kai's eyes beamed with laughter and wonder. "What happened?"

Curiosity piqued as I tried to imagine what Tao had experienced. "What kind of women dare to attack a warrior?"

"Did you do something inappropriate?" Kai gave him a playful punch on his arm.

"I'm not like you." Tao shook his head as embarrassment flushed onto his face. "They came out of nowhere."

"Tell me they were pretty." Kai smirked.

Tao rolled his eyes and turned to me. "I scouted the area like you asked. When I didn't see any Bloodshade Bandits, I thought the river was safe. So I took out some bottles to retrieve the water." He gestured to the wrapped package on the table. "But a woman whacked me on the back with a stick and a pail."

Kai laughed. "You didn't sense her around?"

"Apparently, she jumped down from a tree branch."

"Why did she hit you?" I asked.

"Because her friend was bathing in the river. I didn't see her!" He met my eyes. "I swear."

"Yeah, right." Kai snorted, and Tao punched him in the arm.

"That's what you get for starting trouble." Tao turned back to me. "More women showed up with bamboo fishing rods, brooms, and baskets. I told them I didn't know their friend was bathing. But they didn't want to listen to my explanation. They just attacked me." He shivered. "Let's just say I got out of there as fast as possible without hurting anyone."

"You didn't answer my question," Kai said, not letting his friend off easy. "Were the women pretty?"

Tao's lips curled into a smirk. "Now that I think about it, they're *perfect* for *you*."

"Oh yeah?" Kai's eyes sparked. "How can they resist this charming package?"

Tao looked at me for help, and I suppressed the smile that wanted to show itself. I didn't think Tao would appreciate that at the moment.

"You probably encountered the River Women," I said. "They live in the Misty Mountains by the river and lake. They're like hermits, keeping to themselves and minding their own."

"Never heard of them," Tao said.

"They don't show themselves often, so I'm surprised you saw them. I heard these River Women have a connection with the water, but I don't know if that's true."

"Why don't they show themselves?" Kai asked.

"To protect them from *nosy* people like you," Tao said.

"They have a disease that deforms their faces," I said.

"Like how?" Kai made a face.

Tao let out a laugh and stared at Kai as though he were formulating a sly remark for his comrade.

Kai jutted a finger at him. "Not asking you, asshole."

"I'm the asshole?" He sneered. "You started this as soon as I entered the room."

Kai shrugged. "That's because I was worried about my friend looking worn and torn."

Ignoring Kai, Tao said, "They had warts or something like that. I didn't stay long enough to examine. But yeah, their faces were all messed up."

"So . . . not pretty," Kai said, more to himself.

"They had some disease that couldn't be treated, so they moved to a secluded area to settle. People weren't kind to them on the outskirts of Luklum," I said. "I think the Green Fog River allows them the seclusion and peace they needed."

A part of me yearned for that lifestyle right now. The city was too noisy, and I hadn't been sleeping well.

Tao nodded. "Well, that was my adventure." He turned to Kai. "So what did you find?"

Kai leaned back in the chair. "I wish my trip was like yours. Mine was mostly death and destruction." He continued describing the situation at Sun Wheat Village.

Looking pissed, Tao huffed. "What do we do now? We can't let them kill our people and take over our land."

Pride swelled in me as I sat with these men. Their loyalty to the country was an excellent example for all soldiers at the camp.

"They'll pay for sure," I said. "But not right away."

"Do you have a plan?" Tao asked.

Kai shook his head. "Seems like you got hit hard in the head with the pail. How long have you worked with Hung? He always has a plan."

Tao studied me. "You look like you could use some sleep."

"We could all use that." I sighed, offering them a glimpse into my thoughts. "But there's too much chaos right now. The illnesses caused by the Bloodshade Bandits . . . Are there new diseases on the rise? What's Ru Malik planning next? We have to be prepared."

Tao nodded. "Do you think he's in Luklum?"

"If he isn't, he will be soon," I said, remembering Su's comment.

The thought of her soothed me, something a woman hadn't been able to do in a long time. I pushed her beautiful face out of my mind, focusing on the matter at hand. "Get an update from the other generals to ensure our borders are well protected."

"Will do," said both men.

"For now, go home and get some rest. Can you bring the river water to the military physician and ask him to test it? But keep it discreet. I need a status on all the wells."

When they left my office, I should have gone to my bedroom to rest, but I was restless. A walk would be helpful. I strode to the Harmony Well and saw Su retrieving water and pouring it into a small bucket. She kept glancing around, and I made sure I didn't move from my spot hidden in the shadows under a vendor's awning.

She couldn't look more suspicious. Why was she taking the water? A thought popped into my head. Was she *contaminating* it? Was she working for Ru Malik?

A healer working for an apothecary would be the best spy. She had access to the military camp and the palace. So if she wanted to poison the defense system in Luklum, no one would suspect her.

A part of me wanted to confront her, but something told me to wait and watch. I followed her as she retrieved the water from another well. It was getting late, and I wondered if she was also going to the other wells. They were far away. A horse or carriage would get her there faster. It didn't matter; I would see this through if it took all night.

To my surprise, Su didn't go to the other wells. She brought the jars to an old shed near the apothecary. I walked to the back, using the lanterns hanging from nearby businesses to guide me.

Was she meeting someone in the shed?

CHAPTER FIVE

SU

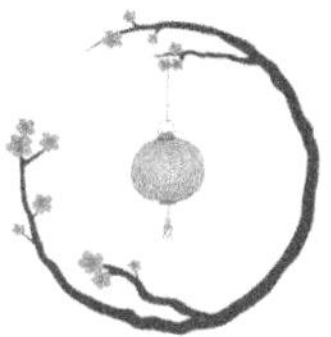

IT WAS TOO late in the night for me to test the water sample for poison. I could do that tomorrow at the apothecary. What was in the water? If the poison was still present, the authorities should close all the wells, right?

I placed the oil lantern and the two water bottles on the table. The City Apothecary often used this shed for extra storage, and I came here when I needed privacy.

The apothecary used rainwater we collected from barrels in the back. Healer Churan placed shungite crystals in the water to help purify it. Due to all the recent storms, we'd had plenty of water to use without needing to go to the wells.

It was late, but I was too wired to sleep. Maybe if I focused on rejuvenating my energy, my body could fight off the poison in me more efficiently. One day, perhaps I could even harness my essa. I glanced at my palms, imagining what the gold essa would look like if it appeared.

Besides the lantern, the crescent moon offered extra lighting for my martial arts practice. Crickets sounded nearby, and the warm night air created a calm mood. I straightened my spine, squared my shoulders, and inhaled deeply. Holding my breath for a moment, I envisioned it moving to the pit of my stomach, settling there. I cleared my head of all my worries, released the breath slowly, and anchored myself to the present moment.

Stretching out my arms, I stepped forward, formed a fist, and punched into nothingness. I repeated the steps a few times, switching up my feet and arms. My body warmed, and my heart rate increased. Muscles cramped all along my right rib, but I pushed through. Damn this poison. After an entire year of honing my life force and training my body to adjust to the various martial arts formations, I'd fallen back a few steps.

"Stupid Ru Malik!" Anger pulsed through me as I punched the air, imagining his masked face. "I'm going to destroy you! It's all your fault!"

If he hadn't made people sick, I wouldn't have investigated. I wouldn't have been at that abandoned temple and gotten sick. Even now, I couldn't figure out how I'd gotten poisoned.

I let out a series of curses, something I refrained from doing while working at the apothecary.

After a while, my body warmed, and my formations flowed easily. This would be the perfect opportunity to practice the sword stance I'd seen the soldiers performing in Gong's lesson. I once saw it when I dropped herbal medicine at the military camp. Instead of returning to the apothecary, I had stayed to watch them from behind several tall trees.

Glancing around, I spotted a twig on the ground and grabbed it. I swung it around, testing its weight on my hand. Once I felt comfortable with it, I tried to mimic the moves I'd seen.

I swung the sword out, cutting into the air. But it didn't feel right. I tried swinging it to the side, moving my feet for balance. Something was still off. I wished I had someone to tell me what I was doing wrong.

Who would teach a woman how to fight? A healer should be working in an apothecary. She should be caring and gentle and not align herself with weapons or violence.

She should be this—she should do that. Society loved to invent rules that made little sense at all. But many people didn't question norms or why they'd come to be. They just accepted it as though it were the air they breathed. I didn't understand it.

I could still be a caring person with self-defense skills, couldn't I? What was wrong with having the ability to defend yourself? If my parents had those skills, they wouldn't have died. Thinking about those ruthless people made me angry, but I needed to calm my mind and body to activate my essa.

A flash of light illuminated the dark sky like lightning. I paused my practice and glanced up at the few clouds that didn't look stormy. A few stars twinkled from where the flash of light had just occurred.

"What's going on up there?" I asked no one as I sat down on a wooden stool. "Thank you for being my sword." I dropped the twig on the ground.

I turned my attention to the stars, fascinated by the sea of lights. What was up there besides the stars? It seemed so vast, magical, and mysterious. I remembered my parents telling me bedtime stories about dragons, phoenixes, heavenly bunnies, tigers, snakes—all the animals in the zodiac. I used to imagine all of them sitting around an ornate dinner table, talking about silly things.

Like the mysterious sky, a child's mind was vast and magical. But now, I was an adult who had fears, doubts, and limitations. I'd experienced grief, seen too much suffering and too many deaths. How much could I contribute to the community? Were my healing abilities good enough? I paled in comparison to my parents' skills. If I'd spent more time mixing medicine blends rather than practicing my kung fu, I'd probably be better now.

Mẹ and Ba, please don't be disappointed with me.

I continued studying the sky, wanting to see another flash, but nothing showed up. As a child, I'd always wondered what was beyond the sky. Wouldn't it be amazing to look down on the landscape from up there? What would the mountains and valleys look like?

A bug flew by the lantern, casting a shadow. I stared at the light for a moment, feeling relaxed. Resting my head on my palm, I studied the sky. I'd always wanted to sleep outside under the stars. There was something magical about it. The crickets sang louder, and the night air cloaked around me, making my eyelids heavy . . .

I glance around the dark tunnel. Lights twinkle around me. For a moment, I feel like I'm standing in the night sky. It's quiet and peaceful. The starscape continues on and on into an infinite vastness.

Where am I?

Something nudges me, and I turn my head. Colorful lights radiate in the distance. The lights appear like a doorway or a tunnel to something. The lights radiate, streaming out and casting a soft glow to the atmosphere.

I'm standing on a massive tree branch that extends all the way to the light. Around me are more tree branches with magical leaves. They're hidden in the darkness. I don't see them until streams of light move past them. Energy zips up and down my body. I gasp as my mind registers the energy as essa. I study it closely—there are textures and patterns within the energy. The patterns shift to create an intricate mandala.

I know that I'm dreaming and things shouldn't make sense. But somehow, a part of me understands the surrounding complexity.

More portals of light emerging? Or were they the emergence of new stars?

Geometric shapes sparkle and float around me like little lanterns. They mesmerize me. As a flower mandala passes over my head, I reach up to touch it. My hand jerks from the surge of electricity that runs from my finger to my toes. My body trembles from this newness.

The flower mandala I touched glows brighter and brighter as though I've turned something on.

A growl echoes in the far distance, followed by another. Some-

thing twists in my stomach before a peaceful sound hums around me, making the fear disappear.

The colorful lights and geometric shapes fade away, leaving only a single portal of light. The soft pinks, purples, and blues pulse, beckoning me. I make my way toward them and look down at my feet. I can't see the tree branch anymore, but I know it's there. There's so much darkness around me with areas filled with light. I'm not sure where that door of light will take me. But I'm curious.

As I approach, sparkles flash everywhere, adding more colors to the spectrum.

Where am I? A memory of me retrieving water flashes through my mind. Then another image of me standing close to General Wen appears, and my heart thumps loudly. The images fade, and I'm sad. A headache blooms as I try to remember his face. He's so handsome.

"Su . . ."

Someone calls me. I've heard this voice before.

The scar on my forearm twitches and tingles. I look down, and the scar is illuminated. What's going on?

"Su . . ."

I look around but don't see anyone. It's just darkness and stars all around me. "Who's there?"

A large animalistic eye flashes into my mind like that time I meditated in the woods.

"Su!"

My body shook awake as my heart pounded in my chest. I glanced around at the dark night.

"You're going insane, Su," I said, realizing I'd fallen asleep. "This isn't your bedroom."

I grabbed the oil lantern, gathered the water bottles, and headed home.

CHAPTER SIX

HUNG

THE NEXT TWO days left me with little time until I finally stole a moment to eat.

Needing the quiet, I brought the container that held my wonton soup and entered my office. I closed the door, sat at my desk, retrieved the soup bowl, and lifted the lid. The aroma wafted up immediately, making my stomach growl. The soup was from the Blue Phoenix Tavern. They knew my regular favorites.

I'd skipped dinner last night because of an urgent meeting with my men. There wasn't time for breakfast this morning either. With a moment to myself, I didn't want to think about anything that gave me a headache. I wanted to clear my mind and enjoy this lunch before heading to the City Apothecary.

That night at the shed left me with a lot of questions for Su. I'd wanted to visit the shop to talk to her, but more people had gone missing, and I had to deal with that issue first. How could people disappear without a trace? There were no signs of theft in their homes. Fear stirred within Luklum, and I could understand why.

On a positive note, the water testing from the wells showed no traces of the poison. That was a tremendous relief.

I dug into my wonton noodle soup, and my mind wandered

back to Su. Did she see the flash in the sky last night? I had thought I was imagining things. But the way she'd stared at the sky told me she also saw something. I had stayed in the shadows watching her, but she didn't do anything that would connect her to the Bloodshade Bandits.

But what was she doing with the well water? Did she know Ru Malik? Was she working for him? If they were working together, why was she cursing at him?

What surprised me even more was seeing her practice martial arts. How long had she been learning it? I could see room for improvement, but that wasn't my place. Who was her teacher?

Despite the many questions brewing in my head, I wanted to wait before confronting her. If she was working for Ru Malik, the extra time would hopefully reveal what kind of relationship they had. Maybe she'd make a mistake somewhere that would give me clues to apprehending him and his Bloodshade Bandits.

Disappointment stirred in me as I imagined arresting and imprisoning her. I shouldn't be attracted to her. The last thing I needed was a criminal sweet-talking me so that she could get away with crimes. And even if she were innocent, Ren wanted her. I couldn't do that to him.

From what I gathered, Su was twelve years younger than me. A young woman like her would want someone her age. We'd have nothing to talk about, nothing in common. She was more inclined to like Ren because he was four years younger than me.

I choked on a noodle and drank some jasmine tea to help it go down. That was probably a sign from the heavens telling me to stop this ridiculous yearning. Maybe I could meet up with a lady friend at a man's tavern to get rid of this itch. But the thought of another woman didn't electrify my body the same way.

Why was I spending my lunchtime thinking about things that confused me? I was trying to clear my head, not clutter it. Yet I couldn't stop myself.

Ren was a respected scholar, more suitable for a healer.

However, based on what I'd witnessed the other night, she was no typical healer. She had a warrior's spirit.

Stop thinking about irrelevant things. She'll be your prisoner soon.

What the hell had gotten into me? I'd never been distracted because of a woman until now. I blamed it on the lack of sleep and the multiple investigations that were exhausting me.

Though I got a little sleep last night, it didn't seem to help keep the distractions away.

Despite having my men keeping an eye out for the bandits, I wondered how they'd gotten past our border so easily. How had they infiltrated Sun Wheat Valley to take it over without me or any other general hearing about it until it was too late?

I knew the bandits were already in Luklum, probably disguised as normal citizens. Had Samo and Jie assisted the bandits? How long had they been working with Ru Malik?

I had to go interrogate their families for more information. This was an urgent matter, and I'd given them enough time to grieve. But first, I needed to stop by the City Apothecary.

On my way there, Lina Zhou stopped me in the street. She stood with her maid, Ting.

"Hung!" Lina beamed, her cheeks flushing pink, matching her dress. "Ren said you'd be in your office."

Lina was General Zhou's daughter and Ren's younger sister. When we were younger, Lina used to tag along with me and her brother.

"Do you need something?" I asked.

Lina had opened Heavenly Reflections with two of her friends in the market, selling jewelry, hair accessories, and talismans.

"I had this talisman made for you." She stepped up to me and held out an intricate gemstone with a tassel. "It's for good luck."

"I don't need it."

"Yes, you do." She hooked it onto my belt. "It looks wonderful on you."

I knew she had feelings for me. Everyone knew. She was a beautiful woman and many eligible bachelors had come to her father expressing an interest in marriage, but she had declined.

When General Zhou asked me if I'd be interested in marrying his daughter, I said no. Settling down wasn't for me. I was a warrior, and I belonged in the field.

Before I could make an excuse to leave, she looped her arm in mine, leading me to Heavenly Reflections. "Help me pick out a talisman for Ren."

"I'm busy. Have one of your friends help you."

"But they're not men." She smiled up at me. "I need a man's perspective. Please? It won't take long."

Before I knew it, I was inside the busy shop. The swarm of women in the store surprised me. Why did they need to buy so many hairpins? Women giggled as they saw me and Lina.

A familiar energy entered the store, one that made my body tingle. Without looking around, I knew it was Su.

"What color are you looking for?" Su asked Yunxi.

She stood on the other side of the store, looking like a polished gem—incomparable to everyone.

She's going to be your prisoner.

I shoved away the thought and studied her demeanor. She seemed like a different person from the other night. Right now, she wore a baby blue dress with a dark blue belt that had intricate embroidery. Two floral hairpins gleamed in her hair. They were simple yet stood out to me more than the complex designs.

Su picked up a gold hairpin with pink flowers. She'd look beautiful in it.

I blinked at my ridiculous thought.

What the fuck was wrong with me? Since when did I care about what women wore in their hair? Silly little hair trinkets had nothing to do with capturing enemies, solving crimes, or perfecting war strategies.

But it can be used as a weapon.

I heard my retort and knew I needed to take a few days to come to my senses again.

Lina grabbed my arm and dragged me over to a table filled with all kinds of talismans. She picked up a royal blue sigil with gold tassels.

"How about this? It's made from the orange opal from the Eastern Empire."

At that moment, Su met my gaze, and my heart raced. Though she didn't stand close to me, I still sensed her energy as though she were right next to me. My skin warmed, and an odd sensation rushed through me—making me hard.

Fuck.

I didn't want to bring attention to my dick, but it was as hard as stone. I'd never reacted to a woman like this. The more I tried to shove her from my mind, the more she lingered.

Su smiled at me, and I offered her a nod. She turned to look at Lina, who was placing various talismans on me, testing them out as though they were for me.

"Do you like this?" Lina asked me.

"What do you think, Su?" I asked, catching her off guard.

CHAPTER SEVEN

SU

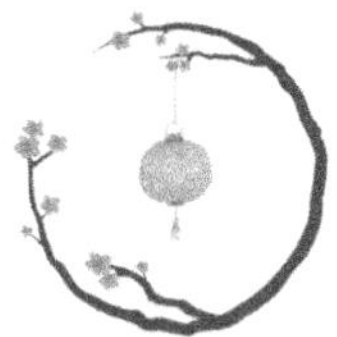

GENERAL WEN'S question took me by surprise. I stalled for a second, unsure of how to respond. Everyone in Luklum knew that Lina from the prestigious Zhou family adored the General. She didn't hide her affection for him, but I couldn't tell if he reciprocated it. Did he like her?

Why did I care anyway? A man like him wouldn't be interested in a commoner like me. He had a wide selection of noble daughters to choose from. Jealousy squirmed inside me, making me feel uneasy.

I didn't like this uncomfortable feeling. Yearning for someone differed from fantasizing about it, right? My fantasies about General Wen were private thoughts I indulged in when I had time alone. I knew he was beyond my reach. But seeing him with a beautiful woman from a privileged family made me want to be with him. What would it be like to be held in those powerful arms? To be the sole object of his attention? To be kissed by him?

I shuddered at the outrageous thought, which surprised and annoyed me. I should know better than to want the impossible.

"Are you okay?" General Wen asked.

Lina stared at me with an arched eyebrow.

"Yes, I'm fine," I said, trying my best to subdue my embarrassment. I gripped the talisman, admiring the royal blue color and the gold tassels. I wasn't sure if he wanted my opinion on the talisman for him or for her. "The color is bold and regal. Perfect for anyone who receives it."

I couldn't tell if he liked my reply.

"See, Hung?" Lina beamed at him. "I'll get one for you and one for Ren."

"You already gave me one." General Wen glanced down at the talisman dangling from his belt. "I don't wear things like that."

An ache grew in my chest, and I didn't like it.

"But you should. It looks good on you." She poked him in the chest. "It's for your protection. You need it when you're in battle or catching criminals." She tilted her face up at him. "Trust me."

Like me, she was a head shorter than him. I heard she was a year older than me, but her flawless skin made her seem much younger. Even her hands appeared delicate and soft. Some people got lucky and didn't have to labor like others. They had maids doing everything for them. I didn't blame Lina for being blessed— I just understood how different we were.

My parents had taught me to be self-sufficient at a young age, which had come in handy when they passed.

Yunxi came over and held up a peace blossom hairpin. "What do you think of this for Aunt Yin?" Aunt Yin was a client at the apothecary who always brought us food whenever she stopped by. Tomorrow was her birthday, and we wanted to show her our appreciation.

"I think she'll love it."

"Let's get it!" Yunxi beamed.

Lina dragged General Wen's arm to another table, looking at hairpins. They acted like a loving couple. The ache in my chest flared up again, and I sucked in a breath.

"Are you feeling okay?" Yunxi leaned in and whispered, "Is the poison bothering you?"

Could I blame the jealousy on the poison? Maybe it was the

combination of the poison and the stress of seeing my dream man with another woman.

"I'm okay," I said, heading to the counter to pay for the hairpin.

Su . . .

A voice echoed in my head. It sounded close by, but when I glanced around, I didn't see anyone. It was the same voice that had called me in my dream the other night. Who was it?

I looked around once more and saw General Wen staring at me suspiciously.

CHAPTER EIGHT

HUNG

AFTER WALKING LINA HOME, I began to make my way to the City Apothecary, but Kai approached me in the street with a concerned expression.

"Three dead bodies were just discovered."

"Where?" I asked.

"At the Pearl Forest Rest Stop," Kai said. "The merchants reported as soon as they arrived in the Market Square. They stopped at the rest stop after a long day of traveling and spotted the bodies. The merchant feared for his family's safety and rushed to report the crime at the Imperial Court today."

Pearl Forest was just outside of Luklum. The popular rest stop gave travelers a place to pause, eat, and sleep before continuing on their journey. The Pearl Forest Road was a common path that led to the adjacent cities and towns.

"Gather some men to join us." I turned around, walking toward my home to retrieve my horse instead of continuing to the City Apothecary. My visit there needed to be postponed.

"I already sent two men to cover up the bodies and block off the area until we arrive."

I nodded as thoughts spiraled in my head.

Could the bodies be those of the missing townspeople? Who was behind these crimes?

Kai lifted an eyebrow as he flicked the talisman. "Who's that for?"

I yanked off the talisman, placing it in Kai's hand. "For you. It's supposed to keep you safe from dark energy."

"Shouldn't you keep it?" Kai stared at it.

"The dark has already seeped into my soul. There's no saving me."

"True." Kai chuckled. "The dark needs its own talisman to protect itself from you."

I admired his sense of humor despite the chaos swirling around us. I didn't mind the dark. Some of my best strategies emerged from immersing myself in the quiet dark of the night.

"Joking!" he piped up when I didn't respond quickly enough.

"I know, asshole."

On the way to the Pearl Forest Rest Stop, I surveyed the surroundings. Merchants and civilians traveled on foot or used carriages pulled by horses or oxen. Nothing appeared out of the ordinary at a glance, but I sensed a lingering darkness.

When we arrived, an odd scent stirred in the air.

I turned to Kai. "You smell that?"

Nodding, he covered his nose and mouth with his hand.

"The bodies have a strange smell." Two guards approached, offering me, Kai, and the four soldiers who had come with us handkerchiefs to cover our noses and mouths.

I placed my handkerchief on and glanced around the rest stop. Tables and chairs sat beside a large bamboo gazebo that offered shelter for travelers. Various trees and bamboo surrounded the area. Cobwebs covered the four empty vendor stands, which told me no one had used them in a while. This place had been busy two years ago when I passed by. Despite that, the well-worn path proved travelers had been using this rest stop.

Were these people killed here? Or were they killed elsewhere and moved here?

Several scenarios emerged in my head as I stood over the three bodies covered in blankets. I removed the blankets and studied the corpses: they had distorted facial features, hollow cheeks, and their eyes were missing. Their bones appeared to be sucked out of their bodies.

Based on the clothing, one body was a child. He lay beside a man and a woman, possibly his parents.

"What happened to their bones?" Kai asked, staring at the piles of soot where bones should have been.

When had they died? For this kind of decomposition, it must have been a while ago.

"I don't know." I walked around the bodies, careful not to step on any soot. "Looks like dark magic. We'll need to remove the soot and clean up this area. Take some soot back for examination."

"Okay." Kai took two soldiers with him.

I waved over the rest of the soldiers, including the two guards who had come early to block off the rest stop.

"Can you look for any signs of soot?" I pointed to the surrounding woods. "Let me know if you spot any."

"Will do, General." They bowed their heads and walked off the assignment.

While my men wandered into the woods, I studied the area around the dead bodies. It didn't look like a fight had taken place. The grass appeared untouched. There were no markings on the dirt near their bodies. If bandits had attacked this family, there would have been signs of a scuffle. My suspicion leaned toward the theory that the family had been killed elsewhere.

"General Wen!" a soldier hollered from the woods.

I rushed into the woods and encountered the soldier. "What happened?"

Hope sparked in his eyes. "We found the missing girl from the Shen Family."

CHAPTER NINE

SU

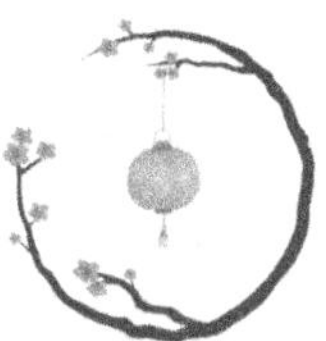

"GO GET SOME REST," said Healer Churan.

"I can help you sort the dried herbs and put out more essential oils." I glanced over at the basket of herbs and the bottles of oils. "You need more lavender, lotus, and rose oils."

"Your color looks much better." She studied me. "I don't want you to overexert yourself. Are you in pain anywhere?"

"No," I said. "I've been monitoring my body too. The sporadic fever is finally gone."

Though my energy was stable, there was something different about it. But I didn't know how to explain it. Healer Churan had plenty to do, and she didn't need to worry about me.

The number of sick people had diminished drastically over the past few days. The apothecary could catch up on the tasks pushed aside when we had to focus on treating the patients. Aside from treating sick people and selling all kinds of remedies, we also sold essential oils, bath soaps, and fragrances.

"It's not too busy today. Take advantage of it. Get some fresh air."

"Are you sure?" I could use the time to practice my kung fu and cultivate my energy.

She grabbed a basket of yarrow and astragalus and sorted them. "Yunxi and I will be fine. It's slowed a lot here today. Go."

The door opened, and the Empress's maid, Mei, entered. The two braids enhanced her friendly face.

Wearing a soft pink dress, she walked up to me. "Empress Jayaatu would like to see you today, Healer Su. She's running out of her *self-care* concoction." She smiled and patted the empty basket in her hand.

The self-care concoction was the code for Empress Jayaatu's pregnancy. She didn't want anyone to know about her pregnancy because she'd experienced a miscarriage last year that had devastated her. Everyone in Lin Din Ni had known about the pregnancy and had celebrated. So when the baby didn't make it, the entire country mourned. I understood why she was extra careful this time.

I walked to the back room and gathered some prepared packages made of ginger, raspberry leaf, peppermint, angelica root, Schisandra berry, and astragalus. I also took a pack of dried ginger dipped in sugar cane. Empress Jayaatu had been experiencing morning sickness, so these ginger candies would help ease the nausea.

I placed the herb packages into Mei's basket. "You can take these to her. I'll stop by after I pick up a few more things at the market.

"Thank you." Mei beamed.

As I walked through the Market Square, I passed the bulletin that announced the well water was safe to drink. They had all tested negative for any poisons.

Though the announcement eased my worry a little, I still had questions. It didn't make sense to me. That night, I'd heard Ru Malik ordering Samo and his friends to poison the wells, but now the officials stated there was no trace of any poison. What had happened?

Did Samo and his friends fail? If they did, maybe Ru Malik

poisoned them as punishment. Various scenarios popped into my head.

"Are you feeling better?"

My body jerked at the voice, and I turned to see Ren smiling at me.

I didn't know what he was referring to. "What?"

"You weren't feeling well the last time I saw you."

That was the day I'd met him and General Wen in the Market Square. "I'm better, thank you."

"Glad to hear it. There's a Lantern Blessing Festival coming up in a few months. Would you like to attend?"

I hadn't even thought about the festival at all. The Lantern Blessing Festival was a fun event where everyone bought or made lanterns to illuminate the night. Each lantern brought more light into the world. Some said magic happened on that day. I used to enjoy the festival, but I stopped attending when my parents died. We used to make lanterns together and hang them outside our home to welcome in the blessings. We'd go out into the streets and enjoy delicious meals and chat with friends. That tradition died with my parents.

"I'm not going," I said.

"Why not?" he asked, looking disappointed.

Ren had a handsome face, and a lot of women wanted to marry into the Zhou family. They were a noble family who was part of the military. But I wasn't attracted to him and had never given him any indication that I was. Some women liked the attention and played along. I didn't have the patience for games.

Somehow, that didn't deter Ren from pursuing me. Perhaps I should be clearer to him?

"Scholar Zhou." Two beautiful women strode up to him. "Will you be offering that poetry class again? We missed the most recent signup." A lady wearing a soft green dress twirled a strand of her long hair.

"Perhaps after the Lantern Blessing Festival." He grinned. "I'll have to see what my schedule is like."

The lady with the pink dress beamed. "Are you going to the festival? Will you be giving out the paper lotus flowers like last year?"

Ren smiled, loving the attention. "I plan to."

"I hope I get the lucky lotus and can attend a class with you!" The lady wearing the green dress clapped with excitement.

A dark energy pricked me as though a thorn were scraping gently down my arm, and my body stiffened.

I looked around and spotted a man with a slight beard in a brown outfit standing beside a group of people by a fried noodle vendor. The way his eyes scanned the area told me he wasn't buying noodles but searching for something.

What was he looking for?

When our eyes connected, he turned and darted from the crowd. I rushed after him, ignoring Ren's call for me. If this man was part of the Bloodshade Bandits, I had to find him and alert General Wen.

But when I came to the street intersection, he'd disappeared. He could've gone down any of those paths.

"Su!" Ren approached, looking out of breath. "Are you okay? What happened?"

"I thought I saw a Bloodshade Bandit."

"Really? Where?" His eyes widened. "How do you know it's them?"

"Just a guess." I shrugged. "We need to alert General Wen."

"I'll let him know when he returns," Ren said.

"Where did he go?" I asked, even though it wasn't my business. "I mean, is there another crime he's investigating?"

Had he discovered something new about Ru Malik?

Ren rolled his eyes. "Hung is always investigating something."

I wondered what it would be like to address General Wen by his first name.

"He's trying to protect Luklum," I said, trying to defend the General.

My forearm itched, and I lifted my sleeve to scratch it. My

scar had gotten darker, and the shape had changed. What used to be a subtle scar now appeared like a dark floral design—a unique mandala. I brushed my hand over it, and the color faded in and out. I shoved my sleeve down and looked up to see Ren staring at me.

"What happened?" he asked, looking concerned. "Did that man hurt you?"

"No," I said. "Just an itch."

Most women would love Ren's protectiveness, but I wasn't one of them. My heart had only been moved by one other man. Since I saw General Wen training his soldiers in the field two years ago, I hadn't stopped thinking about him.

"Why aren't you attending the festival?" Ren asked again. "It's fun."

I didn't want to explain my history with him.

"Not in the mood. There've been too many deaths in the city, and I've been working a lot. I just want peace and quiet."

As we headed back to the Market Square, a group of women swarmed him with questions about the festival and the lotus flower prizes.

"I've got to go." I waved goodbye and headed to buy some pastries for Empress Jayaatu. Like me, she loved her sweets.

On my way to the palace, I sensed someone following me, but I didn't see anyone suspicious. To be cautious, I remained within the Market Square and pretended to shop for miscellaneous things.

When the strange sensation disappeared, I entered the majestic palace filled with fancy decor, beautiful paintings, regal courtyards, charming fish ponds, intricate gazebos, and exquisite bridges. A magical world existed within these walls because of Empress Jayaatu. Some called her The Seamstress because of her ability to extract energy from plants and animals, weaving their life forces together to create a more potent energy. This thriving energy moved around the palace, reflected in the flowering trees, bushes, and grasses.

As I walked down several hallways, I nodded as the passing guards recognized me. I made it to the Empress's section of the palace and walked toward her mesmerizing garden. Her weaving of essas had created rare plants that only grew in Luklum. I glanced up at the tall, twisty trees with flowers hanging from the branches like illuminating curtains.

Wanting to enjoy this peaceful moment, I slowed my steps and sat on a bench with floral vines twisted around it. Was someone following me, or was I being paranoid? With all that had happened, I had every reason to be paranoid. What if someone spotted me disguised as a man at the abandoned temple that night? Had Ru Malik figured out it was me? Did he send that man in the brown outfit to watch me?

Stop it. You're scaring yourself.

I pulled up my sleeve and glanced at the mandala etched into my forearm. The scar I'd gotten as a child was growing. Why was it expanding now?

Fear slithered around me, whispering terrifying scenarios. I'd seen diseases that affected the skin. A change of color, texture, or shape could signify the diseases had worsened.

Was the poison intensifying inside me? If so, why didn't I feel weakness or other symptoms? My pulse appeared fine, and my energy wasn't erratic.

Healer Churan would have sensed something dire. But I hadn't shown her the changes to the scar on my forearm yet.

Tonight, I'd examine the scar in more detail. Right now, I had to check up on my pregnant friend.

CHAPTER TEN

SU

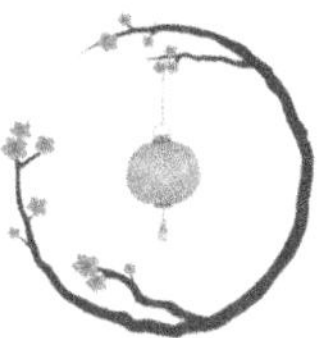

AS I APPROACHED the Empress's garden, I walked by the nascynth bush, native to Lin Din Ni. Nascynths were star-shaped flowers that resembled jasmine flowers but were smaller. Their pink petals normally spiraled, sending outbursts of light. But the flowers on this bush were dried up. The Empress was usually good at maintaining her garden and removing dead buds so they didn't use unnecessary energy, but her pregnancy must have been occupying her mind. She enjoyed tending to her plants instead of having her maids do it.

I stopped and plucked off all the dried flowers from the bush. The dead flowers would only use up energy from the plant. My skin tingled as I removed the last dry flowers. Maybe the tingling sensation was the plant's gratitude for my assistance.

"You're welcome," I said. "You can breathe easily now."

I found my best friend pruning another nascynth bush. Threads of golden essa swirled around her. A table of supplies stood beside the Empress. Walking up to the stone table near the bamboo gazebo, I placed the bags of pastries and ginger and lemon candies there.

I ambled over to Empress Jayaatu, trying not to disturb her.

The flower bushes glowed around her like a sea of pink stars. The way the petals spiraled mesmerized me. Enchanted by the magic, I stood there studying my friend.

At twenty-seven, Empress Jayaatu was five years older than me. She had long dark hair with a natural wave. Yeeva's family came from a small valley that no longer existed. The Emperor had saved her from demonic beings years ago. She was the last member of her family who could tap into essas and weave them together.

Today, she wore a lilac gown that flowed in the gentle breeze. The soft color added warmth to the lovely glow that emanated from women who were with child. Her intricate earrings that matched the mesmerizing necklace glistened when they caught the light from the flowers. The simple gold crown with gorgeous gemstones added to her beauty.

Yeeva and I met years ago when we both chased after a blue rabbit into the woods. It was a color I hadn't seen before. We didn't want a wolf or any other beast hurting it. I'd considered the rare sighting auspicious because the Empress and I became friends that day.

Though the rabbit disappeared in the woods, Yeeva and I continued to discuss the rabbit and every other topic that came to mind.

Empress Jayaatu held a flower branch in her hand, and the glow from the flower fluctuated. It dimmed and glowed and dimmed again, reminding me of dying candlelight. I hadn't seen that before.

"Is everything okay?" I walked up to her, pointing to the flower. "The flower looks like it's struggling to light up."

Smiling, she placed her shears on the table beside the bush and offered me a hug, which she didn't do in public. An empress had to keep her distance from commoners to prevent gossip and the impression of favoritism.

Pulling back, I studied her pale face. "You're not feeling well?"

"I should ask you that question." She looked at me with worried brown eyes as she gripped my hands. "Your energy is unstable." She squeezed my hand. "It's fighting something."

The poison.

"You can see that?" I asked, jealous of anyone who could see energy.

"Not as clearly as I used to." She rubbed her flat stomach, which showed no signs of her pregnancy even though she was about four months along.

I didn't want to worry her about my health. Based on my observation, she was also weak.

"It's nothing serious," I said. "Healer Churan made a concoction for me. I'm feeling a lot better."

"What did you have?"

"Probably caught something from one of the sick patients." I lifted a shoulder. "We had a surge. Did you know the well water was contaminated?"

"I heard it's safe to drink now." She nodded. "General Wen also checked the Green Fog River to ensure it wasn't contaminated."

I hadn't even thought about that. Streams from that river ran through several small villages around Luklum.

"I'm glad he thought about the streams. I was focused on the major wells in Luklum."

"General Wen is thorough like that. Wei trusts him." She slid me a curious look with a slow smile. "He's an eligible bachelor. Very handsome, strong, powerful, and charismatic." She stared at me as though asking a silent question.

"What?" I asked, pretending not to know what she was doing.

One time, I accidentally blurted out that General Wen was handsome. Yeeva hadn't forgotten that slip and kept teasing me about it. He was beyond my reach.

"You should ask him to teach you kung fu. I'm sure he'd do it."

I snorted. "He's busy investigating on top of his regular duties. I'm sure his soldiers need him more than I do."

"He needs a good woman like you to distract him from working too much. Do you want me to write a decree, forcing him to teach you?" the Empress asked without blinking. How could she send out an official decree for something so trivial?

"No!" I exclaimed. "There are more important things for you to do than force the Prime General to train a healer."

"But the healer is my *best* friend."

I rolled my eyes. "Seriously, don't do it. Or I won't give you more ginger and lemon candies *or* egg custards." I narrowed my eyes and gestured to the bags on the stone table. "Besides, I haven't had time to practice like I used to."

Laughing, she took my hand and ushered me to the stone table. We both sat down, and she peeked into the bag of egg custards. Her eyes shone as she took one out, bit into it, and sighed. "So good. I've been craving these. Thank you!"

"How are you feeling?" I studied her.

She chewed, swallowed, and placed a hand on her stomach. "I feel her energy. She's a strong one."

"You know it's a girl already?" I stared at her stomach.

She nodded. "We didn't do the pendulum magic to guess the gender. It doesn't matter to us whether the baby is a boy or a girl. We'll love her or him the same." She reached for the bag of ginger candies and took one out, popping it into her mouth. "I had a dream about a strong yet lovely energy embracing me. Intuition tells me it's a girl."

"That's wonderful, Yeeva." I reached for her hand and squeezed. "Addressing her by her first name had taken getting used to. It took me almost six months before I was comfortable doing so. But it was the Empress's order.

Friends address each other by first names.

"Do you have a name for the baby yet?" I asked.

"Not yet." She glanced down at her belly and smiled. "I'll let it come to me."

"When do you plan on announcing it to everyone?"

"I'll have to soon because my belly is growing." Concern splashed on her face.

"What's worrying you?" I asked.

"There's something in the air." She lifted her fingers and wiggled them. A stream of light emerged from her index finger, flickering on and off like the glowing flowers.

"You're weak." I met her eyes.

She nodded. "It's the pregnancy. My energy is divided between my baby and me."

That was true, but I sensed something else was worrying her. Yeeva gave light to the plant life around her by energizing it with her essa. I glanced around, admiring the trees and flowering bushes. Despite their beauty, they lacked the luster that used to radiate from this garden.

"Make sure you rest," I told her.

"Right after the archery competition." She rubbed a hand over her belly. "I'll be announcing my pregnancy on that day as well."

I arched a brow at her. "Shouldn't you be focusing on resting?"

She sighed. "You know Wei loves martial arts. With each competition, he wants to concentrate on a specific skill. One year, it was sword fighting. Another year, spear sparring or various kung fu formations. This year, Wei wants an archery competition."

A few years ago, I'd watched adept warriors from all over the world come for a chance to win a weapon from the Emperor's Weaponry.

"I've always wanted to learn archery," I said. "What's the prize?"

"A weapon forged from the blue fulgurite stone."

Blue fulgurite was a rare crystal created by the power of lightning piercing through the earth's surface, formed entirely by power and heat. I'd heard the fulgurite stone was found in other parts of the world, but Lin Din Ni was the only place where it was blue.

"That's a precious stone to Lin Din Ni," I said, not under-standing why the Emperor and Empress would want to give some-thing that priceless away. "People have been trying to steal blue fulgurite for years."

"And they've failed." She rose from her chair, stretched her back, and walked over to a pot of flowers on a stone pedestal. "What they don't know is that the fulgurite has intelligence. It will activate when it resonates with a specific energy." She plucked off some dried flowers and tossed them into the trash. "So even if a warrior gets a blue fulgurite sword, if the stone doesn't agree with his energy, the sword won't be as effective."

The way she described the event told me there was another agenda beyond a simple martial arts competition.

"What are you aiming at?"

"Wei wants to recruit more adept warriors to join his council or military." She smiled. "It's hard to find skilled and loyal men. Plus, the winner with the new fulgurite weapon would be a new attraction, leaving Lin Din Ni out of the spot-light for a while."

The blue fulgurite stone was located behind the palace in a sacred space that no one visited except the Emperor and Empress.

"That's a great idea," I said. "The more skilled warriors we have, the better. I'm in awe of the stone's versatility." I gestured to the crown with the three blue jewels on her head. "It can be a decorative jewel or a powerful weapon."

"Look." Yeeva reached behind her neck and removed the necklace. "There's blue liquid fire in it, kind of like an opal. But it's lightning energy." She dropped it into my hand.

Its weight surprised me. "It's heavy. How can this pendant be comfortable for you to wear?" I examined the oval gemstone encased in a delicate gold setting. As I shifted the stone from side to side, the blues flashed. "It's a rare stone indeed."

An idea sparked in my head, and I debated on whether I should share it.

Yeeva looked at me. "What is it?"

I twisted my lips, still unsure of how she'd respond to my thought.

She placed a hand on my shoulder. "We're best friends, Su. You can trust me."

"You're going to think I'm insane."

"Which means you're not boring." She smiled. "What is it? Don't make me force you to tell me the truth." She narrowed her eyes.

"I want to participate," I blurted out.

She knew I had a love for martial arts and had been practicing on my own for some time.

"Why not?" Joy and approval sparked in her eyes.

Hope surged in me. "You think so? What if the judges won't allow it? What if the public demands you remove me from the competition?"

"There has never been a female participant from Lin Din Ni. I'm excited to have one this year. Go for it!" She narrowed her eyes. "No one will dare question who I allow into my competition.

Self-doubt crept in. "What if I make a fool out of myself?"

"You will be the first woman—the first healer—to participate." She clasped her hands together with glee. "Use the competition to show that a healer can also be a warrior."

That had been my intention. Fear and excitement rushed through me.

"Now I'll really need to practice."

Winning a fulgurite weapon would be amazing, but being the first woman to participate was even better.

"Come on." Yeeva pulled at my hand. "We just got some new bows and arrows. Take a look at the lightweight bow and arrow from our arsenal. You can have one."

"I can't do that!" I stopped in my steps.

"Of course you can. You're my healer, my friend. There's nothing wrong with showing my appreciation by giving you whatever I want." She huffed. "Besides, Wei will agree with me."

"Okay, but I'll need to give you an exam after. My visit today was to make sure you're healthy. All we've been doing is talking about weapons and competition."

"And a handsome general." She poked me in the ribs. "I like the idea of you and him together. Have you envisioned him and you while flipping through *The Art of Intimacy?*"

"No!" I said too quickly as heat burst on my cheeks.

Yeeva roared with laughter, knowing my quick reply was a lie.

CHAPTER ELEVEN

HUNG

ARRIVING IN THE MARKET SQUARE, I scooped up the girl from the carriage and rushed into the City Apothecary, hoping to find Su. But the Grand Healer spotted me and the little girl in my arms.

"Bring her in here." She gestured to the bed. "What happened?"

I placed the unconscious girl on the bed. During the journey, she'd regained consciousness for a few minutes but lost it again. I didn't see any injuries on her, but I hadn't given her a thorough exam.

"She's the missing girl, Luzi Shen. Everyone in her family is dead." I stepped back to allow Healer Churan to examine her. "We found her in the woods."

"Okay. I'll take a look."

"Let me know if you need anything. I'll be in the waiting room." I stepped out of the room to give her privacy.

I couldn't help but compare myself to this girl. She now had to face the cruelty of this world on her own. She'd have to find the strength to survive.

When my parents died, I had Uncle Seeto to guide me. Did

she have anyone? Was she close to her uncle's family who had reported her missing?

Anger simmered in me. I had no doubt the Bloodshade Bandits killed her family. But why? They weren't wealthy citizens. They didn't hold any Imperial positions. Ming Shen worked at his brother's restaurant while Mai Shen worked as a teacher where her son Bao and Luzi attended school. These were commoners living a simple life.

Su emerged from the back room and rushed up to me. "Yunxi said you brought back a little girl. Is she okay?"

"I hope so." I looked into the exam room. "She's the only survivor of her family."

"The Shen family?" Surprise flashed in her eyes.

A scream erupted outside the apothecary. Su and I exchanged glances and hurried out. It surprised me how quick she was. I'd met several healers while traveling over the years, and Su's reflexes weren't that of a common healer.

How much kung fu did she know? What else was she hiding?

We stepped outside and saw a man wearing a black and red hooded outfit. He plunged his sword into a man and yanked it out. Blood splattered, and onlookers screamed, hiding behind vendors' carts.

I reached for the dart on my weapons belt and whipped it to a nearby pole, triggering the bell to ring. That was the signal for my men to do what was needed.

Drawing my sword, I charged at him. He whirled around and blocked my sword. Swords clashed as metal screeched against metal. He wore a snake mask, as expected from Ru Malik.

I tapped into my essa, drawing power from the pit of my stomach, and fought him. Gold energy swirled from my hand, adding force to my attack.

"Why are you here, Ru Malik?" I snarled.

"You know why!" he growled.

Our swords clashed again. With my free hand, I threw a fist to his face, and he blocked it easily. I wanted to see the actual face underneath the mask. Who was this fucker?

Ru Malik was an adept warrior. The gold of his essa appeared darker than what I was used to seeing. Perhaps the darkness in him affected his essa. It was too bad he was my enemy, otherwise we could've spent time analyzing martial arts skills.

What would he do if he knew he'd fallen into my plan? I'd expected him to show up sooner. But it didn't matter—he was here now. Today, he'd pay for his crimes.

We fought with our swords, legs, and fists until I harnessed my essa and channeled it into my arms, hands, and fingers. The energy sent my sword swinging with so much power it knocked his weapon to the ground with a loud *clank*.

I aimed my sword at him. "Take off your mask."

No one knew what he looked like. "Don't be a coward. Reveal who you really are. You'll be imprisoned in Luklum for all to see anyway."

He laughed. "You're too confident, General Wen. You know what they say about overconfident people: they'll die a torturous death."

"A threat from a rival means nothing to me. It only confirms that you're afraid of me." I paced the street, still holding him at the point of my sword. "A true opponent doesn't hide behind a mask in battle."

The longer I could carry on a conversation with Ru Malik, the more time my team had to come and apprehend him.

Su cleared the area by helping people leave the street. She dragged the bleeding man to the side and treated him. He'd lost too much blood, and I knew he wouldn't make it.

"So righteous," said Ru Malik. "You can't rescue everyone. Just like you couldn't rescue your parents."

My heart raced at his words. Of all the things he could have said to me, that comment surprised me the most. My parents' deaths weren't worthy news to someone like him unless he had something to do with it. Did he?

I had always assumed the Deathcap Clan was responsible. They were one of many rebel groups the Imperial Army was after that time. The country rejoiced when the army obliterated the Deathcap Clan a year after my parents were killed.

"What did you say?" I asked, trying not to reveal my emotions to him.

He cocked his head to the side. "I heard your parents called for you with their last breaths."

Emotions and intrigue whirled in me. What did Ru Malik know about my parents?

Ignore him. He's trying to rile you.

This was a tactic used in battle to distract the opponent so you could attack him when he least expected it. I didn't want to fall into this trap.

"How do you know this? Don't you have enough to do in the Rebel Territory? Why are you so interested in the lives of Luklum civilians?"

"You have no idea what's coming, General Wen. Let me make you an offer now—join me." He pressed a clenched fist to his chest. "Join the Bloodshade Bandits, and you'll be rewarded."

"You should know I have no interest in awards or accolades." I studied him, desperately wanting to know what he knew about my parents' deaths. Apparently, I'd missed something important. "I'm only interested in protecting the civilians of Lin Din Ni."

"Don't be too invested in something that will fail." He let out a laugh. "You're a smart man. Make the right decision."

"And if I don't?"

"Then you too shall perish." He took a slow breath and stared at me. "You can achieve more with me. Don't settle for being the Prime General. The horizon is endless for ambitious warriors like us."

"You obviously don't know me." I pursed my lips. "Why is the leader of the Bloodshade Bandits snooping around in my boring life? Do you admire me or something? Like a big brother? Like a *Sifu*?" I smirked. "Sorry, but I don't accept students who kill innocent people. But if you *kneel* and *beg* me"—I jutted my finger to the ground—"I might consider taking you on to clean the bathroom at my military camp."

He cursed and charged at me.

A battle erupted between us. Screams and chaos rose from the citizens still in the area. I swung my sword at Ru Malik's. Infuriated, he aimed a punch squarely at my face, which I blocked. But something came from his fingernails that I hadn't seen before. Black soot floated up from his hands and lingered in the air. This wasn't essa—this was black magic.

Five men dressed in red attire with hoods covering their masked faces emerged from seemingly nowhere and attacked me. One of them rushed toward Su, and fear surged in me. But she grabbed a rod from a vendor stand and blocked the attack.

Galloping horses sounded, and I knew my men had arrived. The soldiers helped Su and assisted the frightened civilians, blocking off the area. Kai leaped in and fought off the bandits with me. Ru Malik retrieved his sword from the ground and stood by to watch. He was probably waiting for me to use up my energy so he could attack me.

"Sorry, they ambushed us on the way here. Don't worry, they're all fucking *dead* now!" Kai shouted, wanting Ru Malik to hear the news about his men.

Using the iron rod like a sword, Su cut into the bandit's arm. It injured him, but he threw a fist at her face. *The fuck!* Rage spiraled in me. Ru Malik barked something at his men, and they focused on me while Ru Malik charged after Su.

Why her?

She dodged his attack, but his fist slammed into her shoulder, knocking the iron rod out of her hand. Concern soared in me. She wasn't ready for this kind of violence.

With all my might, I gathered my essa, leaped over, and punched Ru Malik, sending him skidding away from Su. A bandit swung an arm at her, but I brought my sword down on it, chopping it off. I broke his legs with two powerful kicks, sending him to his knees. With a forceful swing, I beheaded him. His head rolled and slammed into the wheel of a vendor's cart.

I ran over to Su, who stared at the severed head with widened eyes.

"Are you okay?" I asked.

She didn't answer, and her eyes shifted to something behind me. I immediately shoved her aside and whirled around to dodge a flying dart.

At that moment, Ru Malik charged at me as well.

Two more bandits arrived but were met by Kai. I focused on battling Ru Malik.

"No!" Su cried as I sensed her body behind me.

Kai jumped in to help me fight Ru Malik. I spun around to find Su wincing from a dart sticking out of her right shoulder.

She'd taken a dart for me . . .

A wrath I didn't understand erupted in me. I glared at the bandit, who had held two more darts in his hand.

I'm going to fucking kill you.

"I'm fine," she said, yanking the dart out of her shoulder like a brave soldier. Pain splashed onto her face, but she didn't cry. She'd earned my admiration.

"Go capture him," she said as her face paled. "I'll be fine."

Suddenly, thunder roared, shaking the ground. A flash of lightning sliced through the sky, surprising everyone. Dark clouds had formed above us, but the sun shone not too far away.

"Don't move," I told Su and leaped over to the bandit.

He whipped another dart at me, but I caught it, whipping it back at him. It cut into the side of his neck. Darkness spread onto his skin.

The bandit screamed and gripped his neck, yanking the dart out of him. Black blood dripped down his neck.

Su.

Terror escalated when I realized the dart was poisonous. I turned to my soldiers and pointed to the injured bandit. "Apprehend him. I need the fucker alive."

I rushed over to assist Kai, whose arm was injured.

Ru Malik's fighting skills had improved from the last time I'd encountered him years ago. I blocked a powerful fist from Ru Malik, shoving Kai aside.

"Take Su to safety," I ordered Kai.

He rushed over to Su as I continued my fight with Ru Malik. He knocked my sword out of my hand, and I knocked his weapon away as well.

"Who are you working with?" I threw a tiger claw at him, wanting to rip off the snake mask and the dark hood. He deflected my attack and stepped back.

"Join me, and I'll tell you." He waved his hands around, and clouds of soot emerged from his fingernails. Together, they formed into a dark ball of power. A terrifying face with a mouth faded in and out of the ball. Then he whipped it at me.

"No!" Su screamed.

Time stopped for a split second as a strange force yanked me out of harm's way. Sounds faded around me. I couldn't make out what Kai was saying, his mouth and bodily movements slowed. Not only that—a field of energy blocked the ball of darkness, absorbing its blackness into the wall of energy.

Streams of peach essa emerged from Su's fingers, wrapping around my waist. Other streams were connected to the wall of energy. Everything around us was still in slow motion. Ru Malik cocked his head, probably as baffled by this phenomenon as I was.

What kind of power did Su have? Had she always known about it? The perplexed look on her face answered my question.

Her body trembled as the essa cords disappeared. Su collapsed to the ground, and time resumed its normal flow. Ru Malik leaped onto the roof of a house and disappeared.

Fucking hell!

I didn't chase after him and rushed toward Su.

CHAPTER TWELVE

SU

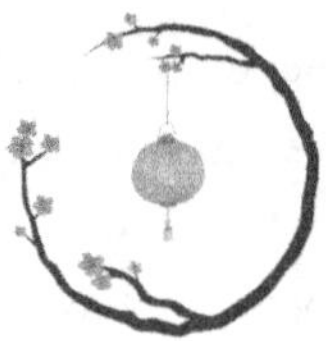

THE POISONED DART had done something terrible to my body. Pain burst in my lower stomach, like a bad menstrual cramp that came in waves. I was in and out of consciousness. I couldn't open my eyes.

A conversation occurred beside me. Voices drifted in and out.

"How is she doing?" I heard General Wen ask Healer Churan.

Su . . .

I need you . . .

Su . . .

It was the same female voice I'd heard that day in the woods and in the shed. I couldn't fully understand her. Back then, the voice had seemed distant. Each time I heard it again, it sounded closer, clearer. But I couldn't hear everything. It was as though something was covering my ears.

Maybe this damn poison was making me hallucinate. Or maybe I was on my deathbed. A flashback of the battle emerged in my mind. I quivered at how I'd fought off those bandits. I'd never been in that kind of fight before. There was no hesitation, even though fear was present. The adrenaline had kept me afloat, obscuring all other emotions.

Voices stirred around me. I sensed it was General Wen and Healer Churan. But I couldn't make out their conversation. Healer Churan was probably monitoring me. But why was General Wen here?

I'd never injured anyone, but that changed today. Guilt cramped my chest. I had been focused on staying alive and making sure General Wen was safe.

As a healer, I'd seen death many times, but I had never killed anyone. Did anyone die by my hands today? Those ruthless bandits deserved death and more for all the violence they'd bestowed on innocent people. They didn't hesitate to attack me, General Wen, or his guard Kai. Still, ending a life changed a person forever.

"Her body is trying to fight it," Healer Churan said. "She has two different poisons in her."

"What? How?" Concern was etched in General Wen's voice. "When did she get the other poison?"

"A few weeks ago." A heavy sigh escaped Healer Churan. "But my medicine has tamed it. It went dormant, but the poison today triggered it again."

"Does Su know kung fu?" General Wen asked.

"I know she has been trying to learn on her own. Why?"

"Just curious," he said. "She saved my life today. She has great potential as a warrior."

The memory of what I'd done emerged. I didn't know how I saved General Wen from Ru Malik. When I saw the darkness, my body tensed with fear, and something shifted in my chest. An inexplicable protectiveness rose in me, fierce and hot. All I wanted to do was to get him out of harm's way.

How had I yanked at his essa? A thrill coursed through me. Had I activated my essa? I saw a peach essa from my hands pulling at General Wen's gold essa.

What power had I invoked? Did I learn something I wasn't aware of? Time had seemed to stand still in that moment. Had I done that? How? Everything happened so fast, I didn't have time to contemplate.

"People with passion achieve great things," Healer Churan said. "Su is the most passionate and curious healer I've ever met."

A storm of hot and cold energies battled within me. Excruciating pain erupted, and my body arched. A second later, the pain subsided.

"Is she okay?" General Wen cursed and gripped my arm. "She's warm."

"She's been like that—hot and cold. But her pulse is abnormally stable."

"Please let me know when she wakes. I'll be back."

Where was he going? I wanted him in the room with me. I wanted to hear his voice. His presence comforted me more than I realized.

A flash of a geometric shape appeared before my eyes. It looked like the scar on my arm, which was heating up.

Su . . .

Be strong . . .

A fresh surge of pain scorched through me, making me feel helpless. My muscles tightened and my skin tingled as movement shifted inside me. I could tell my body was trying hard to fight off the poison. I'd never sensed this kind of awareness before.

Heat rose and sweat dripped down my neck. Was my body losing this battle?

I was dying. This wasn't the painless death I had hoped for later in life. Had I done something awful to deserve this kind of suffering? Heat bloomed around my liver and kidney areas. Were they about to burst?

"I'm sorry," I muttered, trying to open my eyes to check on my body, but they refused to open. Why?

Tears filled my eyes. I was only twenty-two years old. I had so many things I wanted to do—to feel. General Wen's face popped into my vision, and more pressure bloomed in my chest. I never got the chance to confess my feelings for him. Even if he didn't feel the same way, at least he could have known there was a woman who admired him from afar.

I never got to improve my martial arts, either. Tears streamed down my face. Silence thrummed around me. I didn't know if Healer Churan was still in the room. I focused on the chaos within me. Hot and cold. Pain throbbed in my muscles, followed by a strange calmness I didn't understand. Perhaps it was my imagination wishing for something that wasn't there.

My legs and arms twitched from the pain zipping up and down my body. I shivered as a chill embraced me. I tugged at the blanket around my waist, yanking it up to my chin. I curled onto my side, trying to find warmth. A second later, heat blasted, and I kicked off the blanket.

I tried my best to breathe in and out using the technique I learned from the martial arts pamphlet. A beautiful geometric shape emerged in my vision against a dark backdrop. The flower mandala glowed gold as iridescent sparks fluttered around it like tiny flower petals scattering around.

The flower mandala multiplied into various sizes. Some flipped onto their sides, looking like a plate. Others became a three-dimensional circular design. Some even formed into an octahedron shape, created by two three-dimensional triangles attached at the flat base. Healer Churan had a pendant like that.

A spectral shroud seemed to settle over my eyes. I blinked and found myself immersed in a fantastical world with red energy waves moving gently around me. Geometric shapes floated around and filled the space. I was inundated with confusion and intrigue.

Somehow, my body tilted, and I swam in the sea of red energy. The mandalas touched me and bounced away. It felt like I was underwater, but I wasn't holding my breath as I would when I dove into a river or a lake.

What was happening to me? Despite the question, my body somehow knew what to do.

A thought sparked in my mind. Was I swimming in red blood?

My body tingled as though responding to my question. A blob of darkness appeared in the distance. The air thickened as it moved toward me, and I struggled to breathe. The flower mandala glowed brighter, moving through the dark wall. I reached for the gold mandala. It dragged me with it as it swam right into the darkness. A series of sensations overcame me, from hot to cold. When I emerged on the other side, the heaviness in my body lightened, and the air became abundant.

My eyes opened as I breathed deeply. I lay there in wonder and confusion, staring at a peaceful night sky with gleaming stars. Where was I?

I knew my physical body was inside the apothecary's exam room, but why couldn't I see it?

You're in a different realm.

Had I just witnessed my body fighting the poison within me? It seemed surreal, and no one would believe me if I told them my experience.

Su is really sick. She's hallucinating.

I couldn't help but think that the flower mandala was like an acupuncture needle, knowing exactly where to pierce to break through the blockage.

Was this all a dream? I didn't think I was dreaming. It felt too real. Sweat dripped down my eyes from my forehead. I wiped it with my sleeve as I sensed my body calming. The tension in my body loosened as my eyes grew heavy from relaxation, drawing me into a restful sleep.

CHAPTER THIRTEEN

HUNG

EMOTIONS ROILED in me as I stood inside the prison, watching the masked bandit wince in pain. He had whipped the poison dart at Su, and now he had to pay. But I didn't need to dirty my hands because the poison was torturing him for me.

"Do you want to live?" I yanked off the mask that resembled the snake mask worn by Ru Malik. But this one wasn't as intricate.

"Yes!" he cried in agony as dark spots moved under his skin. Like his comrades, who were being questioned by Kai, his hands were secured in manacles that hung from the brick wall.

He'd been infected with the same poison as Su, but his condition appeared worse. He was going to die soon. I had to get information from him to save Su.

The darkness crept down his neck, looking like it was eating his flesh. His panicked eyes flicked to me. "If you get me the antidote, I'll tell you their next move."

"What move?" I asked, trying not to show interest. "Do you think your comrades will offer me the same information?"

I didn't trust anyone from the Bloodshade Bandits. He could make things up to distract me, to buy extra time for someone to save him. No one was getting into this prison. Precautions had already been set in place.

But I played along. "I could consider that option. But it depends on what you have to tell me. Is the information worth your life?"

"Get me the antidote first."

I took an iron rod and prodded him in the neck area where his flesh bubbled. "I don't take orders from you." The darkness covered almost half of his face and neck. "What kind of poison is this?"

"Spewing Pain from the black deathcap."

I'd heard about the Deathcap Clan using this deadly poison a long time ago—they were notorious for using toxins from mushrooms. Who was using their recipe? Were the members still alive?

"Where did you get the poison?"

"I don't know." He seethed as a wave of pain rolled over his body.

Was Su experiencing this pain? Worry and anger consumed me. When I left her, she'd been unconscious.

"Where's the antidote? How do I get it?"

He waited until the pain passed. "There's a pottery shop called Wang's Pottery. The owner is Wang Mo. Go there and tell him you want to buy a custom vase with a snake on it."

"And he'll automatically give me the antidote?"

"He'll tell you there's a special sale on a phoenix teacup set. If you purchase the set along with the custom pottery, he'll give you a discount."

I listened intently to the secret code used to conduct illegal transactions. What else did Wang's Pottery sell?

"You agree to the discount and give him two gold ingots. He'll ask you for the name of the poison. Tell him, and he'll give you the antidote." He winced. "Hurry."

How many antidotes did this asshole carry?

"Does he sell the poison too?" I asked, wanting to kill the fucker.

"Yes." The man groaned as his skin bubbled, spewing out nasty pus.

"Other than Ru Malik, who else does Mo work for?"

He licked his dry lips. "I'm not sure." He reached into his pocket and pulled out a metal plaque with a snake sigil. "This will prove you're a returning customer. He'll think you're part of the Bloodshade Bandits."

As much as I wanted to barge into Wang's Pottery to arrest him, I couldn't. Mo would recognize me as the Prime General. I needed help from someone who wasn't a public figure. How long had he been selling antidotes to Ru Malik? Who were his other customers? I didn't want to arrest him just yet.

Minutes later, I entered the Maroon Meadow to redeem a favor. The tavern outside the Market Square offered lodgings and entertainment for men. People went there for delicious food and pleasant music from a variety of singers and performers. Though the Maroon Meadow was classier than other entertainment places, this wasn't a family-friendly atmosphere.

Despite that, the restaurant drew in a lot of customers. Even in the late afternoon, it was always booming with noise.

I walked up to the counter, and two women dressed in flowy dresses smiled at me. "How can we help you this evening?"

"I'm here to see Blue Orchid. Is she around?"

I didn't have to wait long. Blue Orchid stepped out from the room behind the counter and smiled. Her blue dress enhanced her features. Many men wanted to marry her, but she refused, saying she enjoyed her freedom as a successful businesswoman. Though she offered entertainment at her tavern, she didn't entertain anyone.

"I thought I heard your voice." She walked around the counter to meet me. "What brings you here, General Wen?"

"I need your help with something."

The women behind the counter snickered. Then it dawned on me. Men who entered the Maroon Meadow always needed "help" in one way or another.

I clarified, "Business matters."

The giggles only grew louder. *Fucking hell.*

Blue Orchid grinned but didn't defuse the situation.

The last thing I needed was a rumor that I was spending time here with Blue Orchid. Once a rumor started, it was unstoppable.

"Let's take our *business* to a private room." Blue Orchid smiled and gestured to the room farther down the hallway.

She wasn't helping the situation. "I don't want any rumors."

Once inside, I walked toward the wide window that opened to a lush garden. I approached a round table, removed the sword from my back, placed it on the table, and sat down. "Your office has a lovely view. It's peaceful."

"My private suite. The peace and quiet is perfect for meditation." She smiled. "Don't worry about the girls. I'll ensure they know you're not here for *that* kind of business."

"I didn't know you meditated."

"There are a lot of things you don't know about me, Hung." She poured some tea into a cup and offered it to me. "You had your chance at a relationship with me, but you declined."

I considered her a friend, so I didn't want to break her heart.

"Not interested in a serious relationship." I sipped the tea and placed the cup down. "I can't offer you or any woman the thing they want the most—security."

"So you're going to be single forever? You're not getting any younger."

She didn't need to know about the casual relationships I'd had over the years. But it had been a while since I'd been with a woman.

"Don't worry about me," I said.

I'd saved Blue Orchid from an abusive relationship, so she owed me a favor.

She sat down and considered me. "No woman is good enough for you?"

I grabbed the tea kettle and refilled my teacup. Though Blue Orchid ran an entertainment business for men, she possessed integrity that most men didn't have. For that reason, I considered her a trusted friend.

"More like I'm not good enough for any woman. I'm a warrior who could die at any moment." I crossed my arms. "It's complicated."

As I said that, Su's face flashed into my vision, and warmth spread through my chest. She was the first woman to intrude on my thoughts.

I didn't know what was happening to me.

Liar.

Okay, fine. I knew *exactly* what was happening, but I didn't want to think about it. She stood out from all the women I'd ever met. And she was the first to take a poisoned dart for me.

But things wouldn't work between us. Ren fancied Su. He'd been after her for at least two years. I couldn't do that to my best friend.

Blue Orchid's eyes sparkled as she sipped from her teacup. "You're a complicated man, Hung. Don't you want to settle down and have a family one day?"

"I'm too busy trying to save all the families in Lin Din Ni."

"We all need love. I hope you find a woman who can finally crack that stubborn facade." She sighed. "How can I help you?"

"I need you to get an antidote from Wang's Pottery, a shop in the Market Square." I leaned into the table. "It's a life-or-death situation, and I don't want the person in there to know I'm onto him."

"Do you need me to go as someone else?"

The corners of my lips tilted in admiration. "This was why I came to you. It's safer to be in disguise."

She was also talented with makeup and disguises.

"I'll get it done." She looked at me inquisitively. "Does this have anything to do with the attack by the Bloodshade Bandits earlier today?"

Nodding, I briefed her on the secret code and gave her the metal plaque with the snake sigil.

"When you fetch it, have someone deliver it to me at the Prime General's Villa." I rose from the chair and grabbed my sword, securing it to my back. "Thank you. We'll be even after this."

"But I enjoy owing you something."

"No one likes to be in debt."

She got out of her seat and walked up to me, placing a hand on my shoulder. "I wouldn't mind being in debt to you." She fluttered her eyelashes.

"I think it's time I introduce you to some of my brothers-in-arms who wouldn't mind settling down."

"I'm only testing you, General Wen. Seeing if my charms could work their magic. But it appears you're hopeless." She shook her head. "No need for your assistance. I've got a decent man who loves me." She gestured to the lush garden. "That's for him."

"Really?" I lifted an eyebrow. Blue Orchid was a beautiful woman, and I was surprised a man hadn't snatched her up before. "Who is the lucky man who inspired the garden?"

"A well-respected man who meets all of my criteria." She smiled. "He needs the quiet to stabilize himself."

"Only an eccentric man needs stability." I jerked my chin at her. "Perfect for you."

She rolled her eyes. "I'll let you know when I have the antidote."

CHAPTER FOURTEEN

HUNG

HOURS LATER, I checked on the prisoner, but he'd succumbed to the poison. His body was covered with blisters and smears of black blood. Poison had deformed a large area on the back of his shoulder that extended to his spine and legs. Maybe this was where the poison had settled.

Fucking hell. Was Su all right?

As I leaped onto my horse, heading toward the City Apothecary, a man wearing the black and red uniform from the Maroon Meadow rushed up to me.

"General Wen!" He bowed and gave me a packet. "This is from Blue Orchid."

"Thank you." Hope sparked in me as I opened the packet, thinking it was the antidote. But all I got was a note.

Hung,

Sorry, I don't have the antidote. Wang Mo is dead. His maid discovered his body in the storage room.

I guess I still owe you a favor after all. Let me know if you need anything else.

Blue Orchid

. . .

Fucking hell! I couldn't believe this. I'd hoped for good news, but obstacles kept piling at my feet.

Placing the note back into the packet, I rushed to the apothecary. Upon arrival, I jumped down from the horse and entered.

I spotted Yunxi adding bottles to a display rack. "How's Su doing?"

"She stopped trembling about two hours ago. We're still monitoring her."

"Does she have any skin blisters?"

"No." Yunxi considered me. "Why?"

"The bandit infected with the same poison just died," I said. "May I see her?"

Nodding, Yunxi gestured to the exam room.

I entered the room, and relief settled in me when I didn't see any obvious side effects of the poison on Su's face, neck, or hands. She was sound asleep in the bed. As I sat down on the edge of the bed, she let out a slight snore.

"Get well soon." I took her hand in mine and brushed my thumb back and forth over her skin, loving how warm and soft it was.

I studied her beautiful face and noticed her skin tone had regained some of its color. Sweat beaded on her forehead. She winced and shifted on the bed, making uncomfortable noises. A second later, her breathing calmed again. I took a towel from the side table, dabbing her sweat. Other than the warmth emanating from her hand, her condition didn't look dire like the bandit's.

What if the poison was showing in other areas on her body? She was too unconscious to know. What if it was pooling near her back like the bandit's?

A better man would have waited for Healer Churan to check on Su's back and shoulder, but concern escalated in me. In battle, there was no time for formality. Saving lives was the only goal. Besides, I never said I was a decent man. I was a warrior who had killed many. Blood had stained my hands to the point where I could never completely wash it away. That was the life I'd chosen.

What if my hesitation delayed any treatment that could've saved her life? I didn't have time to waste. I turned her slightly to the side and shoved away the fabric on her shoulder, revealing her shoulder blades.

The tension in my body relaxed when I didn't see any signs of poison on her soft skin. My fingers lingered there a bit too long.

Stop it, I scolded myself. What the fuck was wrong with me?

I covered her shoulder, returned her to her resting position on her back, and continued studying her. Why was her body's reaction different from the bandit's? They'd both been infected with the Spewing Pain. The poison had killed the bandit quickly. But Su seemed to fight it better, and she wasn't a martial artist like the bandit.

I remembered how she had yanked at my essa, pulling me to safety. Her essa had a peach glow to it. What magical ability had she used to yank at my essa? Could that ability be the reason her body was fighting the poison successfully?

I kept my gaze on her beautiful face, not seeing any more signs of discomfort.

What if she was experiencing pain and wasn't aware of it?

"Are you in pain?" I placed my palm on her forehead. Still warm.

It's only been minutes since you last checked, idiot.

Had Healer Churan given her more medication? As I headed to the back room, I passed a room with dolls, drums, and other children's toys.

With everything that had happened, I forgot about Luzi. "Shit."

Get yourself together, General.

I found Healer Churan in the back room, adding herbs into an iron pot and stirring it with a wooden spoon.

She met my gaze and bowed her head. "General."

"How's Luzi doing?"

"Surprisingly well." She placed down the wooden spoon and put a lid over the pot. "She doesn't remember much about the event. It's probably a good thing. Grandma Pham from down the street took Luzi and her grandchildren to the park. Her grandchildren are close to Luzi's age. She'll be back soon."

"That's great to hear. I'd like to speak to her in the next few days. Perhaps she can shed some light on the investigation." When Healer Churan furrowed her eyebrows, I said, "I promise I won't push her if she can't remember anything. But her account would help me."

"I'll let you know when she's ready."

"I can arrange for the orphanage to take her in when you feel she's ready. She can start school and meet new friends."

I'd been in Luzi's situation, so I understood her mental instability and the need for security. Unlike Luzi, I had Uncle Seeto to take care of me. Who did Luzi have?

"Have you reached out to her uncle?"

"I don't think Luzi will be happy living with her uncle's family." Healer Churan scowled. "She didn't want to go home with him. He hinted about not having enough money to feed another mouth because he spent a lot on her family's grave." She shook her head. "Some family members are worse than strangers."

"Do you want me to make arrangements for her at the orphanage?"

Healer Churan sighed. "Let her stay here for now. She seems to like it. We have enough room for her, and I can certainly feed her. We'll discuss her residence later, General Wen."

"Please call me Hung. I've been here enough times over the years. You've treated a lot of my wounds as well. We're friends, aren't we?"

She nodded. "How's Physician Lim? Are the palace and military camps keeping him busy?"

Physician Lim officially oversaw the Emperor and Empress's health, but Empress Jayaatu liked visiting the City Apothecary for her needs. Lim often traveled to several military camps around Lin Din Ni, treating soldiers.

"They certainly are," I said. "Did you give Su any herbal concoctions?"

"No. I didn't dare give her anything because I didn't know what kind of poison they used." Healer Churan lifted the lid, and steam burst out. "Her symptoms could worsen if a concoction reacts badly to the poison." She stirred the pot again as the scent of herbs filled the space. "Certain herbs create different chemical reactions in the body. We have to be extra careful."

That thought hadn't occurred to me. "Su looks like she's getting better. The bandit who said it was the Spewing Pain poison just died."

"That's from a deadly mushroom." Creases formed on Healer Churan's forehead. "But it doesn't appear to affect Su."

"Maybe she's immune to it," I said.

"Something strange is happening inside her. Maybe this poison is battling the other one."

"At least we know the source of one." I remembered how pale she'd been in the Market Square. I had assumed she was just under the weather. Had she been in pain all this time? "What do you know about the Deathcap Clan? Spewing Pain was one of their trademark poisons—before they were all killed years ago."

"I heard the Deathcap Clan were fascinated by poison, that they had poisonous mushroom farms. But sometimes, if you add two poisonous things together, you get a healing product. It all depends on what they're using the toxin on." She looked at me. "You think someone is still alive within the Deathcap Clan?"

"I'm not sure. It's a possibility. Either someone is still alive, or someone in the Bloodshade Bandits was also in the Deathcap Clan."

I sighed. "What can we do to help her?"

"Right now, Su is doing fine. We'll wait and see. I've given her acupuncture to ensure her energy and blood flow are unobstructed.

"Can you please keep me posted?" I asked.

She smiled. "Why aren't you married, General?"

I blinked at the seemingly random question. Blue Orchid and Healer Churan were so interested in my personal life. Couldn't they see I was busy trying to apprehend Ru Malik, investigate Luzi's family's death, and find the antidote for Su's poison, on top of managing my military camp? I had no time for marriage or personal relationships.

"My life is chaotic," I said. "I don't want to put my family through the pain and suffering, you know." I told her the truth. "My mother was constantly worried about my father when he was away in battle. I couldn't do that to the woman I love."

"You can always retire," she said.

Crossing my arms, I stared at her. My mom would've been Healer Churan's age if she were still alive. Perhaps her maternal instincts kicked in with my concern for Su.

"Don't worry," I said. "I won't hurt Su."

"She's a healer with the spirit of a warrior. Curious, dedicated, and passionate." She met my eyes. "I don't want her to assume something that's not there, you know? A woman's heart is fragile. If she loves a man, it's hard for her to move on if it doesn't work out."

I opened my mouth to say something but closed it quickly. What could I say? Was I interested in Su?

Don't answer that.

Was I giving her the wrong impression?

Fuck.

Needing something to do, I ran a hand over the weapons on my belt. I didn't expect Healer Churan to bring up this topic that unsettled me. I wasn't ready to think about it. My concern was Su's condition.

"You have nothing to worry about," I assured her. "I'm worried about her because she took a poison dart for me. I would be the one lying in bed if it weren't for her."

That was partially the truth.

She offered me a warm smile but said nothing. I had to get out of the apothecary before she could ask me more questions.

"Thank you for your time. Please keep me posted on Su and Luzi. I've got to go now."

"You're also curious, dedicated, and passionate." Her eyes sparked.

I didn't know how to respond to her statement, so I nodded and left the back room.

What exactly did she mean by that? Why did women speak in riddles?

CHAPTER FIFTEEN

SU

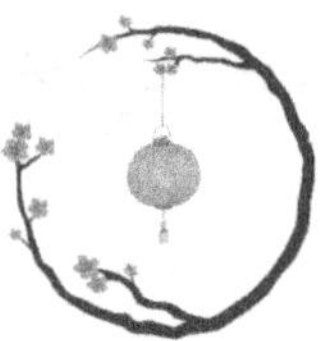

AS I SWAM through the darkness, I heard General Wen's deep voice echo through the space.

"Get well soon."

Heat bloomed in my palm, but when his voice disappeared, a chill set in.

I didn't know why I was swimming. I wanted to wake up and talk to him—to see him. But no matter how much I wanted to break free from this dream—or trance—I couldn't. This had to be a lucid dream, where I knew I was dreaming and could make certain decisions. But my awareness appeared sharper, and my emotions felt too real.

Could this be more than a dream? But what?

Though I had my eyes open, darkness greeted me. A powerful energy pulled me forward, moving my arms and legs as if I were underwater, swimming toward my salvation.

But this wasn't water. I was in the air.

The pain and the hot and cold sensations that had warred in me earlier had disappeared. I couldn't feel any traces of them.

A sea of stars appeared and twinkled in the distance. I gaped at the astounding view. Brightness appeared, dimming the surrounding stars. As I swam closer, I realized it was a blue bunny with a warm glow around it. This was the same creature Yeeva and I had seen all those years ago in the woods. The reason we met.

My heart raced as I approached the bunny. It cocked its head at me, perking up ears that looked like four leaves to form a beautiful crown around its head. The extraordinary bunny sat on a soft mound of darkness that had shades of colors in it. As the dimmed stars brightened, I lowered my feet to the ground—and it undulated. I no longer needed to swim; I could walk on this bouncy, dark ground.

"Hello," I said.

It opened its mouth to say something, but a peaceful sound came out, soothing me. It echoed through the space like a lovely song. The stars responded with their own sound, and I listened to a cosmic song that vibrated my entire body.

"Sorry, I don't understand you."

More sounds came from its mouth as it hopped along the darkness, stopping after a few hops and turning back to look at me.

"Oh, you want me to follow you?"

The four-leaf ears flopped to one side, giving the bunny an adorable hairstyle.

I took that signal as a yes and followed the creature. To my surprise, the flexible ground adjusted to my weight, dipping and bouncing as I ran after the fast bunny.

The sensation sent a jolt of energy through me, invigorating me in inexplicable ways. This fantastical dream had taken me to a world I'd never imagined possible. I was swimming, walking, and running across a starry sky, following a unique bunny who sang with the stars.

If I shared this bizarre experience with Healer Churan, I doubted she'd have a remedy to bring me back to my senses. That was what she'd say. Yunxi would think the poison had gotten to my brain. Maybe it had.

But at this moment, I felt a liberation I couldn't explain. The freedom to explore the sky and hear the stars was indescribable.

As the bunny approached a massive mountain with more mountains behind it, the darkness faded, allowing a magical world to come into view. Wispy clouds spread across the pastel sky. The tranquil scenery wrapped me in peace.

The bunny sat in front of the mountain, wagging its short tail with a little puff at the end.

The surface of the mountain shifted, forming an intricate flower mandala. It looked like the scar on my arm. I glanced down, and the scar glowed. The patterns on the mountains shone gold and shifted, creating what appeared to be fish scales.

An opening emerged within the mountain, like an expanding mouth. I couldn't see anything inside the cave with delicate lights sparkling around. The blue bunny glowed brighter, hopping around. A roar emitted from inside the cave, and my body shook, trembling as though every single organ had swapped places.

"Su, I need your help."

I sucked in a breath at the clarity of the voice. She was the same person calling me.

"What do you need?" I replied. "Who are you?"

Another roar erupted from the cave, and lightning cut through the pastel sky that slowly turned dark. From that single bolt of lightning, more multiplied like brilliant veins running across the sky.

The ground shook, and I woke up.

CHAPTER SIXTEEN

HUNG

AFTER REVIEWING the crime scene at Wang's Pottery and interviewing his mother and sister, I headed back to my villa. Kai and Tao stayed behind to collect evidence and interview the neighbors. Exhaustion tugged at my limbs as I mentally organized what I had to do, including preparing for my meeting with the Emperor in a few days. He'd want a report on what I'd been investigating.

Wang Mo sold various poisons and antidotes to the Bloodshades and other rebel groups. He could've died at the hands of these people. But my gut told me that Ru Malik had gotten to him. The leader of the Bloodshades wanted to protect his business and ensure the injured bandit would die.

Anger and frustration stirred in me. My plan to lure Ru Malik to Luklum had backfired. I had underestimated him that day when he showed up at the Market Square. He had prepared his men to attack mine. Kai had fought them off, but that battle had delayed his help. If more men had been present, perhaps Su wouldn't have gotten hurt.

How had Ru Malik maneuvered around Luklum so easily? This was my territory, and he'd been running an underground business right under my nose. That infuriated me. Samo, Jie, Peng, and Mo were all on his payroll. Who else in the Market Square worked for him?

On top of that, his martial arts had improved with more strength and swiftness. He was probably working with other empires, trying to conquer Lin Din Ni. This needed to be addressed during my meeting with Emperor Tang.

Lin Din Ni had mostly remained neutral over the years. We didn't meddle with other empires, and we didn't go out conquering lands. Though rebels had created trouble along the borders, we'd dealt with them successfully.

But this situation with Ru Malik was different. I felt it in my bones. Who was helping him?

So many things had happened in a short amount of time. I felt like I would miss something if I didn't slow down and review all the details.

When I reached my office, I dropped into a chair, closed my eyes, and breathed. After a moment, the tension in my shoulders relaxed. I rose from my chair and walked over to the table that held the map of Lin Din Ni. I reviewed territories that were vulnerable to threats. The Central Border was monitored by General Zhou. General Li had been successful in managing the border along the Western Empire, and General Pao reported nothing abnormal with the Southern Border, which I also assisted. But something felt off to me.

I'd need to discuss adding more soldiers to the borders at the next council meeting.

I thought back to my conversation with Mo's mother and sister. They claimed not to know anything about his illegal activities. They had assumed his pottery business had increased when he started selling his special snake collection.

Though I believed them, I'd ordered Kai to monitor the mother and sister for a few weeks to be safe. What if a former customer came looking for Mo? This could be an opportunity to catch other criminals. Details mattered right now.

Mo had committed treason, and his family would pay if they had anything to do with it.

My fingers curled into a fist. Ru Malik was steps ahead of me. Needing to pound something, I walked to the courtyard outside my bedroom and practiced my tiger claw, snake attack, and dragon stance. I needed to release the tension in my body. An hour later, sweat streamed down my face, making me feel better.

While I submerged myself in the bathtub, Su's face appeared in my vision. My fingers tingled as I remembered her soft skin, and my dick hardened.

It had been a long time since I was attracted to a woman like this. She intruded into my thoughts whenever she wanted. A man like me preferred control. I didn't need or want the distraction, especially now when there was a storm in my city.

But somehow, I felt like a storm was also brewing within me. Was that a sign I should stay away from her?

It was probably best, given the sensitive situation I was in. Ren was my best friend. We grew up together. He was like a younger brother, and I couldn't hurt him like that. Ren didn't hide his affection for Su, and it would be wrong of me to interfere, even though Su had shown no interest in him.

She didn't show any interest in you either.

But I had a hunch. There was something there. If she didn't like me, why did she take a dart for me?

Because she's a healer; she cares for everyone.

I hated my inner voice. All it did was irritate me.

I shut off my mind, finished bathing, and hopped into bed so I could get the rest my body desperately needed. But as I lay in bed, her face drifted across my eyelids, teasing and taunting me. How was I supposed to sleep when I kept imagining being with her?

CHAPTER SEVENTEEN

SU

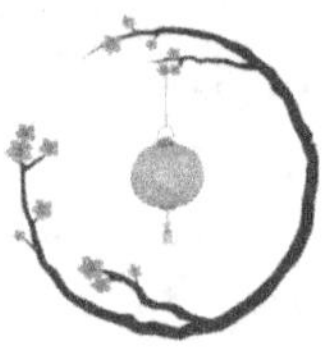

AS I SAT in the courtyard eating a bowl of chicken porridge, I couldn't believe it was already the next day. When I woke this morning, I realized I had my moon cycle while I was unconscious. It came early this month. Healer Churan had placed a towel under me to absorb the leakage.

What I'd experienced the past few days had been a blur. And somehow, everything seemed real as well. Swimming and running across the starry sky, hearing the soothing sounds of the stars. I smiled, wondering what the four-leaf-ear bunny was doing now.

What was beyond the clouds? Was there another world in them? Were they portals?

After waking from the lucid dream, my mind wouldn't settle. Aside from the dream, what I'd done to save General Wen was another mystery that baffled me. Everything happened so quickly, so much that I didn't realize what I'd done at the time.

I had activated my essa! I was both overjoyed and confused. Most people tapped into their essa because they'd studied martial arts, cultivating their energy to a potent level. I was still in training. How had I tugged at General Wen's essa with my own? Mine was a metallic peach, different from the normal gold others emanated.

What had allowed me to call on my essa?

I waved my arms around, trying to mimic the steps I'd taken prior to activating my essa, but nothing appeared on my hands or at my fingers.

I sighed. "Maybe I'm still weak."

I'd never imagined I'd be that close to Ru Malik. Fear tightened my stomach just thinking about him on that day. If I ever had to fight him, he'd kill me easily. But an evil person like him would probably take his time torturing me. I flexed my fingers, desperately wanting to learn how to protect myself.

I needed to dedicate more time to practice my martial arts. That was the only way to defend myself and those around me. But who would teach me?

I stirred the porridge with the soup spoon, blowing at the rising steam. A muscle twitched in my shoulder, reminding me of the dart that had punctured there. At that moment, I didn't have time to think or hesitate. All I knew was that I didn't want him to get hurt.

When the dart hit me, a chill had shot straight down my spine. I knew I'd been poisoned.

The pain didn't last too long, not when I was immersed in my lucid dream. I wasn't sure if it would have been worse if I'd been conscious. I stretched out an arm, rolling my shoulder. A slight soreness sparked, but not unbearable. I'd recovered faster than I'd expected.

Get well soon.

Was that really General Wen speaking to me, or had I been dreaming?

A smile formed on my lips while I stirred the hot porridge.

"What are you smiling about?" Yunxi approached the courtyard, holding a tray with two bowls and a plate. She had on a light green dress with a purple hairpin.

Wearing a pink dress, Luzi walked beside her with an anxious expression. When she saw me looking at her, she offered a little smile and a nod.

"Just happy to be alive," I said and turned to Luzi, pointing at her dress. "You look adorable in that pretty dress." I patted the stool beside me. "Have a seat."

"Thank you." Luzi smiled, but it didn't stretch as far as it could.

This girl had a rough path ahead. She needed love and guidance. I knew that situation well. Thanks to Healer Churan, I grew up with compassion instead of hatred.

Healer Churan told me Luzi was adjusting well despite the trauma she'd experienced. We all wanted to know what she'd seen or heard, but no one had pushed her to say anything she didn't want to. They feared asking too soon could disrupt her recovery. She needed time.

Yunxi placed down the tray, putting a bowl of porridge in front of Luzi and keeping one for herself. She also had some fried bean curd strips on a plate, which were delicious with porridge.

"Can I have one?" I asked.

"I brought extra for you." Yunxi looked at Luzi. "Be careful. The porridge is hot."

Luzi nodded and blew on it carefully.

"How are you feeling?" Yunxi met my eyes.

"A lot better, thank you." I spooned up some porridge and ate it. The savory taste warmed my stomach. "Did I miss anything important while I was unconscious?"

"No. Not that busy in the apothecary. People were probably scared to go out, fearing the bandits might still be around."

"Did General Wen catch them?"

"Yes. But there could be more lurking around." Her eyes sparkled. "He came by to visit you."

"Did I snore or say anything strange in my sleep?" I finished the porridge.

"You sure did." She leaned in. "You said he was the most handsome man you've ever met. Then you drooled, snored, and *farted.*"

"What!?" My hands flew to cover my face in horror.

How could I face him now?

I removed my hands, huffing. What did that poison do to me?

Luzi's eyes widened as she glanced from me to Yunxi. I saw the suppressed smirk on her lips before she ate her porridge.

Yunxi's expression was deadly serious. "I'm sure he understands you were sick. We've all treated people who did those things while they were under. The body has to do what it needs to do. Don't be embarrassed."

I leveled my eyes at Yunxi. "Says the person who didn't drool, snore, or fart in front of her dream man."

Luzi tried her best not to laugh. A shiver ran down my spine as I tried to imagine him in the room with me.

Firehell. If there were any chance of him being attracted to me, that horrifying display would absolutely ruin it.

"Firehell!" I exclaimed, covering my face with my hands. Then I realized who was beside me and clamped a hand over my mouth. "Erase that word from your mind, Luzi. It's not a word for kids to use. Or hear."

Luzi giggled. "I've heard it before."

My eyes widened. "You must forget it until you're old enough to use it."

Nodding, she smiled. "Okay."

"You can apologize to him." Yunxi kicked me under the table. "He's in the back room talking to Healer Churan."

"No." More heat flushed to my face. There should be a remedy for embarrassment. Maybe there was some mystery herb in the forest that could treat it. "I'm not going into that room until he leaves. Let me know when it's safe. I'll be sitting out here eating my porridge."

Yunxi looked into my bowl. "But it's empty."

"I don't care." The embarrassment was too much for me to handle. "I'll apologize *next* month."

Nerves fluttered in my stomach as though a hundred butterflies just emerged from their cocoons. This attraction to him overwhelmed me. A man like him surely had a woman somewhere. He probably didn't even notice me until I blocked the dart from hitting him.

Yunxi winked at Luzi, who looked up with her mouth full of food, clueless about what was happening. Did Yunxi want to rush Luzi along? Or did she want Luzi to go into the back room to get General Wen to embarrass me even more?

"I've seen you stare at Kai." I narrowed my eyes at her. "Is he the most handsome man you've ever met?"

"I know what you're doing." She rolled her eyes, straightened her posture, and shoved a spoonful of porridge into her mouth.

Smiling, I placed a hand on her shoulder. "Teasing you makes me feel better." I sighed. "It's nice to have secret crushes. They make life more colorful, even if they only give us temporary joy."

We both sighed together.

Yunxi's face lit up. "We could reveal our wishes to the Moon Goddess at the Lantern Blessing Festival! People say that if you write your wish on a paper boat and send it down the river, the goddess will fulfill it."

I'd heard of this tradition but didn't believe it was true. Some traditions were made to make people feel better but held no truth. For example, growing up, I knew so many women who wanted to marry into wealth and power so that their children—especially their sons—could carry on the family's legacy. Why couldn't a girl make her own wealth and cultivate her own power while carrying on the family name too? Why did she need to stand *behind* her husband?

Why couldn't she stand beside him and shine just as brightly?

But I didn't want to ruin the celebration for Yunxi or Luzi, who seemed interested.

"Sure. We can try that," I said. "It'll be fun."

"Can I write a wish too?" Luzi asked.

"Of course." I squeezed her shoulder.

Luzi beamed and finished her porridge.

"Want to help me sort dried herbs?" Yunxi asked Luzi. "I can teach you about them."

"Okay," she said, then winced.

"Are you okay?" I asked.

"Just an ache." A hand went to her ear.

"Did those kidnappers hurt your ear?" I examined her ears and the surrounding areas. Everything looked fine. But I was only looking at the exterior. Who knew what internal damage had been done?

She shook her head.

"Let me check your pulse." I reached for her wrist, but she resisted. "It won't hurt. I promise."

"Su is an exceptional healer. Better than me," Yunxi said.

Luzi had gotten accustomed to Yunxi while I was sick. She'd need more time to get acquainted with me.

Luzi held out her wrist for me. I placed my fingers on her pulse, and the energy there seemed erratic. After a moment, her pulse calmed.

"All is well," I said. "It's going to take time for you to adjust. If your ears are still aching, I can treat it with acupuncture."

She nodded. "Okay."

Luzi wasn't ready for General Wen to ask her questions yet. The earache could've just been from anxiety.

After Yunxi and Luzi walked back into the apothecary, I stared at the entrance, wondering if General Wen was still inside chatting with Healer Churan.

My face flushed as I imagined the horror he had experienced. What an unforgettable impression I made.

Though I wanted to see him, fear of his judgment stopped me. *You're being ridiculous, Su.*

Well, I had a good reason to be. My crush had seen the worst of me. How was I supposed to react?

If I saw him, what could I say? Sorry about being gross?

I squeezed my eyes shut and took a deep breath. When I exhaled, I opened my eyes and tried my best to look at things from a different perspective.

I was making things more complicated than they were. He

was a general who had been in countless battles. He'd probably seen worse things in his life.

Be courageous. Take charge of what you want.

Hope surged in me even while nerves multiplied. I grabbed my empty bowl with the spoon, got up from the stool, squared my shoulders, and strode into the back room to face the handsome general who had seen such a vulnerable side of me.

CHAPTER EIGHTEEN

SU

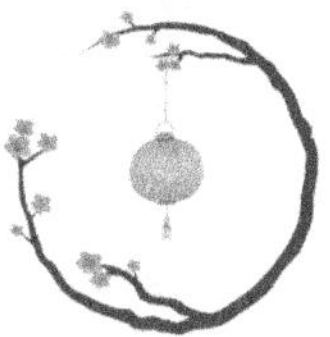

WHEN I ENTERED the back room, no one was there. One table was full of dried herbs that needed to be sorted. Another held seedlings that needed to be planted. In addition, a supply of dried fruits had arrived from a nearby farm. Those needed to be divided and packaged too.

I walked over to the basin of water by the window and cleaned my bowl and spoon. Courage still lingered in me, and I feared that if I didn't take advantage of it now, it might not come back. Leaving the bowl and spoon to dry next to the ones Yunxi had cleaned earlier, I strode out to the front area with my heart pounding in my chest.

What was wrong with me? I'd never felt this way before. The usual nerves when I saw an attractive man were nothing compared to the monsoon within me.

The entire situation unsettled me.

I should worry about more important things than the general's opinion of me, like what he'd done to the bandits. Had he learned more about Ru Malik? What was Ru Malik's agenda? Who else was he working with?

All these questions were so much more important than my vanity. Yet I couldn't help it.

Voices boomed as I neared the front counter, and my heart rate increased. I walked by an exam room and saw Healer Churan performing acupuncture on a male patient. She met my eyes, then looked me up and down once.

"I'm okay," I said. "Don't worry."

She nodded.

I left her to the patient and stepped into the front area filled with merchandise. The shop had gotten new products while I was out.

"*Su.* So happy to see you," Yunxi emphasized loudly enough that General Wen turned around from the talisman stand. The popular talisman created by the Chens had sold out a few weeks ago. I was glad to see them stocked again.

General Wen met my eyes, and my entire body tingled. He didn't wear his military uniform today, just a blue cotton outfit with a metal belt, still looking as handsome as ever. I imagined he'd look good no matter what he wore.

He walked over to me. "How are you feeling?"

Standing only a few inches away, his brown eyes fixated on me. A kaleidoscope of brown and copper burst from those inquisitive eyes, making my heart twirl.

"Better, thank you."

"Thank you for saving me." He raked a gaze down my body, from my head to my toes. "Does your shoulder still hurt?"

"It's a little sore, but nothing I can't handle."

More questions sparked in his eyes, and I could tell he wanted to ask me something. But then a voice interrupted him.

"What do you think of this lavender soap?" Lina asked him.

The joy that had been stirring in me died. I'd been so focused on General Wen that I didn't even see her at the soap and lotion display. Did he come to the shop with her?

General Wen flicked his eyes to the lavender soap in her hand and shrugged. "I don't know. It's soap."

Like always, she looked beautiful. She wore a silk gown made by the Imperial dressmaker, which only noble families could afford. Gorgeous hairpins gleamed in her hair, and the perfect makeup increased her attractiveness.

Feeling insecure, I glanced at myself. Why hadn't I changed my cotton outfit? My plain clothes couldn't compare to those worn by prominent families.

The front door opened, and Ren stepped in, holding a food carrier. Like his sister, his scholar's outfit was made from the finest materials.

"Ren!" Lina called and glanced at his carrier. "Is that for me?"

"No," he said and walked up to me, beaming. "I heard about what happened. Glad to see you're feeling better."

Then he looked over at General Wen and slapped a hand on his shoulder. "Did you reward her for saving your life?"

"There's no need for that," I interjected.

"Of course there is," Ren said. "You took a poison dart for him. He could've died."

"That was you?" Lina studied me, probably comparing my simple clothing to hers.

I didn't know her well, but I knew enough about her group of snooty friends who co-owned Heavenly Reflections. I couldn't afford anything there.

Did these women know what it was like to work hard? I looked at her flawless hands. They were probably softer than mine.

Did General Wen prefer this kind of woman?

Lina stared at me, and I remembered I hadn't answered her question. "Yes, that was me."

"What's your name?" she asked, studying me.

"Su."

"You're a healer?"

"One of the best healers here!" Yunxi said, standing at the counter, assisting Aunt Ying with her purchase.

"Su healed my awful rash three months ago. Before coming here, I went to three healers who couldn't help me," Aunt Ying said. "The City Apothecary is the best."

"They have the most talented healers," Ren smiled. "And she took a dart for General Wen."

Not again.

I didn't save him because I wanted the attention.

Feeling uncomfortable, I said, "He was fighting a bandit leader when a rebel attacked him from behind. I had to do something."

General Wen looked at me, and something stirred in his eyes. But I could have been imagining things.

Lina lifted a perfect eyebrow. "You know how to fight?"

"Not really." It wasn't a complete lie—I was still learning. "I acted on instinct. You would've done the same if you'd been there."

"That's right." Lina turned to General Wen. "I would've saved you too."

Her brother snorted, and a hint of a smirk slid onto General Wen's face.

"What?" Lina slapped her brother's arm.

"You scream at the sight of a tiny mouse." Ren laughed.

"It wasn't tiny!"

"Don't you think General Wen should reward Su for the pain she's suffered?" Ren asked his sister.

She twisted her lips, thinking. "I could get her something at the jewelry pavilion."

"Thank you," I said. "But I don't want anything."

"There's no need." General Wen lifted his hand. "She saved my life, so *I* should give her something."

Lina pouted, looked at her brother, and pointed to the food carrier. "What's in there?"

Ren lifted it. "Food for Su. I asked the kitchen staff to make her soup. There are some pastries in there too."

"Oh, I want some."

Minutes later, we all sat inside a gazebo outside the City Apothecary. Ren placed a bowl of soup in front of me. "This is a special egg drop soup with cilantro and mint."

"I haven't had that in a while." Lina scooped a spoonful into her mouth.

"There's more at *home* for you," Ren said.

Lina narrowed her eyes at him and smiled as though she understood a secret no one else knew.

She reached for two lotus bean buns and offered one to General Wen. "Let's take a walk, Hung."

I knew Lina was trying to give her brother some privacy. She didn't know I wasn't interested in him.

General Wen looked at me. "You'll get your reward soon." Then he looked at Ren. "Thanks for the pastry."

My heart sank as I stared after them as they walked into the street.

"Finish the soup, okay? It'll help rebuild your strength." Ren eyed me and the bowl. "The chef added a lot of healthy ingredients."

I appreciated his thoughtful gesture more than he knew, but I didn't want him to get the wrong idea. After tasting the savory soup, I said, "It's incredible. Thank you." I placed the spoon down and met his eyes. "Ren, I appreciate your kind gesture, but we can only be friends. I don't want you to waste your time on me."

"I know," he said. "We're *friends*. Don't worry."

"You're not mad at me?"

"Extremely angry," he said with a straight face. "I'm only teasing. Friends can still spend time together and share a meal, right?"

I smiled. "Yes, we can."

A casual conversation followed as I finished the delicious soup, wondering where General Wen and Lina had gone.

CHAPTER NINETEEN

HUNG

I RETURNED to the City Apothecary right before they closed.

Yunxi stopped wiping the counter and smiled at me. "Are you looking for Su, General Wen?"

"Yes. Is she around?"

"She's in the courtyard or the herb garden." Yunxi gestured toward the back.

"Thank you," I said.

Sensing that someone was looking at me, I turned and saw Luzi sitting on a low stool in a corner with a book in her hand.

I walked over to her and crouched. "How are you?"

She swallowed, looking a bit scared. "Okay."

"I'm glad to hear that," I said. "I'm going to catch those bad people who hurt your family. You're safe now, Luzi."

Her lips trembled, but she didn't cry. I wanted to ask her more questions, but tonight wasn't appropriate. I didn't want to trigger anything before she went to bed.

"Are you enjoying your time here at the apothecary?"

Luzi looked over at Yunxi and then back at me, nodding. "Everyone is very nice here."

Then she yawned, looking tired.

"We'll head to bed as soon as I'm done," Yunxi said and

turned to me. "We're taking her to the Lantern Blessing Festival. She'll have fun there."

"You'll enjoy it. Get some rest." I rose to my feet and walked over to the talisman stand. There were so many colorful options to choose from. I unhooked a talisman with a twisted knot and gold tassels. It had iridescent beads that glistened when they caught the light. "I'll take this."

"Beautiful choice. It's one of my favorites. This is for protection, good luck, and joy." She placed it inside a silk pouch. "Who's it for?"

"Someone who deserves all those virtues."

"All set." She dropped the silk pouch onto my palm and asked, "Are you giving this to Kai?"

"No," I said, trying not to show my surprise. Did Kai have an admirer? "Do you think he needs one?"

"All the soldiers need one," she said. "You're protecting the country, and that means you have to deal with evil people."

"You're right. I'll let my men know they should come here to pick out a talisman. I'll pay for it."

Her eyes widened with excitement. "Thank you for your support, General Wen! When you're done talking to Su, you can use the back door in the courtyard."

"Thank you." I walked toward the back and heard chatter erupt between Yunxi and Luzi.

"Wait until I tell Healer Churan!" Yunxi squealed with excitement. "We need to place another order with the Chens. Want to come with me?"

"Okay," Luzi said.

My men could definitely use the protection of those talismans.

CHAPTER TWENTY

SU

DISAPPOINTMENT LINGERED in me as I plucked herbs from the garden and placed them into the basket. I should rest, but I couldn't sleep. There was too much noise in my head. Most of it had to do with General Wen. What had he and Lina spoken about yesterday? Did he have feelings for her?

It was none of my business, but I couldn't help wondering.

The insecurity and confusion from yesterday still clung to me now. It made it difficult for me to concentrate on anything. I thought time would allow me to feel better about my feelings for General Wen, but I was wrong. After they left together, the jealousy only got worse.

I didn't like this version of myself. I used to wonder how anyone could let one emotion control them. *Just shove it aside* was what I used to think. That it could easily be dismissed.

I was wrong.

Now, I was a victim, and I didn't know what to do. What would Healer Churan think of me if I asked if there was an herbal remedy for jealousy? She'd laugh at me, no doubt.

I looked at the Calming Waterfall bush with its tiny pink flowers cascading like a waterfall. "Are you my remedy, pretty little thing?" I held the delicate buds in my palm. "Will you help me get rid of this emotion?"

The flower didn't answer me. I didn't expect it to, but in my mind, we were having a deep conversation witnessed by the night sky, the earth, and the other plants.

I walked over to the Soothing Wishes shrub and admired the gorgeous clusters of purple flowers. I was going insane and talking to plants, but I didn't care. Right now, they eased the tension in my body. I was immersed in a fantasy world no one could understand but me. The freedom to say or think whatever I wanted stirred in the air. I brushed my fingers along the stem of the Soothing Wishes, a plant used to reduce inflammation from a wound.

"I'm wounded," I told the plant, placing a hand on my heart. Then, I put the basket onto the table so I could free up my hands to enjoy the plants.

My emotions were in turmoil. Maybe this ingredient would make the perfect addition for my no-more jealousy concoction. It would be a bestseller at the City Apothecary. People from all over the world would come and buy this drink since it was such a universal emotion.

You're absolutely going insane, Su.

I didn't listen to my inner voice criticizing me. I recognized this dilemma staring me in the face. It was time to meet it head-on. I couldn't deny my attraction to him, but what if he wasn't interested in me?

Even so, I had to know. I had to nip it in the bud and move on. There was no point in secretly admiring someone from afar. I'd been doing that for too long. My heart was exhausted from the yearning and not knowing.

"Will you help me cure my strange illness?" I tapped the flower cluster.

"I don't think the plant is going to reply." His deep voice cut through my fantasy, sending a shiver down my spine.

CHAPTER TWENTY-ONE

HUNG

WHEN SHE TURNED to look at me, I saw something other than surprise on her face. Was it a spark of joy radiating from those brown eyes? Was she as thrilled to see me as I was thrilled to see her? Or was I imagining all of this?

I was never a man saddled with these kinds of emotions. But I'd never encountered a woman who made me want and wonder to this degree. She confused me. She made me uncertain of myself. Though I didn't like it, I was extremely curious. No woman had touched me in that way, and now I wondered what else she could lure out of me.

Something flashed across her face as though she just remembered to be courteous to a guest.

"General Wen." She offered me a nod and a slight dip.

"Call me Hung," I said, walking over to her. "There's no need for formality."

She blinked at the comment but eventually nodded. She clasped her hands in front of her as though she needed to do something. I enjoyed knowing I unsettled her. It made me want to pull her into my arms. But that was just a fantasy, right?

I stepped closer to her, and an intoxicating floral scent surrounded me. It snuck up my nose and traveled all over my body. The sensations that rippled through me were indescribable. My skin felt charged and my senses keener as I breathed in more of her unique scent.

Fucking hell.

My body was acting on its own accord, forgetting who I was.

"You don't know that," she said, tapping the purple cluster again. "It could've replied by releasing an energy you can't see."

"Then how would you know what it said?" I studied her exquisite face.

Her determined eyes held passion and curiosity as a hint of pink bloomed on her cheeks. Her pink tongue peeked out from her full lips, licking the bottom portion. My gaze didn't deter me from her lips. I wanted to taste them.

I yearned for this woman like the swordsman yearning to explore a magnificent weapon gracing his presence. I'd been with women during my travels over the years, but they'd been temporary fun with no attachments or responsibilities. Su wasn't like them. I couldn't seem to let her go.

It didn't make sense. How could I let her go when she was never mine to begin with?

"I can assume what it says," she said, her tone changing to a slight annoyance. Then she turned away from me to look at the floral shrub.

Something seemed off. "Are you not feeling well?" I placed a hand on her forehead.

"Why do you care?" She looked at me, and I could almost see invisible daggers coming out of them.

I arched an eyebrow at this odd shift in character. The healer with a normally calm demeanor was revealing herself to me.

I like it.

She stood a head shorter than me, and I loved the way she looked up to meet my eyes. The dark curtain of lashes added to her beauty and mystique.

"Why wouldn't I care?" I inquired. "You were injured because of me."

Sighing, she walked over to another flower bush illuminated by a lantern hanging on the wooden pole. I had leaned on that pole earlier while watching her talk to the plants. That delightful image had been the highlight of my day—one I'd never forget.

Then she turned to me. "So you're only being nice because I took a dart for you? If Lina had gotten hurt because of you, what would you have done?"

Ah, so this is why she's irritated.

A small smile crept onto my lips. Su just answered a question that had been occupying my mind. She *was* attracted to me. Jealousy had never brought me so much joy.

I stared at her for too long because she said, "You don't have to answer if you're uncomfortable. I know she really likes—"

I yanked Su flush to me, loving the way her eyes widened with surprise.

A breath escaped her lips, but she didn't push me away. Instead, her body relaxed, molding into mine.

"She *wouldn't* take a dart for me," I said. "It would ruin her dress and her hair."

Su smiled, and warmth spread throughout my chest. "So there's nothing between the two of you?"

"She's my best friend's younger sister. The only feelings I have for her are those for a sister."

Relief beamed on her face, and her hand skimmed my jawline, sending a trail of heat with her every touch. I gripped her hand in mine, loving how small it felt in my large palm. She stared at our joined hands, then tried to pull hers away.

I held it tight. "Your hand is like the perfect handle to a sword's grip."

She smirked. "Are you trying to be poetic?"

Was I?

"It's the first thing that came to mind."

She squeezed my hand. "The way you hold my hands is like a leaf cradling a drop of morning dew."

My lips stretched into a smile. "You're a lot better at poetry."

She stared at me for a moment as though I'd done something abnormal.

"I love the way your hand feels in mine." I rubbed my thumb against her skin.

She sucked in a breath, and her lips opened slightly.

"And I know you like it too."

"You're so arrogant." Defiance sparked in her eyes. "How do you know what I'm feeling right now?"

"Because I can feel your heart racing. That wild energy practically radiates from you." I reached for a lock of her long hair and twirled it around my finger. "The pupils in your eyes are so wide."

She arched an eyebrow. "That can be a sign of fear too." Her lips tilted to a smirk. "Or of a *predator* preparing to attack its prey."

I laughed at the way her mind spun.

She stared at me with intrigue. "Do that again."

"Do what?"

She extracted her hand from my grip, and I didn't like it. Then she placed her index fingers at the corner of my lips, pushing them up.

"Smile more. Laugh more," she said. "It transforms your face. You're very handsome when you do that."

Joy—or whatever it was—sprouted in me. Though I'd heard women say all kinds of things to me, something about her words sank deep into my soul. It was as though she knew the most effective way to touch me.

It had been a long time since I found the energy to smile or laugh. All the bloody battles I'd experienced and seeing my men sacrificing their lives to keep Lin Din Ni safe had created a concrete barrier around my heart. Grief added more rigid layers over the years, making it hard to feel anything worthwhile.

But now, this captivating woman had penetrated the impenetrable with her honesty.

Emotions surged in me, and I gripped the hand that had escaped from mine, pulling her to me.

"I like feeling your heartbeat and seeing the passion in your eyes." I kissed each of her fingers slowly.

She sucked in a breath and watched me intently. A low moan passed between her lips as more pink flushed her cheeks.

Su yanked her hand away but kept her eyes on me. "I'm a lot younger than you."

"Is that a problem?"

"Not for me," she said. "But you're an experienced man. Wouldn't you want someone your age?"

A laugh escaped me—and surprised me. In one night, she'd made me laugh more than anyone had in years.

"Are you calling me old?" I asked, even though I knew she wasn't referring to that.

"No!" She bit her bottom lip. "It's just . . . Look, you're the esteemed Prime General. You could pick any woman you want. Women from noble families. Why would you want a simple healer like me? I can't help you succeed the way a noble daughter could. I don't have the influence you need."

My wildflower didn't know me well enough yet.

"First, you're not a simple healer. Second, do I look like a man who cares what others think? I became who I am because I did what *I* wanted. Does that settle your concerns?"

Her eyes sparkled. "Yes." She walked over to the stone table where her basket sat.

I followed her like a puppy. There was no other path for me but the one that led to her. That was another aspect I had to think about. My path had always been to protect Lin Din Ni and to serve the Emperor and Empress, but now things were shifting . . .

"Why are you visiting at this late hour?" She pulled out the herbs in her basket and plucked off the dried leaves, putting them in a pile.

I glanced up at the evening sky, gathering my thoughts and calming the heat swirling in my body. I could still feel her fingers on my bottom lip and remembered the inappropriate thoughts that had surfaced when I'd kissed her fingers. But this wasn't the place to act on them, nor was it the right time.

"I came to thank you for saving my life." Reaching into my chest pocket, I pulled out the silk pouch and slid it over to her. "I hope this will keep you safe from now on."

She opened the pouch, took out the twisted knot talisman, and smiled. "Thank you. Is this my reward?"

I nodded. "I don't want danger around you."

She twisted her lips as though disappointed.

"You don't like it?" Had I made the wrong choice?

"I love it. But . . ."

"But what?"

CHAPTER TWENTY-TWO

SU

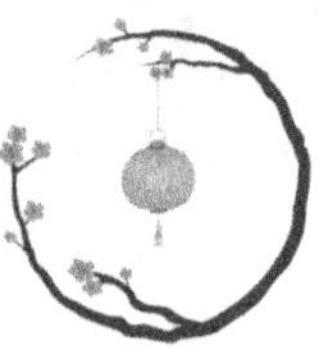

I LOVED the twisted knot talisman—I truly did. It was a beautiful charm and incredibly thoughtful, especially coming from General Wen. I'd cherish this gift forever.

But since he mentioned the reward, I could only think about him being my mentor. That was what I really wanted. Proper lessons would help me enhance my skills. I'd been doing things on my own and didn't know if I'd been practicing correctly.

How should I explain what I wanted from him? Nerves tumbled in my stomach, fearing he would say no.

Hung was the Prime General responsible for his soldiers and other Imperial duties. Crimes were rampant, and he was busy investigating them. If I asked him to teach me, would that take him away from his responsibilities? Would that endanger Lin Din Ni, especially Luklum?

Guilt tore at me. Then I remembered the upcoming archery competition. An idea popped into my head.

He stared at me, waiting for an answer.

"Let me ask you a few questions first," I said.

He leaned into the stone table and cocked his head, considering me. "Okay."

His powerful energy blasted at me, and a series of tingles

skipped down my skin. The glow from the nearby lantern illuminated his face, creating a beautiful contrast of shadows and light dancing over his high cheekbones, strong nose, and square jaw.

My core tightened at the sight alone. No wonder women found him attractive—irresistible. I wanted to lean into him, inhale his musky scent that teased me. But that would be unladylike and inappropriate.

Another man would have asked me what I wanted already. But Hung waited patiently for my reply. Like me, maybe he didn't want this night to end.

I looked away from his eyes, studying the Soothing Wishes as a firefly glowed around it. My gaze tracked the firefly as it flew to the center of the table.

"Are you a man of your word?" I met his eyes.

"I am indeed," he said. "My brothers-in-arms and I value this."

I nodded. "Do you care whether your soldiers fail or succeed?"

"I certainly do. I created an extensive training course to ensure they succeed. Their success assures we have the advantage during warfare." His eyes narrowed on me, probably wondering why all the cryptic questions.

To be honest, I didn't know why I was asking so many questions either. I just wanted to test the waters to see what kind of teacher he'd be.

Strict. Disciplinary. Someone with high expectations.

Could I handle all of that?

A stream of cold sweat slid down my back when I remembered spying on the soldiers practicing in the field. Men bigger and stronger than me were huffing and puffing, struggling to finish their practice—and I had only seen two training exercises. How would I survive the more difficult routines?

Despite that, I needed an expert in the field to teach me. I'd do whatever it took, even if it took me half a year instead of a couple of months to complete the training.

"Have you ever taken on a disciple?"

He arched an eyebrow. "No. I don't have time."

"Would you consider your soldiers students?"

"All of your questions are hinting at something. Why don't you just ask me?"

I had a feeling he'd say no if I asked him exactly what I wanted, so I spun it around to challenge him.

Inhaling a deep breath, I said, "I dare you to take me on as a student."

Something flashed in his eyes while he considered me. "You can't handle it."

Though he didn't say it in a demeaning way, his comment irked me. Now, I wanted to succeed just to prove him wrong.

"Maybe *you* can't handle me," I retorted. "Let's arm wrestle for it. If I win, you grant me my wish—my reward. If I lose, then you don't have to."

A smirk slid onto his face.

"Come on." I bent my elbow, placed it on the stone table, and wiggled my fingers. "Don't tell me you're afraid of a healer's strength?"

"You yanked at my essa that day. So yes, I am curious if you could do it again."

If I could, I would have already. But I wasn't going to give him any clues.

"Maybe I'll decide to give you a show, General Wen. Let's go."

He shifted and bent his elbow, placing it opposite from mine. Then he gripped my hand with his. Energy zipped between us, and I knew he sensed it.

Our eyes met. "That's my essa tickling you." I made that up, but he didn't know that.

"On the count of three, we start, okay?"

"Okay," he said.

Why was he so calm?

"One, two, three—"

I pulled at his arm with all my might, and he didn't budge. I was going to lose this battle, no doubt. His gaze pinned me, probably wondering why I wanted to arm wrestle when I knew he'd win. Sensing my struggle, he backed off a bit.

I winced and glanced at my injured shoulder. He immediately relaxed his grip, and I pinned his arm to the surface.

I released his hand and clapped with glee. "I win!"

"You—"

"That wasn't cheating." I smiled. "You were just distracted. In war, you need to learn how to distract your opponent, right?"

He shook his head. "Who taught you that?"

You.

"I've heard stories of your victories. Of how you've won over your enemies."

Pride beamed on his face.

"You lose, General Wen. As a *man of your word,* when do I start?"

I'd cornered him, but he didn't seem to mind.

A smirk slid onto his lips. "If I take you on as a student, everyone will know. Especially my soldiers. I would have to put you through the same training exercises I put them through. What if you don't succeed? All of Luklum would know."

I bit the inside of my mouth at the stark truth of his words. He wasn't lying, and he was worried about me. Would I handle the embarrassment well?

It wouldn't have bothered me so much except I didn't want to bring the negative attention to the City Apothecary. If I succeeded, I would inspire Yunxi and other girls and women to learn how to defend themselves. But if I failed . . .

Stop that negative thought.

I shook my head clear of anything that would distract me from my goal.

"Are you too embarrassed to teach a woman? I didn't think a general like you would care about what others thought of him."

Hung stared at me as though he knew exactly what I was doing, but all he said was, "I don't. I'm just watching out for you. After all, you saved my life."

"As your savior, I *dare* you to take me on as your first female student." I lifted a hand before he could say anything. Why were his eyes gleaming? "Give me two weeks to do your required entry-level training. If I succeed after the two weeks, I'll continue to the next course. You can also prepare me to enter the upcoming archery competition."

His eyes widened. "Interesting. And if you fail?"

"If I fail, I'll deal with the shame and embarrassment."

"Deal."

I expected him to ask more questions, but he didn't. "Don't you have questions for me?"

"Do you want me to ask you something in particular? You've already won the arm-wrestling match and become my student. I'm afraid my questions might somehow lead to something I'd regret later."

I smiled. "Do you regret agreeing to teach me?"

"No."

"I just want to make sure you understand our deal so you're not surprised by anything later on."

His eyes intensified. "I'm a man of my word, remember?"

"I'm a woman of my word too. When do I start?"

"When you're healed. Your energy needs to be strong to start any strenuous training. If you start now, you might injure yourself."

Disappointment churned in me even though I knew he was right.

"I have a question. But it has nothing to do with our deal." His expression turned serious. "Healer Churan told me you were poisoned before getting hit by the poison dart. How did you get poisoned the first time?"

Oh no. What would he think of me if I told him I'd seen Ru Malik telling Samo, Peng, and Jie to poison the city wells? Someone who snuck around causing trouble? That wasn't what I was doing. Would he think I was behind other unsolved cases?

But I didn't want to lie to my future teacher, to my *Sifu*. He'd expel me immediately.

"Ru Malik," I said as more fireflies emerged, flying around the Soothing Wishes and then toward us. I caught one, cupped the other hand over it, and looked inside. "Have a good night." Then I let it go.

Hung also held one in his palm before letting it go as well. I didn't realize how long we'd been chatting outside. The sky had darkened. Yunxi, Luzi, and Healer Churan were probably all in their rooms getting ready for bed.

"How did you know it was him?" Hung asked.

"I saw him meeting Samo and his friends at the abandoned temple."

Something flashed in his eyes, but I couldn't read his expression clearly because of the dim lighting.

"Why were you there?"

I told him how I'd overheard Samo talking about Luklum's mysterious illnesses and disguised myself to follow him.

"I didn't get hurt by a weapon or anything. Not sure why I felt fine after that day. So I'm not sure how I got poisoned. I didn't eat, drink, or touch anything."

"Are you feeling okay?" His jaw tightened as he leaned over to check behind my ear. "You don't have the same red dots or blisters like Samo and the others."

I placed a finger behind my ears. I'd forgotten about the red dots.

"Are you sure you're not in pain?" He eyed me, looking extremely concerned. "Has Healer Churan checked your pulse today?"

"I think my body's fighting it," I said.

"Why do you think that?"

"I don't know. Just a feeling. I can't explain it."

"Have Healer Churan check on you again tomorrow. I'll stop by to visit."

"You don't—"

"I do." His voice was firm. "If you're going to be my student, I need to ensure the poisons aren't affecting you. I don't want to inadvertently hurt you. You've been through enough. Are we clear?"

I blinked at the rigid tone. What happened to the man who was just talking to me as though we were close friends? What happened to the man who had kissed my fingers earlier? Not to mention I felt his hard cock when my body was pressed close to his. That was something I'd think about tonight before going to bed.

The strict and taciturn general was back now.

"Are you okay?" I asked.

"I'm fine." He closed his eyes for a moment. When he opened them, his hard expression softened. "You've been poisoned twice and are still sitting here talking as if nothing has happened to you. Instead of resting, you're determined to be my student. On top of that, you want to enter the archery competition. You should take it easy."

"Well, I plan on taking it easy and having some fun at the Lantern Blessing Festival. Are you going?"

Hung studied me for a moment, and my skin warmed again. This man could command my body. "Sure, I'll go."

He stayed for a few more minutes before I walked him to the back door. After he left, I locked up and rushed back to my bedroom to replay the exchange in my head. I was going to be his student!

CHAPTER TWENTY-THREE

HUNG

I REFRAINED from revealing my shock and anger until I reached my office. I kicked the door closed and walked over to my desk, poured some wine into a cup, and downed it.

Then I slammed a fist onto my desk and cursed, "Fucking hell!"

Someone knocked on my door.

"What?" I exclaimed.

"It's me, Kai."

I blew out a breath and contained myself. "Come in."

Kai walked into my office and looked at me. "Are you all right? What happened? I heard you cursing from down the hall."

A man clouded by anger couldn't think clearly and would always make mistakes. Rebels were trying to destroy my cities. I had to remain calm to ensure everyone's safety—yet I couldn't help the guilt that tore at me.

"Have a seat." I gestured to Kai. "Have you heard from Tao?"

I'd sent my other Elite Guard to other cities to search for clues about Ru Malik and his Bloodshade Bandits. Luklum couldn't be the only city they had infiltrated.

"The recent letter I received stated that he'd arrived at Dai

Shan and would be traveling to Ming Shan soon. I'll let you know as soon as I receive anything from him."

I grabbed the Prime General's jade seal from the table and held the knob between my fingers. "Do you remember the day at the abandoned temple?"

He grinned. "How could I forget? Samo and his friends thought we were the Bloodshade Bandits and you, Ru Malik."

I had discovered that Samo, Jie, and Peng were poisoning the wells. But I knew they were working for someone else, so I disguised myself as Ru Malik. I had two reasons for doing this. One, I wanted to extract more information from the men, and two, I wanted to lure Ru Malik here.

Samo and his friends had committed a heinous crime, so they were going to die anyway. But first, I used them as bait. It worked.

Ru Malik had come to Luklum as I had expected. As an arrogant person, he probably wondered who had dared impersonate him, who had used his accomplices to carry out a crime, blaming it on him. Despite successfully luring him to the city, there had been a casualty. Su had gotten hurt.

"Su was poisoned on that day with red thorn poison, just like Samo, Jie, and Peng." I held the jade seal in my hand, wondering if I was worthy of it.

"Who poisoned her?" A ridge formed between his eyebrows.

"I did." I put down the seal and looked at him. "You and Tao chased after somebody that night."

"But that was a man."

"She was disguised as a man spying on Samo and his friends. She overheard them talking about the poisonings and wanted to help."

He cursed. "With two deadly poisons in her, she should be dead."

The red thorn poison was added to the incense holder, and the smoke distributed it into the air. I'd gotten the antidote from the black market enough for me, Kai, and Tao that night. The poison was supposed to be a slow death, which was why Samo went to the apothecary the day after, crying for help. I had to ensure Samo, Jie, and Peng followed our orders before they died. They successfully added the antidote for wandering nightshade poison, which had made people ill for the past few months. It had taken me a long time to find the antidote.

"Su must have an immunity to certain poisons," I said. "She claims her body is fighting it."

But what if the poison was only dormant in her body? Could it be triggered again? I had to make a trip to the Southern Border to find the Humble Hornet, the black-market seller of antidotes and other miscellaneous things. It had been a pain in the ass to locate him, but I heard he came from Emerald Song Valley, a place I hadn't been to in a while. I was indebted to Su. What if she died because of me?

I couldn't live with that. She needed the antidote for the red thorn poison so she could heal from that poison, at least. As for the Spewing Pain poison from the dart, I had to keep my eyes and ears peeled for anyone who had it.

"Do you want me to go search for the antidote?" Kai asked.

"No, I'll head out in a few days." I owed her that much. "You stay and keep watch here. If all goes well, I'll be back in three weeks. I'll check on Tao as well."

He nodded. "Does she know about us on that day?"

"Not yet." I thought back to the day I'd followed her to the abandoned shelter, thinking she was meeting Ru Malik or one of his men. Guilt knifed me in the gut.

I had to find the right time to tell her. I couldn't face her right now. What would she think of me? Would she still want to be my student?

She considered me a respected general who always did the right thing. Sometimes in war, I had to do reprehensible things to protect *my* people. I'd deceived my enemies, lured them to be slaughtered. But if I hadn't done that, the enemy would have killed me and my men without hesitation. That was the reality of war—kill or be killed.

Would she understand that, or would she consider me an evil person?

Yesterday, I thought we might have a chance to be together. But now I wasn't sure. Would she want to be with someone who wasn't the hero she'd envisioned? Another issue popped into my head. I needed to talk to Ren about my feelings for Su. Would she hate me?

I didn't want to think about it anymore and changed the topic. "She asked me to be her mentor."

"For what?" Kai crossed his arms.

"She wants to learn how to fight."

"She did a great job that day in the Market Square. A little guidance would benefit her." He considered me and laughed. "You know, she's perfect for you."

She was, and I didn't want to lose her. "She also wants to enter the archery competition."

"That means she's going to be competing against you. Does she know Emperor Tang wants you to enter too?"

"She will soon."

CHAPTER TWENTY-FOUR

SU

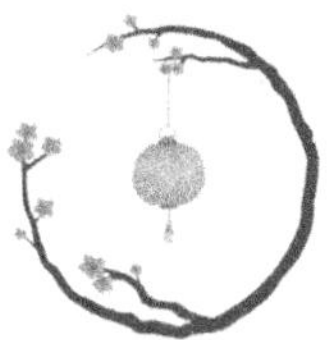

OUTSIDE IN THE BACKYARD, I stood smiling to myself as I sorted the herbs and placed them on drying trays.

I couldn't believe how events had changed so quickly. A few weeks ago, I'd only imagined being with Hung and wondered what it might be like to have him hold my hand or kiss me.

Kiss me.

A shiver raced down my back as heat crept into my face. Women didn't talk about these things in public. But Yunxi and I often discussed relationships and what people did in private. Both Yunxi and I had been in relationships before, but mine wasn't serious, and that had been years ago. Yunxi's relationship lasted longer than mine, but it ended too. We knew what kissing and being intimate with our significant other was like. But I admitted I wasn't that experienced. At that time, I'd been curious about Bolin, a locksmith's son, and wanted to know what it was like. Women usually waited until their marriage to be intimate, but I didn't want to wait. What if I never met anyone? What if I died the next day from some illness and never got to experience that?

More than ever, I wanted to pursue my happiness now. With all the deaths I'd seen lately, life seemed fragile. For those who wanted to wait for the perfect partner, that was wonderful. But I had my own path to walk.

For the first time in a long time, I pulled out a taboo book I'd hidden under my bed. I got it by accident when I visited an old bookstore years ago—after my relationship ended. The bookstore had since moved to another city. The owner's grandmother gave me it as a gift when I purchased three books regarding the body's meridians.

When I opened the book at home, I was shocked at the images and what the book was about. Despite that, I couldn't help but read through it to understand physical intimacy between a man and a woman. Nobody talked about this. There was no class to teach a woman what truly went on in the bedroom.

Last night, I had imagined Hung doing these wild things to me. I paused and glanced around the backyard. Of course, no one was there. Yunxi and Healer Churan were out front treating patients. Still, I felt like I was diving into dark territory and didn't want to be caught there. In the privacy of my mind, I could do whatever I wanted. But I didn't want my curiosity to bring trouble to anyone around me.

I placed dandelion flowers on one tray and the leaves on the other. Then I sorted lavender, ginger, and Goji berries. The City Apothecary was doing well, and profits for the shop had tripled compared to last year. We should probably start thinking about hiring more help.

My mind wandered back to Hung and his concern about my health. Even I didn't understand how my body hadn't succumbed to the red thorn poison like Samo and his friends or to the Spewing Pain like the bandit. With two deadly poisons in my system, I should have been dead or had horrible symptoms. Perhaps I had a super strong immune system. Or perhaps there was something else I didn't understand.

I looked at my palms, moved them around in front of me, invoking the energy from the pit of my stomach, channeling it to my hands. My palms warmed, but no essa shot out like that day in the Market Square. How had I invoked that power?

I'd experienced several inexplicable events lately. Could they all be connected? That mystical voice I'd heard many times seemed so far away and yet so close to me. The animal eye I'd seen during my meditation still gripped me.

I've been searching for you.

The voice echoed in my head. Who had been speaking to me telepathically?

While I was unconscious, I'd delved into an incredible world. What was happening to me?

I had heard about warriors who had elevated their essas to high enough levels that allowed them to tap into different planes of existence. The metaphysical phenomena they described were so fantastical . . . I wanted to experience them too. Had I experienced one of those mystical things without knowing? It was possible since I was able to tug at Hung's essa with my own.

A smile formed on my lips again.

"What are you smiling about?"

"Ah!" I jumped at the sudden voice.

"I guess you've been thinking about inappropriate things." Yunxi laughed, holding a basket with more herbs to be sorted.

"You need to stop spying on people." My cheeks burned with embarrassment. "Don't you have patients to see out there?" I jerked a chin toward the front of the apothecary. "Doesn't Healer Churan have enough for you to do? I can talk to her about it."

"My patients are all taken care of. All is well, my friend. I came back to accompany you—keep you out of trouble." She winked.

I rolled my eyes. "I don't need any company."

Smiling, she placed an arm around my shoulders. "Did you know that General Wen placed a large order for talismans for all his soldiers?"

"Really? That's thoughtful of him. All warriors should carry one with them."

"Last night." She tugged at my twisted knot talisman. "After he purchased this for you. Now you don't have to wonder if he likes you or not. The answer is pretty obvious."

"I guess so." I looked at the talisman for a moment longer, feeling joy sprout in my heart.

"Look what I have for you." Yunxi pulled out a packet of herbs from inside her basket. The pretty packet was wrapped in paper with dried flowers on it.

I arched a suspicious eyebrow. "What kind of trouble are you in? Why are you being so nice? You need my help with something?"

Yunxi poked me in the ribs. "Between the two of us, *you're* the troublemaker. Why can't I buy my friend a gift to celebrate her happy heart? She's captured the man of her dreams."

"I don't know about that," I said. "But we're both attracted to each other."

"And that's the first step in any relationship. Let's take a quick break."

She ushered me to the stone table and sat down. "We're ahead of schedule with inventory. I'm sure Healer Churan wouldn't mind us taking a few minutes to rest." She pointed to the packet in my hand. "Open it."

I sat down beside her and opened the gift. It was a pink book called *The Art of Intimacy* by Pink Rose. The front cover had a painting of a single rose. It looked similar to my book, *The Art of Seduction* by Cherry Blossom. Could these books be part of a series? I had no doubt the authors' names were fake.

I flipped to a page and gasped at the provocative illustrations. The next page depicted even more acts that had me turning red.

I clamped a hand over my mouth and whipped a gaze at Yunxi. "What are you doing?" I meant to ask a more direct question, but that was what came out.

She laughed. "Making sure you know what happens in a relationship."

"I know enough." Yunxi didn't know I had a similar book in

my room, and I wasn't going to tell her. "But thank you. Do you have a copy of your own?"

"Of course I do." She beamed, not even a little embarrassed.

"I thought the bookstore moved to another city?" I asked.

"It did, so I asked a friend to get me two copies when she visited her family."

More women were reading these books than I expected.

"As healers, we know the anatomy of the body pretty well," Yunxi said. "But when it comes to sexual pleasure, it's a different study."

She grabbed the book from my hand and flipped to a page. "Look at *this* position. How is this even possible?" She giggled. "The woman must be boneless."

She turned to another page, and her eyes widened. We shared a glance and burst out laughing.

"I know you've been fancying a certain Elite Guard. Want to tell me about it?"

She placed her elbows on the table, resting her chin on her palms and sighing dreamily. "He's so gorgeous. I bet he has a marvelous dick too."

Laughing, I shook my head at her honest words. "Be careful what you say. Healer Churan or a patient might hear you. You've got a filthy mouth."

"It's not filthy. I'm just describing a man's anatomy as is." She bumped shoulders with me. "Most men say they prefer their women to be virgins. But deep down, I think they want someone with experience." She shrugged. "Maybe there are some men who want an inexperienced woman. I prefer my man to know what he's doing. Don't you?"

I couldn't believe I was having this forbidden conversation with Yunxi at the back of the City Apothecary.

I didn't disagree with her. But I wasn't a man, so I couldn't be certain. I often wondered about noble daughters. Were they as pure and disciplined as they made themselves seem? I doubted it.

Emperors from other lands had several concubines. It was

normal to have a harem of women. But our Emperor Tang wasn't like the others. He was true to Yeeva. I wanted a man who was dedicated to me. Besides, I couldn't even fathom having multiple partners. How would I even remember details about them? I'd probably end up calling them by the wrong name.

Did Hung want a woman who was pure?

Yunxi leaned in and said, "I bet General Wen is excellent in bed." She pointed to an unimaginable position that made me blush again.

Did couples really do that? The man had to have powerful arms for that to work.

"You're crazy. Get back to work." I pushed her away, and we both started laughing.

"What's so funny?"

I stiffened at Hung's voice, glared at Yunxi, whose eyes widened, and mouthed, "See?"

I immediately shoved the book into my chest pocket, inhaled a breath, rose from my seat, and turned around to face him. Like always, he was gorgeous in his uniform, looking regal and powerful.

"Nothing important," I said with a slight bow. "We're sorting dried herbs. Yunxi often gets giddy for no reason."

"Su is worse." She walked over to Hung and offered a slight bow. "General Wen. Nice to see you again. The talismans you wanted for your men should arrive this week."

"Thank you. I'll let my men know to come in and choose one."

When she disappeared into the apothecary, he walked up to me. "How are you feeling?"

"The wound on my back is healing well. My energy has improved since yesterday."

"Are you sure?" He stepped closer and placed a hand on my forehead. "Did Healer Churan examine you today?" He looked at the back of my ear, probably checking for the red dots. "I want you to tell me if you're feeling unwell. Okay?"

"Okay," I said, taking in his masculine scent.

He brushed a finger down my cheek, trailing my jaw, and heat zipping through me. He paused at my chin, tipping my face up to meet him.

I studied his face. His eyes looked tired. "You didn't sleep well last night?"

"No," he said. "I'll be gone for a few weeks."

"Where are you going?"

His brown eyes bore into mine. For a moment, I saw a swarm of emotions in them.

"Is something bothering you?"

"No." He interlaced his fingers with mine. "I'm going to ensure you're completely healed before we start our strict training." Then he lifted my hand to his lips.

My heart palpitated as warmth bloomed on the spot where his lips contacted my skin.

Despite his comforting words, I could tell he was hiding something from me.

"Let me show you a way to harmonize your energy. You can do this at night before bed and in the morning."

Hung took two stones and placed them about three feet apart. He ushered me to stand in the middle, between the stones. "This is the zero point, the beginning and ending, also referred to as the intersection of energy flow."

From behind me, he ushered me to walk around one rock, turn around to cross over, and walk around the other rock. He followed me for a few rounds.

"It's just like the infinity symbol with our feet," I said.

"Exactly."

"My parents taught me to envision this loop of energy flowing when I was feeling unwell, but I'd forgotten it until now."

Sadness clung to me. How could I have forgotten all the precious lessons my parents had taught me?

You were young, and grief clouded your memory.

When you were a child, you didn't listen to everything your parents told you. If I had paid more attention when I was younger, I would probably be a better healer now.

"It's a powerful symbol that radiates harmonious energy." He paused and pointed to the ground. "When you walk the Infinity Loop, don't forget to breathe in and out. The intake is like absorbing the earth's energy. The exhale is removing the negative stuff inside you. This flow harmonizes the energy of your body, allowing it to rebalance itself and heal faster."

"Will this help my kung fu?"

"Absolutely."

"Who taught you this method?" I asked.

"My kung fu teacher. He passed away seven years ago. I was his only student."

"And now I'm *your* only student, right?" I asked. "Aren't the soldiers your students too?"

"In some way they are, but there are other teachers besides me showing them the skills, like Gong and other guards who have experience. The basic teaching guides have already been established for their training." A glimmer appeared in his eyes. "But you're the only one who gets my personal attention. I have to customize a training session for you."

A thought occurred to me. "Will your soldiers or guards find this whole thing strange? I mean, you're my teacher, but you're also. . ."

His eyes sparked. "Also what, Su?"

I narrowed my eyes at him, wanting him to confirm our relationship—or whatever this was between us.

"My *friend*," I emphasized with a pout.

A muscle twitched on his jaw. "We're more than friends." He gripped my chin with his thumb and index finger. "You're my beautiful flower, my dahlia." He lowered his lips, brushing them gently over mine, sending electricity from my head to my toes. Then he drew back, his eyes darkening. "Is that confirmation enough for you?"

My heart raced, and happiness burst inside me. I'd heard men referring to their significant other as flowers or gems as forms of endearment. But I didn't think General Wen was that kind of man.

"You are my bamboo." I smirked.

His lips tilted, and wild butterflies multiplied in my stomach. "I've never heard that phrase before."

"I'm your flower, so you're my plant—versatile and strong." I placed a hand on his cheek, feeling the slight stubble on his chin. "Actually, you're my *warrior*. Do you like that better?"

"I do."

"You know something?"

"What?"

"You should never stop smiling." I traced his lips with my fingers. "You're more handsome when you do."

"You make me smile."

My heart swelled, and an extra burst of joy swirled in me. I never knew a relationship could make me feel like this. I wrapped my arms around him, feeling his sturdy body against mine. He secured me in a tight embrace. He was a lot taller than me, probably over six feet. I rested my head on his shoulder, feeling his racing heart. I inhaled his musky scent of myrrh, frankincense, and wood. So masculine and seductive.

For the first time in so long, I felt safe, wanted, and loved. I couldn't explain this wave of emotions. After my parents died, I always felt incomplete. That my life was in pieces, never truly connecting to anything. I lived my life as though I were trying to find my perfect spot—a place where Zhao Mei Su could call home and do whatever her heart wanted without the judgment or regulations from society.

Right now, I felt like I'd found my place.

Not all good things last.

I shoved the negative thought away, not wanting to taint my happiness.

After what seemed like a long moment, he kissed the top of

my head and drew back. "Time to meet with the Emperor." He pulled a hairpin from his chest pocket and dropped it into my hand. "What do you think?"

"It's gorgeous." I held the gold hairpin with pink and blue flowers. The gemstone glinted in the sunlight. This wasn't a simple hairpin bought off a street vendor. Maybe he got it at Heavenly Reflections. "Where did you get it?"

"I had it made for you." He took it from my hand and twisted the knob on the flower end. A small blade gleamed. "For dire situations only."

I gaped at the blade. "It's a weapon hairpin."

"Perfect for my warrior dahlia."

I'd never seen anything like that. No one had ever given me such a precious gift. "Thank you."

"I don't want you to get hurt again." His expression turned serious. "When I saw the hairpin mockup, I thought of you. I asked the maker to add a hidden blade." He slid it into my hair, stepped back, and studied me. "Perfect."

"Thank you." I felt it with my hand, making a note to check myself in the mirror later. "You've given me two gifts already. But I haven't given you anything."

"You already gave me your life when you blocked that poisoned dart. That's a priceless gift to me. There's no need to get me anything. We can have a warmup lesson tomorrow. It's not real training, though."

"That's okay." I grinned. "It'll be a starting point for me."

When he left to see Emperor Tang, I rushed into the back room to look at myself in the mirror.

Healer Churan entered. "That's a gorgeous hairpin."

"Thank you." I beamed. "Are there a lot of patients today?"

"Nothing we can't handle," she said. "Can you spend time with Luzi today? Take the afternoon off. She's been asking about you. I think she's interested in how you're healing fast. She heard about your bravery—fighting the bandits and saving the general. I told her that you lost your parents when you were young. She probably feels a connection with you."

"Yes, I'd love to spend time with her."

"It'll help her recover. General Wen wants to interview her when she's ready."

I wanted to know who had destroyed Luzi's family too.

CHAPTER TWENTY-FIVE

HUNG

AS I WALKED down the hallway with pots of glowing plants, Gong appeared wearing his purple cloak. His wavy dark hair had a hint of purple today. He was the most radical council member, but I liked that he was different.

You couldn't pay me to color my hair purple or red. Not even a thousand gold ingots. I'd probably die of shock before I could spend the money.

"Are you in this meeting too?" he asked.

"Yes," I said. "It's our monthly meeting, right?"

"This one is different, though."

"How so?"

"Three-Eyes just came back from his assignment. The Emperor also called back the three generals."

I was the Prime General, and Generals Zhou, Li, and Pao usually reported to me. But that didn't mean the Emperor couldn't have asked them to do something without my knowledge. Still, I wondered the reason for this urgency.

"I heard about the incident with Ru Malik," Gong said, "What's your plan? What happened to all the captives?"

"They're dead. They didn't offer useful information, and I won't waste food on them," I said. "Ru Malik's kung fu has improved substantially. He's got powerful support somewhere. I'm going to find out who."

I looked over at Gong, fifteen years older than me, making him forty-nine. He'd had more experience with training than I had. I'd heard he used to have a few disciples before joining the Emperor's Council.

"How many students did you have before?"

"Two. That was a long time ago." He lifted a bushy brow. "Why?"

"Have you ever taught a woman kung fu?"

"I have." He stopped in his steps and considered me. "But she gave up and never continued."

That wasn't what I wanted to hear. How should I approach my lessons with Su? Though tomorrow's lesson was just a warmup, I needed to plan.

"What happened?"

"It didn't work out." He shrugged. "I suppose I was too hard on her."

Gong was tough, but so was I. I appreciated his assistance—and any other experienced warriors volunteering their time—in the training camp. This way, the soldiers could get an overall view of different fighting styles. We had to prepare the Imperial army for battle, and they needed realistic training in all kinds of weather.

"Are you planning on teaching a woman?"

I nodded. "What's the best technique?"

"Is she determined to learn?"

I remembered that she'd spied on my soldiers. What would Gong think if he knew my student was also my significant other?

"She's very determined," I said.

"Then I recommend you treat her like a soldier. Have her undergo strenuous training. But keep in mind she won't be as strong as they are. Adjust as you go along." He rubbed his chin. "This could be historic, Hung."

"What do you mean?"

"If your student succeeds, more women might want to join the army."

I couldn't see that happening unless we made a lot of changes to accommodate female soldiers. If successful, it would be the first military to have all genders.

"That's farfetched. I just want to focus on teaching *one* woman."

"Who is she?"

"You'll find out soon." We entered the royal chamber where Emperor Tang held his council meetings.

Three-Eyes sat toward the front near the Emperor's seat at the head of the table. Emperor Tang wasn't present yet. General Zhou wore his navy uniform with red accents. He'd grown a beard since I last saw him. He met my eyes and rose, placing a fist on his chest in greeting.

General Li and General Pao—both in uniform—joined him, and I returned the gesture. General Li looked older than the last time I saw him. I'd heard his son had been ill, so that could've added to his stress. General Pao had piled his hair into a man-bun with a metal accessory. He was the youngest of the three, and I'd promoted him myself.

Gong and I sat across from the generals.

"Welcome," I told them. "How are the borders? Keep it short. You can provide more details when the Emperor arrives."

"We've pushed back the rebels, but they're getting more brazen," said General Zhou, who monitored the Eastern and Central Borders. The Bloodshade Bandits had taken over that territory, with plans to expand.

"Let me know if you need more troops," I said.

General Zhou had joined the military with my father. The two had been great friends, just like Ren and I. He'd helped guide me with my military endeavors.

"Something odd occurred two days ago at the camp, but I'll share that later," said General Zhou.

"One rebel group attacked us at the Western Border a month

ago, but we defeated them," said General Li. "It's been quiet since."

"How are the Southern Borders?" I asked General Pao.

"Nothing unusual," he said. "I heard about Ru Malik's attack in the Market Square. That's close to the palace. Are you okay?"

"Yes, thank you. The Bloodshades are probably hiding in cities and towns near you. Monitor them. They're planning something."

"Have you apprehended him yet?" General Zhou tented his fingers. "Seems like his rebel army has increased."

While my generals shared stories about the events around their territories, Three-Eyes talked with Gong.

Three-Eyes could see beyond the veils, which made him beneficial to the council. He had a head of silver hair that matched his eyebrows, the long hair tied at the back of his head. The third eye sat on his forehead in a vertical position. It only opened during specific situations, but I didn't know what those were. I saw it open once, but that had been an accident when I'd entered an Imperial room looking for the Emperor and found Three-Eyes sitting in the chair, murmuring something to himself. When the third eye looked at me, I sensed a strange stillness I'd never experienced before.

The Scarred Hallows attacked the Western Border that day and almost breached our forces. I wanted to inform the Emperor but found Three-Eyes instead. I'd assumed the sudden attack was the reason his third eye opened. But the Emperor told me an evil force had possessed the Scarred Hallows' army, pushing them to destroy us. The possession didn't last long, and our army survived the assault.

There was something about Three-Eyes I didn't trust. Though he served as a seer for the Emperor, he never revealed much about himself. All I knew was that he had a brother but hadn't been in contact with him. But then again, I was a private man too. He probably thought the same about me, which was why he always gave me a strange look.

Conversation erupted between the generals and Gong, but Three-Eyes kept his gaze on me. His eyes emitted an intensity that showed he could see things no one else understood. A tingle rushed down my arm, but this was nothing like the feeling when Su looked at me with those loving eyes. Though I was uncomfortable, I didn't show it. In war, you should never reveal your weakness to the enemy.

Though Three-Eyes wasn't my enemy, I didn't want to show him how uncomfortable he made me. Why was he looking at me like that?

Perhaps he was doing this on purpose. *Fucking hell.*

Did he sense the darkness around me? I wouldn't be surprised; I'd just battled Ru Malik.

Emperor Tang had sent Three-Eyes on a covert assignment that no one on the council knew about. What had the seer discovered?

I had a feeling Three-Eyes didn't like me. Not that his opinion mattered. But knowing you were disliked made it awkward during meetings.

My loyalty was to the Emperor.

"How was your trip?" Gong asked Three-Eyes.

He slid his gaze away from me. "Interesting."

"What exactly does that mean?" General Zhou asked, making the other two generals smirk.

"You'll find out when the Emperor arrives. I don't want to bore you by repeating myself."

Two servants emerged with trays of food. Another pair of servants brought in two containers of wine and mugs, placing them on the table.

At that moment, Emperor Tang strode in, changing the energy in the room. A few years older than me, he was also a warrior, and we'd become friends through dueling with each other. His dark hair was swept back, secured with a gold accessory with no crown.

We all rose from our seats and bowed to him. Emperor Tang wore a gold cape draped over a navy and gold uniform. I didn't know if the other men noticed his attire, but he only wore that uniform during battle. Was he in a battle today? If so, where? Were his guards with him?

Emperor Tang lifted a hand and walked over to his seat. "Sit. Sorry I'm late." A crease formed on his forehead.

"Is everything all right?" I asked.

"Just a minor thing. It's resolved now."

When more food arrived, filling the table with all kinds of delicacies, he opened his arms. "Eat. We can talk while doing so."

The servants filled his plate for him, but he only glanced at the food, seemingly lacking an appetite. He asked the generals for updates, and they told him what they had told me earlier.

"Good. Keep a close eye. There's a darkness working hard to penetrate the energy wall I've put up around the palace."

The Emperor possessed the magic of time and space, which meant he could bend or manipulate them at his will. But he hadn't done that in a while because it used up a lot of essa storage, making him weak.

His council members knew he had cast an energy cloak around the palace for many years. Years ago, he'd extended the protective cloak beyond the palace, but that exerted too much of his energy. The Empress convinced him to limit it to just around the palace.

Emperor Tang looked over at General Zhou. "I heard something strange occurred at your base."

"Two days ago, our guard fought a rebel. When he died, his eyes disappeared, leaving dark holes for the eye sockets. Dark ashes floated from them." General Zhou looked at me. "I was going to send word to you but got the alert to come back for this meeting."

I nodded, understanding the urgent situation. As the Prime General, I had to know what was happening near the borders to assess the security of the entire empire.

"Do you still have his body?" I asked.

"Yes. I brought it back with me."

"Excellent," I said. "I'll look later."

I had a feeling the same dark magic was used to kill Luzi's family. The details of their corpses weren't revealed to many, and I didn't intend to share them now. Limiting the investigation to only a few people prevented rumors and the potential for public panic.

I'd never seen this kind of power before. I shot a glance at Gong, who sipped his wine contemplatively.

Did he know anyone with that kind of dark power? When I looked at Three-Eyes, he was staring at the food on the table. But I had a feeling he wasn't seeing food.

"I called for this urgent meeting because I have something to share." The Emperor turned to Three-Eyes. "I asked our seer to investigate the energy around the borders of Lin Din Ni and beyond, and he discovered something alarming. You can share it with the council now."

Three-Eyes rose from his seat and reached for the fabric-covered box in front of him. He untied the fabric covering, revealing a wooden box. Abstract inscriptions were carved into the wood. Some glowed as if lit from within.

Silence filled the room as everyone stared at the unique box and what it held.

"What are those carvings?" I gestured to the abstractions.

"A light language."

"A what?" General Li asked.

I'd never heard of it either.

"A form of cosmic language," he said. "Most people won't understand it. All you need to know is that it's imprisoning the force in this box."

He waved a hand, and the wood faded, revealing glass panels. Fluctuating darkness moved inside the glass box like fog or smoke. The abstract symbols lit up against the glass panels, casting light into the box. The moving darkness shrieked—a sound so evil that goosebumps shot up my arms and legs.

The generals gasped, and Gong rose from his seat, staring at the box. "What is it?"

Three-Eyes looked at everyone. "Soul Extractors. Beings that feed on the soul's energy to strengthen theirs. It's a powerful darkness that is slowly penetrating Lin Din Ni. It can infiltrate the body, take it over."

"Like a possession?" Gong walked over to stand beside Three-Eyes. "Where did it come from?"

Three-Eyes offered a nod. "But most people won't recover from it. These dark beings aren't from this world."

The generals glanced at each other with worried expressions.

"Our men aren't prepared for this kind of battle," said General Zhou.

"We will prepare them. Am I correct, General Wen?" Emperor Tang looked at me, and I knew it was an invitation for me to meet him after this council meeting.

"Yes." I ambled over to examine the demonic energy. It floated around, taking on various shapes.

"If it's not from this world, where exactly did it come from?" General Pao asked.

"From a dark world that breeds evil forces," Three-Eyes continued. "This being was hiding in a cave. I lured it out and imprisoned it."

Another shriek erupted, making me shiver this time. The third eye on the seer's forehead flipped open, glancing around.

General Zhou gaped at the eye, which was larger than the other two.

The eye glared at the evil thing inside the box. The iris and pupil disappeared for a moment, and a moving darkness swam across the eye with sparkling stars in between.

I briefly looked over at Gong, but his face showed no surprise.

Were we looking at the same thing? I returned my gaze to the eye, but the night sky had disappeared. The eye blinked a few times, and the evil sounds from the demon faded along with the color of the smoke. Had the eye weakened it somehow?

Three-Eyes dropped into his chair when the third eye closed, looking paler than before. More wrinkles appeared on his forehead and around his mouth, making him seem years older.

The Emperor rushed over, offering him a drink. "Take this."

Three-Eyes took the cup with a shaky hand and gulped it down.

"What just happened?" Gong asked.

Three-Eyes took a few breaths, drew some symbols onto his chest, and muttered a mantra. After a moment, color returned to his face.

He looked at the Emperor. "There's a pocket of darkness."

"Where?" The Emperor furrowed his eyebrows.

"Emerald Song Valley." He swallowed. "Those Soul Extractors are more powerful than this one." He pointed to the box. "This demon tried to call for help, but I weakened it."

"That's what it was doing with that eerie sound?" General Li asked.

Emerald Song Valley was where I had to go to retrieve Su's antidote.

"How do we destroy it?" I asked. "I had plans to go there for an investigation."

Three-Eyes looked at me. "Not with a regular weapon."

"See me after this," the Emperor said, sitting back down. "I'll give you something that will help you."

CHAPTER TWENTY-SIX

HUNG

AS I HEADED to the Emperor's office, Ru Malik's words about my parents' deaths echoed in my head. What did he know that I didn't? His arrogance had opened a door that made me question the thoroughness of the investigation of their murders. That was another reason to apprehend Ru Malik.

Heaviness clung to me as I strode down the wide hallway full of potted plants decorating the place. Small flowers glowed among them, but they weren't as bright as they used to be.

I walked up to the door, and the two guards recognized me. They placed a fist on their chests, nodded, and announced my presence. When they opened the door, I stepped inside and shut it behind me.

The Emperor turned and met my eyes, and I greeted him. He stood at the window, staring out at the garden below. I ambled over to see Empress Jayaatu walking around it with her maid, tending to their flower bushes.

He'd removed his regal cape, hanging it over the rack beside his chair.

The Emperor sighed, and I could feel the tension in the air. The crown he often wore sat on his desk, which proved he'd been outside the palace.

"Where are you going?" I gestured to the navy and gold uniform. "Or rather, where *did* you go?"

He looked at me. "Do you regret being the Prime General?"

The Emperor and I were friends outside of my responsibility to his court. It all started when he was in disguise visiting Lotus Crane Harbor with his new bride, showing her around. He had guards but had sent them out to pick up some necessities for his wife. Two rebels destroyed the restaurant he was eating in, demanding everyone offer their belongings. The Emperor could have killed them, but he wanted to remain discreet—just a visitor admiring the flourishing area.

I stepped in and killed the rebels before the situation worsened. At that time, I hadn't been a general, just part of the military, working my way up. When I realized he was the Emperor, we had a conversation. He discovered who my father was, a general who had devoted so much of his time to Lin Din Ni. We often dueled and compared our fighting skills. Over the years, he confided in me in several dire situations, asking for my insight.

When he promoted me as the Prime General to oversee this military, no one protested. Not that they could change the Emperor's mind.

"No," I said. Why the strange question?

"Because your responsibility to oversee the safety of Lin Din Ni has just gotten far more difficult."

"It comes with the job. No regrets from me." I gestured to his warrior attire and asked again, "Why this uniform?"

He placed a hand on my shoulder. "I checked out the Shadowcrest Mountains."

My mouth dropped. "Alone?"

The Shadowcrest Mountains harbored dark energy that repelled most people. Some adept warriors had dared to travel into those mountains but were never seen again.

Nodding, he lifted his hands, moving them around. The space between them shifted, and malleable energy formed.

"I manipulated time and space by creating a portal that took me there." He expanded the space between his hands, and the malleable energy stretched. An image of the mountain range appeared within the energy. Dark clouds hung low around the peaks. "I couldn't take anyone with me. It would've used up too much of my essa."

My brows creased, not liking that he'd placed himself in danger.

Emperor Tang saw the concern on my face. "Even if I had deployed some guards or a troop to meet me there, it would've taken them weeks to get there. Time was of the essence."

"What did you find out?"

"That mountain range is breeding darkness. The heaviness is worse than before." He jerked his chin toward the direction of the Imperial conference room we had just been in. "Some beings were like the darkness trapped inside the box. But I encountered a powerful being who could shapeshift. For a split second, I saw his human face with a serpent's body. He sensed my presence even though I was traveling between spaces."

I didn't have the power to travel to another plane of existence, so I couldn't fully understand what he was describing.

"What kind of demon is that?" I asked.

When the Emperor looked at me, fear appeared in his eyes. "No one else has ever sensed me. We fought, and I injured it with my dagger. Then I rushed out of the cave and hid in the woods. But then, a flash of lightning sliced through the sky, and a roar rattled the ground. The roar unsettled the evil entity trying to search for me. I took that opportunity to create a portal to come back."

"Why did you go there? Did something happen I was unaware of?"

So much shit had occurred in the last few months. I wouldn't be surprised if I'd missed something important.

"I sensed the darkness brewing there. It wants to come here, so I had to investigate."

"Why here?"

The Emperor turned to a pot of glowing nascynths. A unique light radiated from them, which other lands didn't possess. Most of the glowing flowers flourished in Luklum, where the palace was situated. Today, the glowing flowers appeared muted. Did they sense the impending darkness too?

"Because it wants to destroy the light here."

My stomach twisted.

He jerked his chin toward the garden where his wife tended the plants. "Yeeva senses it too, and it's making her weak." Then, his eyes brightened as he changed the subject. "Yeeva is pregnant again. I'm going to announce the news on the day of the archery competition. We're keeping it quiet for now."

I squeezed his shoulder. "Congratulations."

Their last pregnancy didn't go well, and the entire country mourned with them. I understood why they kept it quiet this time.

Then it occurred to me. "Do you think she's weak because of the pregnancy and not the darkness?"

"That's a possibility," he said. "She is giving more energy to the baby, so there isn't much left for her. But something else is happening *here,* in Luklum—in the palace even. I *feel* it. I just have to find its source and eliminate it." He walked to a wall and opened the wooden door to a room filled with weapons.

He walked in, reached for a sword on a rack, and drew it from its scabbard. The blade was made from blue fulgurite.

"Yeeva wove her light energy into the mother stone. This sword is made from a piece of that gem."

The mother fulgurite stone sat in a secluded area behind the palace.

The Emperor touched the blade. "Not everyone can activate the sword."

"Why?"

"Because it reads energy. I want to see if it resonates with you. I'm touching it, but it doesn't activate for me."

"No?"

"I already have a dagger, which I used to fight off the entity."

He walked out of the armory, stepped over to his desk, and placed the sword down. Then he reached for a dagger on the other side of his desk, removing it from its decorative scabbard. It had a gilded handle with abstract symbols glowing on the illuminated fulgurite blade. "This weapon likes my energy, so it activates when I touch it."

"So the stone has its own intelligence?"

"Yes. The crystal seems to have a mind of its own." He let me hold his dagger.

I gripped the handle, and the light on the blade and abstract symbols disappeared immediately.

"What does the light do?" I gave the dagger back to him.

"Burns like fire." He inserted the dagger back into its scabbard. Then he reached for the sword again. "Yeeva added sacred geometric shapes she'd seen in her dreams onto his blade. Try it." He offered it to me.

I grabbed the handle, and the abstract symbol immediately flashed brightly, followed by the entire blade. A powerful blue aura radiated from the sword.

The Emperor grinned. "It's yours, Hung. Use it to kill those dark energies. The light will burn the dark more effectively."

I held the sword, feeling the energy zipping through my body. Even though this was my first time holding the sword, I felt a camaraderie with it.

"Are you sure?" I asked, studying the sword. I've never had a weapon this precious before. "Do you want to have other warriors test it out too?"

He placed a hand on my shoulder. "There's no one more worthy of this sword than you. This sword knows this. You deserve it, and it's my gift to you. Make good use of it."

"Thank you." I slid it back into its scabbard.

He looked at me. "Why are you going to the Emerald Song Valley?"

How much should I share with the Emperor? I didn't want to lie to my friend, but I also didn't want him to know what I'd done to lure Ru Malik into Luklum. Would he have approved of my methods? I'd used three civilians—criminals—as bait. But Su had gotten hurt. She was the Empress's beloved healer. Now that Empress Jayaatu was pregnant, what would happen if she knew her healer was poisoned?

Right now, the Emperor had too much on his shoulders to worry about my personal problems. I'd tell him after I made things right.

"Need to follow up on a clue regarding Ru Malik," I told him a partial truth. "Now I'll look into the Soul Extractors too."

When my visit with the Emperor ended, I made my way to the morgue to examine the soldier's dead body that General Zhou had brought back. The decomposition was exactly like the members of the Shen family.

Was that being the Emperor saw in the Shadowcrest Mountains responsible for the possession? Or was this the work of another devil?

CHAPTER TWENTY-SEVEN

SU

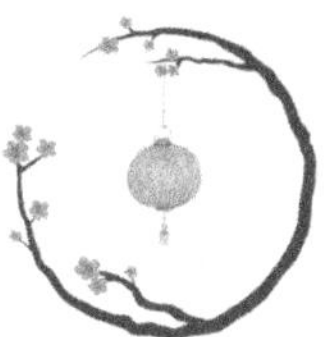

I WOKE up at the crack of dawn and snuck into the storage shed
to practice archery. I'd bought a target board and a beginner's
book to help me. Hung wouldn't approve of this, but I couldn't sit
around and waste time. I felt fine, and no one knew my body
better than me.

The sky glowed a soft orange, signifying I had a few hours to
practice before heading back to open the apothecary. The bow
Yeeva had given me was made of bamboo, silkwood thorn, and
wild mulberry bound together using silk and animal matter. The
arrows she'd given me were made of bamboo with copper arrowheads. I also saw some with bronze and iron arrowheads.

I gripped the bow and then the arrow, testing their weight and
familiarizing myself with the weapon. I stared at the target, aimed
the arrow, and shot it. But the arrow flew past the target board,
landing elsewhere. *Not a very good start, Su.* I didn't realize
pulling the bow back required so much strength.

According to the book and what Hung had mentioned, I
needed to develop upper body strength, especially my arms. I
didn't have any weight handy, so I found two large rocks nearby
and followed the instructions. With each rock in my hand, I positioned my arms out, keeping them straight while squatting. This

position would build strength in my arms and legs. I focused on my breathing technique while my arms and legs burned, trying to remain in position. Minutes later, I took a break and repeated the weights, squatting, and mixed in the practice with various animal kung fu styles.

After a few hours of practicing, my body zinged with energy. But I knew my body would pay for it tomorrow. If I repeated this every other day, my skills would improve.

CHAPTER TWENTY-EIGHT

SU

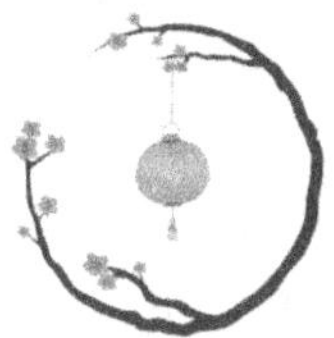

THE NEXT DAY, my body ached as I had expected, but the muscles relaxed after I practiced the Infinity Loop for a while until the soreness subsided. Then I put on a casual tunic and pants and added a belt. I wasn't sure what Hung would teach me today, so I chose loose clothing that would allow me to kick and jump with ease. A dress would limit my movements.

Tucking my worn-out kung fu pamphlet into my pocket, I walked to the front desk, looking for Healer Churan. Two ladies browsed the essential oil stand. When they saw me, they approached me immediately.

I recognized them as Wong Beibei and Lu Cailing, daughters from noble families, as impeccably dressed as ever. Beibei's dangling earrings glistened from the sunrays streaming through the windows. She wore a pink dress with a rose hairpin. Cailing had on a light green dress that matched her intricate hairpin.

"Is it true you're learning martial arts?" Beibei asked.

How had the news spread so fast? I glanced over at Yunxi, who was busy helping a customer. She saw me, likely overheard the conversation, and shrugged. Yunxi liked to gossip with me, but she was careful with people outside the shop.

"Yes, I am," I said, not feeling ashamed of my interest. I'd been dreaming of this day for the longest time.

"Why?" Cailing asked with a disapproving expression. "It'll roughen your hands, you'll get blisters all over, and you'll be sweaty and smelly! No man will want to marry you."

I wanted to roll my eyes but stopped myself. These women kept the shop busy, so I needed them to continue buying from the City Apothecary.

"I'm learning kung fu so I can defend myself if I have to. The world is a dangerous place. Did you hear about the bandits?" I widened my eyes at them for dramatic effect. "I don't want to rely on someone else to help me. What if the guards aren't unavailable?" I organized the bottles of essential oil on the stand. "And I don't want to feel *useless*. And if no one wants to marry me, that's his loss, right?"

Beibei studied me for a moment. "You're so brave."

"But you could die if you fight back," Cailing said.

"You'll *definitely* die if you don't fight back. But learning kung fu can help you navigate dangerous situations too. Maybe you'll see a way to escape and avoid the violence."

"I've seen General Wen and other warriors leap into the air as though they're flying." Beibei waved a hand. "It looks hard but so cool."

"My dad says that takes a lot of energy to master," Cailing told her friend.

"Everything takes time to master," I said. "That's why people practice."

Beibei and Cailing looked at each other as though they shared a common thought.

I could tell that they hadn't considered they could protect themselves. Like most people, they thought they needed someone else to help them. I gave them a glimpse of something they never thought possible.

"Can you let us know if you like it?" Beibei whispered.

"Maybe I can learn it from you? But I don't want my family to know. They won't approve."

"I'm interested too," Cailing said. "When I was younger, there were these mean kids who kept throwing things at me. My brother knew martial arts and always protected me. But he's married now, so his priority is his wife."

These women understood far better than I expected. Maybe my passion could inspire other women to do as they desired instead of waiting for someone else's approval.

"Sure." I beamed. "I'll let you know how it goes."

Beibei smiled. "Thank you."

The two women giggled as they walked to the counter to pay for their purchases.

When they left, Yunxi said, "I don't know how everyone knows about you taking lessons. It didn't come from me."

"It's okay," I said. "Everyone will know once they see me at the training camp with soldiers for the basic lessons. Once I master the basics, I'll get customized lessons."

Healer Churan entered the apothecary with bags of pastries in her hands. "We're celebrating today."

"Celebrating what?"

She tapped me on the shoulders. "You—the healer who defies the norm. Everyone in the Market Square is talking about you learning from General Wen. It's a big deal."

"Why?" I knew people would be curious, but I didn't realize the magnitude of it.

"It's something that hasn't happened before, something they've never even considered."

"I'm only learning martial arts."

"How many female martial artists have you met?" Healer Churan asked.

"There was that warrior who accompanied a noble family from the Northern Empire to one competition."

"That warrior came from a family of brothers who are also warriors." Healer Churan placed the bags on the counter. "I know other female warriors are out there, but they're rare in Lin Din Ni. People don't give female warriors the same respect as the males."

"It's a stupid rule," Yunxi said. "It's not fair."

"I agree, and it's not a rule. It's more of a mentality." Healer Churan tapped her temple. "This is how things were and are. People know nothing else." She looked at me. "But you're changing that."

Joy surged in me. I thought about Beibei and Cailing seeing the possibility of the impossible.

Healer Churan took the pastries from the bags and placed them on a plate. "You're defying the odds, bending the rules. More importantly, the Prime General is your teacher. He's bending the rules too, and the Emperor and Empress aren't rejecting the idea."

"The Emperor could stop him." I feared.

"He could order a decree, but that won't happen. The Empress loves you. The Emperor loves General Wen. They understand his style. He's different from the other generals. He's paving a fresh path for himself too." She grinned. "Maybe the military will accept female soldiers soon."

Yunxi propped an elbow on the counter, looking dreamily at the ceiling and muttering, "I wonder if Kai would offer lessons."

Healer Churan and I exchanged smiles.

It thrilled me to see some people being receptive to this idea of me learning from my warrior. But I knew the majority hated the idea.

"Just ignore the hearsay when you walk out to the Market Square," Healer Churan said. "You'll get stares and questions in the streets."

"She doesn't need to wait for that," Yunxi said. "Two noble daughters were in here earlier and already asked Su questions. But our magnificent Su is very skillful. Instead of being offended, she inspired them! They even asked her to teach them once she's gotten her lessons."

"Is that right?" Healer Churan asked with amusement.

"They're good patrons." I shrugged. "It was better to have them on our side."

Healer Churan gestured at the plate of pastries, and I grabbed an egg custard while Yunxi took a pork bun.

"I told those women the truth." I bit into the egg custard and chewed. "That they need to rely on themselves. My honesty resonated with them."

Healer Churan smiled, placing a hand on my shoulder. "Your parents would be so proud of you."

"I hope so."

Healer Churan glanced around. "Is there anyone in the exam rooms?"

"No," Yunxi said. "A patient just left about thirty minutes ago."

"Slow morning," I added and finished my custard.

"Good." Healer Churan stretched out her elegant arms and danced. Her feet moved across the floor like she was floating. Her body twirled and dipped gracefully around the room, mesmerizing me and Yunxi.

"I didn't know you could dance." I watched her fluid movements, wishing I had her skills.

"You're so talented, Healer Churan." Yunxi clapped.

Healer Churan paused in her steps, curtsied, and bowed her head in gratitude.

"We all have our passions," she said. "Dancing was mine."

"Why did you stop?" I asked.

"It's hard to make a living as a dancer," she said. "The men look at you differently. They think you're a product and not a person. They don't respect you the way they should. In their eyes, you're only good for entertainment."

"That's awful," I said, understanding her well. The sadness in her voice stirred in the room.

"I wanted respect, so I learned to heal. Everyone needs a healer, even judgmental people." She looked at me. "Your parents taught me when I first started. I learned a lot from them. When they died, I learned from books and other teachers."

I knew my parents were close to Healer Churan, but I didn't know they had taught her. I understood her predicament. Most of the dancers I knew were part of an entertainment group that often came to the palace for celebrations. Sometimes, they offered shows in taverns and pavilions, but that was how people viewed them.

I could see why men would view Healer Churan differently. She was a beautiful woman in her mid-forties. I could only imagine how attractive she had been in her youth.

"You should start a dancing school for women," I said. "Bend the rules and teach healing and dancing. They're both forms of art."

"They certainly are. But some would argue against that." She laughed. "Why am I not surprised you would make the connection?"

"I'll learn from you," Yunxi said. "Dancing looks fun."

"Me too." I wouldn't mind some of those graceful movements.

"Focus on one thing at a time." She tapped my forehead. "Perhaps I'll do it one day. But right now, the energy is too unstable. There's danger lurking—I can feel it. My priority right now is ensuring we're safe and the shop flourishes."

She was right. This wasn't the time to start something new. Ru Malik could come back any time. His spies hid amongst our people. We had to be cautious.

With that thought, I wiped my hands with a napkin and drank some jasmine tea. "I'm heading to class. Can't be late on my first day. That would look awful. I'm sure people are waiting for me to fail so they can start the next gossip."

"Have fun," Yunxi said. "Don't worry about us here. Learn all the martial arts skills so you can come back and protect us." She laughed along with Healer Churan.

As I walked across the Market Square, people stared and whispered.

An older man shook his head at me. "Women should stick to the kitchen."

"Or healing," a man said to his friend, who stood beside him. "They have delicate hands for delicate things." He offered a sleazy smile that made me want to slap him.

His friend raked a gaze down my body and chuckled. "Women belong in the kitchen *and* in the bedroom. It's what they're born to do. I think General Wen just wants to see the body underneath her clothes." He licked his lips, and his friend laughed.

A mother walking by covered her young daughter's ears. Anger thrummed through me. Their ill words didn't bother me, but that little girl reminded me of Luzi, who needed someone to look up to. If I didn't defend myself, I was inadvertently condoning their obnoxious behavior.

I stalked up to the two men and lifted a clenched fist. "Do you want to know how *delicate* my fist can be?" I glared at them, ready to take a swing at either one of them.

The men glowered at me, but they stepped back.

"You should apologize to Healer Su," said Beibei, who held a basket of pastries. "Otherwise, the next time you get sick, don't bother coming to the City Apothecary."

"She's right." I smirked. "The next time you come in for treatment, I might be too busy being insulted to attend to you." I held up my hand. "Or I might be *inspired* to poke my acupuncture needle into your critical meridian points where the blood flow will rewire your mind. That'll help you show some respect and decency." I tapped on my body to show my intention. "Or my delicate things might stab the needle where you'll die a slow and painful death."

The two men widened their eyes, cursed, and stalked away. I didn't expect them to apologize, nor did I need them to. I was certain the next time they saw me, they'd walk in the other direction.

I turned to Beibei. "Thank you."

"You're welcome. I can see how knowing kung fu would benefit that situation," she said, then waved to Cailing, who stepped out from a paper store, probably looking for her friend.

Feeling inspired, I entered the military campsite. "I'm here to see General Wen."

The guard looked at me, arched a red eyebrow, and smirked. "He told us to escort you to the back room." He crooked a finger at a guard standing by another post. "Can you watch this entrance for a bit? We'll be right back."

"This way." The guard with a round face gestured for me to walk down a hallway, away from where the training field was located.

CHAPTER TWENTY-NINE

SU

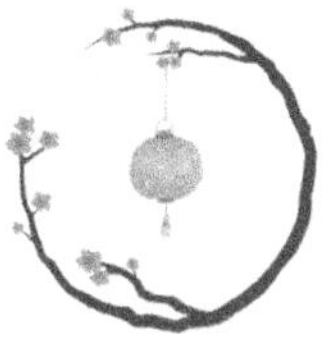

"I DON'T THINK this is the right way to the training field." I glanced at the dark hallway with no one around.

The guards grinned.

"You must undergo an initiation process to learn at this military camp. All the soldiers have to do this." The guard with the red eyebrow walked ahead of me. "Let's go."

I'd never heard of such a thing. But then again, I didn't know all the details of military training. Why didn't Hung mention this to me?

He's the general, Su. He has to be fair. He can't give you details ahead of time.

These guards didn't seem like they wanted a woman entering their training camp. As I walked down the hallway that seemed to lead me farther away from the main entrance, Red Eyebrow stuck out his foot, trying to trip me. I kicked him in the shin with so much force that he wailed and limped in pain.

Did they treat everyone like this? Or were they testing me because I was a woman? They probably assumed I didn't have a clue about self-defense. Did they want to stop me from learning?

Red Eyebrow pushed me against the brick wall, his eyes blazing with fury. "Bitch has some fight in her."

"Women aren't welcome here." Round Face leaned his shoulder against the wall and smirked. "You should know your place."

Did Hung know his men acted like this? Did he condone this kind of behavior? I'd never encountered a guard or soldier behaving this way when I'd visited the palace.

Irritation pricked my skin. "And what place is that?"

Round Face crossed his arms over his chest. "Stay in the house, the kitchen. Learn to cook better meals. *Please us* in bed."

He laughed, slapping a hand on his comrade's shoulder. They were a lot taller and bigger than me. I could get a few attacks in before I had to escape.

Though I should be afraid of what these two men could do to me, I was too angry to entertain fear.

"Do you know *your* place?" I asked, curling my fingers into a fist. "Soldiers like you should defend and protect the citizens of Lin Din Ni despite their gender. Didn't they teach you this in training class? If not, let me speak to General Wen about his methods. Better yet, let me bring this up to the Emperor and the Empress."

"She needs a lesson." Red Eyebrow's nostrils flared as dark clouds entered his eyes.

I looked over at Round Face, and his eyes were also pitch black. What was wrong with them? Their bodies twitched eerily, and I ran.

"Get her!" Red Eyebrow yammered.

"Kill her!" Round Face exclaimed.

"Don't kill her. I need her alive." The voice sounded familiar, but I didn't know who it was.

I turned, and Red Eyebrow drew his sword, but his hands remained frozen. "Keep her alive."

The voice came from his mouth, but it wasn't his voice.

"Help me!" I shouted as I ran down the hallway toward the main entrance.

I heard their footsteps give chase, and I pushed myself to run faster.

Then I heard a cry, and something thudded to the ground. I turned to see Red Eyebrow on the ground and Hung whipping a dagger at Round Face.

"Are you okay?" Hung approached, pulling me to his side.

"Yes. What's wrong with them?"

As they bled, dark soot filled their eyes, and their flesh decayed right before my eyes.

"It's dark magic." He drew his sword and stabbed each of them in the chest again. "They were possessed."

I'd heard about various types of magic used by sorcerers, sorceresses, and warriors around the world, but I'd never seen it. It occurred to me there was so much about the world I still had to learn. The growing evil taking over Luklum astounded me.

While Hung and his guards moved the bodies to examine them, I sat on the bench facing the training field, waiting for him. Who had possessed those soldiers? Were there others out there?

I tried to look on the bright side of things. If another woman had come to the office to report an incident with these guards, would she have died? My stomach twisted at the thought, so I focused on the soldiers training in the field.

I'd watched them before from the other end of the field, where the trees hid me from view. Today, they practiced the bow and arrow. *Excellent.* I wanted to learn archery too.

Gong walked out from a tent onto the training field, watching a group of soldiers practicing kung fu. Then he strode over to the men, who were shooting arrows toward the target at the other end.

His purple cap billowed in the breeze. Yeeva told me Gong was an exceptional warrior and an intelligent man who often came to train the soldiers with Hung.

He turned to me, lifted his arm, and waved me over. At least, I thought it was me. I glanced around, but no one else was near the bench.

I rose and walked down to the training field. When I got to him, I offered a bow. "Did you need my help with something?"

"I heard Hung was taking on a student. Is that you?"

"Yes." I looked toward the hallway where the possessed soldiers had been. "He's busy right now. I'm just waiting for him."

He laughed. "General Wen is always busy. I'm surprised he agreed to teach you."

Would he have agreed if I hadn't taken the dart for him? Did he agree to help me because he felt he owed me? I had used that as leverage. But a deep part of me wanted him to *want* to teach me regardless of the incident.

"Maybe he sees potential in me."

"What do you want to learn?" His eyes fixated on me. "More importantly, *why* do you want to learn?"

A purple gemstone earring glistened in the sunlight. I'd heard people say Gong was handsome, and I agreed. However, in my eyes, no one was more attractive than Hung.

I looked out at the soldiers doing drills in the field. Some were dueling with each other. I watched as a soldier shot an arrow, hitting the target successfully.

"Everything." Straightening my posture, I declared, "I want to learn how to protect myself." I looked at him and saw the other part of the question. "Because I don't want to depend on someone else." My parents' faces flashed in my mind. "I want to protect the people I love."

He looked at me for a moment. "Who did you lose?"

"My parents."

He inhaled a breath. "Grief and sorrow can be powerful forces. I can see the passion in your eyes. Hung is an outstanding teacher. Do you know how to shoot an arrow?" He walked over to the basket holding the arrows.

"No. But I'd love to learn."

He grabbed a bow from a table and took an arrow, demonstrating the process to me. His arrow pierced the center of the target with great precision.

"Try it." He offered me the bow.

I clasped it, trying to mimic how he had held it.

Gong approached, took my hand, and placed it properly.

"I'll take over." Hung's voice draped over me like a protective cloak.

Gong smirked. "You abandoned your student, so I figured I'd give her a head start." He looked at me. "If he mistreats you, I can make an exception and teach you."

Hung slid him an annoyed look. "The dead bodies are in the morgue for your review."

The amused expression faded, followed by a serious look. "I'll take a look."

After Gong walked off, Hung still looked annoyed.

"Is everything okay?" I asked. "If you need to go with Gong, I can come back."

He looked at me for a while as though he were trying to sort something out.

Then he sighed. "No. It's fine." He walked over to the supplies table and returned with a pair of gloves for me. "They'll protect your hands, but these might be too big for you. I'll get you a smaller pair next time."

"Thank you." I pulled them on, and they were big.

Standing close, he offered a lesson. "Use your dominant eye. It's like being righthanded or lefthanded. You'll have a better aim once you know your dominant eye."

I listened to his every word as he demonstrated the stance, grip, drawing the bow, aiming, and releasing the arrow.

"Got it."

Pride gleamed in his eyes. "Let's try it." He stood behind me, and the scent of myrrh and sage stirred around me, sending tingles down my spine.

"You smell nice," I whispered, inhaling his scent.

He looked down at me and smiled. "You do too." He clasped his hand over mine, helping me aim.

I knew it wasn't the proper stance, but I leaned back into him for a bit.

"You're not standing straight enough."

"Can't help it." I tilted my face up at him, beaming. "I just like your body against mine."

"Is that right? Then why did you let another man teach you?"

Oh. So that was the reason for his irritation. He was jealous of Gong and me. What an absurd idea. Still, my heart galloped with glee.

"You weren't here, and he offered to show me. I thought you liked Gong. He's been training your soldiers."

His lips curled. "I have nothing against him."

"But?" I asked, nudging him on.

The mischievous side of me wanted to see all his facets.

He flicked me a frustrated look. "I don't like seeing other men touch what's mine."

I didn't know why, but I loved this possessive side to him. There was more to my warrior than the exterior he showed the world. Like all of us, he had vulnerabilities.

"Would you battle him for me?" I looked up at my handsome warrior.

He narrowed his eyes at me. "You're causing too much trouble as it is."

"Never," I said. "I just like unraveling you."

"I know what you're doing." He pursed his lips, but I saw a wicked gleam in his eyes. "If you keep this up," he leaned into my ear, "I'll be *unraveling* you. It's a punishment for making me want you."

Smiling, I patted his cheek, loving the annoyed look. "You're cute when you're jealous."

"I don't like the feeling." A crease formed between his eyebrows. "It makes me lose control of myself."

"And that confuses you. A man like you needs control, logic." I placed my finger on the crease and stroked it gently. "A serious relationship is unfamiliar terrain for you to explore, General

Wen." I tapped his forehead. "I want you to remember this. The only person I want teaching me is *you*—my warrior."

He looked at me with eyes that seemed to smile. "You can start with archery today. Tomorrow will be some light practice. I don't want you doing the obstacles until later."

I glanced over at the soldiers, and they quickly looked away. They'd been watching us all this time. More rumors would spread about us. But that wasn't a bad thing. It meant this relationship was also important to him.

Hung demonstrated how to shoot the arrow a few more times before I tried it myself and missed the target.

"What am I doing wrong?" I asked.

"Your grip is too tight." He tapped my fingers, which were squeezing the bow. "Relax your fingers a little. Now try it."

I drew the bowstring and released the arrow, hitting the target dead center.

Leaping with joy, I threw my arms around him. "I did it!"

Muffled laughs erupted nearby, and I looked over to see the soldiers giving me a thumbs-up before quickly returning to their training.

Embarrassment flushed my cheeks. This wasn't the private courtyard at the City Apothecary. I should refrain from showing my affection. People weren't used to these things in public.

"Sorry," I muttered to Hung. "Did I embarrass you?"

"I don't get embarrassed easily." He touched my face.

Remembrance surfaced. "I have something to show you." I reached into my pocket for the kung fu pamphlet. "This is what I've been using to study. What do you think?"

Hung flipped through the book, and his eyebrows furrowed. "Where did you get it?"

"At an old bookstore."

He flipped to the last page and pointed to a small drawing of a sword. "That's my drawing."

"What? Really?" I grabbed the book to look at it again.

"I gave my old books away years ago." He smiled. "I'm glad

you found it. This is an excellent basic book to start with. Now I know why your movements are quick for a beginner."

He returned the pamphlet, and I tucked it back into my pocket, cherishing the book even more.

"Did those guards hurt you?"

"No. You arrived at the right time. I should have known their behavior was abnormal."

A muscle twitched in his jaw. "They're new to my camp. We recently took in some additional guards from other military sites. I'm not sure if these men were possessed prior to entering the camp or during their stay here."

"A voice told them not to kill me. It came from Red Eyebrow's mouth, but it wasn't him speaking."

"I've never seen anything like it." He looked at me. "There's something I want to teach you, but it will take you some time to learn it."

"What's it called?"

"Dim Mak, also known as the death touch."

CHAPTER THIRTY

SU

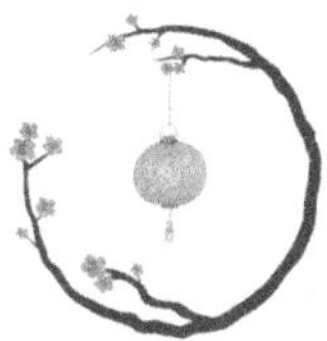

I GASPED EXCITEDLY. "I once saw that during a competition. A warrior pressed his fingers into his opponent's shoulder, and the opponent became immobile—paralyzed."

Hung demonstrated by using two fingers to strike the air. "Dim Mak is effective when used correctly. It can also kill a person if the appropriate pressure point is targeted." He looked at me. "Knowing this technique would benefit you because you know all the acupuncture points."

"It's like acupuncture with my fingers instead of needles, right?"

"Exactly, my smart dahlia." He tapped my chin. "How are you feeling?"

"Fine. Why?"

"I want you to walk the Infinity Loop." He reached for two rocks on the ground, placing them three feet apart. "Do this loop a hundred times. It's gentle enough on your body."

"That's easy." I looked over at the soldiers running laps up and down the stairs. "Why can't I do that?"

"You've been poisoned, remember?"

"Yeah, but I feel fine."

"Your *Sifu* says no. That's final."

If only he knew what I did in the early mornings before work. I didn't share it. What if he thought I was overdoing it and decided not to teach me as punishment?

I glared at him and walked the loop a few times. He sat on the bench, watching me the whole time. My body heated not from the walk but from his stare.

"Aren't you bored?" I asked.

"No."

When I finished my lesson, he rose from the bench. "You did an amazing job today."

"Though that was fairly easy, I know my body will be sore tomorrow."

"It's a good sore. I want to ensure your body acclimates at its own pace. Running the stairs is too strenuous."

He placed a hand on my back. "Balance your energy tonight in bed so your body can heal during sleep. The chapter in the pamphlet is excellent."

"I don't know if I've been practicing it correctly, though."

Hung showed me the breathing technique, and it was how I'd been doing it. Then, he demonstrated a few fighting styles, asking me to study where he positioned his hands and feet.

"Don't do any of these physical movements yet. This is just for your future reference, okay?"

"I understand," I said, not making any promises.

He showed me how to tap into my stored energy to punch, kick, and leap. A lot of it was paying attention to my body, allowing the essa to form and circulate within and around my body. It sounded easy, but it required a smooth communication between my mind, body, and energy for the kung fu to be more effective.

"When I get home, I'm taking a long hot bath with flowers and herbs. That's how I'm healing my body."

He flicked me a look. "Do you need any company?"

I rolled my eyes. "The tub is not big enough to fit you. Besides, I'm not sure if it's appropriate to have you there. Healer Churan might take a broom to you."

"You didn't say no, so I assume it's a yes if the tub was bigger." He smirked. "I have a large tub at my place whenever you feel like taking a bath there."

Intrigued by the thought, I narrowed my eyes at him. "We'll see what I learn tomorrow. Maybe I'll use the Dim Mak on *you*. Keep you in place while I pour rose petals all over your body."

"You don't need to paralyze me for that." He tossed me a look that had my loins tightening. "I'll do it willingly."

Heat spiraled from the center of my core, spreading all over me. I enjoyed having flirty conversations with him. It chased away the darkness that loomed over the city.

"What's going to happen to those corpses?"

"Gong and Three-Eyes will take a look at them. I'll station extra guards around the city and send an alert to other military barracks."

"Three-Eyes is a strange man," I said. I'd only seen him walking around the Market Square a few times. He seemed to live in two different worlds at the same time.

"He is, but the Emperor values him."

As we walked by the City Garden, a roar of laughter erupted. A group of women sat at a table inside the large gazebo. They giggled as a woman with a yellow dress recited something in front of what appeared to be a class. Beibei and Cailing were also sitting at a table.

Ren clapped and gestured for the woman to sit down. He looked over, saw me and Hung, and waved.

Beibei spotted me and walked to the railing. "How was your training?"

"It was tiring but good," I admitted.

She laughed and told the women I was learning self-defense to protect myself and that I was strong and brave.

All the women gasped, glancing my way.

Ren gave the women an assignment and walked over to us, slapping a hand on Hung's back. Then he looked at me. "How was training?"

"He's starting me out slowly," I said.

"That's good. You're still healing, so don't push yourself."

Hung looked at his friend. "Can we talk after I escort Su back to the apothecary?"

Ren nodded. "My poetry class will end soon. Come back here." He smiled at me. "I see a future warrior in you."

Hung was quiet during the walk to the City Apothecary. I knew what was on his mind.

"Ren will understand and accept our relationship."

He sighed. "I have to talk to him. He's been after you for so long. I knew this, and yet I couldn't stop . . ."

I placed a hand on his chest. "I see him as a friend or a big brother. That's it. I already told him I couldn't reciprocate."

"You did?"

I nodded. "When he brought me soup that day."

"It's good he's aware." Relief settled on his face. "But I want to ensure he's okay."

"He's a handsome man. All those ladies who signed up for his class aren't there for the poetry."

"You're right."

After Hung left, I submerged myself in the warm bath. My body sighed with relief and gratitude.

Leaning back against the wooden barrel, I closed my eyes, trying to keep my mind blank.

Su . . . Su . . . Su . . . The moon.

My eyes flipped open, and I glanced around, thinking someone was in the bathroom with me. I didn't see anyone. The voice was closer now.

Though I should have gone to sleep to prepare myself for more training tomorrow, I felt an urge to go outside to look at the moon. We just had a new moon. The full moon wouldn't occur for another two weeks.

Warmth bloomed on my arm, and the scar had grown yet again. The mandala shape looked bigger, more intricate.

What was happening to me?

CHAPTER THIRTY-ONE

HUNG

I SAT across from Ren and said, "I don't know what to say other than sorry I hurt you."

What else could I say?

"No need to apologize, Hung. You're like my big brother." He poured some tea into my cup and offered it to me. Then he poured tea for himself. "Su doesn't have any feelings for me. So we're good."

I nodded and drank the tea.

His expression changed. "Just so you know, I'm interested in Beibei now. She's beautiful and smart, and we both like each other."

A burden finally fell from my shoulders, and I felt like I had my best friend back again.

CHAPTER THIRTY-TWO

SU

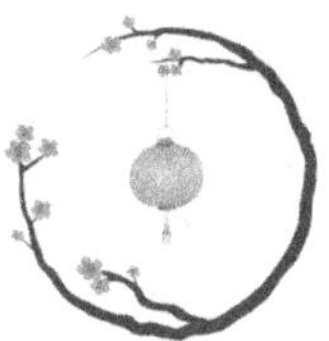

I DRESSED QUICKLY, rushed to the courtyard, and glanced up at the evening sky. A sliver of a moon greeted me.

What did the voice want me to know? Why couldn't I hear more of the message?

I was about to turn back to my room when I saw the blue rabbit sitting beside the flower bush, staring at me. When two leaflike ears fanned out into four, it blinked at me and hopped away. This was the blue rabbit Yeeva I had seen all those years ago. The same rabbit I'd seen when I was swimming in the starry sky.

I sucked in a breath when the rabbit hopped through the locked door. How had it done that? I opened it, thinking I'd lose the animal, but it was waiting for me. The body glowed with soft luminescence. It hopped once, then turned to look at me.

It wants me to follow it.

Was this the voice that had called me?

"Did you call me telepathically?" I asked.

No response.

The bunny hopped down a street away from the Market Square. It was dog hour, so most people were probably at home having dinner and getting ready for bed. Was Hung still talking to Ren at the City Garden?

Two people walked by me and said they heard about my training. They didn't seem to notice the rabbit sitting in the middle of the street like a little blue lantern.

When they were out of sight, I continued.

The rabbit hopped to the edge of the woods behind some bushes and sat by a tree trunk.

I walked over slowly, fearing I would scare it away.

Surprisingly, the bunny didn't move as I sat down beside it. "Did you want to see me tonight?" I pet its back, loving the soft fur. Its ears perked up as though they responded to my question.

"You have very interesting ears. Can I hold you?"

I scooped the rabbit onto my lap, and it snuggled against my thigh. The four ears fused into two, and it seemed to relax. Then, the rabbit released an energy akin to a warm hug. The scar on my arm glowed brightly.

A twig crunched nearby. "Why aren't you in bed?"

The rabbit leaped out of my lap and disappeared.

I rose to my feet and walked onto the street to find Hung talking to Luzi.

She beamed when she saw me. "I was looking for you."

I walked up to her, placing a gentle hand on her small shoulder. "Why? You should be in bed."

"You rushed out quickly." Her lips twisted. "I thought something was wrong."

"Nothing's wrong." I tipped her face up. "I don't want you going out by yourself ever again, okay? Especially at night." My mind went wild imagining terrifying scenarios. "It's not safe. The next time you see something that worries you, find an adult, okay?"

She nodded. "Sorry."

"It's okay." I patted her head. "I know you were just worried about me."

Hung glanced around the woods, looking for something. Was

he investigating? I didn't want to ask him questions because Luzi was here.

"I'll walk both of you back to the apothecary," Hung said.

I clasped Luzi's little hand in mine. It was cold, so I wrapped an arm around her.

As we walked, Hung took on that stern appearance that kept others away. He was acting like a general now—on guard, ready to defend.

We arrived at the back door of the courtyard of the apothecary. "Thank you. I'll see you tomorrow at training."

When I closed the door, I lifted the metal slit and peeked through.

Hung stood in the street, looking right at me. "Go to sleep."

How did he know I'd peek?

After rolling my eyes, I grinned and took Luzi to her room.

CHAPTER THIRTY-THREE

HUNG

I WOKE UP EARLY, tossing and turning. I should go back to bed, but too many thoughts were swimming in my head. So I got up, washed up, walked out to my balcony, stretched, and inhaled the morning air.

After my conversation with Ren last night, I scoured the area for any strange things. The deaths of two guards and the body General Zhou had brought back still clung to my mind. Why had the guards come to my military camp? I wouldn't have seen Su running away if I hadn't gone to the storage room for supplies. What would've happened if I hadn't been there?

She mentioned a voice telling the guards not to kill her. Why? Was the voice targeting her, or did it need her for something else? This brought me back to when she had tugged at my essa. Su had some magical powers that were probably still dormant within her.

On my way home last night, I spotted a moving shadow from the corner of my eye. A man dressed in black had swiftly moved across the rooftops of several homes and businesses. Could he have been Ru Malik?

I had lost track of him when I approached the woods. Then I'd heard Su talking to a rabbit. It glowed on her lap. At first, I thought I'd been hallucinating, but it was real.

I wanted to go over to Su but didn't want to make any sound, fearing the spy could be nearby. As long as I remained still, I could watch over her.

But then I saw Luzi wandering alone in the street. The stakes were too high, so I'd announced my presence.

What was Su doing with the blue rabbit? Where had it come from?

Stop worrying. Clear your head so you can train her properly.

I pulled an old pamphlet on Dim Mak from my desk. She could refer to it when I wasn't around. Su had a curious mind, and I knew she'd be thinking about her lessons on days off. I couldn't believe of all the people who ended up with my former kung fu pamphlet, it was her. We were destined to be with each other.

I smiled as I remembered how she had leaned against me during the archery lessons.

I like the feel of you on my back.

My body warmed, remembering the feel of her against me.

You smell nice.

I took a deep inhale, remembering her floral scent that intoxicated me.

The jealousy that had surged through me surprised me. I couldn't control it. I'd never felt possessive about any woman, but Su unsettled me to the core. She had lured raw emotions from me I hadn't felt before. She made me feel alive, and she was becoming too important.

For the first time, a woman both comforted and terrified me. I didn't want to lose the only person who had captured my heart.

Intuition told me that Su was somehow connected to the darkness lurking in Lin Din Ni. I had to find out what it was so I could protect her.

After Su walked several more rounds of the Infinity Loop, I had her practice breathing and stretching. I had expected her to complain about the easy lessons, but she didn't. She probably knew it didn't matter what she said. I was firm on her starting easy.

When her breathing and stretching techniques were done, I took her to the Prime General Villa to teach her Dim Mak.

"Why can't we learn in the training field?"

"The soldiers don't know Dim Mak. It's a special technique that involves concentration and knowing certain locations on the body. I'd rather them focus on other techniques."

She nodded. "I can't wait to see your villa."

I arched an eyebrow. "You've been wanting to see it? Why?"

"I'm curious about you. What does the Prime General's house look like? How does he decorate his courtyard?" I shrugged. "I want to see what strange things you have in it."

I laughed. "Like what?"

She'd be disappointed if she were expecting something fancy. Was she? Should I have cleaned my bedroom, office, and the courtyard? Insecurity stirred in me.

She studied me. "What's wrong?"

When was the last time I cared about someone's opinion of my house? *Never.*

"What did you do to me?" The thought slipped out of my mouth before I could stop it.

"What do you mean?" she asked innocently.

"I've been transformed," I admitted.

"Is that a good or a bad thing?"

I stared at her for a moment, and the truth rang clear. "I think it's a good thing."

She smirked. "That's the *right* answer."

When we arrived, I opened the door for her to enter. It occurred to me that no woman had been inside my home. Well, the maids had, but they were different. The only two people who visited me here were Kai and Tao. They understood my need for privacy and only came when necessary.

Today, I brought Su to my home without hesitation. What did that mean?

You know what it means, said my annoying inner voice.

She surveyed my home. "You have a beautiful living space. It's clean and spacious."

"It was a gift from the Emperor after winning so many battles for him."

"You deserve it." She walked around the space, stopping to admire the paintings on the walls, running her hands over my wooden furniture, and making her way to my office.

Su stood in front of my library, then approached my desk. "So this is where you work." She placed a hand on my chair. "This is where your war strategies come to fruition."

The image of her standing at my desk giving me feedback on my work did something to my chest. I could see her in my home, and that made my heart race.

I was changing, and that confused and excited me. I was no longer the same person. Did I like this new version of me?

Su made me want more than I ever imagined. Being with her made me feel whole—that my life had a purpose. All my senses seemed sharper, and my path ahead seemed clear. Whereas before, I just . . . existed. Su was now the substance of my empty well.

I now saw a future for myself. I could raise a family here with her. We could teach our kids kung fu. A shiver ran through me at the thought.

"Some areas could use a feminine touch," she said, gesturing to an empty corner and a table with nothing occupying it.

"Like what?"

"Some plants or vases. Maybe a silk pillow for the back of your chair for when you work late."

"You're welcome to help me," I said.

"I'll be happy to. We have a lot of plants in the apothecary. I'll repot a few of them for you." She tapped her hand on the table. "For someone as busy as you, you've maintained a spotless home."

"I have the maids to thank for that."

She looked around. "Where are they?"

"They work here in the mornings, and then they go to the Military Pavilion to help. We'll be practicing in the courtyard. This way." I walked down the hallway toward the arched doorway.

We passed by my bedroom, and I imagined her in my bed. A thrill rushed through me, and my cock swelled. This attraction between us increased every time I was near her. How would I survive the lessons?

We rounded the corner and stepped into my courtyard filled with floral trees, bushes, bamboo, and a stone table with matching stools. Lanterns hung around the wooden poles. A few birds flew off as we disturbed their peace with our presence. But they returned soon after.

"It's a quaint courtyard with a lot of ground space," she said. "Do you want a lavender bush? The fragrance would be lovely out here."

"This peaceful space is conducive to my martial arts."

She walked up to me and placed a hand on my chest. "So this is where General Wen improves all his skills? How many people have you brought here?" Her eyes bore into me. "How many women?"

"Ten."

"Oh." The joy in her eyes faded, and she extracted her hand from my chest.

I gripped it back and interlaced my fingers with hers, smirking. "What's wrong?"

"Nothing." With furrowed eyebrows, she tried to yank her hand from mine.

"You're lying." Why do women always say the opposite of what their faces are expressing?

"I thought you took me here to learn something. Why are you wasting my time?" she asked with an edge to her voice.

"I'm learning something right now."

"What?" she exclaimed with a spark of defiance in her eyes.

"That you're jealous."

She twisted her lips. "What's wrong with that?"

"Nothing. I like it. I lied about the ten women." Lifting her hand to my lips, I said, "You're the first woman to be in my home—and my courtyard."

She smiled, then added, "I guess the maids don't count?"

"I have no interest in them." I drew her close to my body so she could feel what she did to me. "Only *you*." I pressed my lips to hers, softer than I imagined.

She gripped my tunic with both hands and kissed me back. Then she drew back with lust in her eyes. "You're not supposed to kiss your student. But you're breaking the rule, General." She bit my bottom lip, sucked on it, and then kissed me again. I'd never encountered someone like her. She took what she wanted without regret.

Her tongue teased mine, and I responded with the same fervor. I angled my mouth, deepening the kiss. If dreams could be tasted, she was that farfetched dream I didn't think I could have.

So fucking enticing.

My hands traveled down her body, discovering her. I gripped her ass in my hands, squeezing it possessively. I explored the curves and valleys of her body.

She whimpered. "I love the way you break the rules."

My hand skimmed up her body to claim a breast. "Like this?"

She gasped and opened her mouth to say something but moaned instead. Her breast was the right size, fitting perfectly in my palm. I wanted to toss her over my shoulder and bring her to my bed—to strip off her clothes and devour every inch of her. But I reminded myself why she was in my courtyard today. I didn't want to move too fast and scare her. Based on her reaction to me, she showed no signs of fear or hesitation.

"I enjoy breaking the rules too, General." Smiling, she palmed me, and my cock jerked. "I think this particular stalk likes me." She stroked me, and I almost burst on the spot.

I clasped a hand over her wrist. There were things I needed to teach her today. This wasn't it. It took all my willpower to pull her hand away.

"There's no doubt about that, my dahlia. It wants you more than you can imagine. But you're here to learn the death touch, not how to make me lose control."

She licked her lips, her chest heaving. "There's some heavy sexual tension here."

"Agree."

"How are you so calm?"

"If only you could see the storm inside me."

She inhaled a deep breath and released it slowly as though to calm herself. I did the same. We exchanged a silent understanding and smiled simultaneously. It was like a quiet promise for another day when we could deal with this tension.

"So where were we?" She tapped my forehead. "I lost my train of thought."

"Rules," I reminded her and myself. "The basic rules don't apply to you."

"Why not?" She pouted with swollen lips from kissing me. "You're my mentor, and I'm your mentee."

"You're not underage. And we have no Imperial document that spells out the official rules about a woman training in the military," I said. "You're not in the military. You're not a normal student."

"What exactly is normal?"

"A student who's been recognized by the military and is documented in the books. You're in a different category."

"What category is that?" She traced her finger along my jaw, distracting me.

"The kind that makes me want to do a lot of inappropriate things to you." I leaned into her ear and whispered one of my fantasies to her.

Her body jerked, and her face blossomed pink. "So you're creating your own inappropriate document?"

I let out a laugh, loving the way her mind worked. "I am." I took her hand, guiding her to the stone bench on the side of the courtyard.

When we sat down, I briefed her on the basics of Dim Mak, how to cultivate the energy, home in on it, and channel it to the fingers.

"I've heard your Dim Mak technique differs from others."

She's been studying me.

"I've cultivated my energy long enough to push my essa to my fingers, adding more power to my death touch."

I yanked at the energy storage in my body, moving my hands in specific formations that called to my essa, and swiped my index and middle finger into the air.

With gold essa glowing from my fingertips, I pressed them gently to her collarbone, gliding along the skin, down toward her chest, being extra careful not to touch any pressure points.

"So much heat on those fingers." She breathed as she looked at me with so much passion. "What could that Dim Mak do to someone just now? I know you were just giving me a soft version of it."

"If I aim it at the right meridian point, it can immobilize someone for a long period or cause bodily harm by cutting off their energy flow. If your life force is blocked, then it's dangerous. But the Dim Mak isn't like a sword that can physically 'cut' you right away. The death touch works beneath the surface. It can damage you internally, breaking down your bodily systems one stage at a time."

"So if an enemy wants to kill me, then I should use a weapon? But if there's someone I want to subdue to question later, the Dim Mak is more appropriate?"

"That's one way of looking at it," I said. "If you don't have time or don't want to kill your opponent, you can immobilize them to give you time to escape. The paralysis will release after a few hours, depending on the force you've applied to that pressure point."

"That makes sense." She swallowed. "I don't want to kill anyone unless I have to. I'm a healer first, remember?"

"You're not killing people for no reason. Consider the technique as a form of protection. Use it only when necessary. But like any other form of martial arts, you'll exert energy. So make sure you recharge as often as possible."

"Okay," she said.

"There's something else to keep in mind. If your opponent is an adept warrior with powerful essa, they can unlock your Dim Mak and release themselves. In this case, you shouldn't use the death touch on someone stronger than you."

She nodded, absorbing the information.

I held up my index and middle finger to her. "You channel your energy into these fingers and strike your opponent. I have this for you to study at your own pace." I reached into my pocket and pulled out the pamphlet on the Dim Mak. "It's easy to understand."

She took the book, flipped through to the end, and looked up at me. "No cute sword drawings in this one."

"No," I said. "But you can draw something in it. It's yours now."

Her eyes sparked. "I might use the Dim Mak on you."

"We can have a duel one day. If you can use the death touch on me, then you can do whatever you want to me."

Amusement sparked in her eyes as she bit her bottom lip, a gesture I loved.

She stuck out her pinkie finger. "Promise? You won't go back on your word?"

I hooked my pinkie with hers. "Promise."

"I have a goal now." She winked. "To *paralyze* my mentor."

"You're a dangerous student. Maybe I should reconsider teaching you."

"Too late. Everyone knows I'm learning from you. As the Prime General, you must keep your word. Otherwise, you'll lose everyone's respect."

Shaking my head, I rose from the bench. "Let's practice cultivating your energy."

CHAPTER THIRTY-FOUR

SU

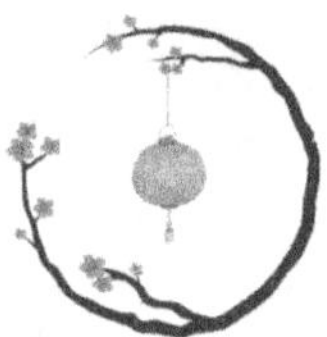

IN THE BACKYARD, Luzi watched me as I placed two small rocks on the ground. After learning and practicing the Infinity Loop, I wanted Luzi to benefit from it. The energy in my body was more balanced, and I attributed that to doing it every night before bed.

"What are you doing?" she asked in her adorable voice.

"We're going to practice a magic walk." I took her small hand in mine. It felt cold. "Do you need a jacket?"

"No," she said.

Some people naturally had cold hands and feet. Maybe Luzi was one of them.

"The walk will warm up your body."

She looked up at me with curious eyes. A dark spot in her right eye caught my attention. "Hold still, Luzi. I want to check something."

I asked her to look down, up, and side to side. No other dark spots were there.

"Something wrong with me?"

I released my grip on her face.

"No. You just have a little blemish on the white area of your eye. Have you always had it? Did you ever injure your eye? Did your parents ever mention anything about it to you?"

I wasn't sure if she'd remember anything, but I had to try. Sometimes, a blemish in the eye could signify a hidden illness that had been missed or one that had recently developed. But it could also mean nothing. I'd seen healthy people with blemishes in their eyes. Perhaps I was too concerned and protective of Luzi. She was an orphan with no family to care for her.

Luzi shook her head.

I tapped her head. "It's okay. I'm just being extra cautious because I care about you. Let me know if your eyes hurt or you can't see properly, okay?"

"Okay," she said.

Though Luzi was still cautious of other people, she was slowly opening up to me, Yunxi, and Healer Churan. I couldn't blame her for the wariness. Her family was killed, and her life had changed in an instant.

"How do we do the magic walk?" She pointed to the rocks.

I held Luzi's hand and walked to the center, between the rocks. "Just follow me. We're going to walk around one rock and loop back to cross this center to walk around the other rock. Then we repeat the steps."

"Okay."

As we walked, my body and mind calmed, as though the energy wiped away all my tension. I researched more on the Infinity Loop walk, but there weren't a lot of books on it. The information that stood out to me said the technique connects the person's energy to the energies of the Cosmos, helping your body heal itself faster.

We chatted about random things, and she seemed as relaxed as me. I discovered she liked red bean buns, pork and mushroom dumplings, and fried rice with Chinese sausage and scallions.

"We'll get you some of those after the walk."

"Really?" Her eyes widened.

After a few more loops, I heard sniffles and looked down to see Luzi crying.

Crouching, I dabbed her tears with my sleeve. "What's wrong?"

"Why are you so nice to me?" She threw her arms around me, hugging me tight.

Laughing, I drew back and met her eyes. "I like nice people—don't you? Besides, I'm a healer. Who would want to be treated by a mean healer? Do you like the magic walk?"

"Yes. A lot."

"Good. You can do this before bedtime or when playing in the courtyard. It's like medicine for the body."

"Will it keep . . . evil things away?" she asked with fear in her eyes.

A child like her should never have to include the word evil in her vocabulary.

"I believe it will do its best. Bad things are afraid of good things. So we must give more power to the good by believing in it."

As an adult, I knew that statement could be debated. Sometimes, believing wasn't enough. But I wouldn't squash the hope of a child.

Luzi thought about my statement for a while. Then a small smile stretched onto her lips. "That makes sense." Her expression changed. "Is General Wen a good person too?"

His face appeared in my vision, and my entire body zinged with energy. *My warrior.*

"Oh, he is." I cupped her face in my hands. "He has a very important and very dangerous job. General Wen and his men have to protect the entire empire. If he seems unfriendly, it's because he's seen a lot of evil and sadness in this world."

"A lot of people die in war?"

I nodded. "Too many."

"I know he has questions for me," she said. "Do you trust him?"

"Yes, I trust him. He wants to catch the people who killed

your family. I do too. We need to ensure they don't do it to anyone again."

"What if they're not . . . people?" Her hands gripped the side of her dress.

I took this opportunity to extract some information from her.

"What do you mean they're not people?"

She twisted her lips. "Like they have magic or something. And you can't touch them." She swiped a hand in the air. "Like dark smoke." Fear splashed onto her face. "I don't want to talk about it anymore."

I brushed a comforting hand down her back. "There's no rush to talk about it. You take your time. You can live here at the apothecary for as long as you want."

Hope gleamed in her eyes. "I can live here with you forever?"

I hadn't yet realized it, but I adored her. Helping her was like helping me back when I had no one. I didn't know what was required to take care of a child, but I would give it a try.

I nodded. "Yes, you can."

She hugged me again. "I can play with you and Yunxi forever."

I smiled. "Yunxi would like that. We can train you to be a healer if you'd like."

She nodded and asked, "What if those evil people hurt General Wen?"

"Don't worry about that. General Wen is a powerful warrior. He'll know what to do. He's traveling soon, but we can sit down and talk to him when he returns. Would that be okay?"

"Yes." Her stomach growled, and she placed a hand over it.

I rose to standing and grabbed her hand. "Let's go get you some food."

After buying red bean buns, dumplings, and fried rice at a food cart, we sat on an outdoor bench nearby. Luzi smiled as she ate all her favorite foods. I also enjoyed some dumplings.

Two guards sat beside our table, discussing some darkness lurking in the Emerald Song Valley.

"I'm glad we're not being dispatched there," said the guard with the crooked eyebrows.

"Yeah," replied the one with a big mole on his face. "There's some evil thing there."

"Where did you hear this?" Crooked Eyebrow asked.

Big Mole leaned into the table. "My brother, who's a guard inside the palace, overheard a conversation between the generals. Something is trying to infiltrate Lin Din Ni."

"We have to be extra alert. I heard General Wen is on his way to the valley."

"I can't believe he's going by himself." Big Mole bit into his pork bun.

"He's investigating quietly. If he brings too many people, whatever demon is there will know he's coming."

"True."

Nerves churned in my stomach. Did Hung know about the pocket of evil there? He had to know. So why was he going by himself?

A sick feeling seized my stomach.

"Are you okay?" Luzi asked. "You're not eating."

"Want the rest of my dumplings? I'm not hungry."

After Luzi finished my serving, I bought some dry jerky, dried fruits, and pork buns.

"I thought you weren't hungry." Luzi stared at the bags of food in my hands.

"It's for later."

I wouldn't sit around worrying about Hung. I had to go with him. What if he needed help and no one was there to help him? I didn't take a dart for him just to let him die at some evil force's hands.

"Where are you going?" Luzi looked at me with concern.

"I'm going to take a little trip. Make sure you practice the Infinity Loop. When I come back, I'll show you some self-defense moves."

"You know how?" Her eyes brightened.

"I do." What if she knew I had to help my teacher? What if he didn't survive this journey? Would I see him again?

When I arrived at the apothecary, I informed Healer Churan and Yunxi about my journey. They understood why I had to go. General Wen was the Prime General of the Imperial Army. If something happened to him, the enemy could use that opportunity to attack us.

They suggested I ask the Emperor for guards to take along the trip. But I explained that this was a discreet operation and that I'd be extra careful.

"Disguise yourself as a man on the road," said Healer Churan. "It's safer."

I already had some clothing I could reuse.

I rented a carriage so I could rest during the trip. It would take a few days to get there. I looked up at the dark clouds looming in the sky. It could storm soon. Healer Churan wanted me to go at dawn, but right now, every minute mattered.

After tucking the round talisman that I wanted to give to Hung into the satchel, I headed out.

CHAPTER THIRTY-FIVE

HUNG

I WASN'T DRESSED in my armor for this trip. Instead, I wore clothing reserved for long and dangerous journeys. The loose tunic had hidden pockets within the sleeve, chest, and pants. These pockets held knives, darts, and daggers. The sword the Emperor had given me hung on my back.

I didn't know what to expect when I got to Emerald Song Valley, but I had to be prepared. A murder of crows suddenly flew out of the forest and startled me, and the horse screeched to a stop.

"It's okay." I patted the horse's neck.

Dense forests surrounded us. An eerie feeling stirred in the air as dark clouds loomed above. The sky would get dark in two hours.

When the horse calmed, I galloped on.

Kai wanted to come with me, but I needed him in Luklum to monitor the palace.

Tao hadn't sent any updates on his whereabouts, which I found strange. He was supposed to be in Ming Shan, a city known for its silk fabric. Both of my Elite Guards knew how to conduct an investigation. So when a few steps were missed, that told me something was wrong.

I'd also sent men to look for him, but no word had come back from them either.

Kai wanted to look for his friend, but I ordered him to remain in the capital. I couldn't risk losing another man if something had happened to Tao. The pigeons we'd trained to deliver messages had always been dependable, but we'd received nothing from Tao. The pigeons hadn't returned either.

I had to make a trip after this one to check up on him.

That's if you survive those Soul Extractors.

What if I didn't come back alive? That possibility scared me. But what was more frightening was when Su popped into my vision. Our relationship had just started, and I wanted to see where it would lead.

I'd never been afraid of going into battle. I'd come too close to death several times and had wounds to prove it. Death had surrounded me for too long. Seeing my men die and not being able to help them had disillusioned me.

Was there meaning to all this pain and suffering? The answer never arrived, but I kept going because I refused to let the enemy win. They would win if I gave up.

But Su had changed my perspective. The fear of losing her—of not being able to see her again—made me tense. I had never desired anyone the way I wanted her.

She was the sunlight that sliced through my dark clouds. She'd brought comfort into my life when I thought it was impossible to feel such a thing. Ren used to write lovely poetry of longing and devotion, and I used to roll my eyes at it. But now I understood what inspired a poet to create something like that.

Su was both my strength and my weakness. The thought confused me, and I didn't want to ponder it too much. It could cloud my judgment. I needed clarity to fight these fucking Soul Extractors.

My stomach growled, and I cursed myself for not bringing enough dry goods. I thought there would be food carts along Emerald Road to grab a quick bite and rest for a moment, but so far, I hadn't seen another soul. The last time I'd been this way, there had been several vendors. Emerald Road wasn't popular as wild beasts roamed these forests and mountains. The mountains separated Lin Din Ni and the Rebel Territory. There had been too many attacks, and I could see why travelers avoided this path.

But isolation could be the perfect breeding ground for evil, right? I'd seen too much shit in the world to take things at face value.

Thunder boomed, and a few drops of rain slashed against my face. I'd made good progress on my journey. Shelter was a good idea before the rain poured. Hopefully, the storm would pass soon. I didn't want any delays.

A tavern appeared in the distance. *Food!* I could almost hear my stomach cheer. As I approached, I saw horses secured to a wooden railing under a canopy. The carriages were stationed not too far from the horses. A few people sat outside eating on the benches beside a food vendor cart.

Food and wine would do me well right now. The horse needed food and rest too. I hopped off my horse and secured him to a tree.

The old man feeding his two horses nodded at me. "Storm's coming. The tavern doesn't have any vacancies." He gestured to his carriage. "I'll be resting there until it passes."

Fucking hell. I could rest in their storage or in a corner of their kitchen. It didn't matter. I just needed shelter until the storm passed.

"Is this the only tavern around here?" I asked.

He nodded. "Unfortunately, yes. There's another inn farther down the road. But I wouldn't go there."

"Why?"

"Bandits ransacked it about a year ago. I heard they killed the owner for refusing to hand over their jewels." He sighed. "It's haunted. People claim to hear crying voices."

I offered the old man some money to feed my horses and entered the tavern.

"Welcome, sir." A maid gestured to the only unoccupied table in one corner.

A glance showed me most of the patrons were travelers. But then again, I was dressed casually too. After Ru Malik had escaped, I suspected his men were everywhere. Maybe one of these men was in disguise.

Another curly-haired maid walked by with a tray holding two dishes that made my stomach rumble. My eyes followed the maid to a table with a man in casual brown clothing wearing a hat.

When the maid returned, walking past me, I asked, "What's he having?" I gestured to the man with the delicious-smelling meals.

"Wonton soup and ginger scallion chicken."

"I'd take those meals and a container of wine. Do you have a spare room for the night?"

"Sorry, we're booked," she said.

"Is there a place I can stay just for the night? It's hard to travel in a storm."

Thunder boomed as though it were helping me out.

"Let me ask the owner."

While I waited for my meal, I took in my surroundings. Laughter and chatter filled the room. My attention swung back to the man with the hat. As a seasoned general who had experienced many battles, I often relied on my intuition. There was something about the man that had me on alert.

A woman walked by his table, tripped on something on the floor, and fell toward him. But he gripped her arm, rose from his seat, and straightened her up.

"Are you okay?" he asked.

"Yes. I'm so sorry," said the woman whose husband swiftly came to her assistance and thanked the man.

The man's quick reflexes told me he was no ordinary traveler. Only a skilled fighter could react so easily. Who was he? Why was he in this tavern?

The Emerald Road branched off to smaller paths up ahead. Was he heading to Emerald Song Valley or another area?

Unlike me, he kept his attention on his food.

The maid brought over my food and wine and smiled. "The owner said you're welcome to take cover in the supply shed for the night. That's all we have. He'll give you a discount for that."

"Wonderful. I'll take it." I'd slept in many places worse than a shed.

By the time I finished eating, rain pounded on the roof, creating another form of chatter that increased the noise in the tavern.

The maid showed me the supply shed. "Do you need anything else, sir?"

"No, but thank you." I placed the oil lantern on a wooden stool and glanced around.

Bags of rice and beans were piled in the corner. Broken furniture took up another corner. I sat on the floor, placed my sword beside me, and leaned against the stacks of hay.

What was Su doing right now? I remembered our embrace and wondered when I'd get to feel that again. The image brought comfort to this uncomfortable setting. The hay poked my back, but I ignored it. At least I was out of the rain.

Was she thinking of me? The smile that spread across my face surprised me. She'd given me meanings to things that had once been meaningless. I held her in my thoughts as I blew out the lantern.

Closing my eyes, I drifted off to sleep. When a soft noise sounded, my eyes popped open. My hand immediately went to my sword and gripped it. My body became alert as I stared out at the door and the closed window with a paper covering.

I shifted and quietly created a pile of hay that looked like a body. Then I ambled to the far corner to hide behind the stacked furniture.

The door opened quietly. Whoever this person was knew I was staying out here and had waited for me to fall asleep.

The blade of a sword gleamed under the lantern hanging outside in the hallway. He stabbed the pile of hay with the sword and cursed when he realized it wasn't a body.

I threw a broken chair at him. He kicked it away and turned in my direction. I drew my sword and charged at him.

A battle erupted in the room and broke out into the hallway. He jumped onto the roof, ran across it, and jumped down to the road. With the rain pouring down on me, I followed behind and caught up to him. Jumping in front of the man, I aimed my blade at him. Abstract symbols glowed on my sword, and he stared at it.

"Who sent you?" I asked the man with a brown hat.

I'd been right. He was no ordinary traveler but an assassin sent to kill me.

CHAPTER THIRTY-SIX

SU

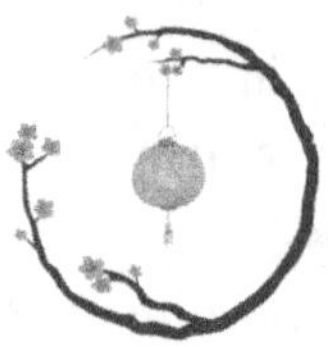

AS THE RAIN poured and the wind howled, I heard voices crying. But it could be fear making me imagine things. I'd never traveled this far alone during a storm. I hadn't expected the Emerald Road to be quite so empty.

Help! . . . Someone, help us!

No!

Was someone calling for help?

More wind whipped across my face, and I wiped a hand to clear the water from my eyes. Even though I had a small canopy over me, it didn't protect me from the wind. Hope sparked when I saw lanterns swaying in the distance.

I flicked the reins on the horse. "Come on. I'll find you shelter soon."

As though the horse understood me, it galloped faster.

The small oil lantern hanging under the canopy only offered me a little light. Fear skated down my back throughout the trip, but I pushed it aside and kept going. Was Hung safe? His safety and the need to see him helped me focus on the journey.

As the carriage moved toward the tavern, I heard shouts and the sounds of screeching metal.

Was that the voice calling for help? Curious, I maneuvered

the horse toward the sounds. The heavy rain had diminished, and the wind had also died down. The fighting sounds rang clear now.

As I neared the back of the tavern, two silhouettes fought on the ground. The lanterns glowing from the roof cast the two men in soft light.

When one man faced me, my heart leaped as I recognized Hung. His clothes were all drenched. Without hesitation, I grabbed a sword I'd brought to practice and rushed over. A glance at Hung's body didn't show any injury. Relief settled in me.

I swung the sword at the attacker, but he dodged it, spun around, and blocked my second attack with his sword. The powerful force cleaved my sword in two. Hung jumped in, blocking the attacker's aim.

Shit. I should have known my practice sword wasn't strong enough. I glared at the man as he continued battling Hung. He'd been in the crowd on the day Ru Malik attacked us.

Hung threw a powerful kick at the attacker and rushed over to stand in front of me. "Stay back. I don't want you getting hurt."

I nodded, knowing I was now a distraction. My stomach twisted at how unhelpful I was. This man was a better fighter than those Bloodshade Bandits. His moves were swift and precise.

The man charged at Hung, and he swung his glowing sword up and over, cutting from the enemy's stomach to his thigh. The man fell to the ground, bleeding profusely. Puddles of rain spread the blood into the earth.

For a moment, guilt tore through me. As a healer, it was my responsibility to help and heal those in need. But right now, I stood frozen in place, watching the man bleed out. Would the gods punish me? If he were an innocent citizen, I'd rush to help him. But I knew this man worked for Ru Malik, and that made him my enemy. How many innocent people had he killed so far?

Hung walked up to the man, and I stood beside him.

Hung aimed the sword at him. "Who sent you?"

"Go to hell!" Wincing, he gripped the blade of the sword and pushed the blade into his chest.

I gasped as blood gushed out of him.

Hung yanked the sword from his chest, flicked the blood from the blade, and turned to me with concern in his eyes. "What are you doing here?"

"I came to help you."

"What?" The worried expression softened as he examined me. "Are you hurt anywhere?"

"No. You're drenched. I've got a carriage and some towels." I took his hand, dragging him to my carriage.

Inside the carriage, I offered him a towel to wipe his face.

"You use it first," he said. "You're drenched as well."

"I have one too." I reached into the compartment under the bench holding my supplies and dry goods and grabbed a towel.

"We need to get away from here." He got up from the bench. "I'll be back. I'm going to grab my horse."

After Hung got his horse, he rode beside me farther down the path.

"Do you think the Bloodshades are close by?" I asked.

"Maybe," he said, surveying the surroundings. "People will find the man's body at dawn, and whoever sent him will probably send more people."

"I saw him at the Market Square the day Ru Malik attacked us."

"What was he doing?"

"He was just standing in the crowd. I followed him to an alley-way, but he disappeared."

Hung pointed to a small trail. "Let's go in there and get some rest."

The carriage moved down the dirt path. "Is that a shed?" I squinted my eyes.

As we approached, Hung said, "It's an old shed that merchants probably used at one point in time." He hopped off his horse, reached for the lantern on my carriage, and offered me his hand.

I took it as he helped me leap to the ground without using the wooden steps attached to the carriage.

With one hand, Hung lifted the lantern to cast light for us to see the ground. He gripped his sword with the other, ready to defend.

Though I didn't have a weapon, I found a stick on the ground and prepared to fight if necessary.

Hung kicked the door open on the shed. When nothing came out to attack us, he said, "Stay here." He entered first and looked around. "It's safe to come inside."

I stepped inside, and a musky and earthy scent greeted me. Hung placed the oil lantern on a dusty stool. The lantern cast a soft glow to the shed. Broken tables sat in the corner. Old pots, rusty pans, and miscellaneous items were piled on a long table covered in cobwebs. More cobwebs hung across the wooden beams on the ceilings.

The light from the lantern created linear shadows on the floor. It was dark, and the dangerous incident I'd just experienced should have made me afraid, but I wasn't. Hung made me feel safe.

"Do you need help?" I asked, watching him unroll a bamboo mat and shake it free of dust and debris.

He found a broom and reached up to clear the cobwebs hanging above us. Then he cleaned a spot for us on the floor and placed the mat down.

"No." He leaned the broom against a cabinet and gestured to the mat on the floor. "We'll take cover here for now. Get some rest."

"Are you hungry? I have dried fruits, beef jerky, and containers of water in the carriage."

"Oh yeah?" He smirked, placing a hand on my cheek. "You risked your life to come all the way here to bring me food?"

"See what a great and loyal student I am?" I rested my hand against his rough hand. "I knew you'd be in danger."

"You weren't scared on the road?" His stare intensified.

I saw the image of myself reflected in his eyes and loved the look of it.

"It was scary, but I had to keep going." I chewed on my bottom lip, feeling a little embarrassed for being so open about my feelings. "I wanted to see you as soon as possible."

His eyes fixated on my lips. "You missed me?"

I nodded as my heart raced.

"I missed you too." His eyes met mine, and the passion in them sent heat churning in my core. When his lips crashed down on mine, my body fell into his. His lips were perfect—masculine, curious, and greedy. I moaned, wanting more of his hunger for me. His cock grew hard against my body.

My fingers curled into his wet tunic, and a moan escaped me. His tongue slipped into my mouth and dueled with mine. I'd kissed a man before, but not like this. He elicited sensations I'd never experienced. A powerful current zipped through me as his tongue circled mine. Then he dropped kisses along my jaw and neck.

His eyes darkened with lust.

"I want you," I muttered. "I've been wondering about us . . ."

He was on a dangerous journey, and we'd just escaped a threatening situation. What if we never had the chance to be together? I wanted to know what it would feel like to be with him.

A wicked smile curved onto his lips. "My lascivious dahlia."

"Perfect for my impressive warrior."

He pulled away, then walked to the corner to drag over two chairs and dusted them with the broom. "Let's dry our clothes on these chairs."

"I brought some dry clothes. Only one set for me and one for you. I'm not sure if they'll fit you, but I got the largest size available at the shop."

Amusement flashed over his face. "So prepared."

"I didn't know what to expect, so I took a lot of things. Let me get them."

"No. I'll go. You stay here and . . ." His eyes flicked to mine with mischief. ". . . prepare yourself for an unforgettable lesson."

The muscles in my stomach flipped with excitement.

"Grab some food too." I smiled, loving this unfamiliar side of him. "There's also a blanket in one compartment." He walked over to the stool to grab the lantern but then retracted his hand. "You'll need light to dry your clothes."

"Take it," I said. "I'll wait for you to come back."

"You want me to remove your clothes, don't you?" He tossed me a look that aroused me.

That wasn't what I was thinking at all. I didn't want him to trip on something in the dark. But now that he had planted that wicked thought in my mind, more heat coiled in my core.

He smiled as though he understood what went on in my head and opened the door to the shed. I stood in the dark, entertaining the many questions blooming in my mind.

Did everyone know the serious general could tease like this? Was he like this with other women? How many had he been with? The thought soured my mood, so I pushed it away for now.

Would my parents have liked Hung? I knew he would protect me. But his life—his duty—was to protect Lin Din Ni, and that came with certain responsibilities. I placed a hand on my heart, closed my eyes, and whispered to my parents.

Ba, Mẹ, *I want you to meet Hung. He's making me braver every day. I've never felt this way with any man. He's also teaching me kung fu. I'm learning how to defend myself. These skills will allow me to help those who can't defend themselves. I think you'll really like him.*

The memory of their deaths flashed before me, and sadness overcame me. Tears streamed down my face as Hung returned. I wiped my eyes, but it was too late.

"What's wrong?" He walked up to me.

"Nothing." I dried the rest of my tears with my wet sleeve. "It's just a memory from the past."

"I want to know what that memory is." His eyes bored into mine. "I want to understand you."

I'd never shared my past with anyone. Healer Churan only knew part of it, but that was because she took me in when my parents died. I knew it wasn't my fault that my parents died, but I still felt guilty. They saved me. I got to continue living, and they were buried beneath the earth.

Perhaps sharing it with Hung would ease the guilt.

"Okay," I said.

He returned the lantern to the stool, placed the dry clothes on the bamboo mat, and walked up to me, tipping up my chin. "Let's kill two birds with one stone."

"What do you mean?"

"I know what we can do to chase away that sadness." He placed a hand on my shoulder and massaged it.

I had an idea of what he was referring to.

"We're dueling. The first one to remove the opponent's clothes wins." His eyes sparked with a challenge.

"Win what?" I asked, loving the idea. At this moment, nothing would make me happier than to *defeat* my mentor.

"You get to ask me one personal question." His gaze raked down my body before returning to my eyes. "If I win, I get to ask you a personal question."

I had too many questions to ask him. Perhaps this was how we'd get to know each other. I didn't mind. Images from *The Art of Intimacy* and *The Art of Seduction* popped into my mind and made me gasp. I knew what I wanted to ask him, but I could only do that if I won.

His eyebrows arched with suspicion. "No cheating."

"I don't cheat, *Sifu*."

"Good. Because as your mentor, I would have to *punish* you." A wolfish smirk slid onto his face. "Come this way. We don't want to ruin the bamboo mat before we sleep on it."

CHAPTER THIRTY-SEVEN

SU

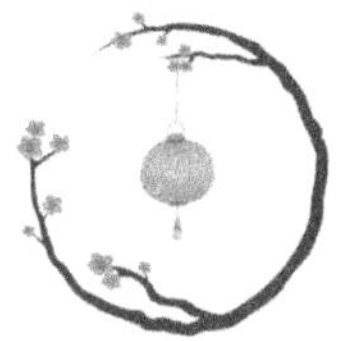

HUNG STEPPED AWAY from the mat, and I followed him. There wasn't a lot of room in the shed for me to run from him. I knew I'd lose.

Before he could prepare himself, I charged at him, using the crane strike I'd learned from his pamphlet. He blocked my attack, gripped my wrist, and yanked me close. Then he pulled my belt loose. I reached for my belt in his hand instead of trying to grab at his clothing. It was a natural reaction to retrieve my clothes if someone took them.

Take his clothes. Ignore what he does to yours.

He waved my fabric belt in the air while wearing an arrogant smirk. I shifted my feet, and my tunic opened, revealing my *dudou*. It was one of my favorite undergarments because of its silkiness and intricate designs. His eyes were fixated on the floral embroidery no one had ever seen but me. All he had to do was tug at the ties on my lower back and neck and he'd see my bare chest.

I pretended to throw a tiger claw at him. When he sidestepped, I swung low and undid his belt. Hung tried to clasp my hand, but I poked him in the ribs with my other hand—one, two, three times. He squirmed from my tickling, and I pulled at his tunic with significant force. He shifted, trying to loosen my hold on his tunic. But I held on tight as he turned and removed himself from the tunic. Before I knew it, I held the tunic and the belt in my hand like tokens of victory.

Though pride gleamed in his eyes, he glanced down at his undergarment, a second tunic, thinner and shorter than the outer one.

"I didn't realize you were so skilled at removing men's clothing with tickles."

"This is my first time, *Sifu*. If you behave, I can teach you this unique skill. Then you can call me *Sifu*." I wiggled my eyebrows.

"That's not going to happen, my lovely dahlia. I'm going to show you a lot of moves tonight that will have you begging."

Arousal surged as the provocative images from those books emerged in my mind. Did he know all those moves?

I lifted his outer tunic, feeling its heavy weight. "Why is this so heavy?"

"Be careful with it. There are weapons inside the pockets."

"Oh. I like a man who's good with weapons." After examining the many hidden pockets in his tunic, I draped it over the chair to dry.

"I've got a weapon you can examine." He smirked.

I rolled my eyes. Did all men consider their body parts as powerful weapons? Despite that, I wanted to see all of him.

From the corner of my eye, a dragon claw reached for me. I dodged it but tripped on something and fell back. His arm caught me as I looked into his brown eyes, which had darkened considerably. His face was inches from mine, and my heart throbbed at how handsome he was. Then his other hand reached to untie my *dudou*. Because he held me close to him, the garment didn't fall away but loosened over my body.

I placed a hand on his face, tracing my finger along his jaw. While his eyes stayed on mine, I used the death touch on a location on his shoulder, holding him in place for a few seconds.

When I stepped away, my *dudou* fluttered to the floor. My nipples immediately pebbled from the chill. His eyes flicked to my chest, and the look on his face reminded me of a wolf ready to feast. Heat bloomed all over me.

I reached for his trousers and yanked at the ties. They fell to the floor, and I gaped at his magnificent cock, throbbing for me. It was a weapon, indeed.

"You win." He broke free of the Dim Mak, which he could have done earlier. Maybe he wanted to see what I wanted to do to him.

He walked up to me and caressed one of my breasts. "As soft and beautiful as I imagined."

His touch was a lick of fire on my skin. It singed and woke nerve endings I didn't know existed. The internal fire warmed my body, making me yearn for more. I loved his hands on me, but he stepped away to pick up our discarded clothes. I shivered, desperately needing his touch again. He shook the clothes free of dust before hanging them over the chairs.

Speechless, I stared at the scars covering his muscular body. *So many scars.* He had slashes on his back, shoulders, arms, and legs. My chest tightened, wondering how much pain he had endured.

I ran my fingers over the long scar. He stiffened at my touch but said nothing. I could almost feel the pain and suffering whispering to me. Then I lowered my lips and kissed each scar.

"What are you doing?" he asked huskily.

"Erasing the pain from your scars." I moved my lips slowly over each one. "Can you feel the darkness lifting? Can you feel them cheering?"

Chuckling, he turned to face me. "I like your imagination."

"The pain and the dark are less scary when you dress them differently." I ran my hand over the scars decorating his lower abdomen.

"Thank you for that."

"For what?"

"For tickling my scars and making them laugh."

My smile widened.

He took my hands in his. "Those scars don't bother me. They're markings that make me remember my victories and how my brothers died. But now I honor them even more because of you."

I ran my fingers over the scar on his shoulder. "Can you tell me how you got them?"

"Yes. But not tonight." He took my hand and guided it down his body. "Tonight, I want you to discover me as I'll discover you."

When my gaze landed on his cock, it seemed to have grown larger than before. I sucked in a breath at how glorious it was. As a healer, I'd seen people's anatomy, but those situations were different.

This situation turned me on, making me want to explore it further. How would this large cock fit inside me? He took my hand and placed it over his hot length. It throbbed in my hand, and I stared at it with wonder and mischief. I stroked and squeezed him, and his breathing changed. As I repeated the steps, he released a long growl. I felt powerful, loving how I could control this warrior with my grip on his cock.

I knew he could have broken free from my death touch earlier, but he didn't. He *wanted* to lose.

"Why didn't you release the death touch earlier?" I asked while stroking him. "Tell me the truth, or I'll stop." My lips tilted.

"You're so wicked," he groaned.

I'd never threatened a man like this. Hung had unraveled the inner Su, and I was grateful for it.

"You haven't seen anything yet. *Tell me.*" I loosened my grip, and disapproval rumbled in his throat.

"Because . . ." He moaned and closed his eyes, wearing an expression of pleasure I'd never forget. When he opened them, he looked at me with intensity. "Because I wanted to know what you would ask me." His husky voice sent shivers through me.

He was my sex warrior, and I couldn't stop loving him with my hand. I'd never felt more powerful than at this moment. He seemed vulnerable to my touch, desperate for more. I loved how his face tensed, watching my fingers tighten over him. My thumb pressed down on his crown.

"*Fuccck.*" He growled. "Don't stop. I love your hand on me. What's your consensus, healer Su?"

"He's spirited." I squeezed him. "Healthy." A long stroke. "And throbbing for me." I loved how I could almost feel his blood filling his veins.

"You're killing me, my dahlia." He tugged at my pants—the only other item on my body. Then his eyes roamed to my breasts.

I smiled at the tension on his forehead. "I would never do that."

He gripped my wrist, moving my hand away from his cock.

"If you keep touching me, I'm going to come before I get to do anything to you." He led me to the bamboo mat. "Sit, my lovely dahlia. You had your fun with me. Now it's my turn."

I kneeled on that and watched as he joined me. Anticipation rushed through me as I studied his handsome face etched with desire. He grabbed my breasts with both hands, squeezing them gently, and I arched into his touch.

"I've imagined doing this to you so many times." He rolled my nipples between his fingers, sending waves of heat through me. "You're so beautiful."

When he lowered his mouth and licked a nipple, I moaned loudly. He fluttered his tongue, and I gasped. "More." I loved how he adored each of my breasts.

He suckled my nipple while he caressed my other breast. Pleasure coursed through me.

"Hung!" I cried and gripped his head, holding him in place. The heat blooming in me was so intense I needed to hold on to something for stability. I'd never been devoured like this.

I threw my head back, offering him more of me. Heat spiraled from my core, creating a powerful pressure pulsing to release.

He dropped kisses all over my breasts, making his way up to my neck and jawline. When his mouth met mine, I devoured him, wanting to feel every part of him. Our tongues clashed, and I shifted to straddle him. His cock throbbed against my thigh, warming my skin.

Moans and sighs filled the shed. Heartbeat to heartbeat, we discovered each other. He smelled like magical secrets buried in the musky earth. He tasted like mint and lemon flavors I adored. His arms wrapped around me, holding me close. I looped my hands around his neck, loving the feel of his skin. Then his hands gripped my buttocks, giving it a gentle slap.

We broke for air, and he nibbled my ear. "I didn't realize you were so bold."

"You bring out my wild side. The blame is on you."

He drew back, his eyes dark with desire. "What did you want to ask me?"

Embarrassment flushed to my cheeks. I didn't know why I felt that way—I was sitting naked on his lap. All the things we'd been doing should have made me more bashful than the question.

I looked away from his eyes, trying to gather my courage. Why was he asking me this now? I assumed he would ask me later when we were done and I was lying next to him. At least, that was how I'd envisioned this night.

He gripped my chin, turning my face to meet his eyes. His hair was a gorgeous mess, and I assumed mine was too.

Our position reminded me of an illustration in *The Art of Intimacy*.

Well, I was going to have to tell him eventually. Inhaling a breath, I said, "I have this book. It's not a poetry book. Well, it could be, depending on how you look at it. But this isn't something you would study in a class."

His lips tilted. "What kind of book is this?"

"The kind that teaches you about relationships. There are pictures in there that are . . ."

How could I explain these images?

"Are what?" He pressed on with glee in his eyes. He knew exactly what I was talking about.

"Are very intimate. They show positions . . ." I covered my face, laughing at my ridiculous behavior.

He pulled my hands away. "And you want to ask me if I've tried them?"

"Have you?"

"Yes."

My mood soured, knowing he'd done them with other women.

As though he read my mind, he said. "I want to try them with you." He took my palm and kissed the center. "How many have you tried?"

"Just one. I didn't know what I was doing."

He arched an eyebrow. "From what you demonstrated, I know you're very skilled and creative."

"I'm a fabulous student." Smiling, I remembered he was much older than me and had a lot more experience. "I learn quickly."

In one swift move, he grabbed me, shifting me so I was lying on the mat with his warm body covering me. The cool surface of the bamboo mat didn't even bother my back.

"You've proven that. Let me show you something I desperately want you to experience." He kissed me deeply, making me dizzy with his scent and taste. Then his lips moved to my neck, shoulder, and breast. A trail of heat sparked as his lips moved down to my stomach.

My body quivered at the sensation overwhelming me.

He drew up my knees and nudged them apart, staring at my sex. He placed his palm over me. "Beautiful and all mine."

He pushed the heel of his palm against me, and I moaned at the friction. With a wicked grin, he lowered his mouth and licked me.

Shock and pleasure burst in me. This was one of those erotic images from my book. Hung kept licking me, and I gripped the bamboo mat for stability.

"You taste so good," he crooned.

It felt heavenly, and I didn't know what to do. I'd never experienced this before. I felt like I was flying. My legs wanted to close, but he pinned them in place.

"Relax, my flower. Give yourself to me."

I gasped, loving the image of his face between my thighs. When he lifted my ass with his powerful hands, I got to experience another image from my book.

He sucked on my bud, and my vision blurred. When he shoved a finger inside me, I couldn't help but beg. "I need you, Hung."

CHAPTER THIRTY-EIGHT

HUNG

I LOVED the sound of her seductive voice calling my name. Her moans were the music chasing away the darkness that had surrounded me for so long. I could almost hear the stones in my wall falling, one by one.

I pumped my finger into her, loving her softness and wetness. She whimpered, and I wanted to devour her mouth. I shifted so I could continue pleasuring her while kissing her. She tasted like sweet wildflowers—lush, liberated, and untamed. I'd never met anyone like her. Courageous, kind, and with the spirit of a warrior.

"Please . . ." she begged against my lips.

The lust in her eyes sent more blood to my cock. I extracted my finger and licked it. She watched me as I had expected.

My curious wildflower.

I placed her down on the mat, spreading her thighs apart. "Do you—"

"I've been taking an herbal concoction. It also prevents pregnancy."

I kissed her softly, remembering she'd been poisoned.

"Okay." I guided my cock to tease her entrance. "Let me know if it hurts."

Though I didn't like knowing she'd been with another man, I

wanted to ensure she'd never forget this night with me. I knew it would be forever etched into my memory.

As I slid into her, her facial expression transformed. God, I loved seeing what I did to her.

I groaned with every inch. "Are you okay?"

"Wonderful." She smiled and wrapped her legs around my waist, taking me in deeper and deeper.

I hovered over her as her muscles squeezed my cock. The friction intensified, and the tension grew. I thrust harder and faster. Sweat-slicked skin slapped against each other. We were having a sexual battle of our own, but one where we could both win.

I sensed her orgasm building.

"Look at me." I brushed the wet strands of hair away from her forehead. "I want to see you in bliss."

Her eyes darkened as her face transformed. "Hung!" Her body trembled with the powerful release.

I muffled her cry with a kiss. I'd never wanted a woman the way I wanted Su. She not only saved me, but she also endured the dangerous Emerald Road to look for me. All because she was worried about me.

No one had cared for me like this. My life had been lonely until her. She had opened my heart, and now I could see why men would kill for a woman—why an emperor would go to war for his empress.

Then I chased my orgasm, pumping into her.

"You're a sex warrior," she muttered against my shoulder, nipping me.

She didn't release her legs from my waist. Instead, she clung to me more tightly, fusing us together.

"I love the feel of you inside me," she admitted.

"Good. Because I'll be inside you often. From now on, I'm the only man who will be inside you. Understand?" I pumped harder.

"Yes," she moaned and placed a hand on my face, watching me as I had watched her.

The wave of my orgasm surged and surged until it shot out of me like a geyser, making my entire body shudder. *Fuck.* I'd never experienced an energy force like this—powerful, invigorating, and inexplicable.

I dropped to the side, half on top of her and half on the mat. My heart continued to pound. I needed a moment to gather myself. The explosion sent my body scattering. I wouldn't be surprised if my limbs were located elsewhere in the room.

"Oh. Look." She waved her hand in the air, but I was too content nuzzling her neck.

"What is it?" I inhaled her sweet scent.

"Your essa and mine. Is this normal?"

"What?" I looked up where her fingers were twirling with my gold essa and her peach essa. I blinked at the surreal sight. "It's not normal. I've never seen essa twirling together like this."

"They're twisting into each other . . . fusing. Are they mating?"

I chuckled at the ridiculous thought. But I could see why she would think that. The twisting and the coiling did look like they were mating.

"Maybe my orgasm was so powerful that it's messing with my head," I teased.

"That's a possibility." She laughed. "But I'm seeing it too, and I'm swimming in bliss. The gold is you. I remember tugging at your essa that day."

"I've only seen gold essas. This is my first time seeing peach essa. You're unique."

"So are you." She kissed my forehead. "We have a magical connection."

My cock was still inside her, and I made it twitch. "It was more than magical. It was *heavenly.*" The hairpin I'd given her was about to fall out, so I adjusted it. "Let's do this more often."

She flicked me a seductive look. "When we don't have enemies wanting to kill us."

"I've read that sexual energy is a powerful force. It's the process of creation. But I don't think that's why we saw our essas tonight. Maybe they resonated with each other on a different level."

The swirling essas faded. I reached to touch it and felt a slight zing of energy. I couldn't grip it the way Su could. "How are you able to yank it like a thread?"

She shrugged. "I don't know. My first time doing it was when I pulled you to safety."

She looked at her palms, turning them from side to side. That was when I noticed a floral design illuminating her arm.

"Why is that thing glowing on your arm? How did you get it?"

She glanced at it. "It's an old scar that's growing. The glowing is new, though."

"It's too refined and the geometric design too accurate to be a random scar. It could be a branding tool. Did someone do this to you?" The edge in my voice surprised me. I wanted to kill whoever branded her.

"No. I got hit by lightning when I was younger." A shiver ran through her.

"Let me get you some clothing to keep you warm. Then you can tell me about it."

I extracted myself from her, cleaned her with a towel I'd brought from the carriage, and gave her the new set of clothing to put on. Despite all the intimate things I'd done to her, her cheeks still flushed while I was wiping her. I appreciated her sincerity. Her emotions were clearly written on her face.

After cleaning myself, I dressed in the spare clothes she'd brought for me.

"They fit you." She ran a hand over the tunic as I sat down beside her.

Though I wanted to hear her story, I wanted her to get some more rest. I didn't want to overexert her and trigger the poison. I should've been more delicate with her.

"Are you sure you're feeling okay? No weakness? No dizziness?"

"Still some weakness and dizziness." She pinched my cheek. "But that's all from bliss."

"We should try to get some sleep before dawn approaches." I wrapped an arm around her.

She leaned into my shoulder. "But I thought you wanted to hear my story."

"I do." I kissed her head. "But I want you to get enough rest for tomorrow's journey. Who knows what's waiting for us? We have to be prepared."

"But I'm not sleepy." She pouted, snuggling closer.

"Then tell me." I draped the blanket over her. "And when you get tired, stop. Okay? You can resume tomorrow. We'll have time for the rest of your story during the journey."

She placed a hand over my heart. "Okay. Will you tell me your story too? I only know that your parents died when you were little. But I also know you've seen a lot of death on the battlefield."

I pressed my lips into a thin line. It had been a long time since I'd talked about my parents' deaths. I'd never shared with any women before. But when I looked into her eyes, I couldn't say no. I couldn't deny this woman who had a grip on my heart. It was both terrifying and liberating.

"Okay," I said. "But you go first."

CHAPTER THIRTY-NINE

SU

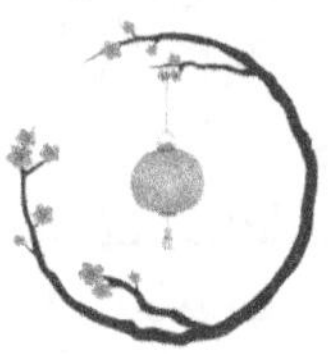

I COULD SEE his hesitation at my request. But when he agreed, joy burst inside me. Hung didn't know how happy I was tonight. The changing scar on my arm didn't scare me, even though a raised scar could be a sign of a deadly disease. But I wasn't afraid. There was this innate happiness rushing through me. I couldn't explain it.

Everything felt . . . right. Like I was in the right place with the right person.

With my heart pounding, I shared my past with him.

"We're just healers." Ba is on his knees, begging a masked man. "Please let us go. We have nothing worthwhile for you."

I can see the man with a mean face through the slit in the curtain from the carriage window. The wicked soldier holds a lantern, casting a glow over my parents.

A flash of lightning lights up a wooded path, and I see three other men dressed in black with masks. A small lantern hangs from a pole secured to something on their horses. It's dark, and I can't see clearly.

Fear twists my stomach. I know something bad is going to happen. Thunder roars in the sky as rain pours down.

Then a man hits my father, and he falls to the muddy ground. I want to scream, but Mẹ *clamps a hand over my mouth and shakes her head.*

"Liar! This jade is worth money!" He rips off the jade tassel from my father's belt.

Mẹ *and I had gotten it for him last year on his birthday. Anger and fear surge through me.*

"Shhh." She points to the barrel that holds our fabric and dried herbs. "Remember what we discussed last year?"

She takes out the fabric and herbs, emptying the barrel.

I nod, slip into the barrel, and crouch. I'm only eight, so I can fit in the small space.

Mom stuffs fabric around me, creating a cushion. Then she kisses me on the forehead. "I love you."

"I love you too," I whisper.

Mẹ *has prepared me for emergency situations, and tonight is one of them. She closes the lid, which has a security latch on the inside for me to unlock when I'm ready.*

"Stay in here. No matter what happens, keep quiet, okay?" she whispers to me as tears well in her eyes. Then she exits the carriage. "Please don't hurt my husband. We also have herbs you can take."

I hear more horses approaching.

"Hurry and kill them! The Imperial soldiers are arriving!" someone shouts.

I hear my father scream, and I reach for the fabric in front of me, shoving it in my mouth to muffle my cry. I'm so scared.

Noises erupt as my mom cries for my father. I can tell from her awful sobs that my father is dead. I don't know how I know, but I do. Pain bursts from my chest, shooting down my body.

Something hits the carriage, and it topples over. The barrel bounces to the ground, and my head hits the wall of fabric protecting me from the hard barrel. The barrel rolls somewhere, making me dizzy.

"Leave us alone!" I hear my mother's voice in the distance.

I hear the men laugh. Is Mẹ *okay?*

The barrel bounces and hits something. Then it rolls again. I feel sick. A loud boom smashes into the barrel, and I see a flash of lightning. The lid to the barrel breaks apart, and I fall out. A burning pain blasts my arm. Heat fires up my skin as I cry in pain.

I remember those mean soldiers, so I suppress my cry. What if they hear me?

I'm in a ditch in the woods. I think it's the woods. It's dark and I'm scared. I want my parents.

The rain comes down hard, blending with my tears.

"Be strong, Su. Go get help."

I hear horses approaching, but I'm scared it's those rebels. I crawl to an enormous tree trunk and peek around it. The soldiers have lanterns on their horses. I recognize the navy uniform with a red belt on the soldiers—the Imperial Army! Hope bursts in me as I dart out of the woods screaming. "Please help me! Please help my mother and father!"

A soldier on a horse spots me and hops to the ground, rushing to me. "Are you okay, little one?"

"The rebels are up that way!" I point, wanting to say more. But something's wrong with my body. Heat explodes in me, and I tremble. My vision blurs, and I faint.

"They sacrificed themselves to save you. Now I understand why you want to learn kung fu." Hung wiped at the hot tears streaming down my face. "I would do the same." He touched the scar on my arm. "I don't think this is a simple scar."

"Why do you say that? I thought the same, but I can't seem to find logic to it."

"Maybe there's no logic." He ran his fingers over it. "Does it hurt?"

"No. Sometimes, it lights up and changes shape."

He nodded. "You should keep a record of what triggers the change just to be on the safe side. What if the poison is triggering it? Making it worse?"

"I've thought about that too," I said. "But I should *sense* something's wrong with my body. I don't feel unwell. I just feel . . . different. Enough about me. I want to know about you."

CHAPTER FORTY

HUNG

"ARE you sure you're not sleepy?" I asked. "It's late. We only have a few hours before dawn."

Listening to her story helped me understand her strength and drive. Some people emerged from an unfortunate event carrying bitterness toward the world. But my dahlia emerged with inspiration and motivation.

She leaned into me. "I want to know about you. Sleep can wait."

How could I say no to that? After I told her about my parents' murders at the hands of the Deathcap Clan, I shared another story that gave her a glimpse into me.

Battle cries boom around me and my men are falling. The Iron Resistance attacks us unexpectedly. They're rebels with iron masks and excellent weapons. How did they know we were taking this route behind the mountains?

Who's the fucking traitor? I vow to skin him alive.

The stench of blood fills my nostrils as I race over to assist my soldier, Mudpie. I plunge my sword into the opponent's back before his sword can come down on my man. I twist the sword, yank it out, and plunge it in once more.

Mudpie's wounds are severe. Blood gushes from his arms, stom-

ach, and legs. Worry, fear, and rage collide in me. But I push them aside to help him.

He joined my camp five years ago and has become one of my loyal guards, along with Kai and Tao. They took a different route. I pray for their safety.

I drag Mudpie to the side, leaning him against a boulder. "Stay here."

"You should escape, General." He winces. "You can't die here."

"Neither can you."

"We need you alive," he breathes. "Someone knew we'd be here. Find out who."

I'm not leaving him.

A boom slices through the air, and fire and smoke billow near me. More rebels appear, and three of them meet my eyes. I flick my sword to remove the blood already on it, ready to kill.

They charge at me, and I fight with all my might. I see my men being stabbed and beheaded. Rage thrums in my blood. Where's their fucking general? I need to kill him first. But the sea of dead men, the burst of fire and smoke create too much chaos. The smoke stings my eyes.

I blink, trying to focus as rebels swing their weapons at me. I deflect a blow and stab one rebel. Then I pierce my sword into another. The third fighter holds a spear in his hand. I bend down, grab a handful of sand, and whip it at him.

Then I leap and plunge my sword into his chest, all while looking him in the eyes.

"How did you know we were here?" I push my sword deeper, waiting for him to reply. But of course he doesn't as he wails in pain. I extract my sword as more soldiers arrive.

I only see three of my men still standing. Something sharp slashes my back, and pain spikes. I whirl around to find an enemy smiling as he pulls back the sword that had just injured me.

I gut him with my sword.

More rebels arrive, but then something explodes.

Mudpie limps to me. "Go! I won't survive! But you can." Pain and rage splash on his face. "Please."

The Iron Resistance shouts with glee. I know my remaining men are gone.

Tears fill Mudpie's eyes. "Please."

"I'll find out who did this. I promise."

As I run down the crooked path into the woods, I hear Mudpie declare, "Lin Din Ni!" Silence follows, and the cheers from the enemy erupt once more.

I know they'll come after me, so I don't stop. Mudpie didn't just die so I could get caught. I discover a small nook beside a cave. Too injured to fight them, I slide into the nook and stay hidden. I have to survive. My men won't die in vain. Guilt rips into me, but I can't think about it. It will only enrage me. How can a general like me leave my men to die like that?

It's not your fault.

Guilt is a sword that continues to stab me from all sides.

My body is covered with the blood of my men and the enemy. A darkness brews in me as I lie waiting for the silence. When silence comes, I crawl out of the nook, following the stream toward my country. This is a small stream that connects to the Green Fog River. Outsiders stay away from there because of the infected people. But that's a risk I'll take.

I don't know how long I've been walking. My vision blurs and pain overwhelms me. Thirsty, I sit at the river's edge, scoop up some water, and drink it. I hear voices farther down the river and walk toward the sound.

But my body trembles as I lose control of myself and pass out.

My body jerked as though it remembered that moment. Su embraced me, comforting me with her warmth. "Did you find who the traitor was?"

"Two soldiers from the Bronze Barracks confessed to being spies for the Iron Resistance. They had been paid for the information about where my troops were heading. They were executed for treason." I released a breath. "But I knew there were more traitors. After that battle, I was cautious about sharing details about anything with anyone."

"Greed can make people do unimaginable things." She snuggled closer.

Our conversation continued about random things until I asked her a question, but she didn't reply. A soft snore escaped her lips, and I smiled down at the marvelous woman sleeping against my body. She was so beautiful, so smart, and so perfect for me.

I didn't know where our relationship would go. I feared her reaction if she knew I had poisoned her. Would she reconsider being with me? I should have told her sooner, but I wanted to wait until I found the antidote. She didn't show any adverse symptoms, but sometimes, the deadliest symptoms were dormant until something triggered them.

I shifted her so she was on her back and covered her with the blanket. Like me, she had endured fear, pain, grief, and guilt. The world was a cruel and dark place, but now I got to see a glimpse of the light. I skimmed my hand down her cheek. She was the flame that filled my heart with warmth and hope. She was also my fierce bow and arrow and my dangerous death touch. As a warrior, she was the only weapon I'd ever need to win any battle.

Tomorrow, I'd continue on my search for her antidote and destroy the Soul Extractors.

I smiled as I drifted off to sleep.

CHAPTER FORTY-ONE

SU

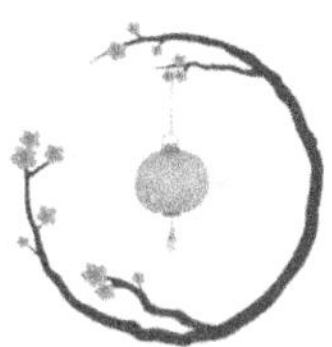

THE HORSE CARRIAGE JERKED, and I bounced in my seat. Scooting toward the front, I pushed the curtain aside and peeked out at Hung sitting on the horse, steering the way. He had secured his horse to the carriage, and it trekked along the side.

"Everything okay?" I asked, looking around at the desolate road.

Hung turned to the side. "Sorry, the carriage ran over a small hole in the road. Are you okay?"

"I'm all right. I was worried about you."

He turned to the side, revealing his gorgeous profile. "No need, my dahlia."

I loved that name—I could sense the affection in it. When I'd overheard couples speak to each other like this, I used to wonder if a man would ever dedicate a flower to me.

Last night had been the best night I'd ever experienced. Though it wasn't in the comfort of my bed or his bed, the experience was unforgettable. I had no regrets. I wanted more.

My heart swelled as I studied him. His shoulders shifted from side to side on the horse. His sword was slung on his back, making him appear like a dangerous warrior. I peeked at the round dragon talisman I'd given him earlier this morning. He'd attached it to the side of his belt.

Hung was a powerful warrior to those who didn't know him well. But there was so much more to this fascinating man. Like all of us, he carried wounds and vulnerabilities. But he also possessed a depth that called to me. We had a special connection I couldn't explain. Our essas had interlaced as though they understood we belonged together. I'd never seen, read, or heard anything like this. Most adept warriors spent years cultivating essas, but Hung and I had emitted this potent energy while making love. Maybe there were other ways to activate essas.

For some reason, Hung seemed especially worried about the poison in me. I was worried too, but he appeared more concerned.

"We're almost there. Stay alert," he spoke over his shoulder.

"Okay." I looked around, making sure nothing appeared abnormal. Trees surrounded us on both sides. We passed a few abandoned vendor stands that looked like they hadn't been used for a while.

This morning, Hung suggested I return home because he was searching for the Soul Extractors and didn't want to put me in danger. I'd never heard of them. Apparently, these dark beings had possessed people, which explained why no one was on this road. They were either possessed or dead.

But how could I leave him to face this peril alone? Even if I were to head back, I could also be attacked. So I used that angle to force him to let me stay.

An eerie feeling gripped me, and I shivered as I looked at the growing blanket of mist in the distance.

"Do you see the mist?" I asked Hung.

"Yes." He pulled the reins and stopped the carriage. "We don't need to go any farther. They're here."

"How do you know?"

He hopped down from the horse, walked over to me, and drew the sword on his back. It glowed brightly with golden abstract symbols.

"When the sword senses something, it heats up. I can feel it thrumming on my back."

I gripped my dagger, another weapon I'd brought with me. "Do you think the Dim Mak would affect the Soul Extractors?"

"I don't think so," he said, standing protectively in front of me. "The possession probably distorts their energy, so it won't be as effective. We should kill them immediately."

Perhaps we could keep one for interrogation, but I didn't want to risk it. Five people emerged from the fog. They appeared like normal merchants and farmers. But their dirty shoes didn't match the clean clothes they had on.

"Are you here to help us, sir?" said the man holding a rake.

"What do you need help with?" Hung asked. His sword continued to glow, making a strange zing sound.

The man with the rake glared at the sword. "We need food. There are sick children in the village. We need medicine too." He looked toward the carriage. "Do you have some with you?"

Was this how they tricked people into captivity? Who wouldn't want to help sick children? Dark energy emanated from these people, and a chill scraped down my spine.

"Sorry, we don't have any right now." Hung walked toward them, and Rake Man stepped back. "But if you help me, I can get food and medicine."

The four other people who stood behind Rake Man stepped forward.

"What do you need?" asked the woman with the messy hair. "Perhaps you can come to our home to discuss." She pointed beyond the mist.

"Why is the mist moving?" I asked no one in particular.

The mist had darkened to gray, moving in layers, trying to form something. Fear clawed at my throat, but I remained calm and vigilant.

The woman turned away from Hung and looked at me. My body jerked, and the scar on my arm heated. It burned, and I clamped a hand over it.

An awful cry that didn't belong on earth seared through the air. The woman's face distorted, taking on an unrecognizable appearance. One side of her face dropped like her skin was melting. Rake Man and the other men's faces were also distorted. When their eyes turned black, they charged at us.

The woman leaped toward me while the men attacked Hung. She threw a tiger claw at me, but I dodged it. Her techniques were ruthless. I deflected, spun, stabbed the dagger into her stomach, and retracted.

Black blood ebbed out of her, but she kept fighting me as though the dagger didn't affect her. Hung slashed at the men with his blade, and they dropped to the ground. Their flesh turned to soot, leaving nothing but a pile of bones. The woman wailed angrily and threw herself at Hung. But he cut her in half, and her flesh turned to soot while her bones thudded to the ground just like the others.

Noises erupted from the fog, and silhouettes of people emerged. The fog darkened, blurring the area. Hung grabbed my hand and ran into the woods. Terror gripped me as I ran at his heels. Twigs crunched under our feet as we hopped over logs and pushed away vines draping from the trees. The wind picked up, and a chill coated the air.

"You can't run from us!" someone shouted. The sound echoed on and on.

I hear footsteps approaching. Someone jumped in front of us, and Hung stabbed the man. Three more came at us, but Hung pushed me behind him as he battled them. These men were better fighters than the others. Their uniforms showed they were possessed Imperial Army soldiers. These were Hung's men.

"Watch out, Su!" screamed a child's voice.

I turned to see Luzi running toward me, pointing at a man to my right. He held a large butcher's knife, glaring at me. Shock and confusion slammed into me. I dodged and slashed at his back with my dagger, but it did nothing to him. My weapon was useless against these Soul Extractors.

Another possessed soldier appeared and kicked me in my stomach. I fell onto my back, and he charged me, holding a sword, ready to plunge it into my chest.

Luzi rushed up to him, and I knew what she planned to do.

"No!" I shouted, but it was too late.

She stabbed him in the back. He whirled around and swung the sword at her, slicing her in the stomach.

"*Luzi!*"

Fear and shock gripped me as I rushed over to her. What was she doing here? She should be at the apothecary right now. Black blood flowed freely from her wound too, but I couldn't worry about that now. She wasn't one of them. She came to *help* me. Tears streamed down my face as I ripped off a part of my tunic's hem, putting pressure on her wound.

Hung leaped over and beheaded the butcher. "Hold this. I'll carry her." He gave me his sword, and its luminosity faded.

He lifted her little body into his arms, and we ran farther into the woods that weren't blurred by the fog. I heard running water in the distance, and my feet moved faster.

Dear God and all the Great Ancestors, please save Luzi.

"There's a bridge!" Hung exclaimed.

Eerie cries echoed behind us as we arrived at the rope bridge. A powerful river flowed below us, separating this landmass from the one across from us.

"Be careful," Hung said as he stepped onto the moss-covered wooden plank.

If we slipped and fell, we'd have died for sure. With caution, I followed close behind Hung.

When we reached the other side, Hung gently placed Luzi on the ground. Then he opened his hand. "I need my sword."

I gave it to him, and the sword came to life. While I held my tunic scrap to Luzi's wound, he walked up to the bridge and waited. When the swarm of possessed people arrived, they rushed over the bridge. He swung his sword when they were halfway across, chopping the ropes that secured the bridge to the posts beside him. The rope bridge broke off, and the bodies dropped like pebbles into the wild river below. One man stood at the edge, watching his comrades die. He looked over at us and let out an awful cry. Then he turned and ran into the woods.

Relief settled in me as I focused my attention on Luzi. She was bleeding too much.

"Her blood is black." Hung crouched, studying her.

"I'm not like them . . ." She winced. "I *was*."

Sweat beaded her forehead, and I dabbed it with my sleeve. "What do you mean?"

"They captured my family. . ." she said, panting.

I didn't want her to exert too much energy. Blood continued to pour out of her, also trickling from her nose.

"I don't know what to do, Hung." I added more pressure to her wound. Then I glanced around to see if there were any yarrow or mugwort to help stop the bleeding. I didn't see any. "I need to search for herbs."

"No . . ." Luzi said, tears streaming from her eyes. One of them looked darker than the other. "It's too late. I knew I would die coming here to look for you."

My heart shattered. "Why? What happened?"

"I'm sorry." She flinched as her legs twitched. "They told me if I spied on you and General Wen, they'd bring my family back." She looked at Hung. "They told me you were an evil man. That you kill a lot of people." Then she turned to me. "But *you* trust him. You told me he's a good person." She winced as more blood streamed down from her nose. "I believe you. You really care about me."

How could anyone not care about her? I wanted to keep her safe and teach her martial arts so she could protect herself. Who had done this to her?

Hung tore off the hem of his tunic and dabbed the blood from her nose. "Conserve your energy, little one. You can tell us more later."

"No. You're in danger . . . I have to tell you now."

I wiped the tears from my eyes. "What is it?"

"I was possessed like those people, but not completely. You taught me the Infinity Loop, and it made me feel better. So I did it every night. It cleared my mind, broke their control." She paused for a moment as her eyes fluttered. When she opened them, the left eye had darkened. "They're going to kill me." Tears rolled down her face. "They lied about bringing my family back."

"How did you get here?" Hung asked.

"I heard a possessed soldier talking to someone about you heading this way. He was supposed to capture you. I hid in a trunk in his carriage. He stopped the carriage when he heard fighting. I snuck out and followed him." She breathed. "They're sending more possessed people after you, General." Another pause. "I was so happy when I saw both of you . . ." Her left eye turned completely black.

"No," she said, her right eye looking elsewhere. "I won't listen to you anymore."

Was the darkness trying to control her now?

A loud cry pierced the air as a foul energy burst from her eyes, mouth, ears, and nose. The darkness ate up her body. I watched as her flesh crumbled into soot, exposing her fragile bones. I wanted to stop the demonic process, but I didn't know how.

"No!" I cried, reaching for her—wanting to gather her up.

But Hung held me back. "We can't help her now. Whatever is hurting her could hurt you *through* her. Don't let her die in vain." He tightened his arms around me as soot floated where her body had been.

I couldn't believe what I was seeing. My little Luzi was waiting for me to teach her things. My body trembled from anger and hopelessness as a breeze blew in, taking her from me. Embers of her soul floated away, and I lifted a hand toward them.

"Luzi," I cried as grief tightened my chest. Pain bloomed, but I shoved it aside to focus on a little girl who saved me. She was only a child. She came to me because she was worried about me. I wanted to kill whoever did this to her.

I sobbed against Hung, overwhelmed by grief, sorrow, and anguish. Luzi's bones were strewn on the ground like tree limbs that had broken after a storm.

"We'll avenge her," Hung said as his features took on a sorrowful mask.

There was no doubt about that. A wave of malice surged through my body, forcing my fingers to clench. I now understood the desire to kill. It was different from the day I witnessed my parents' deaths. I'd been young and frightened then. But I wasn't that child anymore.

I dropped to the ground, gathering up her bones. She just wanted her family back. I vowed to destroy whoever had used her vulnerability for their evil cause. How many more people were under their control?

"Can you help me?" I rose with her bones in my arms.

"Of course."

We found a peaceful place in the woods surrounded by flowering bushes. Hung helped me dig a hole to bury Luzi's bones. I found a stick and twisted the surrounding vines to make a pretty design. When I was done, I pierced the stick into the ground and said a prayer.

An awful sound erupted, and we glanced out of the woods. A group of possessed people had returned. One of them was attached to a large kitelike thing, soaring in the sky.

"Fuck," Hung said. "Let's go. They're flying across the river."

I took one glance at the makeshift grave. *Rest in peace, Luzi. I'll make them pay for what they did to you and your family.*

We rushed into the woods. The pain in my chest increased.

"Are you okay?" Hung asked.

"Just some pain in my chest. But I can keep up."

"Okay." He gripped my hand tighter and ran forward.

I wasn't sure where we were going. Heat flared on my arm, and I knew it was the scar. I didn't have time to glance at it.

"Look!" Hung pointed ahead at the blue rabbit.

The ears perked as it looked at us. "Follow me." A faint voice echoed in my head. Was that the bunny talking to me?

"Over there!" someone bleated.

Fear escalated as we kept our eyes on the blue rabbit. It led us around a circle.

"We're not getting farther," I said.

A thread of light appeared where the rabbit had hopped, creating this circular geometric design. We stood at the center.

"It looks like the floral design on your arm."

The rabbit sat on a patch of grass, looking up at us. Its entire body glowed. Then its head turned to the right. A rift opened in the air in front of us, the inside glowing gently.

Su . . . I need your help. Come in.

"Do you hear her calling me?" I asked Hung.

"I only hear sounds, but it doesn't make sense to me."

"Someone needs my help. She wants me to enter." I looked at him. "I think this is our way out."

"We'll take our chances there," Hung said.

I walked up to the rift and opened it with two hands, like parting curtains. I clasped Hung's hand, and we both stepped into it. As the blue rabbit hopped in, I saw a swarm of possessed soldiers appearing around the geometric design. But they couldn't enter the center and watched as the rift closed.

CHAPTER FORTY-TWO

HUNG

SU GRIPPED my hand and rushed through the dark tunnel, following the blue rabbit as our light. I realized I had underestimated the Soul Extractors. Some of them were experienced fighters. I didn't know if I could have protected her if they had swarmed me.

The fulgurite sword was beneficial, but it could only activate when I held it. If I were injured or incapacitated, Su would've been in danger. She wouldn't be able to use the sword.

I shoved all those fears aside as we slowed down in the dark tunnel. Or was it a cave? The space wasn't as dark now. Soft light appeared, but I still couldn't see my feet or the squishy ground.

The glowing rabbit hopped along beside us, shedding light on areas that had been dark to me. It looked like the creature was hopping on clusters of stars. No, that couldn't be it. I glanced around, and stars glistened around us. Why hadn't I seen them before?

"Are you seeing what I'm seeing?" I asked her. "I could be hallucinating."

Sue looked around, and the anguish that had strained her face diminished. "I've seen the starry night before."

The rabbit leaped to a cluster of stars. The stars burst, casting more light around us. To the left, a wave of colorful lights fluctuated in the sky, looking like silky fabrics swaying beautifully. Where were we?

I'd been in caves and was familiar with the musty, earthy scent. Some caves even smelled moldy with damp air. But I didn't sense any of that here.

Su squeezed my hand. "I've been here before." Her eyes brightened.

"When?"

"When I was sick in bed from the poison dart. I heard a voice calling me and was transported to this place. There was buoyancy to the ground too." She bounced on her feet.

I did the same, and an energy shifted under my feet, pushing me back.

Su . . .

A voice echoed in the distance, but I couldn't understand it.

She whipped me a look. "Did you hear that? She's calling me."

"I only heard a jumbled sound," I said.

I wished I could understand it to ensure whoever was calling her wasn't deceiving her. With all that had occurred, I couldn't dismiss the idea that the Soul Extractors had something to do with this. Su mentioned she'd heard a voice talking through the soldier who had attacked her. What if that voice had entered this space?

Who was behind the Soul Extractors? Was the demon from the Shadowcrest Mountains responsible? I had to figure out a way to destroy it.

I concentrated on my sword. It didn't heat as it did when it had warned me about the approaching darkness. My caution lessened a little.

Out of nowhere, geometric shapes of all sizes appeared in the air, radiating a soft gold light. They looked like the floral design on Su's arm. They flipped, turned, twisted, and some even merged to look like three-dimensional flowers. Stars twinkled more prominently.

The mandalas began moving toward something. The rabbit looked at me, made a cheerful noise, and rushed forward. It jumped on one of the floral discs, then another, and another. The rabbit let out adorable sounds as its four ears perked in various directions. The floral designs replied with swooshing noises.

"Are they talking to each other?" I asked.

"Sounds like it." She beamed, glanced down at her arm, and shoved up the sleeve. Her scar glowed just like the mandalas.

"Does it hurt?" I studied it.

"No. Just warm. I think it's responding to them."

I'd seen many wild things during my travels and battles, but this one baffled me. It took me to a whole new place that required my mind to think differently. I felt as if I'd just stepped into a new world.

We followed the rabbit and the floral designs until the night sky and the designs faded and were replaced by daylight. A serene, scenic view spread out before me. An immense mountain range took my breath away, standing like gods in the distance. The mountains were so tall that I couldn't see the tops. Clouds dotted the soft blue sky as a peaceful energy embraced me.

"It's so heavenly." Su inhaled a deep breath, looking more vibrant than she had earlier.

The blue rabbit hopped toward a mountain with a textured, light gray surface. It also had a seashell-like luminosity. Different colors became more prominent depending on where I stood. If I stepped to the side, I saw more blue. If I moved back, a light green or pink appeared.

Moss and other plant life grew in random places in the mountains. An arched doorway emerged from the surface of the mountain, rising tall. Abstract engravings glowed around the arched frame, revealing a hallway filled with golden light.

The blue rabbit hopped in, stopped, and turned to look at us.

"Let's go." Su took my hand and followed the rabbit.

CHAPTER FORTY-THREE

SU

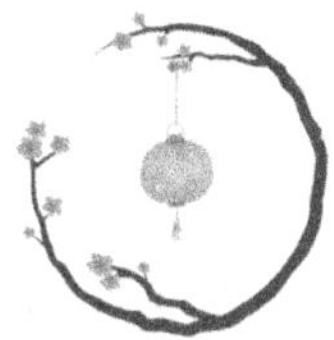

THE ARCHED DOORWAY closed as soon as Hung and I stepped inside.

I didn't know where this blue rabbit was taking Hung and me, but I trusted it. It had saved us from danger. The peacefulness in my heart from this place was the remedy I desperately needed. It was my sanctuary. I could easily ignore my grief and vengeance to focus on who was calling me.

How could I understand the voice and Hung couldn't? What did this creature want from me? A part of me wondered if it was some sort of trick, luring me and Hung to our deaths. But my intuition told me differently. Whatever—or whoever—was waiting for me meant no harm. I felt that in my bones.

The gold light in the hallway came from flowers growing on either side, making the hallway appear mystical. A bird flew in front of me, looked at me, blinked, and flew away.

"Do birds blink?" I asked Hung, wanting to double-check what I knew about birds.

"I don't think so."

A white cat with five tails jumped out from somewhere, startling me. It came up to us and meowed. It had eyes with blue flower-shaped irises. The cat saw a mouselike creature and chased after it, fading into the air.

Images floated around me and on the walls of the hallways. People dressed in strange clothing, holding odd devices that glowed, rushed on a street with a smooth black surface. The busy street looked nothing like the Market Square. The brick homes, tall buildings, and the sidewalks looked different. Peculiar architecture with many windows that weren't made of paper stood like warriors. I'd never seen anything like that.

The images disappeared as quickly as they had come.

"They look like people from a different world," Hung said.

My imagination expanded, welcoming things I didn't know were possible. Was there a world like that? Where was it?

We walked by a shrubbery with glowing fruits the size of peaches. Their skins were transparent. I paused to inspect them.

"Hung!" I gasped, gripping his arm. "There's a little girl inside the fruit reading a book!"

The adorable girl had brown hair, light brown eyes, and iridescent wings.

She placed her book on the desk, and the top of the fruit opened, allowing her to fly out and over to us. "Hello."

"Hi." I stared at her. She could fit into my palm. "Who are you? What's your name?"

"Willowwish. I'm a fairy and work for one of the cosmic libraries." She turned as more of her friends approached. Female and male fairies fluttered around us with colorful hair and eyes to match. "These are my friends."

A cosmic library? What else existed that I didn't know?

Hung and I exchanged perplexed glances.

A roar erupted from up ahead. A powerful wave of energy flowed through the space, and the surroundings appeared to warp or shift. Though the shifting only lasted for a moment, it was long enough for me to notice.

The fairies flew back into the fruit homes and resumed whatever they had been doing. Most of them were reading or organizing tiny books.

"Oh no," Willowwish said. "She's in pain again."

"Who?"

"Rayonaa Theoaa Serakaa, also known as Roar of the Sky. She's pregnant."

Another roar sliced through the space, and the vibration rippled through my body. My internal organs felt like they had traded places. A surge of energy entered my bloodstream. I couldn't explain how I knew that.

The flower mandala on my arm warmed further, and a subtle sound came from it. The fairy fluttered over to my arm and waved her small hand over my sleeve. It rolled up for her, revealing the thrumming floral design.

What the hell was going on?

Willowwish looked up at me and smiled. "She's been looking for you. Hurry! Go to her. She needs you."

The blue rabbit rushed toward the sound, and we ran to keep up with it. Its four leaflike ears glowed brighter, and abstract symbols appeared on its body.

Another roar erupted, sounding like a giant beast. The ground trembled, and my body tingled from the powerful vibration. I should've been used to some of these powerful energies by now, but apparently not yet.

The rabbit rounded the corner and raced down a hallway that increased in size. Not that the other hallway was small or anything, but this was colossal. A gust of wind came from my right, and I glanced to see an exit in the distance.

But my attention returned to the bunny as it rushed into an entrance. When Hung and I entered the room, my heart pounded as I stared at a massive midnight blue dragon lying on the ground with its body winding around and around, making it hard to gauge its true size.

"Is it real?" I asked.

"There's no doubt about it," Hung said. "Look at its body."

I remembered the books and paintings depicting these fantastical creatures. The divine dragon was made up of nine animal body parts. The descriptions in the books did not measure up to this unique creature.

The dragon lifted its head, looking regal and magnificent. It dipped its neck and opened its eyes wide as it stared down at us. An abstract etching that looked like a dragonfly appeared on its forehead and brightened. I studied the immense creature, checking off the nine body parts in my head. It had the head of a camel, the neck of a snake, the horns of a stag, the ears of a cow, the belly of a clam, the scales of a carp, the claws of an eagle, the paws of a tiger, and the eyes of a demon. The books described this detail, but I never understood it.

Those eyes didn't look evil to me. They looked . . . mystical.

It had scales the color of midnight blue, ranging in size and radiance. The horns glistened gold on the top of its head. A beautiful mane of blue hair cascaded around its powerful face. Long iridescent whiskers flowed around its nose. When its belly pulsed and glowed, another roar escaped its mouth.

The blue rabbit hopped close to the dragon, and I shouted, "Be careful!"

What if the dragon thought the rabbit was food?

The rabbit hopped between the dragon's claws and snuggled in. Four ears flopped to the side as it rested its head on the dangerous-looking claw.

A laugh escaped the dragon's mouth, echoing through the room. The sound bounced from the wall and ceiling. I glanced up and saw an opening at the top that gave me a peek at the night sky. That couldn't be the same night sky Hung and I had traveled through earlier, could it? But it was daylight here now. The opening from the cave on the other side even showed daylight. There were so many confusing things happening all at once. How could day and night exist simultaneously in the same spot?

I didn't have time to contemplate further because the dragon got to its feet and lifted itself into the air. I gawked at the majestic serpentine body flying, or rather, swimming, above us. Energy pulsated from its body as it dove up and down, moving like a snake in the air. It looped around and came to face us.

I stepped back from its immense size. Hung wrapped an arm around me protectively.

"You're finally here, Su." Its blue eyes pinned me to the ground.

I turned to Hung to see if he heard the same greeting, but his confused expression told me what I needed to know.

"You can talk," I said.

The blue rabbit hopped to the wall and snuggled by a plant bush, watching the scene unfold.

Hung drew his sword. "Stay away from her."

"I won't hurt her." The dragon looked at him.

I swore the dragon looked amused, but it was hard to tell because this was my first meeting with a dragon.

"What?" Hung stared at it. "I can't understand you."

"She said she won't hurt me." I placed a hand over Hung's arm and reminded him. "If she wanted to hurt us, we wouldn't be standing here."

It was a natural reaction to Hung's protectiveness. I would've done the same if I couldn't understand the gigantic beast.

Despite this, nerves still tumbled in my stomach. I wasn't sure what to feel or how to react to this situation. Dragons existed in books and stories. My parents used to tell me bedtime stories of warriors battling some evil dragons, and the good-hearted dragons emerged to assist them. But those were stories to entertain curious minds back then.

I looked into its eyes but didn't see what the books had described. "You don't have demon eyes. They're not scary."

"Who says I do?"

"Books. Scrolls. Stories from a long time ago."

The creature nodded. "Define what you believe to be a 'demon.' A beast is considered terrifying to most, but that's because people don't understand it. The eyes are merely portals to other worlds." The dragon swam around us, making a swooshing sound. "But I'm not the dragon you're describing."

"Then what kind of dragon are you?"

"I'm an Infinara Dragon from the Infinara Matrix, a realm you can't comprehend yet. My eyes are made of gems you've never heard of. My heart is that of a lion, and my brain is that of an ancient dolphin."

"A dolphin?" I asked.

Hung looked baffled, and I briefly told him what I just heard.

I'd never seen a dolphin but had heard from fishermen who had encountered them. These smart creatures had saved many people lost at sea.

"You may address me as Roar of the Sky. It's a pleasure to meet you, Su."

"I have a lot of questions."

"I'm sure you do." She took a deep breath. Her exhale became a large gust of wind in the room. "I apologize, but I'm exhausted. My eggs are due at any time now."

I didn't know why, but I heard the dragon's heartbeat along with her babies.

"I can hear your heartbeats. You're pregnant with six other dragons," I told her. "How is it possible that I can hear the heartbeats?"

"Because you're connected to me." Her paw brushed her stomach gently. Her eyes flicked to my hand, and the scar heated and glowed. "You have my dragon scale. It's embedded in you."

"That's impossible." I looked at my scar.

"What's impossible?" Hung asked.

"She said this scar is her dragon scale."

Hung gripped my arm to study the scar in detail.

"I lost it during a cosmic war."

"You've been calling me. Why?"

Hung's gaze flicked to me and the dragon. His lips tightened, probably frustrated that he couldn't understand us.

"Why can't he hear you?" I asked.

"Because he doesn't have my dragon scale." She looked at my arm. "May I have it back?"

It belonged to her, so it made sense to return it. "Yes. You could've taken it back earlier."

"No, I can't. I would have to tear your skin to remove it. But if I asked for your permission, it would be a seamless and painless extraction."

As a healer, I should have considered the practical steps in removing something from my skin. This magical place and talking to a dragon had made me forget basic things.

The dragon lowered to the ground, creating a slight tremor when she landed. She walked up to me, lifting a paw close to my arm. My arm glowed brighter than usual, and the scar vibrated.

"What's happening?" Hung stepped closer to me, placing a concerned hand on my shoulder.

"I'm returning the scale to her."

The dragon flexed its paw, and a tingle bloomed on my skin. The floral scale lifted from my arm and floated to the dragon's palm. Then the scale rose on its own, moving to the dragon's body. It was only then that all the scales on the dragon transformed. A flower mandala design appeared on all of them. The mandalas glowed gold against the various shades of midnight blue. I noticed an area on the dragon's body that was missing a scale and, therefore, disrupted the flow of the textured pattern.

"I have a strange question to ask." I kept my eyes on the scale reinserting itself into the dragon's body, completing the pattern.

The dragon sucked in a breath as it rose into the air. A beautiful ripple from the scales created a heavenly sound that couldn't be explained. It was like celestial music shooting straight to my soul.

I looked over at Hung, who was studying it in awe.

When the sound faded, the dragon returned to the ground, looking at me with eyes that seemed different from before. There was a mandala design within its iris, making it look like lace or some intricate design. There was so much to this dragon . . . I didn't think I'd be able to absorb everything I was seeing.

I didn't want to forget my question, so I asked, "Do you track down every scale you lose?"

"No. Most of my scales can grow back, but the one I lost can't." The dragon lifted its head, revealing a long, curved neck and a round belly. "That scale is part of the shield around my heart. It encompasses a unique energy that can't be replicated."

"Oh." I looked down at the light imprint of the floral design on my arm. A dizziness swept over me, and I stumbled back.

Hung caught me. "What's wrong?"

The dragon looked at him. "I need him to get some water from the stream. Can he do it?"

I repeated the words to Hung, and he glared at the dragon. "Where is it? If it'll help her, I'll do anything!"

Understanding him, the dragon glanced down a hallway I hadn't noticed before. "That will take you there. I need two large pails."

Two metal pails appeared before us.

Hung assisted me to a bench I also hadn't seen earlier and situated me. "Will you be okay?"

"Yes," I said. "I'll be okay. Maybe I just need some water."

"What if it's the poison acting up?"

Doubts snuck into my head. He could be right, but I said, "I'll be fine. Don't worry."

With the two pails, Hung rushed down the hallway.

"Tempo, go with the warrior and help him as needed."

The blue rabbit perked its ears and leaped after Hung.

"Why does it need to help him retrieve water? It's a simple task, right?"

Roar of the Sky shifted closer to me and looked out the main hallway from which Hung and I had come.

"With everything you've seen so far, does anything appear simple, Su?" Amusement gleamed in her eyes.

CHAPTER FORTY-FOUR

HUNG

AS I NEARED THE OPENING, the pails grew heavy. My pace slowed as it took more energy to lift them despite them being empty.

Fucking hell.

Tempo hopped ahead of me and stopped at the opening. The pails only kept getting heavier, and I reflexively dropped them to the ground.

What the fuck?

With all my might, I had to drag the pails one by one to the opening. What was in them that I couldn't see? I had to get the water for Su. The poison could've been activated. Sweat beaded my face as I lifted the weighty pails.

Tempo angled his head, looking at me. This was ridiculous. Had the dragon manipulated the weight? What was its intention? Su's life was on the line, and I had no time for jokes.

Irritation clung to me as I nudged the second pail to the opening. I shook off the strain in my arms and hands, straightening my posture to breathe and gather my strength. I'd envisioned the same scenic view from earlier, but this was a fucking desert. A few cacti loomed, along with some desert plants. The ground was mostly dirt, sand, and some rocks. It didn't look like any rain had come through the area.

Where was I going to get water for Su?

The dragon mentioned a stream. I did not see any stream. Was the dragon testing me? But why?

Questions sparked in my head, but I didn't have time to entertain them. Su needed water.

I grabbed the pails again and stepped onto the dirt path, surveying the area for any signs of a stream. I came to a set of boulders and climbed on top of them. Below the cliff was a vista that spread out before me. A few trees were scattered across the landscape, but no water.

A dark cloud loomed in the distance. Was that a raincloud? How long would it take for it to arrive? It might be too late for Su. I had to find a different path.

A bird cawed as it soared in the sky. I turned down a path with cracking soil, hoping to locate a stream. After two miles of walking with the pails and the rabbit, I stopped, breathed, and revisited my plan.

I'd been so focused on searching for water that I didn't realize how light the pails were now. The weight had lessened drastically. Not only that, the pails also didn't feel as hot as they should, given the heat beating down on the metal. Sweat drenched my entire body. I wanted to strip my top but decided my tunic protected my skin from burning. I needed water too.

My sword had been quiet ever since we entered this dragon realm, or whatever it was. As long as it remained quiet, I didn't have to worry about unexpected attackers.

My mouth grew dry, and I feared I might pass out from the dehydration if I didn't head back soon. But I couldn't return without the water. My chest hurt thinking of her suffering. I wanted to protect her, to love her.

Love her.

The words rang loud and clear. The emotion had been building and building, and I'd been afraid to face the truth. It was time I admitted it to myself. I'd fallen in love with Su. She was the first woman to make me feel alive and worthy. I'd do anything for her.

At first, I doubted my feelings. Did I feel for her because I'd poisoned her? She had saved my life from that poison dart. I owed her more than she knew. I didn't know if my emotions were just me feeling sorry or guilty. Or both. The sexual attraction was real. But love was another thing entirely.

Right now, as I stood alone in this desert with only a blue rabbit as my companion, I could hear my heart speak louder. My mind was uncluttered, allowing me to understand that I truly loved her. There was no confusion or doubt.

Did she feel the same way about me? What if she knew the truth about how she'd been poisoned?

You're overthinking it.

Was I, though? These were logical thoughts.

I was a warrior who entered a battle without fear, but now I was afraid of what would become of us after I told her the truth.

These negative thoughts weren't going to help me fetch water for Su. Regardless of what happened, she needed this miracle water, wherever it was.

"Come on, Tempo. I need your help. Where do I go?"

The creature made a sound, and the strange ears took on different positions. When it hopped down another dirt path, I followed it. We came to an area with some desert plants. Dunes loomed in the distance.

"I don't see any water."

Tempo leaped over to an area, hopped around it, and jumped back to my feet.

The ground quivered, and the area where Tempo had hopped sank. Something sparkled in the sunlight. Then a pool of water filled the hole. The pool glistened as though gems blanketed the surface. Gold streams of light emerged from the water, flowing everywhere. This was the magical water.

I rushed over and filled each pail with water. Then I scooped some with my hands to quench my thirst. A powerful gust of wind emerged, blowing dirt and sand everywhere. Something blocked out the sun, casting darkness over the area.

I looked up, and the dark cloud I'd seen earlier was right above me.

Dark tendrils grew from it. The tendrils looked like the soot snakes from the Soul Extractors. The rabbit raced back to where we'd come from. I grabbed the pails and rushed after it, but the tendrils yanked at my arm and foot. I fell and dropped one pail. The water spilled everywhere.

Fuck!

The pool where I'd gotten the water had disappeared. Infuriated, I secured the other pail and drew my sword. It glowed but didn't heat like before when the Soul Extractors had attacked us. Was something blocking its power here?

More sooty tendrils descended from the clouds. The snake heads screeched with sounds that made my skin crawl. They morphed into three enormous monsters with giant mouths that could devour me whole.

Angry that it made me spill Su's water, I leaped at it with my sword. "Give me back my water!"

The monsters dodged me and released a sound that reminded me of mockery or laughter. That only made me angrier. My sword sliced into the sooty tendrils, cutting off a few heads. The heads rolled and formed into a wolflike creature with blood dripping from its fangs.

The wolf swiped at me once and missed. I swung my sword at it, but it moved away too quickly. It charged at me and clawed my right shoulder. Pain sparked, and blood seeped through my clothing. More wolves joined the monsters. My heart pounded in fear as I realized I could die right now. What would happen to Su? I couldn't leave her alone.

A wolf jumped onto me. I plunged a sword into its chest, and it dispersed. Another two attacked me from behind, while three jumped at me from the front. I pierced one wolf with my sword while the others clawed my back, arms, and legs.

Time slowed, and Tempo appeared before me. The wolf monsters became immobile as though I'd used the Dim Mak on them. Tempo leaped to a flat rock I hadn't seen before. The slowness allowed me to follow. Then I was somewhere that was completely dark. I couldn't see my feet or my hands. A few seconds later, strands of light appeared around me like a web of glowing threads. The threads pulsed and shifted, and images of my past and present flowed within the web.

I saw a gold thread interlacing with a peach thread. The image reminded me of my essa intertwining with Su's that night. Something tugged at my leg, but I couldn't see it. A second later, the intertwined thread appeared closer, so I grabbed onto it. It tossed me across the dark space, and the force sent my sword flying somewhere.

CHAPTER FORTY-FIVE

SU

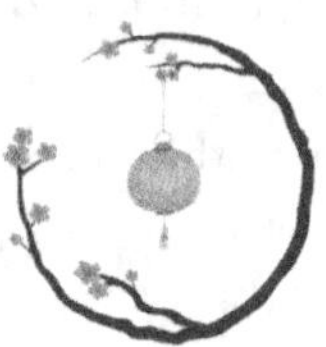

ANXIETY KNOTTED my stomach as my concern for Hung increased. He hadn't come back from retrieving two pails of water. How hard could that be? Had the dragon sent him elsewhere?

"Do we need to go check on Hung?" I asked.

"There's no need to worry," said the dragon as she shifted her body, probably trying to get comfortable.

"He's been gone for a while, though. Do you think he needs help?"

"Do you love him?"

The blunt question took me by surprise. Why was this dragon asking about something so personal?

She looked at me, and I felt this odd sensation of maternal love. Did she care for me because I had her scale all these years? Or was there another reason behind her question?

I was having a conversation with an immense dragon from another realm as though it were something people did every day. I didn't know if this profound experience would ever seem real.

"Why do you want to know?" I asked.

"Because I care. We have a special connection. My scale *chose* you when it detached."

"It chose me? How? How did your scale do that on its own?"

The dragon looked up at the opening in the sky. "There are wars in the sky, in several dimensions. Wars between beings you can't comprehend."

"What are they fighting for?"

She chuckled, and her massive body trembled. "Power. Control. Domination." She stretched her neck, moving her head closer to me. "The light."

"What do you mean?" I knew what she meant, but I had a feeling there was more to my simple understanding.

"The battle between the dark and the light has been ongoing for eons. A powerful darkness has snuck into several realms. It's as old as time and very intelligent. It's been recruiting an army of followers to do its job."

"What's the job?"

"To destroy the light." She lifted her paw, and streams of iridescent essas flowed from it. They weren't just gold but other metallic colors. "I'm not only referring to the light of the sun, which we need to live. I'm referring to the potent light within us—essa. The important life force in you, me, and everything around us."

"Basically, energy, right?"

"Yes. But essa is elevated energy, which means it holds more power. The dark will want to eliminate what threatens it most."

"Is that possible?" I swallowed, fearing her answer. "I mean, can the darkness achieve that?"

"It already has achieved this in one realm, which is why it's strong now."

Fear squirmed in my stomach, probably showing on my face.

"But there are a lot of us who won't let that happen." The dragon searched my face. "We also appreciate humans and this Earth. You possess emotions that have more power than you know." Her head jerked toward my chest. "I sense the strength of your heart." She smiled. "It's mighty."

I placed a hand over my chest. Fate had linked me to Roar of the Sky in an unimaginable way.

"Why couldn't I have met you sooner? I heard you calling me many times. But the communication wasn't always clear."

"I tried finding my scale for a while. But it liked your energy and remained dormant. Because of the dormancy, I couldn't track it. When it activated, I could connect to you beyond time and space."

"What exactly does that mean?"

"There are spaces, folds, and secret places that exist between the realms and the spiral of time. I know it sounds confusing, and your mind is trying to find logic in what I just said. Don't fret about it." The scales on her body shifted, taking on a teal color.

How could I not try to understand it? My curious mind spun, trying to connect all the dots into one cohesive understanding. Though my mind had trouble grasping the various realms and what she meant by the spiral of time, a deep part of me understood her words.

"You don't have to understand everything, Su. Sometimes, the truth is felt, and that's all that matters. I could reach you because your essa was open to receiving information. Energy can open doorways, but it needs a trigger. Pain, grief, fear, joy—anything that radiates a powerful burst from your heart opens a doorway."

"How did your scale choose me?"

"It resonates with your energy—your essa. Where most people emit gold essa, you naturally have a metallic peach color. My heart scale felt at home with you."

The faint imprint that now looked like a smooth tattoo on my forearm warmed. I couldn't believe how my skin had already healed from the extraction. Even though the scale was no longer physically in me, its energy still lingered.

Sighing, the dragon walked over to the other side, where there was more room for her to sprawl her immense form.

Once settled, she said, "You need to learn how to protect those doorways. Create a filter, or else anything can come through. Some things are deadly and irreversible."

"Like a possession? Like the Soul Extractors?"

"That's one example."

I thought of the pain I felt at Luzi's death. The anger and vengeance had twisted my gut and burned my chest. "A little girl died because she wanted to save me. She was just a child." Tears welled in my eyes. "That's not justice."

"I know." She nodded. "Justice is a category up for debate. If it were that easy, we would have no wars. I'd just eliminate all the darkness in one sweep."

"Why won't you?"

"Because I'd be inserting myself into a situation already written in the stars. There are cosmic laws we all must abide by. Free will is something we can't touch." Her eyes softened on me. "Luzi chose to face those monsters. She chose to help you. Her choices led to certain results. The darkness has found ways to manipulate free will, but there are consequences for those as well." Her scales rippled. "Sometimes justice takes longer to show up. But it eventually arrives."

My shoulders sagged; I felt helpless. I didn't comprehend what went on in the dragon's world or the diplomacy she had to deal with. Why couldn't life be simple? I'd learned that life had so many gray areas filled with dangerous traps.

"Luzi's death changed your energy. Your grief broke through the barriers between the realms, so I took that opportunity to create a rift in space for you to escape."

"Why didn't you save her?" I asked.

"Because it would change a part of history that isn't mine to play with. Luzi's contribution to this world ended there because it has served its purpose."

"What purpose is that?" Anger rose in me at how she made the life of a child sound meaningless. "Every life is important."

"I didn't say it wasn't. We all have a purpose—a role—in this life. What we do is a cause and effect to something else. I'm not trying to belittle Luzi's death at all. Trust me." The warmth in her voice washed over me. "Luzi had an important role, and she completed it. She has my admiration and respect. I'm only trying to explain how things work from a macrocosmic perspective."

The dragon was using words I didn't fully grasp, but I assumed she meant something beyond the world I lived in.

"Know that Luzi is in a happier place now." The dragon's eyes crinkled as though she were smiling. "She's already prepared for her next role in another world."

A spark of relief and joy burst inside me. "Really? You can see that?"

"I can. Remember those images you saw in the hallway?"

I nodded, recalling the strange people in odd clothing.

"Those are real-life occurrences from the past, present, and future. For your world and beyond."

I sucked in a breath at the astounding revelation. "How's that possible?"

"Anything is possible in the quantum field. Again, you don't need to understand it. It's energy that connects one thing to every-thing. The Infinara Matrix exists within this field."

My mind already felt full to bursting—I didn't know *how* to process what she just told me.

"Human emotions fascinate me," she said.

"Why?"

"Because they're powerful. They have possibilities you can't even imagine."

Though I understood a portion of what the dragon explained, it still confused me. Didn't she interfere with life's events when she created an escape for me and Hung?

As though she sensed my thoughts, she said, "I would think the same thing. But you see, you weren't meant to die at that moment. One of your purposes was to return my scale so I could ensure a healthy birth for my babies. The world needs you, and they also need these new dragons." She looked down at her belly. "So I'll do what I can to deliver them."

I wasn't sure if I'd ever understand the laws of the universe. At a glance, life seemed so unfair. I'd witnessed innocent people die for no reason. And I'd seen horrible people who committed heinous crimes go unpunished. It was hard to believe in faith and justice.

The dragon tilted its head. "Things are happening behind the scenes that are beyond me and you, Su. Don't fret about knowing everything. No one knows everything. Even the gods and goddesses." She looked up at the opening and the night sky moving around. Shooting stars shot in every direction. "Just know that there's a plan within a plan within a plan. That plan has many hidden layers that aren't for us to know. We can only do our best with what we're given. The true compass is our hearts." Her horns glowed. "You have a strong and genuine heart. Keep it that way, and it will guide you."

I placed a hand on my chest, feeling my heart thumping.

Her eyes sparked. "You didn't answer my question."

I wasn't trying to avoid her question about my feelings for Hung. I'd never loved anyone like him. I loved him—had loved him for a while now. But the emotion became stronger as I got to know him.

I feared that if I declared my love for him, that knowledge would place him in danger. I knew it was a stupid idea to think that. But the people I loved all ended up dead. My parents died to ruthless thieves, and Luzi died from being possessed.

Should I let fear stop me from living life to the fullest? If my parents were alive, they'd tell me to boldly state my desires. If Luzi had a passion, I'd ensure she declared it. I'd wanted to learn kung fu and achieved that by not allowing fear to hold me back. Loving a man was no different.

Feeling hopeful, I declared, "I do love him." I looked into her curious eyes, which had turned into a night sky with stars. "Do you have someone you love?" I stared at her belly, rising and falling with her breath.

"My mate is fighting a cosmic battle right now so I can be here to rest."

"Oh." I hadn't expected that news. "Is someone helping him?"

"Yes," she said, but I could see the worry in her eyes. A roundness shifted in her belly, and she winced and released a soft roar. "They're coming any day now."

"Your dragon eggs?" I walked over to stand at her belly, placing my hand on her scales.

A swooshing noise sounded above us. I glanced up and saw swirling energy. The next thing I knew, Tempo dropped from the opening and plopped to the ground. Then Hung appeared in the opening and floated down to stand in front of me, looking distraught.

Relief settled in me as I rushed over to him. "Are you all right?" I saw the bloodstains from a gash on his shoulder. "What happened?"

He wrapped an arm around me, placed his head on top of mine, and inhaled my scent. Then he drew back, looking at me. "I was swarmed by Soul Extractors."

I glanced around, trying to find herbal plants to patch up his wounds.

"He'll be fine," said Roar of the Sky. "The Infinara Guards said you were a fantastic fighter.

"What did she say?" Hung shot the dragon with an irritated look.

I told him, and he huffed, "You mean the Soul Extractor wolves who took a bite out of me?"

CHAPTER FORTY-SIX

HUNG

THE TWO PAILS landed with a loud thud beside me. Both were filled with water to the brim, and not a drop of water splashed to the floor. Not even a drop was spilled when I came back through the wind tunnel with Tempo. The rabbit didn't even look scared as it was flipped up, down, and sideways. Despite the wild motion, the rabbit remained at my eye level throughout the transportation. Even though it was lighter, it landed before me. I should have fallen before it. To add to my annoyance, bugs the size of bees now buzzed around me. I swatted at them, but they dodged my attack. Then they entered each ear and stung me!

Fucking hell!

"They just stung me!" I exclaimed with a curse.

Anger pumped through me as I reached for the sword on my back, but it wasn't there. I'd lost it when I was whipped into the wind tunnel.

I wanted to smash the damn bugs against the wall, but they were too fast. Then they had the audacity to hover in front of me after the sting. They had six iridescent wings and eyes that glared at me. They also had geometric designs on their bodies—and a long stinger that gleamed. I wanted to stomp on them.

"Let me see." Su examined my ears, one after the other.

"They're not swollen. No rashes or anything that looks like you might have an adverse reaction. Do your ears hurt?"

"They shouldn't," said the dragon.

I blinked and whipped my face toward the creature. "Say that again."

The dragon repeated the words.

My mouth dropped open. "I can hear you now."

"That's a gift from me and my buzzing friends. You can now understand the cosmic language."

The bees flew off somewhere.

It was strange to hear the dragon's voice. Magnetic, regal, mystical, and warm.

"Why did your Infinara Guards attack me?"

"You passed the test." The dragonfly etching on its forehead glowed.

"What test?"

"For one, you need to earn your ability to understand the cosmic language. It's not a gift I give out easily. Two, it proves your dedication to her."

I narrowed my eyes. "You could've just asked me, and I would've told you."

She laughed. "Actions are more believable than words, warrior."

"Why did you send me to the desert to retrieve water for Su?"

"Did I?" The dragon's eye squinted with amusement. "I remembered Su was feeling sick, and I simply asked if you could retrieve water from the stream. I didn't give a reason why I needed it."

I replayed the scene in my head. She was right. I'd assumed it was for Su. I wasn't sure how to react to this cunning dragon. Should I be angry or grateful to her? She obviously saved us and cared about Su. But the battle with her guards and the damn pails irritated the hell out of me. I only had so much patience.

She'd been right. I was consumed with Su's well-being. It didn't even occur to me her request meant something else.

"What caused her dizziness, then?"

"The scale extraction was a traumatic experience for her body." The dragon's eyes settled on me. "It had been embedded in her for years, so her body was used to it. When it suddenly left, the body had to adjust itself quickly. This drastic change caused a temporary imbalance. She's okay now."

I swept my gaze over Su's body, and she smiled. "I'm okay."

"If the water isn't for Su, who's it for?" I asked.

"Me," said the dragon as she shifted. Her belly appeared even larger and her breathing had changed.

Su rushed over to her stomach, which glowed. "Are you okay?"

The dragon winced as her serpentine body unwound itself. The tail curled forward, revealing the leaves at the tip. They all shook, creating a powerful vibration that filled the room.

"What's going on with your tail?" I asked.

"Please bring over the pails of water," the dragon asked me and then looked at Su. "The eggs are coming sooner than expected."

"Is everything okay? What accelerated it?" Su asked.

"Remember what I said? That no one knows everything?"

"Yes."

"This is one of those moments." She laughed and winced. "I guess they're just ready."

I placed the pails closer to Su and looked up at the dragon. "Can I help with anything?"

"Yes," she said as her tail flicked up and around. "When you see the flames on my tail, douse them with that water."

What? An awful image popped into my head, and I wanted to ask her for clarification, but it was too late. Flames burst from each of the five leaflike attachments to the tail.

The dragon roared, and her breathing increased as flames grew from each leaflet, each offering a different color.

I lifted one pail and tossed water over the flames. Water immediately refilled the pail. Droplets bounced off the flames like a dance. Colorful essas from the tail traveled around the dragon's body to settle on her belly. The dragon's body trembled, and she growled.

"Are you in pain?" Su rubbed her hand over the dragon's belly. "What should I do?"

"It's hard being a female, you know?"

Su laughed and flicked a glance my way.

"I'm still learning," I said. Women's emotions and the mysteries of their bodies baffled me.

The dragon let out a laugh. "Thanks for trying to make this experience more tolerable, Hung."

This was the first time she addressed me by my first name.

The dragon turned to Su and let out a slow breath. "When the eggs arrive, please help me secure them in a safe place. I might not be conscious." Then she looked at me. "I need you to help wash the eggs using the water from the other pail."

I nodded. "Okay."

The water wrapped itself around the tail like a magical balm, slowing down the flames.

I'd never seen a chicken give birth, never mind a dragon. I assumed her body was transforming on the inside.

"Is it always this painful?" I asked.

"This birth is different." The dragon said, looking tired.

"How?" Su asked.

"The six eggs are gifts from the Cosmos to Earth. They are drawing essas from the leaflets on my tail. Each leaf is connected to one of the five elements of life: fire, water, earth, air, and ether."

"What's ether?" Su asked. "And why isn't there an element for wood?"

"We consider wood as part of the earth element. Ether is space, essa, sound, spirit, emptiness, and the Cosmos—however you want to look at it. It lives within the invisible plane. It energizes and empowers all the other elements."

"The life force within a life force," I said, understanding her.

The dragon gave me a light nod as a burst of energy coursed

through her. A roar escaped her mouth, and the ground trembled. Sparkles of light surrounded her belly.

I didn't know what to do. I took a few steps away but stayed close enough to help if necessary. I turned away, giving the mother dragon privacy as Su worked on her. Another roar erupted, followed by heavy breathing.

"Hung! Can you help me? The first egg is here!"

I'd never been present for any kind of birth. Nerves spiraled in me, but I rushed over to assist Su. The textured blue egg was about half the size of Su. It sat beside its mother with goo all over it. I spotted a pile of cloth beside Tempo, who looked as astounded as I was.

More roars filled the space.

I grabbed a cloth and brought the pail of water closer. Dipping the cloth into the water, I cleaned the blue egg. Energy zinged around it, and it had intricate geometric designs on its surface.

When I finished and turned, five more textured eggs surrounded Su, glowing in green, red, orange, yellow, and purple.

I looked at the exhausted dragon, who had fallen asleep. A quiet energy hummed from her and the room.

The tension in my body relaxed.

"Are you all right?" I asked Su, dabbing the sweat from her face.

"Yes." She smiled, looking at the eggs. "We just delivered six new baby dragons."

CHAPTER FORTY-SEVEN

HUNG

THE CASUAL WAY she said those words made it seem like she'd done this many times before. But we both knew how special this experience was.

When I had a quiet moment to myself, I'd reflect on this magical day. How fate had lured Su and me to meet this magnificent dragon who shared her wisdom with us. We got to be a part of her offspring's journey into life.

"How does it feel to be a midwife-warrior?" Su smirked and placed two hands on her hips as she stared at the eggs that still needed to be cleaned.

"I don't know yet," I said. "I guess there's a first for everything. You did most of the work."

"It's an unforgettable experience." She looked at me. "We helped deliver these dragon eggs. How many people can say that?"

Tempo hopped around the eggs, sniffling. Su patted its head, and it responded with a lovely sound.

"Let me help you clean them." Su grabbed a cloth.

It took us some time to clean all the giant eggs. Once we were done, Tempo used its magic to help us roll the eggs to the grassy area near the dragon. The magic lifted the eggs above the ground, ensuring we didn't accidentally crack or drop any eggs. Once situated, I dug up some bushes to create a boundary, preventing the eggs from rolling elsewhere. A powerful energy pulsed from the eggs.

"Do you think they'll look the same?" Su asked, washing her hands in the water that somehow purified itself even though I'd been dipping the dirty cloth into it. The water also refilled itself for our unlimited usage.

"No." I joined her and washed my hands, absorbing the vibrant energy of the water.

"I think they'll look different. Each one will have a unique quality to them."

"Why do you think this?" I asked.

"Because of what she said earlier." She glanced over at the mother dragon, who was still sound asleep. "This is a different kind of birth empowered by all the elements. Their birth is significant."

We both sat against the wall, taking a moment to breathe.

"Are you tired?" I asked. "You can sleep. I'll keep an eye on the eggs."

I wrapped an arm around her, and she placed her head on my shoulder.

Su tilted her head up at me. "Sorry you had to go through all that to retrieve water for me, even though it wasn't for me."

"Are you still dizzy?"

"No."

I kissed her head, remembering what I'd admitted to myself in the desert.

Tell her.

Should I share it with her now? Was it better to wait? What would happen when we returned to Lin Din Ni? Would we be too busy fighting the Soul Extractors? If I didn't tell her now, when would be a good time?

Stop doubting yourself.

A strategy I'd used in battle sprung to mind. What would I do if an opportunity presented itself for my army to apprehend their enemy?

"I'd do anything for the woman I love."

A beat passed, and silence surrounded us except for the dragon's snoring. Even Tempo had fallen asleep beside the eggs, looking like a cute guardian.

Su sat up, placed a hand on either side of my face, and smiled warmly. "What did you say?"

She heard me. I could see the mischievous gleam in her eyes.

"I love you, my wildflower." The words flowed out of me effortlessly. I supposed when you told the truth, things came easy.

But an ounce of self-doubt stirred in me. What if she didn't feel the same way? What if she thought things were moving too fast?

I'd never been in this situation before, so I didn't have a backup plan. This wasn't a war strategy where I had a map of the terrain and knew where to go if one path didn't work out.

I had no clue about relationships. This wasn't a casual fling that I was used to.

Smiling, Su continued to stare at me while her fingers traced my jawline.

"Are you sure?" she asked, bringing her face closer to mine.

"Never been more certain about anything in my life," I admitted.

That confession sparked something in my chest. I could feel my heart shift as though windows from it burst free from whatever had held them closed.

A flood of joy poured out of me, energizing my body. The experience reminded me of how the dragon—despite its immense power and size—trembled from the elements coursing through its body. There were forces beyond us that were incomprehensible.

An expression I couldn't read splashed onto Su's face. Then

she pressed her lips to me. The kiss was gentle, but I felt it everywhere.

Su drew back with tears in her eyes.

Concerned, I opened my mouth to ask, but she pressed a finger to my lips.

"I'm okay," she said. "I'm just overwhelmed with emotions." She looked me in the eye. "I love you too."

Another wave of energy erupted from my heart. I grinned, repeating her words. "Are you sure?"

She laughed and nodded as her face remained serious. "I've been in love with you for a long time. I never thought it was possible for us."

"Why?"

"Because you're a well-respected general who could have any woman he wanted. Countless noble daughters want you to marry them. So being with you has only been a dream until recently."

"There's no nobility that could compare to you, Su." I took her hand and kissed it. "You reign supreme in my heart."

She was the perfect talisman that brought me luck, hope, courage, and protection—all the virtues a warrior needed for survival.

More tears flowed from her, and she threw her arms around me. We embraced each other, letting this moment settle in us.

"Are you done with the heartfelt talk?" Roar of the Sky asked.

Su gasped and drew back, looking embarrassed. "I thought you were asleep. How are you feeling?"

"I was asleep, but my ears are always open, listening to things that happen here and there."

Su flicked me a glance, probably grateful we didn't do anything else besides kissing and pouring our hearts out to each other.

"There's no need to be embarrassed. I've lived a long time, and I've seen and heard everything. Love is the most powerful energy in the Cosmos." The dragon lifted her head to look at her safe eggs.

"They're beautiful," Su said.

The dragon nodded as she examined them. "Life is a miracle, isn't it? The power of a new life and its potential is incredible. My babies will have a monumental task to fulfill when the time calls for them."

"When will they hatch?" I asked.

"Whenever they're ready to explore this world." She pressed her nose to each of them. "Each egg resonates with a certain energy—an essa that calls to it. They'll respond appropriately." She looked at Su. "Just like how your energy responded to mine, and vice versa."

"So they're meant for someone?" Su asked.

The dragon nodded. "Remember what I said about the plan within a plan? My pregnancy was a miracle in itself. I knew the moment I conceived them. My mate felt it too. Together, we assisted a multidimensional conception allowing dragons that don't look like me to come alive. The Cosmos has a plan, and I was merely a vessel."

That idea baffled me. How could an animal give birth to a different species? The dragon looked at me as though seeing the question in my eyes.

"Nothing moves faster than the speed of light. *Nothing.*" She glanced toward the sky. "This is why there's an intricate plan with so many layers intertwined. The Cosmos is the most intelligent choreographer. Sometimes things make no sense, but it will align you with life's perfect dance."

"It's hard to see life that way when innocent people are dying in front of you," Su said.

"I know," the dragon replied. "I don't have all the answers for why suffering exists. All I know is that with each pain, a new gem is born in the earth, a new star is created in the Cosmos, and a new petal buds from the bloom of your heart."

When my men died in a battle, a piece of my soul broke. I supposed seeing it from the dragon's perspective made things easier to endure.

Su remained silent, probably trying to process the wise dragon's wisdom.

"Gems are made from extreme pressure. The more pressure, the rarer the gem." The dragon moved her head closer to Su. "Your heart cracked open when your parents died. That opening radiated a powerful energy that called to the scale in my heart." Then the dragon turned her attention to me. "The sorrow for your parents and the grief for your men also opened your heart." Her eyes met mine and then Su's. "Your essas understand each other on an unfathomable level."

I placed a comforting hand on Su's back, and she smiled warmly.

Tempo made a sound, hopping to the dragon's foot and back to the eggs. The ears perked and darted in several directions.

"Thank you, Tempo." The dragon looked at us. "It's time for you to return home."

"What happened?" I asked.

"Tempo's ears can hear things from the various directions in this world and others. He said the darkness just broke through an energy barrier protecting Luklum. Your people need you."

Tempo hopped to my foot and then Su, making adorable sounds.

"Thanks for accompanying us." I bent down to pet it. "Why can't I understand you?"

"Tempo is from a different dimensional matrix. His energy differs from mine. But you will hear him again."

"What do you mean? I heard him before?"

The dragon offered a slow nod. "During your meditation. You overheard our conversation. That was when I located your energy."

Revelation splashed onto Su's face. "I remember now! But I thought it was a little boy with that adorable voice. But his words made him sound old."

Tempo's ears perked with amusement as it stared at Su.

The dragon laughed. "He *is* an old male inside a cute body. Tempo is an immortal from the thirtieth-dimensional matrix."

Thirtieth? I couldn't even fathom the idea. "What dimension do we live in?" I gestured to me and Su.

"Right now, Earth exists on a third-dimensional matrix."

"That's it?" Su gasped. "No wonder we have so much to learn."

"In time, it'll strengthen to a fourth and even fifth-dimensional matrix. But it won't happen during your lifetime."

I knew we had to get going, but I still had questions. "What do the higher dimensions mean?"

"The higher the dimension, the higher the frequency." The dragon lifted her claws. "But that doesn't mean we don't have problems. We just have different problems. Imagine a being that can maneuver around a higher dimension but has a dark agenda. What does that mean?"

"He will create bigger issues," I said as my mind wandered to the being with the human face and serpent body that Emperor Tang had encountered.

"Did you send Tempo to find us?" Su gathered the rabbit into her arms, and he snuggled there like a baby. "I saw him in the woods years ago."

"He's been my friend for a long time. He knew I was searching for my missing scale, so he was helping me track you down. But the energies didn't align for better communication until recently. Only those whose energy resonates with Tempo can see him."

A swooshing noise sounded to my right. I turned and saw my sword with its scabbard flying toward me. Reaching up, I clasped my hand over it. I remembered losing the sword but didn't know when I'd lost the scabbard. It was probably during my fight with the fake Soul Extractors.

"Thought I lost you." I drew the sword.

Power thrummed from it as the brilliance of the blade brightened more than I remembered. I swung it, and power sliced through the space like a bolt of lightning.

"That's different," Su said, watching me while still petting Tempo.

I met the dragon's gaze. "What did you do to my sword?"

"Added power to it. Your sword has been dipped in the Infinara Pond. It's a cosmic body of water collected from the ether. This sacred water resonates with Luklum's fulgurite stone."

"Thank you," I said, sliding the sword back into its scabbard.

"You're welcome. Everything you experienced while you were here confirmed why you're with Su." She looked at each of us. "Your essas complement each other in a way I haven't seen before. It's powerful and magical."

I remembered Su saving me by yanking at my essa as if it were a rope. So I asked the dragon for clarification.

"When the heart is involved, anything is possible. She transformed the essa with her heart. She turned it peach too."

Su said she'd been in love with me for some time. Perhaps in that dire moment, fear opened her heart.

Tempo hopped out of her arms. "I don't know how to do that again." She glanced at her hands.

"That's something for you to learn on your own. I think you just created your own martial arts skill."

Su's eyes widened with disbelief. I could see the joy bursting inside her. She'd always wanted to learn kung fu and pave her own path. She'd developed her own technique without knowing.

A chill overcame us, and I shivered. "What's that?"

"The darkness that's in Luklum now. You should head back."

"Will you be okay?" Su asked.

"Don't worry about me." The dragon smiled. "This is a sacred space no one can enter without my permission. Tempo will keep watch over the eggs. I have some things to do."

"You just gave birth," Su said, looking worried. "Your body needs to rest."

"My nap did just that. A dragon's body differs from that of humans. I'll be fine. *Go.*"

A rift opened in the space in front of us. I clasped Su's hand, moving toward it.

"There's going to be a shift in time. Don't be alarmed. You'll catch up just fine."

"Will we see you again?" Su asked.

"You won't be able to get rid of me," she said, flicking a claw at us, sending a powerful energy that tossed us into the rift.

CHAPTER FORTY-EIGHT

SU

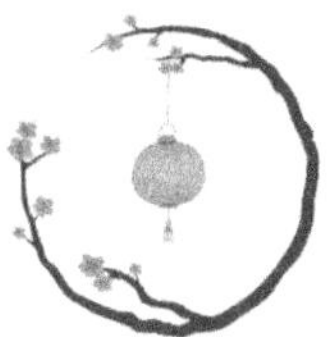

I GRIPPED HUNG'S HAND, thinking it was a repeat experience from the last time we went through a rift. But we stepped through and onto a dirt path right away. There was no tunnel filled with magical things to walk through. No unique beings who lived inside fruits greeted us.

The rift closed immediately. And just like that, we were transported back to Luklum.

"Do you think we'll see her again?" I asked.

He squeezed my hand. "She said you can't get rid of her, so yes. You're connected to her. Maybe you'll hear her in your mind soon."

"But that was because of her scale. Now that she has it, she doesn't need to search for it." I didn't know why, but I missed her already.

I glanced at the slight imprint on my arm. The flower mandala was still there. Roar of the Sky was like a friend who had been with me for a long time, even though I didn't truly get to know her until now.

"I don't think we should mention anything about meeting her to anyone," Hung said.

"Why?"

"Roar of the Sky said the darkness had broken through a barrier in Luklum, which means it could be anywhere." The lines on his forehead deepened. "We don't know who could be a Soul Extractor or a dark being."

My stomach knotted. "They could hide their possession." Then I glanced at his sword. "Do you think your sword can find the dark energy?"

He looked over his shoulder at the sword slung over his back. "Yes, but I don't want to make it too obvious. If they know that we know, it could make them more difficult to lure out. I need to find out how the darkness broke through. So we need to play the game as though we know nothing."

Hung had been in many battles; he knew how to maneuver these dangerous scenarios better than I could. I imagined Yeeva, Healer Churan, or Yunxi being possessed and felt sick to my stomach. I thought of Luzi. I didn't want those I loved to die.

"It seems like the safest path for us," I said. "I don't think anyone would believe we met a dragon if we told them."

"It'll create an uproar. The darkness will take advantage of any chaos," Hung said, assuming the demeanor of a general again.

"Okay." I glanced around the familiar path just outside of the Market Square. Noises boomed in the distance.

Sadness overcame me as I figured out how to inform Healer Churan and Yunxi about Luzi's death. "I want to create a memorial for Luzi." Anger and vengeance sparked again as I remembered what the darkness had done to her.

Understanding, he embraced me. "I'll help you."

As we walked toward the Market Square, a couple strode by.

"General Wen! It's so good to see you back," said the man pushing a wagon full of vegetables.

"I didn't believe the rumor that you were dead," said the woman carrying a basket of rambutan fruits.

"That's an awful rumor," I said, wondering what they said about me. We'd only been gone for a little over a week, most of it traveling.

The lady placed a hand on her curvy hip. "That's what I said. When no one saw you for the last three months, people started whispering." She looked at me. "We missed you at the City Apothecary. Everyone was worried about you. Some said that you were kidnapped by the bandits and killed."

We'd been gone for *three* months?

My jaw dropped, and I stole a glance at Hung, who wore an impassive expression.

"People like to make up stories to entertain themselves," he said. "As you can see, Su and I are safe and well." He clasped my hand. "Without Su's help, I wouldn't have escaped the bandits. She helped me kill a lot of them. It took us time to escape them. Sorry to worry everyone. We didn't have time to send a notice back."

"It's fine. We're glad you killed those evil bandits. They deserve to die." The woman glanced at our joined hands and smiled at her husband. "You make a great couple, by the way."

"Thank you," Hung said.

"We'll see you later," said the man. "We have a lot to prepare for the Lantern Blessing Festival in five days."

As the couple walked off, Hung and I slowed our steps. His hand was still clasped in mine.

"Now everyone knows we're together," I said.

People had probably assumed something was going on when I started my martial arts lessons with him.

He kissed my hand. "That's the idea. It will stop all the rumors."

Though I wasn't worried about our relationship, my heart warmed that he wanted everyone to know about us.

"I'll keep searching for an antidote for you."

"It's not a priority. I feel fine."

He looked at me. "It's better to be safe than sorry."

I knew he wouldn't budge and dropped the subject. My mind wandered back to the revelation that we'd experienced a time jump.

"I can't believe we've been gone for three months!" I exclaimed.

"The dragon warned us about the time difference," he said. "It makes sense. We were in a different realm."

It still baffled me.

"I'll walk you back to the apothecary. Then I'm heading to my office to meet with Kai. I'm sure he has questions for me."

Hung came up with a story that was more of a half-truth to tell people when they asked about our disappearance. He wanted to make sure our stories matched to prevent more rumors.

"We'll resume our lessons in two days. Same time at my place. If anything changes, I'll let you know."

I didn't know why, but I immediately thought of how he'd touched me during my first class at his villa.

"Are you sure you'll be training me *appropriately*?"

A smirk slid onto his lips. "That depends on how well you've improved on the lessons."

I laughed, needing the teasing more than I realized. There had been too much death and sorrow around us recently.

"I've been a good student, *Sifu*." I smiled. "I've been practicing my kung fu and strengthening my muscles whenever I had time."

His eyes gleamed with pride. "My determined student will soon surpass her teacher."

My lips twisted with amusement. "I yearn for the day when my warrior submits to me."

He laughed and kissed me on the cheek. "I'd love to surrender to you and let you have your way with me."

Lovely images popped into my mind, making me blush.

"I can't wait for the Lantern Blessing Festival." I squeezed his hand. "Hopefully, the atmosphere will generate some positive energy."

"Our first festival together." He gripped my hand tighter, swinging it back and forth as we headed into the Market Square.

Handholding was usually reserved for private settings. It

wasn't customary for a respectable man and woman to hold hands in public. I was glad my warrior didn't care when people whispered and giggled as we walked by. He gave them one look, and they turned the other way.

I loved how Hung had redefined the word respect. By doing so, he also placed me on a respectable pedestal.

CHAPTER FORTY-NINE

HUNG

AFTER A QUICK VISIT to the Military Pavilion and reassuring my men that I was safe, I walked to my office. My sword had thrummed on my back since I walked through the Market Square. This confirmed that the dark lurked in every corner.

More people had gone missing in Luklum since my departure. No one had found their bodies. Could this be the darkness that penetrated the capital?

I thought about Luzi and her family's demise. I had to eliminate this darkness. But how? I needed to visit the Emperor to update him. He was probably worried I'd succumbed to the Soul Extractors since he knew I was heading to the Emerald Song Valley.

I placed my sword on the table as a knock sounded on my door.

"Come in, Kai," I said, recognizing the way he pounded on the door with urgency.

Kai entered, clasped a hand to his chest, and bowed in greeting. Then he stood in front of my desk. "Where the hell did you go? We've been searching for you."

All formalities went out the window. I didn't mind because we were like brothers. I understood the concern on his face.

"Sorry. I was stuck battling some powerful Soul Extractors. While escaping, we entered this strange place with a time warp. As soon as we got out, it was months later."

I didn't want to lie to him, but I had to keep my story consistent and light on the details. How would Kai react if he knew the truth? Besides, I wanted him to focus on protecting the capital.

"The fuck!" He stared at me. "Are you sure you're okay? Did something happen while you were in the time warp?"

I rose and walked around my desk so he could see me. "I'm fine. See? Su helped me kill a Bloodshade assassin."

"Our men fought a rebel group along the Green Fog River. They were apprehended quickly. I heard the military camps from the other generals have been battling the onslaught of new rebel groups. So far, we've been successful at holding them off."

"Any more signs of Soul Extractors?" I asked.

Had the Emperor discovered a way to help the army fight off the Soul Extractors? We had discussed it during our council meeting. I had assumed I'd return to help him figure it out.

"Not in the city," he sighed. "We encountered one near the Green Fog River, though. It extracted one of our soldier's souls. I saw it happen. A possessed man placed a hand over Boli's head, extracting his life force, which empowered the Soul Extractor."

"So that's how the possession occurs."

"Looks like it," Kai said. "I took some men to the river because a traveler had discovered Tao's sword discarded near the Green Fog Lake."

"I thought he was supposed to be in Ming Shan." Concern tightened my stomach. I'd planned on searching for him, but the turn of events brought me back to the capital.

"Did you find anything when you were there?"

"I didn't have time to go there yet."

"I'll make a trip to Green Fog Lake."

"I'm coming with you this time. Don't want you disappearing again. I need you here in Luklum—if anything to keep Lina at bay. She's been visiting the military camp *every* single week, asking if you were back. She's worried about you. Ren too. Does she know about you and Su?"

"She should. If she comes again, send her my way."

"We need to prepare for the Lantern Blessing Festival too. But with so many deaths and people missing, I'm not in the mood to celebrate."

"But we have to," I said, understanding where he was coming from. War and death had hardened me. My perspective on life had been dark until Su came along and showed me the possibilities of hope. "The people need it. We don't want them to panic. We need to give them hope."

Love is the most powerful energy in the Cosmos.

Certain things were out of our control. We could only respond to the information available to us. Fighting the darkness required strategy, patience, and diligence. Most of all, it required love—the most powerful weapon.

Love for my land and the people ran through me. More than that, my love for Su empowered me. I wanted a life with her here. I wanted her to be my wife.

Kai spent the next hour reviewing the security plan for the festival with me.

"Increase the guards around the Market Square." I pointed to the map. "Position some guards near the lake and the palace. Have them dress as normal civilians to blend in while staying alert too."

"Any luck on finding the antidote for Su?"

"No. I found a village of Soul Extractors at Emerald Song. Su hasn't shown any symptoms, so hopefully, her body has fought it." I didn't want to mention the dizziness Su had experienced. This wasn't the right time to discuss the cave and the dragon.

"That's good." He looked at me. "Do you need anything from me? I'm going to head out to get some incense for my room."

I arched an eyebrow at his new interest. For as long as I'd known him, Kai had never had incense in his room. Apparently, something important happened while I was gone.

"You were never into incense before. What happened?"

He waved a hand. "With all that's happened lately, I need to clear my space. Sage and palo santo can dispel evil energies."

"Is that right?" I smirked. "Is there something you want to share?"

"No. Do you need any palo santo?"

"No thanks. I have my talisman with me." I gestured to the round charm dangling from my belt. "Didn't you get one from the apothecary? I paid for a talisman for every soldier."

"I got a tiger one." He beamed.

Who had caught his interest? I supposed he'd tell me when he was ready.

"I don't need anything else from you. Get all the incense you need. I'll be heading over to see the Emperor."

"Shouldn't you be resting?" Kai asked.

"I've been missing for three months. The Emperor will have questions."

I needed to make one stop before visiting the palace.

CHAPTER FIFTY

SU

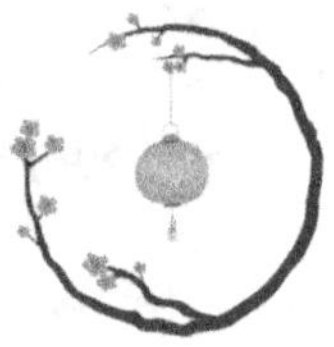

I SAT in the back room with Healer Churan and Yunxi, crying over Luzi's death. We closed the shop for today and tried to keep busy with minor tasks, but our sorrow filled the space. How could we not grieve? Luzi lived with us for a while. She became part of the family. We were supposed to help her recover from her trauma. I'd promised to take her to the Lantern Blessing Festival.

"I should've kept a closer eye on her . . ." Yunxi sniffled.

"It's not your fault. I should've been more diligent too." Healer Churan wiped tears with her sleeve. "That poor girl went through so much. I can't believe they possessed her."

"We went to look for her." Yunxi dabbed her eyes with the back of her hand. "But we couldn't find her."

Her death wouldn't be in vain. I'd make those responsible pay. But I didn't want to share that with my apothecary family. I didn't want them to worry about me too.

"We'll plant a tree in the courtyard for her." Healer Churan glanced outside.

"I love that idea," I said. "She was like our little sister."

"And my adopted daughter." Healer Churan grabbed a handful of herbs and placed them in paper bags. "I'm too old to be her sister." She laughed, changing the energy in the shop.

"You're not old." Yunxi patted Healer Churan's face. "You have better skin than women younger than you. I wish I had your skin. It's flawless."

"Be consistent with your skin routine, and yours will be smooth too." Healer Churan tied up one bag with a loop and started on the next. "I'm forty and haven't been married. People consider me old and past my prime."

"They're just blind and jealous," said Yunxi.

"I don't care what they think." Healer Churan swatted her hand as if a fly had flown nearby. "A woman needs to learn that true happiness is when you're comfortable with yourself. You don't need a man to confirm that." Sadness was etched in her voice.

"Did a man hurt you?" I asked. "Want us to find him and show him the power of healers?" I gripped a pair of shears on the table and snipped the air.

They all laughed.

"I had a lover a long time ago," she said. "But his priority was his career, not me. I don't want to be second place in any man's heart. That kind of relationship won't work for me."

"I want to be *his* priority," Yunxi emphasized. "I want him to think of me day and night." She plucked petals from a rose, preparing them to dry. "Most noble girls just want the comfort of status and power. I think that would make me lonely."

"You need to understand your worth," Healer Churan said. "Once you acknowledge that, other people will value and respect your stance." She smiled at us. "Even if it costs you your relationship."

Was I Hung's priority? He was a general, so he had an important responsibility to the people of Lin Din Ni. They depended on him. Was it selfish to want him to push everything aside for me? Did I want him to do that?

Why were relationships so confusing?

"I think Luzi knew her worth even though she was young," I said. "She knew what was wrong and right, despite the threat and the lies told to her." Tears brimmed in my eyes. "And she held onto that belief to come find me."

Yunxi placed a hand over mine. "We'll never forget her."

Not wanting to cry anymore, I steered the conversation to the battle with the Soul Extractors.

"Please show me how to fight when you have time," Yunxi said.

"We can all practice the basic skills after work in the court-yard," Healer Churan said. "I know some basics."

"You do?" I asked.

"Like you, I was a curious young woman." She smiled. "But I'll still need you to show us the more advanced moves."

"I can show you what I know. I don't consider myself advanced yet. That's going to take time and a lot of practice. But you should prepare yourselves."

I had a sinking feeling that something terrible was about to happen. But I didn't want to worry them.

After a long hot bath to wash away all the negative energy, I sat in my bedroom, flipping through Hung's Dim Mak pamphlet. I hadn't had time to read it since he'd given it to me. Holding the pamphlet to my chest, I smiled like a fool.

What was he doing now? Was he thinking of me? Probably not. I imagined he had a lot of issues to catch up on.

How was Roar of the Sky doing? Was Tempo still watching over the eggs? My experience with the dragon felt like a dream. My skin warmed, and I glanced at the flower mandala imprint on my skin. It now looked like a subtle birthmark on my arm. I closed my eyes, trying to connect to the dragon.

I heard the rush of the wind and eerie cries, saw flashes of mountains. Then a strange blob of darkness appeared in my vision. I tried to hone in on the blob, but my skin prickled. Then I couldn't see it anymore, as though a curtain had been pulled over my eyes. Was Roar of the Sky blocking me from seeing it? Or was it because I'd lost my connection to her and the realm she was in?

I opened my eyes, glancing around my bedroom. Outside the

comfort of this room lay worlds beyond my imagination. I could try to fathom the multiple dimensions the dragon spoke of. When I had looked into the dragon's eyes, I'd seen constellations. So many stars. She carried ancient wisdom that scholars would give anything to know.

I wondered if the Dim Mak technique would work on a dragon. Not that I wanted to try and paralyze her. I was curious about whether I would meet an evil dragon. I doubted it would work because the dragon's anatomy differed from a human's. What if I inadvertently tapped a pressure point that empowered instead of subdued it?

I shivered and shook off the ridiculous thought.

Focus on the human body, Su. Leave other creatures alone.

I flipped to lesson one of the death touch and began reading and practicing. With my knowledge of meridian lines and acupuncture points, I quickly moved to lesson two. This technique could significantly affect the body's energy flow, blocking certain areas to kill the opponent slowly or unblocking energies to release pain. I couldn't stop reading the section on adding power to the touch. That was Hung's special technique, which he'd spent years cultivating. His fingertips had glowed. I wanted to try it.

Calming myself, I inhaled and exhaled. I gathered energy and channeled it to my fingertips. They tingled, and my peach essa flashed on the tips. I gasped excitedly at the sight. Smiling, I continued to practice until exhaustion finally pulled me under.

CHAPTER FIFTY-ONE

HUNG

"YOU WERE RIGHT." I looked over at the Emperor, wearing his noble gown and crown. He'd called for an urgent meeting when he learned of my return. "The darkness has taken over the Emerald Song Valley region."

Only Gong could attend as Three-Eyes was away working on another assignment. The generals weren't in town; they were busy battling bandits along the border. Emperor Tang hadn't figured out an effective way to assist the soldiers. He had planned on using fulgurite to make weapons, but that would have taken too long, and he didn't know if the stone would resonate with the soldiers. What if only a small percentage of weapons could be used? He didn't want to waste the precious stone.

"All those people in Emerald Song Valley were possessed, even the soldiers stationed there. They also had a few adept fighters who were possessed."

A crease deepened on the Emperor's forehead. "The darkness is here."

"In Luklum?" I asked, but I already knew this from the dragon.

He shook his head. "In the palace."

"What? How can you tell?" I asked, looking over at Gong.

His expression told me he was aware of it too. Was that why Three-Eyes wasn't present at the moment? Was he working on something to clear out the darkness?

"I'm going to cancel the archery competition," said the Emperor.

"Why?" Gong asked.

Emperor Tang looked at us and sighed. "I'm weak."

My eyebrows furrowed, studying him. His face appeared strong, and his eyes remained fierce. His posture was straight, and he seemed to be thinking clearly. Nothing appeared abnormal.

"What's wrong?" I asked.

"This darkness is affecting my powers. I don't know how, but I'm getting weak. So is Yeeva." He got out of his chair and walked around the room. "I'm worried about her. Physician Lim says she's fine. But he doesn't know her powers are weak as well."

The Emperor lifted his sleeve, revealing dark veins in his hand. "I've been using my energy to push this darkness out of my system, but it's taking longer than usual. The energy is thick and slimy. It clings to my body."

Concern surged in me as I studied his hand. This wasn't an illness that could be treated by a regular physician or healer. This was dark magic.

"Do you think you were infected when you encountered the darkness in the cave?"

"I don't know." He sighed. "My essa is too weak. It's hard for me to slip through time and space to find out."

Most people knew the Emperor knew martial arts and a powerful technique that could warp time and space. I didn't quite comprehend the experience until recently, when I traveled through a portal with Su to meet the dragon.

Emperor Tang's powers had been passed down to him by his father. With Yeeva's ability to weave and manipulate light, they were a powerful match. What would happen to Lin Din Ni if the world knew of the Emperor and Empress's weakness?

"Does Three-Eyes know about this?" Gong asked.

The Emperor nodded. "He's been removing the negative energy hiding within the cracks of the palace, as well as empowering me. I told him to go rest and recuperate. He'll be back in a few days."

"He can't locate where the darkness is coming from?" I asked.

"It's coming from many places. The cloak of protection I cast around Lin Din Ni has pores in it now. But the extra cloak around the palace is also torn. Something is eating at the protection."

This was probably what Roar of the Sky meant. *Fucking hell.*

I looked over at Gong. "We'll need to notify everyone that the competition will be postponed until a later date."

"People will ask questions," Gong said, grabbing a teacup and spinning it on the table.

The Emperor placed his hands on the table, looking at us with worried eyes. "We'll tell them Empress Jayaatu is pregnant, and the Emperor wants to focus on their first child." He straightened. "We planned to announce her pregnancy at the event, so use that as an excuse."

"That would make the postponement more plausible," I said.

"We need to focus on protecting the country and repairing the holes within the protective cloak. Yeeva is too weak to weave her light energy into it. She needs to conserve her strength for the birth, which is next month."

A weak shield meant more dark energy could enter, affecting everyone. The darkness could pollute the air and contaminate the water sources. Plants and animals would suffer, which would affect our food.

More importantly, what if the Soul Extractors sensed this weakness and brought their army?

I slammed an angry fist on the table. "How could the darkness break through the barrier so easily?"

The Emperor's lips thinned. "I'm trying to figure that out."

"You think we have a mole?"

"Anything is possible at this point." The Emperor sat back

down on his chair. "I've asked the generals to monitor their guards."

"If any of the guards are possessed, it would be hard to tell unless they revealed themselves. The stronger Soul Extractors can conceal their possession well. We need to lure them out."

"You're right," Gong said.

"If you discover I'm . . . possessed, then you must kill me, understand?" The Emperor looked at me and Gong.

I opened my mouth in shock. How could I kill the Emperor? How could anyone in Lin Din Ni follow that insane order?

He opened the engraved box on the table beside him, pulled out an Imperial decree, and gave it to me. "Both of you, read it."

I unrolled the scroll with his regal stamp, read it, and rolled it back up. My heart pounded as the order echoed in my head. The Emperor wanted us to kill him, his wife, and his unborn child if they were possessed.

The situation was more critical than I imagined.

"We keep this between us." Gong turned to me. "Don't share this with anyone. We don't know who's a spy. They could use it to their advantage."

"That's why I'm only showing it to you. Three-Eyes is aware of my plan. So is the Empress." He tossed me a look. "I haven't told the generals. I'll leave that up to you."

"The more people know, the more you're in danger. I won't share this unless it's necessary. We have to lure the Soul Extractors out and kill as many as we can."

"I agree," Gong said. "Right now, they're hiding like spies. We need them to know we're aware of their presence."

"I've got a plan, but I need to talk to Three-Eyes to see if it'll work."

"The Lantern Blessing Festival is coming," said the Emperor. "I don't want the citizens to panic."

"I understand. If my plan works out, we'll lure them out a day or two before the event. But if it falls on that day, we'll take extra precautions and plan accordingly."

The Emperor offered a nod.

Gong leaned into the table. "Are you going to share your elusive plan or force me to fight it out of you?" He flicked me a challenging look.

I was going to wait until I spoke to Three-Eyes before I shared it with them. What was the point in sharing something that might not work? I didn't want to give false hope, but the look on Gong's face and the curiosity of the Emperor told me they needed something to settle their nerves.

"I'll need your help," I said, briefing them on what could either succeed or fail miserably.

CHAPTER FIFTY-TWO

HUNG

AFTER MY MEETING, I walked home, taking my time to scour the area. Nothing appeared different, but the energy had shifted for sure. My sword thrummed in some areas and didn't in others.

Ren and Lina exited a tavern.

"Hung!" She ran up to me, running a hand down my arm. "Where have you been? We were so worried!" She slipped her hand through my arm.

"Why don't you react like that when I'm traveling?" Ren said, looking tired.

"Because you're not in battle. You're a scholar. You travel to teach, recite poems, or visit Dad. There's nothing dangerous about those things."

I didn't know how he dealt with his demanding sister.

He shook his head. "Don't make me sound so useless." He slapped me on my back. "See how important I am to my sister? Where did you go? We should catch up when you have a moment."

A few people walked by, stared at Lina clasping my arm, and whispered. "I thought he was with Healer Su."

I gently unclasped Lina's arm from mine. "We were swarmed

with possessed people. It took a while to escape them and get back here."

"So it's true." She pouted. "You and Su were together."

"She helped me escape."

"You should thank her," Ren said.

She rolled her eyes. "She should've been working at the apothecary instead of roaming around."

"We need courageous women to fight along with us. I would've died if she hadn't been there." I sighed. "There could be more possessed people in the city. We have to be cautious."

Lina gripped my arm again.

Her brother yanked her off. "Stop being so clingy. He's with Su. It'll just make you look desperate."

"They're not married," she said and looked at me. "He can still change his mind."

"I won't change my mind. There are better men out there for you, Lina."

Tears welled in her eyes. "I've loved you since I was a teen! Why are you so cold?" She huffed. "You'll regret it—she's not good enough for you!" Then she darted off.

Ren called after her, but she didn't stop.

"Make sure she gets home safely," he told the two maids who rushed after her.

I blew out a breath. "Sorry."

"You did nothing wrong. Love is a tricky area. She'll be fine after a few days. My father plans on hosting a tournament to find her a decent husband."

I prayed that would ease any pain I'd bestowed upon her.

"Do you have time for some wine?" he asked.

A conversation with my best friend could lighten the stress and mood. We took a seat at an outside vendor selling noodles. My stomach growled, and I dug into my noodle bowl with a pair of chopsticks.

"You haven't eaten yet?" Ren asked, pouring wine into our cups.

"Not yet." I sipped wine from the cup and placed it down. "Been trying to catch up on everything."

"Is it that bad? About the Soul Extractors?" Concern flashed in his eyes. "Have you located Ru Malik and his bandits?"

"The situation in Emerald Song Valley was awful." I told him about the assassin sent to kill me. "He was probably working for Ru Malik."

Ren furrowed his eyebrows. "Is there anything I can do to help? I wish I knew how to fight. Even Su is better than me."

I smiled. "She is."

He laughed. "Maybe I can have her teach me."

I flicked him a look and saw a tinge of jealousy, which I understood. Ren was my best friend, and I didn't have to worry about him being with her. Still, possessiveness overcame me. Su was my woman now. The idea of her teaching him bothered me. They'd be close and . . . I didn't like it.

Did that make me an awful brother-in-arms? Certain lines had to be drawn with relationships.

"I'm kidding," he said, probably reading my hesitation.

"I can teach you." I offered. "Your father is also an excellent warrior."

He waved a hand. "I'm not swift like you. My weapons are a pen and ink."

"Sometimes I wish those were my weapons too." I finished my bowl of noodles. "I'd probably live a longer life if I changed my occupation."

"Then who would win battles for Lin Din Ni?"

A group of men poured out from the nearby tavern, kicking a drunken man who had tripped over his own feet and fallen to the ground.

"I told you not to come into the tavern when we're around," said a man with a pointed black hat.

"S-s-sorry." The drunk pushed himself up, but the three men pounded on him.

I shot out of my seat with Ren and rushed over.

"What's going on?" Ren asked, helping the drunken man. His nose was bleeding.

The three men looked at me, and fear flashed on their faces.

"He . . . he stole from us." The man with a silk outfit jutted a finger at the drunk.

"N-n-o!" the drunk man held up his hands. "I d-d-didn't s-s-steal. I w-w-was just -e-e-eating at a t-t-table."

"What did he steal?" I asked, already knowing the story. It reminded me of my past with Ren. He glared at them as though remembering too.

"Before you answer," I said, looking at them, "know that I will do a thorough investigation. If you lie to me, you *will* be punished to the fullest extent. Do you understand me?"

The three men glanced at each other, terror etched on their faces. Based on their clothing, these men belonged to wealthy families, whereas the drunken man with the stutter came from a working family.

"They n-n-never liked m-m-me," the drunk slurred. "Since w-w-we were in s-s-school. Look w-w-what they d-d-did to m-m-me." He lifted his sleeve and revealed the burn marks on his arm.

I flicked an irritated gaze at the three men.

"It's just a misunderstanding," said the man with a silver tassel dangling on his belt.

"Yes. We were just kids, teasing him," Silk Outfit said.

"We mean no harm." Black Hat forced a smile.

"There's no misunderstanding," Ren said. "You bullied him, and now you're doing it again."

The three men looked uncomfortable.

"*Apologize*," I told them. "If I find out you're still bothering him, I swear your family will pay for your behavior."

Noble families valued their family names and would do anything to keep them pristine. The three men immediately apologized to the drunken man and rushed off.

"Let me know if they bother you again," said Ren. "You can find me at the Imperial Poetry School."

The drunk nodded. "Th-th-thank you." He stumbled off, bracing himself against the brick wall.

"In his condition, he might not make it home safely." Ren looked at me. "I'll walk with him. Are you heading home?"

"Have you seen Three-Eyes? I need to talk to him."

"No. Keep me posted on . . . things," he said, being cautious of those walking by.

After they were out of sight, I wandered the streets of the Market Square. People were putting their food carts away, preparing to go home. Life appeared normal. The citizens just wanted a life where they could feed their families. It wasn't a lot to ask.

From the corner of my eye, a flowing robe moved behind the rows of trees. Was that Three-Eyes?

The wide hood covered his head, so I couldn't see his face. But I was familiar with his movement. The way he shuffled his feet confirmed his identity.

I kept my distance as I followed him along the secluded path most vendors used during the day to transport goods back and forth. Unlike the main road, the path was bumpy and narrow. He came to an opening I was too familiar with.

I remained in the shadows, away from the lanterns dangling on the poles. My eyebrows arched as I watched him enter the Maroon Meadow.

A smirk slid onto my face. I didn't know Three-Eyes visited these places. Emperor Tang said Three-Eyes was recuperating after overexerting himself. Perhaps this was his way of rejuvenation.

I debated entering the tavern but decided to let him relax tonight.

My issue could wait until tomorrow.

CHAPTER FIFTY-THREE

SU

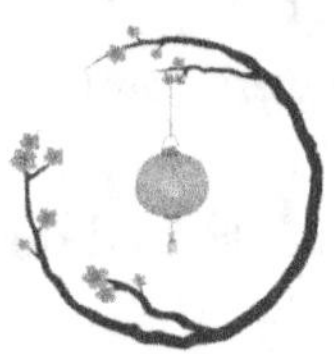

KAI ENTERED the apothecary as I prepared a prenatal herb package for Yeeva.

He walked up to me, handing me a note. "It's from General Wen."

"Thank you," I said.

Kai nodded and walked around the shop.

I ripped the wax seal and opened the letter.

My wild dahlia,

I need to reschedule our lesson for today.
Something urgent came up.
Will see you soon.

An imprint of his seal ended the note.

I grinned, loving this soft side to him—an aspect others didn't get to see. I folded the note and tucked it into the pocket of my tunic.

Kai glanced down the hallway of the exam rooms. A thought bloomed in my head. I'd missed a lot during my time away from my friend.

"Are you looking for someone?" I asked.

"Is Yunxi working today?" he asked.

"She is, but she went to drop off a remedy package to a household. She'll be back soon."

"Do you mind if I wait for her?" he asked.

"No. But she could be a while," I teased. Kai was one of Hung's Elite Guards. It made me smile to know that he and Yunxi had started something special. Yunxi had been attracted to him for some time now. "Is there something I can help you with?"

"Uh . . . no."

The door to the apothecary swung open, and Yunxi walked in.

Kai's face brightened like the sun. Yunxi's expression matched his, and her cheeks bloomed pink. Was that how I looked when Hung was around? I loved seeing that joy in my friend. Love truly changed a person's energy and appearance.

"Healer Churan is out running an errand. She should be back at any moment. I'm going to drop these off for the Empress." I lifted the package to show Yunxi. "The apothecary is all yours." I wiggled my eyebrows as I walked past her. Then I turned to smile at Kai. "Thank you for the message."

He offered a crooked smile, looking a little embarrassed.

As I walked toward the palace, I couldn't help but wonder about what Roar of the Sky had mentioned about the darkness breaking through the protective walls around Luklum. I surveyed the market, which was booming with business and chatter. The sunlight made everything more cheerful. People were preparing for the Lantern Blessing Festival, which was also the harvest full moon. There was so much joy, laughter, and hope in the air.

Was the dragon wrong? I didn't think so, but it was hard to believe any darkness existed in the celebratory atmosphere.

I supposed things weren't always what they seemed.

But I sensed the shift in energy when I entered the courtyard where Yeeva was sitting. The air was unusually heavy.

She spotted me and waddled over. Her belly had grown a lot since I last saw her. She was now around eight months pregnant.

I grabbed her hand, ushering her to the chair. "Sit down. How are you feeling?"

"Fat." She laughed, rubbing her belly. "She's getting so big."

It fascinated me that Yeeva knew her unborn child would be a girl. A mother's bond with her child was beyond my understanding.

I clasped her hand, placing my finger on her pulse. "You haven't been sleeping well?"

"No." She sighed and looked at me. "Something is making me weak. Not the pregnancy, though. The physician confirms the baby is healthy. But my power isn't performing as it should."

Yeeva looked over her flowering bushes, and the glow in the flowers had diminished exponentially. I only saw a few dimly lit flowers in the bush that used to offer a sea of lights.

"I'm channeling all my essa to my baby." She looked at her hand. A spurt of light illuminated but quickly died. "I can't weave power into the plants or the land."

Fear spiraled in me, wondering how I could help Yeeva.

The prenatal packages I brought her would only strengthen her pregnancy. "Is there something I can do to help?"

She placed a hand over mine and squeezed. "Your herbal concoctions and soaps have been helping me stay calm, but your friendship is enough." Her eyes brightened. "I heard a rumor that you disappeared with Hung for a while. What happened?"

I told her the same story everyone else heard. The last thing she needed was more stress.

"People have been talking about your relationship with Hung. Some love the idea, and some don't. Ignore the disapproval from the older folks." She was referring to the age gap between us and our student-teacher relationship. "They're just stuck in their ways. If a dragon roared through the town, they still wouldn't believe it.

Forget the closed-minded people." She bumped shoulders with me. "I mostly hear admiration and applause for you and Hung—a couple that defies the norm."

I laughed, wondering if Hung had heard that.

"You're starting a new trend," Yeeva smiled. "I'm happy for you. Hung needs a woman who can match him in heart and mind. There's no one better than you. He doesn't even look his age."

"True," I said. "He's perfect in every way."

Yeeva laughed, and her stomach jiggled.

A thought occurred to me. "Have you heard of the Infinity Loop?"

"Yes."

"I think you should try it," I said, then described what had happened to Luzi. That loop had somehow disentangled her from the spell of darkness.

"That girl is my hero." Yeeva placed a hand over her heart. "She was so brave to travel that far and *alone* to save you."

Tears filled my eyes, but I didn't want to cry. That would only make Yeeva cry too.

I gripped Yeeva's arm and helped her stand. "Let's walk the Infinity Loop together. We'll loop around the garden."

I didn't fully understand the magic of the Infinity Loop, but it helped Luzi, so it could also help Yeeva.

After a few rounds of walking the wide loop around her garden, Yeeva paused and released a sigh. "You know something? I feel better."

I rubbed circles on her back. "Wonderful. Keep doing it. The walk will also help prepare you for the birth."

"I'd heard about the Infinity Loop, but it didn't even occur to me to practice it."

"You've had a lot of things on your mind. It's understandable."

An unusual sound hummed in the air. "What's that?"

Yeeva sucked in a breath as her eyes smiled. "I haven't heard it hum in a long time. That's a sign."

"What's humming?"

She took my hand, leading me beyond the garden. "Have you seen the blue fulgurite stone?"

"No." My heart raced. "I've always wanted to see it."

I'd only seen weapons made from the stone, like Hung's sword.

"Well, it's time."

The blue fulgurite stone existed in Lin Din Ni. The biggest stone was right beside the palace. We walked along a path with trees and plants. But the brightness in their colors wasn't as vivid. When we arrived at an opening, I gasped at the sight of the massive stone. It looked like a mountain made of gems, with angles jutting out in seemingly every direction. I had envisioned a mound coming from the ground, not something this extraordinary.

"Wow . . ." I glanced up at the stone.

"It's been growing too. Giving birth." She walked over to the side and placed her hand on a section with spears coming out. "These are the new baby fulgurites."

"Could a stone give birth?" I asked.

Yeeva spread out her arms as though giving it a hug. "The stone is a living thing. It has awareness and energy. Like a plant that keeps sprouting."

Of course this could be true. I remembered the fairy Willowwish reading inside a glowing fruit when I walked through the dragon portal. Anything was possible.

I placed my hand on one spear, and it glowed. Fearing I'd done something wrong, I extracted my hand immediately.

Yeeva gasped. "Su, put your hand on it again."

I did, and the spear radiated a peach color, different from the blue that made up the stone.

"It resonates with you. I'm going to have the swordsmith make you a dagger. It's my gift to you."

She explained that the stone only glows when it resonates with an individual's energy. That was why I couldn't use Hung's sword.

"I'll have someone deliver it to you when it's done."

"Thank you." I couldn't wait to see the dagger.

After spending a little more time with Yeeva, I returned to the apothecary. On my way back, I encountered Ren and his sister.

"Su! I'm so glad to see you're well." Ren strode up to me. "I've been meaning to stop by to check on you, but I've been busy."

"Thank you. I'm okay."

Lina stepped beside her brother, whipping me a bitter look.

"Hung told me about the incident," Ren said. "Thank you for protecting him."

Lina rolled her eyes. "So unladylike to chase after a man like that."

Ren turned a disapproving look on his sister. "That's not nice. She *saved* him, remember?"

I let her comment slide. I didn't want her to ruin my day. Why couldn't she be more understanding like her brother?

She flicked her brother an evil stare. "I need to speak to her privately. Can you give us a moment, please?"

Ren looked at me for confirmation. I wasn't in the mood for this, but she and I needed to square things away sooner or later.

"I'll be fine." If she acted up, I would have an excuse to use the Dim Mak on her. Keep her frozen in place for a while so everyone could gawk at her while she screamed for help.

Ren walked over to stand by a vendor selling roasted duck. Lina gestured for me to move to the corner, away from the crowd.

"You should leave him." She crossed her arms.

"Why?" I asked, feeling annoyed but also sorry for her. Why couldn't she let him go?

"He doesn't love you."

I narrowed my eyes at her.

"How do you know?" I wouldn't share that Hung had already told me those special words. I carried them in my heart.

She looked from side to side cautiously. Then she turned her attention to me.

"Did you know he frequents the Maroon Meadow?" Her eyes widened.

Surprise shook me, but I remained calm. How could I be sure she wasn't lying to cause trouble?

"How do you know?"

She glanced over her shoulder at her brother and said, "It doesn't matter. I overheard a private conversation."

Why would Hung visit a well-known men's tavern? Had he been going there before we got together? Was that how he kept himself satisfied? Irritation slid down my back.

Was he still going there?

I shrugged. "Perhaps he's investigating something. Maybe he went to look for one of his men."

She blinked at me. "Do you still want to be with him if he goes there?"

I wouldn't—but I wasn't going to give her the satisfaction of knowing that.

"Would *you*?" I retorted.

She straightened her back. "I've loved him for a long time. We grew up together. Hung and Ren are best friends. So I'll forgive him."

I crossed my arms. "What if he won't ever stop?"

She twisted her lips. "Many men have concubines. As long as I'm his only wife, I'm okay with that. I just want him to be happy."

I knew many emperors and noblemen had concubines. But just because a respectable person did, it didn't mean their actions were right. I would not agree to such a betrayal. I'd rather leave him.

But I knew many women accepted this idea even though deep inside, they knew it was wrong.

"What about your happiness?" I asked.

"If my husband is happy, I'm happy."

I didn't know what to say. Most of all, I didn't understand why she told me all this. What was her agenda?

"I'm not leaving him because of rumors. I'll ask him. And if he still frequents that place, I'll make him pay for the betrayal." I narrowed my eyes at her. "Then I'll leave him."

She gawked at me. "You're brave."

"I just know my worth, Lina," I said. "You should too. If you came here today to bait me into leaving him so you could swoop in, don't bother. Save your energy for something else."

She pursed her lips. "Do you love him?"

"Yes."

With that, I stalked off, leaving her in the corner. Ren called after me, but I ignored him.

As I neared the apothecary, frustration grew, even though I didn't want it to. My heart hurt. I didn't want to enter the apothecary with tears in my eyes, so I found a bench under the willow tree and sat down.

How would he like it if I visited a women's tavern even though I didn't know if one actually existed? Anger surged in me as awful scenarios popped into my head. This was exactly what Lina wanted me to feel. She planted doubts in my mind. She wanted to hurt me, and she succeeded.

Tears brimmed in my eyes, and I let them fall. But I wiped them away quickly in case someone strode by and noticed me. A dark thought trickled into my head. Did he cancel my lesson today because he was meeting someone at the tavern?

There was only one way to find out. I'd stop by the Maroon Meadow this evening to check it out. Renewed with hope and an action plan, I inhaled a deep breath and released it. I shook off any residue of the frustration and headed into the apothecary to plant the cherry blossom for Luzi's memorial. I didn't need Hung to help me. I could plant the tree by myself.

As I used the shovel to puncture the ground, I imagined myself whacking him with a shovel for breaking my heart and lying to me. The violence shocked me.

Give him a chance to explain first. Don't poison Luzi's peaceful cherry blossom tree with dark thoughts.

"We're here to help!" Yunxi's cheerful voice distracted me from my self-loathing.

I pasted a smile on my face to greet her and Healer Churan.

CHAPTER FIFTY-FOUR

HUNG

KAI and I rode our horses to the Green Fog River, searching for Tao. He'd been missing for months. I feared for the worst but clung to hope. After securing the horses to a tree, I walked to the bush where Tao's sword had been found. The sword had a unique design customized for him when he became an Elite Guard. Kai had a similar design.

I glanced toward the river. It wasn't too far. Could Tao have dropped the sword while escaping his enemies? Or had he left it there on purpose? Or had he drowned?

"Have you checked along the river and the lake area in case a body washed up on the shore?"

"We got as close as we could. When we heard the whistling noise, we left."

That was a sign that the River Women were warning us to stay away.

"We didn't want to catch their diseases."

I walked toward the river. Had these secluded people seen what occurred?

My sword didn't heat or make any movement to signify darkness was nearby.

"I'm heading down there."

Kai fell into step with me. "Will you still keep me around if I'm infected with their diseases?"

"I will." I smirked. "But I'm not sure if Yunxi will."

He gasped. "How do you know about us?"

"There are only two young healers at the City Apothecary. One of them is mine. So there's only one left."

"What makes you think it's not Healer Churan?"

"She could be your mother." I stepped over twigs.

"Maybe I like older women," he said with a laugh. "But yeah, Yunxi is with me."

An arrow flew at us, and I dodged it.

"Fuck!" Kai exclaimed, drawing his sword.

I glanced toward the arrow and saw a small riverboat behind some tall bushes.

"We mean no harm," I said, even though I drew my sword. "We just have questions."

More arrows flew toward us, and I deflected them with my sword.

"We need to talk to you, please," I said.

A woman jumped down from a tree branch with a bow and arrow. A section of her face was covered in warts and scars. Another part showed burned skin sagging down to her neck. I now understood what people had said about them. The skin disease had eaten away at their faces. I could imagine what their bodies looked like.

Two women and two men jumped down to stand beside her. They also possessed terrifying faces.

"You need to leave." A woman with a feather hairpin stepped forward. She appeared to be the leader of the group based on how the other women and men stood behind her. She had a long scar on the side of her face.

"Go away!" said the woman with a droopy eye. Her lips only opened halfway because parts of it had melted into her burned skin. "You've caused enough trouble."

I put my sword away and placed my hands in front of me, showing her I didn't mean any harm.

"We're not here to cause trouble. We're looking for our brother. Let me show you his face." I pulled out a drawing of Tao done by the Imperial artist. "Have you seen him?"

The leader took one glance and showed no emotion. "He's not here."

That wasn't my question. Her answer told me everything I needed to know. But I had to play it cautiously. Who were these women and men? Did they have a group of people in hiding waiting to attack me and Kai?

Even if Tao wasn't here, they must have seen something. The two other women exchanged glances, but their facial distortions made it hard to read their expressions.

"He's been missing for a while. We're worried about him. Did a battle occur here?" I watched her expression.

"If you were worried about your brother, why didn't you search for him sooner?"

"We looked everywhere but didn't find a clue until recently. Was there a battle? Is he hurt?"

"Some had uniforms like you." A woman with curly hair pointed at Kai, who wore the Elite Guard's navy armor with gray accents. But the Imperial Army all wore navy with a red belt.

"You saw our soldiers," I said.

"They captured passersby and killed them."

My jaw twitched. "Those were probably possessed soldiers—Soul Extractors. Our men would never do that."

"General, you are blind," said the woman with the feather.

Kai pointed his sword at her. "Show respect for my general."

She laughed with the other two women. "I'm only telling the truth. As a general, you should know what your soldiers are up to." She stepped closer to me. "Do you know why your people have gone missing?"

I lifted my hand, signifying for Kai to lower his sword.

"You've seen them?"

She gestured a hand to the river. "They've tainted this place. The energy used to be more vibrant. Now the air is polluted with cries of the people, and the river is tainted with the tears of the innocent."

She stepped closer to the river.

"What happened to my guard Tao?"

She smirked. "Perhaps he's being tied up and tortured. Someone has to pay for the people's pain."

"The fuck! Where is he?" Kai grunted, charging forward, but I swung out my arm to hold him back.

The sword in my hand didn't pulse with energy. If she wasn't a foe, could she be a friend?

"I'm sorry for what the soldiers did. Our men have been trying to locate all the missing people. Can you tell me where they are?"

"They're dead. Their souls were extracted to empower the hungry Soul Extractors. Those who survived became new Soul Extractors."

"What's your name?" I asked. She seemed to know a lot about these beings. "Do you know how we can destroy the Soul Extractors?"

"Keiya." She stared at me for a moment. "If you sacrifice a body part, then I'll tell you how." I didn't know why, but she reminded me of Su.

"Absurd!" Kai stepped around me, charging at her. But then a hidden net scooped him up, securing him to a thick tree branch.

A man aimed his bow and arrow at Kai while the other man kept his aim on me.

"Don't hurt them!" a voice shouted from the boat.

As the boat moved toward us, I recognized Tao. Relief settled in me to see him uninjured. He leaped from the boat and rushed to stand before me. Tao placed a hand over his clenched fist, greeting me. He wore a brown tunic with matching pants, looking like a farmer.

I gripped his shoulder. "Good to see you."

"Are you going to release me?" Kai shouted from above.

Tao looked over at the leader. "They're my family."

She pursed her lips, shifting the scar on her face. "I thought *I* was your family now."

Tao walked up to her and placed a hand on her cheek. "You are. I'm alive and standing here because of you and your family. I'll never forget that. But these men are my brothers. We've battled in blood and death many times."

"I know." She sighed and gestured to one of the men to release Kai. He shot an arrow up to the rope holding the net, cutting it.

Kai landed on his feet and glared at the river people. Then he whipped his attention to his brother-in-arms. "What's going on, Tao? You've been alive all this time?"

Tao stepped up to Kai and punched him playfully on his bicep. "Long story."

"We've got time," Kai said, looking irritated. "I want to know why you didn't send any messages to alert us. We were so worried. Not to mention all the shit happening in the city."

Tao glanced at Keiya. "I need a moment with them."

She nodded and waved to her people to follow her down the river. A woman appeared from the boat, casting a net into the river.

"They go fishing?" I asked.

"The fish from the river are delicious. Same with the lake," Tao said, looking after them. As though sensing danger was no longer present, more women emerged with nets, fishing rods, and baskets.

Kai punched him again. "If you knew we were here, why didn't you show yourself sooner, fucker?"

"I was tied up."

I arched an eyebrow. "By them?"

"You were tied up by a group of scary-looking women and men? What happened to your fighting skills?"

"A group of *beautiful* river warriors."

Kai furrowed his eyebrows, staring at Tao. "Something

happen to your eyes? Have you *looked* at them? Their skin is practically falling off their faces."

Tao rolled his eyes. "That's not what they look like. They have a connection to the river. I was tied up with magical river weeds as soon as I knew it was you. Keiya wanted to test you. She's witnessed our soldiers in this area killing innocent people and wanted to make sure you weren't some of the possessed ones in disguise."

"What happened to you?" I asked.

"I was on my way to Ming Shan, looking for signs of the Bloodshade Bandits. But then I noticed some of our soldiers moving a carriage and two wagons covered with fabric. I recognized one soldier who belonged to General Li's infantry. He was trekking beyond his assigned location. They didn't take the main road but traveled the smaller paths. Until they stopped by the lake to rest."

He jerked a chin up the path. The Green Fog Lake had some resting areas. But most people kept away from this area, fearing the diseased river people.

"I heard cries from the wagons," Tao continued. "When the cloth covering on one wagon fell off, I saw the missing people we'd been searching for. The possessed soldiers extracted energies from the people. I knew I was outnumbered, but I fought them, trying to save the people."

He explained a voice had come from a possessed soldier, asking Tao to join them. When he declined, they tried to kill him, and he was injured.

"But then Keiya and her people assisted me. They shot them with arrows laced with the ink from the Inca fish, which lives in this river. Their ink killed the Soul Extractors quickly."

"Are those some of the delicious fish you mentioned?" Kai asked.

"No. Incas aren't meant to be ingested. Their ink is poisonous to humans." He lifted his tunic to reveal a long scab. "I was bleeding too much and passed out. When I woke, I was in a bed on a well-camouflaged riverboat."

I glanced toward the river and only saw a small boat. "So there could be a large moving boat I can't see right now?"

He nodded. "Yes."

"That still doesn't explain why you didn't send any messages. We sent off a few pigeons asking for updates from you but didn't receive a reply."

"The possessed soldiers probably killed them. They're watching our military sites from the inside and outside. We have moles. That's why I didn't dare send messages. I don't know who to trust. Plus, I wanted to recover first."

Kai's eyes sparked. "So these are the horrific-looking women who initially terrified you?"

He smiled. "They wear masks to disguise themselves. The disease was real, but they've found a cure that no one knows about. It keeps people away." He looked toward the river. "It's serene here, away from the chaos of war and politics."

I could hear the direction of his heart.

Tao turned to look at me. "But I honor my responsibility to protect Lin Din Ni. Once that is settled, I'd like to retire."

"To go fishing." Kai slung an arm around his friend. "But I'm happy for you. When a man's heart finds its home, there is no better feeling."

Tao flicked him a curious look. "That sounds like you've found a special place too."

"That story can be for another time."

"For now, we'll keep your status as missing," I said. "It's best that no one knows where you are. I have a plan to lure out the Soul Extractors."

"I can help you with that." He pulled out a whistle from his pocket and blew at it. Another whistle sounded in the distance in reply.

A minute later, Keiya walked up to meet him. She didn't have the long scar or burned skin on her face. Instead, she was a beautiful woman. I could see why Tao was attracted to her.

I immediately thought about Su. What was she doing now? I wished I didn't have to postpone our lesson for today, but I had to search for Tao and finalize the plan for the Lantern Blessing Festival. I'd explain it to her later.

"What do you need?" she asked Tao.

"This is General Wen." Tao pointed to me. "And this is Kai. They need our help luring out the Soul Extractors."

"With what?" I asked.

"Fish feces," she smiled.

Kai burst into laughter.

"The Inca is a rare fish with many qualities."

This was exactly what I needed. "How does it work?"

"Based on my observation, the Souls Extractors communicate with their master or the possessor telepathically," Keiya said. "The Inca poop has properties that can penetrate the mind, blurring the communication. During this trance, the mind is lured to follow the unique scent of the dried feces."

"I'd appreciate any help you can offer," I said. "We want to eradicate this darkness so our people can have peace again."

She nodded. "Come this way and tell me your plan."

We followed her down to the river through a small path that made us turn in several directions like a crazy maze. When we arrived at an area closed off to the world, I surveyed the trees and river plants that cocooned this tranquil area. Several homes made of bamboo sat in the distance. Women and men sat on a dock, sorting something in baskets.

Keiya gestured for us to sit at a table, where I shared my plan with her.

CHAPTER FIFTY-FIVE

SU

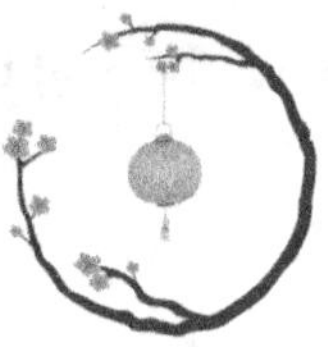

WHEN I FINISHED PLANTING Luzi's cherry blossom tree with Yunxi and Healer Churan, my heart was at peace. We stepped back, admiring the young tree that would probably bloom in spring. We brought over a table and placed her favorite foods on it. Each of us lit incense and spoke to her in our minds.

Hi, Luzi. I hope you like the tree we planted. We brought your favorite foods—even the pastries. I miss you. I know you're with your parents and brother now. It makes me happy knowing you're together. Tears spilled over my eyes. *Hung and I are doing well. He'll visit you soon. Enjoy the food.*

I placed the incense into the holder, pressed my palms together, and bowed three times. Then I dabbed the tears with my sleeve.

I wrapped my arms over Yunxi and Healer Churan's shoulders, pulling them close to me. "We did a great job. I think she's happy wherever she is."

"She'll live in our hearts forever," Yunxi said. "She's part of the family."

Healer Churan and Yunxi reopened the apothecary while I cleaned up in the courtyard. I swept the dirt from the walkway and put away the shovels. A pink butterfly flew by and landed on the cherry blossom tree. My heart swelled, and I couldn't help but think it was Luzi's spirit coming to say hello. After a moment, the butterfly flew off.

Happiness was like that butterfly. It could flit into your life so easily but also depart the same way. I couldn't shake off the sadness that clung to me after my conversation with Lina.

Was my happiness with Hung over?

Stop thinking negatively.

It was easier said than done, but I pushed the doubts aside as I disguised myself as a man and headed to the Maroon Meadow. It wasn't evening yet, but close enough. I wore the same outfit I'd worn the day I spied on Ru Malik in the abandoned temple. This time, I added a bushy beard.

The fear that I might discover something awful gripped my stomach. But I had to know the truth. Who wanted to live a false life? I wasn't one of those women who settled for a relationship just because it looked fancy.

My heart pounded as I stood on the street corner outside of the Market Square, watching the patrons enter and leave the Maroon Meadow.

Should I wait to see if Hung walked in? But what if he was already in there? *Just go in and find out.*

I approached the guard standing at the entrance. He gestured for me to enter.

Two women dressed in pretty clothing greeted me. "Are you here for dinner or entertainment?"

"Dinner, please."

A woman with a blue dress waved me into the restaurant. A maid led me to a table in the corner by a stage where a pretty woman was playing the pipa, a pear-shaped wooden instrument with various frets. I loved pipa music but had never learned how to play.

I had requested to sit at a table with a view of the front entrance. A wide stairwell led up to a second floor wrapped around the entire area. The bedrooms were probably upstairs.

I ordered wonton noodle soup and a pot of jasmine tea. While I waited, I glanced around at the patrons. They were all men enjoying food and wine while listening to the woman playing her instrument. She was wearing a red dress with a low-cut neckline. The tables surrounding her were full of men staring at her.

When my soup came, I ate it. I didn't know if Hung would be here tonight, but I wanted to see what this place was all about. Were all these men single, or did they have families?

From the corner of my eye, I saw Hung at the front entrance. My heart raced as I watched him talking to a hostess. She pointed to a room upstairs. Hung walked up the stairwell as though he'd been here many times. He entered one of the rooms, but I couldn't see clearly. A few seconds later, a beautiful hostess wearing a blue dress and a lot of jewelry walked up the same stairwell, entering the same room.

My heart sank, and I lost my appetite—not that I had any to begin with. But now, nausea rose in me, making me want to puke.

What was he doing here?

That's a stupid question, Su. The Maroon Meadow was known as a place for men to come and relax. They came here to be pleasured.

Tears brimmed in my eyes, but I pushed them back. He canceled my kung fu lesson so he could come here to relax?

I paid for my meal and asked a maid for the restroom. She pointed to a hallway that led to the back room. But I walked up the stairwell even though I wasn't sure what I was going to do. It was obvious what a man and a woman did behind closed doors.

Should I confront them? Then what?

It would only anger me even more if I saw them together. How long had he been with her? Who was she?

I love you.

His words echoed in my head. Lies. Everything was a lie. Laughter rang out from the room. I couldn't do this. I couldn't burst through the door. Shame and rage consumed me. I already knew what was happening from the laughter. So I gathered my strength, turned around, and walked down the stairs.

As I walked back to the apothecary, my heart weighed a hundred pounds of rice. Somehow, I made it to my room and managed to change into my sleeping clothes. As my head fell onto the pillow, I realized I'd been functioning with no thought. My mind, body, and heart were scattered in different places.

I'd believed he was a man who could love me. I'd given my heart to him—and my body. My chest tightened like someone was squeezing the life out of me. I placed a hand on my heart, rubbing it gently.

How could I recover from this pain?

An image flashed through my vision. It was the same blob of darkness I'd seen before. But it had grown. Lightning flashed as Roar of the Sky flew toward the darkness. That image faded, and a new one appeared. Tempo's four ears perked, and fear splashed onto its adorable face. He hopped around as if looking for something.

Was he looking for the dragon eggs? Terror gripped me. Then everything faded, leaving me with the darkness in my bedroom.

Something had happened in the dragon's realm. How could I help Roar of the Sky or Tempo?

You can't. The dragon and her magical pet have powers you don't.

Would Roar of the Sky contact me? There was so much chaos around me and within me. I felt so helpless.

I shouldn't let this failed relationship hold me back. I'd confront Hung soon enough. But for now, I needed time away from him so I could gather the strength to patch up my broken heart. I was a healer, but I didn't know how to best heal myself.

CHAPTER FIFTY-SIX

HUNG

"I CAN'T BELIEVE THIS," I said, gawking at Three-Eyes and Blue Orchid, the owner of Maroon Meadow and my friend.

"Believe what?" Blue Orchid said as she leaned on Three-Eyes' shoulders.

"The two of you." I crossed my arms and looked at Three-Eyes. The gloom I usually saw on his face was now replaced by joy. "Was this why you always scowled at me?"

"What?" Blue Orchid straightened and slapped at his shoulder playfully. "I told you there's nothing between Hung and me."

My eyebrows shot up. "You were jealous? I'm not surprised. I'm a lot younger than you."

He rolled his eyes. This was one of those moments when I wanted to see his third eye roll. But of course, it was closed.

I never imagined the Imperial seer would be jealous of me over a woman. But then I thought about Su. I'd been jealous when I saw Gong teaching her. When a man loved a woman, he was transformed. I believed in that now.

"I'm only interested in my wise man," said Blue Orchid.

I had no comment.

"How did you know I was here?" he asked.

"That's not important," I said, not wanting him to know I'd followed him. "As you know, the Soul Extractors are increasing in Luklum and everywhere else. We need to destroy them."

"They're getting stronger because there are more of them."

"They've broken through the protective barrier around the palace." I leaned into the table. "We need to protect the Emperor and the Empress."

"I can see them approaching from various directions, surrounding Lin Din Ni." Three-Eyes reached for his teacup that Blue Orchid had filled earlier. "I needed time to recuperate before I could think about a defensive plan. This battle requires more than just soldiers on the ground."

"Do you know the source of the darkness?" I told him about the voice coming out of certain possessed people's mouths.

"Not the exact source. But a heaviness is here, hiding in the Market Square. There's a mask protecting the source. It doesn't allow anyone to pinpoint it precisely."

Did that mean my sword could be close to it and not pick up its dark energy? Fuck.

"I have a plan to lure them out for the Lantern Blessing Festival. Do you think it's a good time for that kind of work?"

Three-Eyes could read the stars and the timing of important events. I wanted to make sure the timing benefited my plan.

Before my encounter with Keiya, I had planned on luring the Soul Extractors out by announcing I'd captured a group of them. The Imperial seer would use his magic to extract information from these possessed beings. I'd release information about where I was imprisoning them. Traps would be set up to kill those who came to rescue or kill the captives.

But now Keiya's idea sounded better and posed less danger to my men. Besides, I was curious to see how fish poop would be the demise of the Soul Extractors.

Three-Eyes tapped his fingers on the table, thinking. "It's the harvest full moon. The veils between the realms are thin during this time period. If you play it right, you can use that time to destroy the source. The Soul Extractors are connected by a thread of dark energy. Snip it, and the rest will untangle."

Eliminate the strong one, and the others will weaken.

The idea of luring the Soul Extractors out before the Lantern Blessing Festival wouldn't work now. It would have to be on the day of the festival so I could take advantage of the thinning veil during the full moon. Besides, Tao and Keiya needed time to gather Inca poop to help me.

"Can I help with anything?" Blue Orchid asked.

"No." Three-Eyes clasped a hand over hers. "You stay here. Don't go out. I'll find you after."

"But everyone will be out."

"Yes. We have to let them so the darkness suspects nothing. I'm sure it will be busy here like it is everywhere."

Three-Eyes wanted to keep his woman safe. But I knew Su wouldn't stay put in her room. She was involved in this, and I'd do my best to protect her.

After I briefed them on my plan, I headed back to my villa, walking through the Market Square. A group of men sat at a table playing Chinese chess and drinking tea. Vendors continued to set up for tomorrow's event. I walked by as they set up displays selling lanterns, hair accessories, gemstones, and so much more.

I turned down an alleyway and bumped into a man. His basket thudded to the ground, and fruits and vegetables spilled out.

"Sorry," I said, picking them up for him.

"It's okay," he said quickly, grabbing the fruits and vegetables from my hands without looking me in the eye. His face was deformed, but something was familiar about him.

When he limped away, I noticed the way his shoulders dipped.

"Moo," I called out. It had been a while since I'd seen the three childhood bullies in the Market Square or even in Luklum.

He paused in his steps for a moment before rushing away. I caught up to him and touched his shoulder.

He gasped, dropped the basket, and huddled against the brick wall. I walked up to him, wanting to see what was wrong. But he flinched and lifted a hand to brace for an attack.

I stepped back. "I won't hurt you. It's been a long time. I just wanted to know how you were doing."

After a moment, Moo looked at me. "What do you think? *Look* at me."

He lifted his hands to show three missing fingers on each palm. He had scars on the side of his face and neck. His mouth was crooked.

"What happened to you?"

CHAPTER FIFTY-SEVEN

HUNG

I DIDN'T SLEEP WELL last night. When dawn came, I washed up and replayed my conversation with Moo. I swore I wouldn't reveal his residence, a small house in the woods by the farm where he worked. He went by the name Chen Heng now. I didn't blame him. Guilt nipped at me as I thought back to when I'd encountered Heng and his friends in my youth. My perspective in life had been so narrow. I wished I'd seen more back then. It would have prevented a lot of mistakes.

But now I knew things that had changed the trajectory of my life. My trust in people now wavered as the serrated knife of betrayal cut into me. As a general, I could pivot when an unseen threat emerged. Right now, I needed to reconsider my strategy for the festival and make the necessary changes to protect those I loved.

Once I had a solid strategy, I made my way to the Military Pavilion. I'd been meaning to review my parents' death in more detail. I looked at the old records that dated back to when my father was a general. After I got what I needed, I sat down for a moment to let everything sink in. I welcomed the calm because I needed it to subdue the rage boiling in my blood.

Su's face emerged in my vision, making me feel better. I needed her presence and comfort more than ever.

I returned to my home, waiting for Su to arrive for her lesson. With all that had happened, I couldn't wait to see her. Even though it had been only a day, it felt like a hundred years had gone by. I wanted to wrap my arms around her, inhale her scent, and absorb her warmth.

When our scheduled time had passed, I waited a while longer. Perhaps she had a patient who urgently needed treatment. I practiced my kung fu, concentrating on my Dim Mak technique. Had Su read the pamphlet I'd given her? Had she practiced? Did she have questions?

Worry knotted my stomach when Su didn't show up or send any note explaining her absence. Had something happened? The past few months had been filled with chaos and darkness. Su was the only thing that shed light on my path. If something happened to her, I didn't know what I'd do. I'd never had someone so precious in my life. I could never love another woman the way I loved her. She was the sunlight that cut through my dark clouds.

Did she understand that?

Concerned, I headed to the apothecary.

"She went out to run some errands," Yunxi said while packing herbs for a waiting customer. "I don't know when she'll be back. She took today off. Oh, check out Luzi's memorial in the courtyard. It looks great."

Two more customers entered, asking Yunxi questions.

"Thanks." I headed toward the back as unease twisted my stomach.

I thought Su was going to wait for me to plant the tree with her. What happened between yesterday and today? Was she mad at me for canceling our lesson?

I stood in front of the beautiful cherry blossom tree, admiring the rocks placed in a pretty design at the base. I said a silent prayer and thanked Luzi for her courage and sacrifice. The people you met in life often taught you lessons. Luzi had taught me that courage didn't always come from adults and that children could inspire and motivate us in ways we never thought possible.

With peace embracing me, I roamed the streets, looking for Su. The vendors had prepared the displays, awnings, chairs, and tables for tomorrow's event. Lanterns hung from poles, balconies, and in front of businesses. It was hard not to smile at the festivities.

As a child, I enjoyed this festival. My parents used to buy me all sorts of treats and toys. I hadn't attended these events since their deaths. The Harvest Full Moon was when farmers celebrated their harvest, and people took time off to appreciate their hard work throughout the year. It was a time of rest to prepare for the next season.

I prayed tomorrow's event would go smoothly. I glanced up at the sky, where a cloud covered part of the moon, which was visible during the day. It would be full soon. Noises sounded behind me, and I turned to see a woman pushing a wagon full of firecrackers. She met my eyes, and I nodded, understanding where she was taking the supplies.

"It's going to be an exceptional event," I said.

"I agree. Have a good evening, General," said Keiya, who was dressed in casual clothing with her hair tied into a bun with no hair accessories. She blended in well with commoners rushing to finish their displays.

Another wagon approached behind her, pushed by Dayday and Chuluun, river warriors who had been there that day with Keiya. Dayday had worn the mask with drooping skin and a crooked mouth, and Chuluun had curly hair.

I wanted Su to meet these river warriors. She'd feel right at home with them.

I stood in the street, ensuring they turned down the correct alley. No one paid attention to them as the entire Market Square was busy preparing for the festival.

My sword heated and thrummed for a moment, and I surveyed the area, looking at people. Nothing seemed out of place.

No one appeared suspicious. Soon, the sensation from my sword disappeared. The darkness had masked itself, which made it difficult for my sword to pick up its energy.

I wandered the main roads in the Market Square, including the smaller paths around the area, a few more times. I kept my eyes out for Su, but I didn't see her.

Where was she? Was she avoiding me?

I'd arrive early tomorrow to take her to the festival. Right now, I had to reconvene with Kai, Tao, and Three-Eyes about the adjustments to the plan.

CHAPTER FIFTY-EIGHT

SU

I ENTERED the sanctuary of the forest, where I'd always practiced my kung fu, and sat down on the grass with pretty flowers greeting me.

"It's been a while, my friends." I tapped a tiny purple flower on the bush beside me. Then I looked at the yarrow plant in front of me and ran my fingers along its healing leaves. "I've got a major heartache. Can you alleviate my inflamed heart?"

The plant didn't answer, nor did I expect it to. I just needed to talk out the tension in my chest.

I should have sent a note to Hung, letting him know I wasn't feeling well and needed to reschedule the lesson. But I didn't have the energy to write the note. I just wanted to be alone to sort out my feelings.

If things ended between us, I couldn't continue my lessons with him. What was the point? I'd look at his face and want to stab him for hurting me. I wasn't an evil person, but certain situations call for certain actions.

I yanked at a patch of grass, tearing it up and whipping it aside. When the blades of grass fell to the ground, guilt nipped at me.

"Sorry, grass. I didn't mean to take my anger out on you."

I brushed the bare spot with my fingers. Then I gathered the broken blades I'd torn up and placed them back where I had torn them from. As I held the grass in my hands, I realized some things couldn't be remedied—like these broken blades. How could I reattach them?

There would always be a torn seam in my heart, reminding me of what had caused the rip.

Ask him. Get the truth.

I didn't know if that inner voice belonged to me or someone else. I didn't feel rational, and that voice made too much sense.

I didn't like this anger, confusion, and helplessness. I thought after sleeping on it, I'd feel better. But I was wrong. Images of Hung at Maroon Meadow kept replaying in my head like a bad dream. This wasn't a dream, though. He'd been meeting with another woman even though he said he loved me.

Was it all a lie?

But I love him.

There it was—the truth and the fear that had me running to this sanctuary for answers. Tears flooded my eyes, and in this place where no one could see me, I let them fall. The tears came like a monsoon. My chest heaved, my breath caught, and my stomach quaked.

Was it wrong to love a man who didn't love me? Why couldn't I erase this emotion?

It takes time to heal, Su. Give yourself some grace. Sometimes, things aren't what they seem. Go and talk to him.

My body straightened as the voice cleared in my head. It wasn't my inner voice, but Roar of the Sky.

"Where are you?" I asked out loud.

Patching a rip in the Cosmos.

"How many?" Terror twisted my stomach.

Too many. The darkness is growing strong.

"Are you okay?"

Yes.

"Is Tempo okay? What about your dragon eggs?"

He's moving them around.

"Why?"

The darkness snuck into my space.

That was why Tempo had looked frantic. "Did you destroy it?"

Yes.

An image popped into my head. "I saw a black blob moving toward something."

It's coming to Luklum. Be cautious. I have to go now. Your heart is broken. I can sense it, but you need to find out the truth, Su. Remember, the darkness is very intelligent, and deception is one of its effective weapons. See from different angles. Don't accept things as they seem.

A warmth cloaked me, and I knew Roar of the Sky was sending me her energy. She was a mother to me—caring and watchful.

"Are you still there?" I asked, but she didn't respond.

Looking up at the clear sky, I prayed she was successfully patching up all the rips in the Cosmos. Here I was, moping about my relationship with Hung when she was facing danger to help so many worlds.

She was right. I needed to ask Hung and face whatever was to come. Peace settled in my heart, allowing me to make clearer decisions. I'd ask him tomorrow during the Lantern Blessing Festival. Even if we weren't a couple, I could still help him fight the darkness in Luklum. After all, it was my home too.

As I got up to head home, a pink butterfly appeared. It looked like the same butterfly that had landed on the cherry blossom sapling. Was Luzi's spirit around?

The pink butterfly flew down a path, and I followed it. The butterfly landed on a bush with flowers and purple tepals. Then it flew over to my hand, brushed it, and flew away.

"Wow." I sucked in a breath as I studied the cluster of purple tepals.

These berries had numbing properties effective for illnesses targeting the mouth, tongue, and tonsils. It could help ease toothaches as well. They weren't native to Lin Din Ni.

Healer Churan had received a small supply years ago from a man she'd saved. I'd been with her on that day near the Green Fog Lake. She was teaching me how to distinguish between toxic and nontoxic mushrooms when we stumbled on an injured man with deep gashes in his thighs and legs. A group of travelers were also wounded not too far from him. A rebel group had attacked them, stealing all their belongings. We treated them as best we could, and the man visiting from the Central Empire gave Healer Churan a supply of purple tepals for helping him. This would be a fantastic addition to our apothecary supply.

I looked around but didn't see any more shrubbery. With a stick on the ground, I dug up a small section of the shrubbery with the roots still intact. Healer Churan could cultivate and grow it in our garden.

When I arrived home, Yunxi said Hung had stopped by to see me.

"Where did you go?" she asked, sorting the display of essential oils.

"Errands to run, remember?" I reminded her and changed the subject. "Look what I found."

Healer Churan's eyes widened as she dropped what she was doing, strode over, and grabbed the plant from the bowl. "Where did you find this?"

"In the woods. I was surprised too. Do you think you can grow it?"

"I can try." She gathered up a few purple tepals that had fallen to the counter.

"What are those?" Yunxi asked.

Healer Churan told her about the numbing properties. "But if you ingest enough of them, it can alter your voice."

"Really?"

"Don't try it." She waved a finger. "Trust me. I ate too many once by mistake. They have a sweet taste, so I assumed they were safe."

I laughed. "Too much of a good thing is not always good."

Yunxi bumped shoulders with me. "Ready for the festival?"

"Yes," I said. "Are you attending, Healer Churan?"

"It would be nice to enjoy the festivities."

CHAPTER FIFTY-NINE

HUNG

I WOKE early to go over the plan once more with Kai. Like me, he wore his armor, ready for battle. It wasn't unusual for the military to dress like this during festivities. People often got rowdy after too much wine, and we needed to patrol the area.

I stared at the fish inside the glass bowl on the table. It looked like a sunfish but half the size. "So this is an Inca fish? How could something so small be so deadly?" It flapped a fin and swam to the other side as if offended. A bubble of blackness popped out of its mouth.

"Size doesn't matter," Kai said, scooping out the bubble and placing it into a small porcelain bowl. "What do you want to do with this?"

"I've got plans for it. Just leave it for now." I walked to my weapon closet and pulled out a few daggers.

"I can't wait to eradicate the fucking Soul Extractors." He crossed his arms. "Who knew the river warriors would be our allies?"

"They're helping us because of Tao," I said.

"We'll have a party to celebrate once this is over."

I nodded as I shoved away the uncomfortable feeling that

something might go wrong. But that could be because of my relationship with Su.

I didn't tell Kai about what I'd discovered. I needed more time to think of a plan of action to deal with that earth-shattering issue. For today, my focus was luring the Soul Extractors out with fish poop and destroying them with fish ink.

People should worship this damn fish if all went well.

"I'm going to head out early," Kai said. "See you tonight."

He was probably going to see Yunxi. I couldn't wait to see Su either, but I needed to make something for her first. With a toothpick, I popped the thin layer around the bubble that encased the ink. Ink spilled out onto the dish. Using a sponge, I coated my darts and daggers with the black ink and left them on the side to dry. Then I ambled over to my desk and opened the bamboo box containing the new hairpin I'd bought for Su. Unlike the previous pink hairpin, this design depicted purple flowers. I twisted the purple flower knob and pulled out the small sharp blade, dipping it in ink.

With the danger surrounding us, I had to make sure she had a way of protecting herself.

As I made my way to the City Apothecary, I encountered Ren and his sister.

"Hung!" Excitement splashed onto her face. "Are you attending tonight's festival?"

"I'm going with Su," I said, not feeling the need to be gentle with her anymore.

I'd given her the truth, and she should accept that. Beating around the bush would only make her think otherwise.

The joy on her face died, and I didn't know what to say. Lina was a decent woman. I'd watched her grow up, but my only affection for her was that of a brother.

Being protective, Ren placed an arm over his sister's shoulders. "Dad is holding a tournament for you to find the perfect husband next month. You can find someone better than Hung." He offered her an attentive look. "There are even more skillful men out there for my beautiful sister, right?" He flicked me a gaze, begging for assistance.

I wasn't in the mood, and I didn't have time to deal with this right now. A wave of emotions roiled inside me. But I couldn't stand to see the pain in Lina's eyes. She shouldn't be punished because she loved someone.

I needed to concentrate on today's task. So I had to remove this distraction. Nothing could deter me from destroying the Soul Extractors.

I gathered all my strength and said, "He's right. Adept warriors will line up to marry you, Lina. I'm sorry, but I'm not worthy of you."

"But Su is worthy of you?" She pouted. "What can she offer you that I can't? She's not from a noble family. She can't help your career."

My mouth dropped open at her bluntness. I wanted to explain that love was more than social status. She wouldn't understand the deep connection between Su and me.

"I don't care about social status. That's reserved for those desperate for greed and power. I don't need that. Besides, I love her." The truth glided out of my mouth with ease and relief. Admitting it to someone other than Su was like a mantra to the heavens.

Her nostrils flared, and she took a deep breath.

Ren pressed his lips into a tight line as he placed a hand on his sister's back. "We should go, Lina."

She remained in her spot, glaring at me.

Feeling awkward, I said, "Enjoy the festival." Then I walked off.

CHAPTER SIXTY

SU

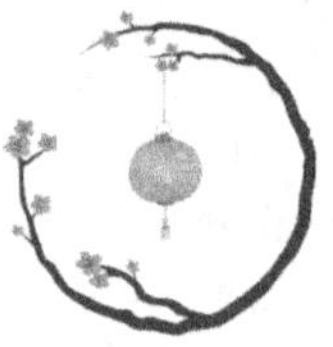

I HAD jitters all morning and afternoon. My conversation with Roar of the Sky bounced around in my head, and images of what I'd seen at the Maroon Meadow flashed through my mind.

Don't accept things as they seem.

But what kind of business did a man have at those places besides—

I shivered as I wiped my mind clear of him being with another woman.

Looking at myself in my bedroom mirror, I put on blush, a little eyeshadow, and chose a pair of purple earrings I'd recently purchased to make myself feel better. As I adjusted the blue hairpin Hung had given me, self-doubts surfaced. How many women had he given hairpins to?

Stop the negative thoughts.

Grabbing two more hair accessories, I slid them into my hair, changing up my look. A fresh look at a new beginning gave me a boost of energy.

I rose from my chair and glanced at myself once more, preparing to head out early to enjoy the festivities. The City Apothecary had closed early as well.

A knock sounded as I reached for the door handle, startling me.

"It's me, Su." His deep voice caressed my body, waking it up.

What was wrong with me?

I was supposed to be angry with him. I didn't like how my body betrayed me as though he had command over it and not me.

Since he was here now, I could get things off my chest.

I opened the door and looked at him. All handsome and magnetic in his Prime General uniform in navy, gold, and red with the navy cape. This look had enamored me all those years ago, but it was more powerful now because I knew what was beneath the clothing. I knew what his touch did to me. My heart pounded as I looked into his eyes.

A quiet silence stirred between us. We both knew something was wrong but didn't know what to say to each other.

"May I come in?" he asked, breaking the silence.

I nodded and stepped aside.

He walked in and turned to face me. His eyes scanned my face, the purple gown, and back up to my hair. He stepped close to me, and the sexual tension thrummed.

"These earrings are beautiful on you." He touched them. His eyes narrowed at my hair accessories. "Who got you these?"

Why did he assume someone got them for me? Couldn't a woman buy her own accessories? Did all men think women *needed* them?

Defiance made me stand a little straighter. "A man bought them for me."

His jaw tensed as a muscle twitched in his cheek. Without hesitation, he yanked them out of my hair and flung them aside. They clanked to the ground.

"What are you doing?" I exclaimed, realizing the stupid question. I knew exactly what he was doing, but I was too angry to articulate.

"They don't suit you," he said. The serious expression I hadn't seen in a while splashed onto his face.

"And you do?" Pissed, I turned to look for my hair accessories, but he grabbed my hand, pulling me flush to him.

Heat from his body melted into mine. I couldn't look away from the intensity in his eyes. Pain, sorrow, and something else swam in them.

"No one suits you better than me." His mouth crushed mine, hot and furious. It was as though he poured all his emotions into that kiss.

I felt his pain and wanted to heal him. My fingers gripped his uniform as I kissed him back with the same need and ferocity. Our tongues clashed as the storm between us exploded.

He broke for breath and rested his forehead on mine. "You're mine, don't forget that."

"How can I be yours when *you're* not mine?" My voice broke, trying to stay composed from the emotional storm whirling inside me. Love, anger, confusion, and betrayal became one big mess in my heart.

He drew back, looking at me with furrowed eyebrows. "What are you talking about?"

I extracted myself from him, but he clamped both hands around my waist. "I'm not letting you go until you tell me."

I wanted to retort by saying I could use the death touch to immobilize him, but he'd release himself immediately. Plus, I desperately missed him. So I betrayed myself at that moment and remained in his grip.

"I saw you at the Maroon Meadow. You were in a room with a woman."

Surprise overcame his face, followed by a smirk. "You were there?" He brushed an errant strand of hair that had fallen out of place, tucking it behind my ear. "I didn't see you. I would've invited you to join me."

Anger surged in me, and I slapped his chest, trying to wriggle free from his embrace.

But he embraced me tightly as he whispered into my ear. "It's not what you think, my wild dahlia. I love that you're jealous."

Then he nipped on my earlobe, sending a jolt of sensation to my core.

"Why were you there?" I asked as he dropped kisses along my cheek, jaw, and neck.

"Looking for Three-Eyes."

"What? The Imperial seer who's part of the Emperor's council?" I couldn't believe it. "Why?"

"He loves the woman you saw. Blue Orchid. She owns the tavern. I needed to talk to him and went there to look for him."

A tremendous burden slid off me, and I released a sigh of relief.

His eyes sparked. "You're very brave for entering a men's den for me. Were you wearing a gown?"

I told him about my disguise.

He considered me. "I'm trying to imagine my beautiful woman with a beard." Then he shook his head. "No beard." Pride splashed onto his face as he gripped my face with his hands, kissing me again. "This is why I love you so much."

My heart jiggled, wiggled, and did all sorts of kung fu formations in my chest.

I placed a hand on his cheek. "I should've trusted you instead of jumping to conclusions."

He gripped my hand and interlaced his fingers with mine. "I would've reacted the same way." His eyes flashed with a serious intent. "But I would've kicked down the door and dragged the man away from you. Then I would have pummeled him."

"But we could've been having a business negotiation."

"I don't care."

I grinned, enjoying this jealous side of him.

He reached into his breast pocket and pulled out a gorgeous purple hairpin. After he showed me how to retrieve the sharp weapon hidden inside it, he inserted it into my hair. "Perfect."

I glanced at myself in the mirror and agreed. "You have an eye for hairpins."

"I have an eye for you," he said, then briefed me on the danger tonight.

It appeared my warrior had been busy scheming to protect Luklum while I was cursing at him. Guilt tore through me.

He told me about the river warriors, and I couldn't wait to meet these women and men. He said he only saw a few men, so most of the warriors were women.

"Do you need me to do anything?" I asked.

"Yes. I'm dividing us into groups to survey the Market Square. The darkness is heavy in the city, which means many people could be Soul Extractors. They've gotten smarter and more powerful, so they can disguise themselves better."

"I don't want anyone getting hurt," I said, imagining Healer Churan and Yunxi.

Hung placed a hand on each side of my shoulders. "I don't either. But tonight's full moon will create a portal for us to destroy the person behind the Soul Extractors. Three-Eyes says the source of the darkness is in the Market Square."

I gasped as I remembered the man speaking through the mouth of the possessed person.

"We're luring them out of the city through the back paths away from the crowds. Tao and the river warriors will be prepared to take them down."

Nerves spiraled in me. "Promise you'll be careful?"

Hung looked at me for a moment. "Before you, I used to charge into battle without fear because I had nothing to lose." He brushed a knuckle down my face. "But now I have everything to lose. I love you. You're the home I want to come home to. You've given me a reason to fight harder."

"Choose what gives you hope and not what makes you fear." My heart raced as I absorbed the meaning of those words.

"Hope is everything that you represent."

Tearing up, I threw my arms around him, loving him more than he could ever know. When I reared back, I cupped his face with my hands. "I never thought I'd understand what love is. But you showed me what it looks like." I rose to my tiptoes and kissed him on the cheek. "Feels like." I palmed him and winked when he twitched against my hand. "Smells like." I sniffed his neck and crooned at the musky scent of frankincense, myrrh, and lemon. "And tastes like." I licked his lips. "I love you. If you come back safe, I'll have a special gift for you." I squeezed his length.

He sucked in a breath. "What kind of gift?"

I smirked. "It has something to do with *The Art of Seduction* and *The Art of Intimacy*."

His eyes darkened. "That's the most enticing reward ever. Those damn Soul Extractors are *dead*."

I laughed, wanting to make light of the dangerous situation for both of us.

"Just be cautious." He pulled a dagger from his belt, drawing the sharp blade laced with ink. "If you encounter a Soul Extractor, kill it with this. The ink from the Inca fish will kill it more effectively."

"Thank you." I hooked it onto my belt, understanding tonight's festivities weren't just a celebration.

"Ready?" He squeezed my hand. "We have a couple of hours before the mission begins."

"Let's make the best of it."

CHAPTER SIXTY-ONE

HUNG

THE MARKET SQUARE boomed with chatter, laughter, and firecrackers. The streets were packed with vendors selling all kinds of celebratory items. We stopped by a stand selling a variety of lanterns.

I chose an adorable rabbit lantern and gave it to Su. "For you."

"It looks like Tempo, but without the two extra ears." She smiled, warming my chest.

It had been a whirlwind of emotions for her, and I wished I could erase all the pain she'd endured.

"I'll take that one, please." She pointed to a dragon lantern with blue and red scales. "That looks like Roar of the Sky, right?" She gave me the stick with the dangling dragon.

"Not as majestic, but it is cute," I said. "Thank you."

The last time I had a lantern was when I was a kid. Su had brought back a wonderful childhood memory for me. After my parents' deaths, I withdrew into a dark cave of grief. Her love was the sacred lantern that led me out of the darkness.

I'd never felt more alive than now. Su was the life force—the potent essa that changed the trajectory of my life. Without her, I'd be a man half-fighting the darkness and half-wandering aimlessly, looking for something I didn't know. I'd found myself and my purpose in her, and I'd protect her with my life.

We both held lanterns as we walked down the streets and spotted Ren with Beibei of the Wong family. Lina strode beside them and saw us but said nothing. Perhaps our encounter from earlier today shifted her mindset.

Beibei smiled and rushed up to us. "Su! It's so lovely to see you. Are you going to make a wish on a paper boat tonight?"

The Paper Boat Prayer was a tradition where people wrote their wishes onto a paper boat and released it into the Harmony Stream, asking for the Moon Goddess to fulfill their wishes. I'd never done it.

"Yes," Su said, turning to me. "We should do it together."

Before today, I had no interest in such a thing. But the hopeful look in Su's eyes swayed my decision. As long as she was happy, I'd do anything.

"Okay."

Smiling, Beibei clapped her hands and turned to Ren and Lina. "We should all send our wishes tonight!" She rushed over to Ren and tugged on his arm. "I'm going to ask her to bless our families with great health and abundance."

Ren nodded. "I like that idea."

Lina just smiled at Beibei, agreeing to the wish. I suspected her wish to the Moon Goddess would probably be something that would hurt me.

Beibei pointed to the rabbit in Su's hand. "That's an adorable lantern."

"It's from the lantern vendor with the red awning." Su pointed down the street.

"Ren, can you buy me one?" She tugged at his hand, heading toward it.

When we walked far enough, Su said, "I think Lina hates me."

"You're not alone. There's nothing we can do."

"I hope she finds someone who loves her. I'll ask the Moon Goddess to bring her an attentive lover."

My warrior had a loving heart. I looked at Su, wondering if Lina would ever do that for anyone.

"I thought you could only ask one wish per year."

"I have everything I need." She touched my face. "So she can have my wish."

"You're very considerate."

She lifted a shoulder. "As long as she doesn't step on my toes."

I tipped her chin up. "I should be careful because I have a morally gray warrior goddess for a lover."

She smirked. "It's because I'm learning from the best morally gray general."

My chest constricted as I realized now would be a good time to share a secret with her. Su had shown no signs of the red thorn poison. Perhaps her body had fought it off.

"There's something I need to share with you."

"What is it?" She adjusted the tassel that had gotten tangled in the lantern.

I took her arm, leading her to the bench that faced a candy stand crowded with children.

"You know that day when you saw Ru Malik in the temple?"

"Yes. He told Samo and his friends to contaminate the well water."

"That was *me*. I was disguised as Ru Malik to lure him out. He was working with Samo, and I needed him to show himself." I looked at her shocked expression. "I didn't give them poison but an antidote. Ru Malik had paid people to contaminate the well water with wandering nightshade."

She wore a contemplative expression as she looked at the ground. "How long have you known I was there on that day?"

"When you mentioned the temple and told me about Samo. You were the person Kai and Tao went after that night. I needed word to spread about Ru Malik, so they stopped the chase after losing you near the woods." I took her hand in mine. "I'm so sorry I poisoned you. That guilt has been eating me alive."

She looked at me for a moment but didn't remove her hand from my grip. "Did you poison me on purpose?"

"No!"

"Then there's nothing to feel guilty about."

"You don't understand." I swallowed. "I've hurt the only woman I love. It weighs on me."

Her expression warmed, and she lifted my hand to her heart. "I *chose* to be there that day. You didn't know. If it makes you feel better, I forgive you."

Her words landed in my chest, entering my heart. I hadn't realized I needed to hear those words out loud for the heaviness to lift.

"Thank you."

"How did you poison me?"

"It's the incense. You inhaled it like Samo and his friends. I only had enough antidote for my Elite Guards and me. The red thorn poison came from a black-market merchant." I looked out at the street which had become crowded. "I heard he was from Emerald Song Village, so I made a trip to look for him and check out the pockets of darkness. But then things took a different turn."

"Look at me," she said. "I'm healthy. The poison didn't affect me. The human body is interesting. One person may react badly to something while another is fine. I used to sense an unfamiliar energy inside me, making me randomly hot and cold. But since meeting Roar of the Sky, I realized it was her scale embedded in my skin. I think the scale—the dragon energy—helped me fight the poisons. It explains why it didn't affect me the same way as others. Still, I've been monitoring myself lately but have sensed nothing abnormal."

"Good. Promise me you'll let me know if you're unwell?"

She released a heavy sigh. "I'm unwell now."

"What? Where?" I examined her face.

She rubbed the area around her heart. "Seeing you worried about something insignificant makes me unwell. So stop it." She pinched my cheek.

I smiled, feeling lighter.

"No more secrets?" she asked.

"No."

"The deeper you love, the more rooted you become." I looked at her hand and placed it on my chest. "A stable heart sees and feels more."

"Didn't realize my warrior is so poetic." She smiled. "Love is an herb that heals." She ran a finger along my jaw. "As long as you're with me, I'll always be okay." She kissed my cheek.

We embraced each other for a moment, then strode through the streets, admiring all the decorations and buying snacks along the way. We gave our lanterns to a little girl and boy who didn't have any as the merchant had sold out.

Before we knew it, the time to depart had arrived. We wandered over to the stand to pick a paper boat.

"Write your wish on this boat." Su handed me one. "We'll release it early."

When I finished writing my wish on the inside of the boat, I handed it to Su. "You can read it if you want."

"No, I won't," she said, even though I could see the curiosity in her eyes.

"You have my permission to read it."

She twisted her lips, thinking. I could see the multiple thoughts swirling in her mind. I loved that I could read her so well now. While she wanted to respect my privacy, she was also desperate to know. But this yearning was because she loved me.

I helped her out. "I insist."

Finally, she said, "Okay. Since you insist."

She looked in the boat and read: *For my love to be forever happy and healthy as she seizes her dreams.*

Tears gleamed in her eyes as she wrapped her arms around me. "I love you, Hung."

I tightened my embrace. "When all this danger is over, let's get married and have a family of our own, okay?"

I was surprised at my question. The thought had swum in my

head for a long time, but I didn't realize this perfect moment had drawn it out of me.

She gasped, drew back, and stared at me. "Are you asking to marry me?"

I nodded. "I'm not a nobleman, so I can't give you status or extreme wealth, but I've got savings that would allow you to live comfortably. Most of all, I'll make sure you're safe and happy."

"I don't want status or wealth. I just want *my* warrior."

"Then it's settled." I kissed her forehead. "I'm yours."

"I'm yours too." She rose to her toes and kissed me on the cheek.

Beaming, she placed the paper boats in the stream. The pink evening sky cast a warm glow around the area, making the atmosphere peaceful and magical. The moon lit up like a large pearl against the dark purple sky. But a darkness lurked in the shadows, ready to destroy this magical moment at any minute. My sword had a quiet hum on my back but nothing strong enough to alert me.

More people arrived to release their paper boats.

Across the stream, Kai stood with Yunxi and Healer Churan. He met my gaze and nodded, signifying it was time. He said something to Yunxi and Healer Churan before taking off.

I tapped Su on the shoulder. "I've got to go. Be careful."

Two soldiers arrived, greeting me. "General Wen, the incense for tonight is ready."

"Thank you," I said. "Stay here with Su and guard the area."

"Why are you lighting incense?" she asked.

"To pray for good health, luck, and prosperity for Lin Din Ni."

My statement was partially true. I wished for all those great things for my land. But the purpose of the incense was to lure out the Soul Extractors. The soldiers didn't know this. For all I knew, these soldiers could be possessed. It was better to be safe than sorry.

But my dahlia knew there was something more. She arched an

eyebrow, waiting for me to elaborate. I pulled her aside and whispered, "You'll see curvy incense sticks. They're made using dried fish poop from the rare Inca fish. The scent doesn't affect a healthy person. But a possessed person whose mind isn't their own will be affected."

"I've never heard of that fish," she murmured. "It should be documented in the history books that fish poop is the most innovative way to take down an enemy."

I couldn't help the laugh that escaped me. Humor was exactly what we needed to lighten up the dire situation tonight.

I straightened my posture and spoke loudly. "Keep everyone safe, okay?"

"I'll do my best," she said and watched me leave.

CHAPTER SIXTY-TWO

SU

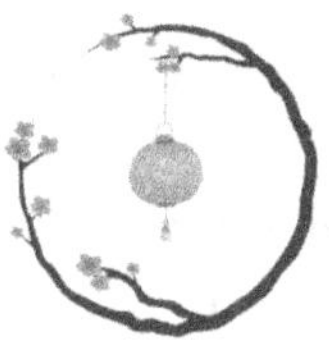

NOT LONG AFTER HUNG LEFT, a fight broke out between two drunken men. The soldiers intervened, separating the men. I scanned the area, looking for any signs of the Soul Extractors, but no one acted abnormal besides the drunken men.

I was curious about this fish poop incense and went to search for it.

A scream erupted, and I rushed to the sound. A woman wearing a yellow dress stood near a willow tree, holding her little white dog in her arms.

"What happened?" I asked.

Trembling, the woman pointed to a pile of leaves and twigs not far from the stream's edge. "I was playing with my dog. He kept sniffing and digging around the pile. Then I saw a leg." Tears streamed down her face.

The soldiers pushed away the leaves and twigs. My heart sank when I saw Beibei's body. I saw her only a few hours ago. What had happened? Her face appeared hollow, as did her body.

Fear churned in my belly as I remembered the Soul Extractors siphoning energy from a healthy human being. Beibei had run into a Soul Extractor.

Where were Ren and Lina? Were they okay?

I asked the soldiers to take the body to their military morgue, inform her family, and increase the guards in the area. Then I rushed to find Ren and Lina.

As I surveyed the crowded streets looking for them, I noticed the incense was placed in holders in various areas on the ground. It blended in with the décor of the festivities. Intuition told me to follow the placement of the incense, which gave off an interesting scent. Usually, I could tell if it was sage, cedar, myrrh, or frankincense, but I didn't recognize the unique scent. This had to be the incense Hung had spoken about. The fish poop incense smelled like a riverweed or something that came from the river.

I stepped up to one and studied it. The brown stick wasn't straight, and it had a bumpy texture to it. The smoke that emerged swirled around before creating a thin layer of smoke in the air. I wouldn't have noticed the smoky stream if I hadn't been paying attention. Anyone could've mistaken it as smoke from fireworks or food from an outdoor vendor cooking.

My heart pounded as I followed the stream of smoke. Then I saw a group of people in some kind of trance also following the smoke. They were soldiers, women, men, and children. From the way they swayed back and forth in rhythm, I knew they were the possessed.

I had no doubt the incense was luring them away from the Market Square. But where?

An idea popped into my head, and I didn't have to convince myself about the danger I'd be in. I rushed to join these people and pretended to sway like them. Their gazes flicked back and forth from the stream of smoke to the ground.

"I'm so hungry," said a woman.

"Smells like a delicious meal is waiting for us." A man lifted a finger, pointing ahead.

"I haven't eaten in so long," murmured a soldier.

As we passed by an alleyway, another group of possessed

people joined us. *Firehell.* I didn't realize there were so many possessed people in the Market Square. I recognized an Imperial guard. Fear skated down my spine. Was Yeeva safe? Was the Emperor and everyone in the palace secure?

Hung would have expected this. He would have measures in place to ensure the safety of the Empress and the Emperor.

Soon, we arrived at the Jade Junction, where roads branched into different directions depending on where people wanted to go. A bamboo forest took over a large section of the area, followed by dense woods of various trees. To my right was the path that led me to the Emerald Road when I'd rushed after Hung that time.

Lanterns hung among the trees, shedding light on an area that would soon go dark.

From the corner of my eye, I saw a figure dressed in black shift as he stood by the edge of the woods. Was that Ru Malik?

I didn't have time to contemplate when someone bellowed, "Now!"

A net of riverweed fell over us, but I darted out of the way at the last moment, rushing to hide behind a tall bush. The possessed people tried to free themselves from the net but failed. The riverweed wound itself around them like snakes. Arrows shot out from somewhere. Eerie screams that belonged to the dark world erupted like hell on earth. Goosebumps rose on my arms as I peeked out and saw soot floating around scattered bones.

As more possessed people arrived, more nets came down on them, followed by a series of arrows. One arrow flew and landed near me. I grabbed it, glanced at the dark arrowhead, and understood. It was covered with the same substance as the dagger Hung had given me.

A group of soldiers escaped the net and arrows and looked around for the lost trail, appearing to still be under the spell. Ru Malik jumped out of the undergrowth, wearing his snake mask and dark outfit. He swung his dark sword in many directions, spreading soot. The soldiers inhaled the soot and broke free of the trance. Their features changed to hollow faces with dark veins and eyes that radiated malice.

"Come out and fight me," Ru Malik declared. "Unless you're afraid, General Wen."

Ru Malik was behind the Soul Extractors?

Hung leaped out to stand in front of Ru Malik. He drew his blade. It glowed and hissed with power.

"It's been a long time," Ru Malik said. "You think this will eliminate the Soul Extractors? You're wrong. We're stronger than you think we are."

"We both know it hasn't been that long." Hung gestured to the group of possessed people turning to soot. "They don't look strong to me."

Though my heart hurt for all the victims, I reminded myself that they were possessed. If they stayed alive, they'd hurt more people.

"You're just wasting your time. Lin Din Ni will fall," Ru Malik said with certainty.

"Why are you doing this? This is your home too."

"You are a fool, General. Lin Din Ni is a weak empire, but it will be stronger when I conquer and remake it."

Did Hung already know who Ru Malik was?

"Join me and the Dark Lorde, and you will be rewarded. Nothing is stronger than the dark. I've tasted its power."

"Not interested."

"Anyone who stands in my way will die!" Ru Malik charged at Hung.

More possessed soldiers emerged, but the trance didn't seem to affect them. Kai, Tao, and a group of female warriors emerged from the woods, fighting them with weapons covered in dark ink.

Hung's sword clinked against Ru Malik's and hissed as sparks flashed from the collision.

Ru Malik seethed. "I'm going to *kill* you."

"I should have let them kill you back then!" Hung cursed. "You betrayed me!"

"There's a price for everything. I want power. No one dares to look down on me again." He lifted his arms to the sky, invoked something with a spell, and opened his palm.

A darkness shot down from the sky and entered his body. He trembled and grew in size as though he'd absorbed a burst of extra energy. His neck and hands looked like snakeskin.

A battle broke out between them. More possessed beings emerged from the woods. I clasped the inked arrow, leaped out from the shrubberies, and killed three possessed soldiers.

Hung saw me, and fear splashed onto his face. During that moment of distraction, Ru Malik sliced his shoulder.

"No!" I rushed over to battle Ru Malik with the inked arrow, but he dodged and didn't attack me like he did with Hung. Why?

"Help Kai and Tao!" Hung hollered. "I'm fine!"

Ru Malik pointed his sword at Hung. "You *poisoned* her, and you made her *infertile*, you fucker!"

Infertile? Was Ru Malik insane? What the hell was he talking about?

"The fuck!" Fury sparked in Hung's eyes as he charged at him. "It's *your* poison! You're the reason she's hurt!" Metals clanked, and Hung's sword radiated lightning energy, breaking Ru Malik's sword in half. An energy burst from the swords' contact, shoving the two men apart.

They glared at each other. I could feel their tension throbbing in the area. Hatred, anger, and resentment appeared in Hung's eyes. I'd never seen this vengeful look on his face.

"Su was poisoned with red thorn incense." Ru Malik pointed a finger at Hung. "But when she took that arrow for you, the two poisons created a deadly reaction. I gave her the antidote in the soup, but it was too late. It saved her but not her ability to have children, you fucker!"

The stomachache and the early moon cycle had been the side effects of the poison. A tidal wave of shock overcame me. Ru Malik was Ren? My dream of having a family with Hung was gone. I could see the shock and pain on Hung's face. It broke his heart. I could *feel* it. It wasn't his fault.

Ren's deranged desire for power had caused him to betray his best friend. How long had this been going on?

I wanted to kill Ren for all the people he'd murdered. Luzi's face flashed into my mind. He was responsible for her death and her family's. He was the leader of the Bloodshade Bandits, who had terrorized and tortured so many people. Lin Din Ni was his country too. Why was he doing this? I didn't understand it.

"Who killed my parents?" Hung asked, and the ice in his voice made me shiver.

"You should've stayed home that day. But you were being righteous, helping me retrieve my talisman." He ripped off his snake mask and tossed it aside, revealing a face strained with darkness and scaly skin. A dark mark sat on his forehead while deepset eyes stared at me. "Don't blame yourself. They were meant to die whether you were there or not."

"Why?" Hung demanded.

"Why does a general want to defeat his enemy?" He grinned, and I wanted to rip that mockery off his face. "There's only one reason."

I didn't recognize the kind scholar who recited poetry. This was a greedy man, desperate for power at any cost. He'd been hiding behind a harmless facade. How did he become this way?

I'd been fooled. Did his family know this?

From the corner of my eye, a soldier rushed toward Kai, who was battling two others. I darted over and stabbed the possessed soldier with an arrow.

Ren drew a smaller sword and fought Hung. With one swipe, Hung destroyed Ren's new sword. He jabbed the sword into Ren's shoulder and pulled it out. Black blood spurted from the wound. A swarm of sooty darkness emerged from his wound, surrounding the area like a storm. It was hard to see now, as nighttime had arrived. The sooty darkness obscured the lanterns in the tree.

"Su!" Hung shouted for me, but I couldn't see him.

I moved toward his voice, but an arm wrapped around my waist. A strange scent snuck up my nose, and my body jerked from an overwhelming chill. The powerful arm didn't belong to Hung. He yanked the arrow from my hand, and I heard it fall to the ground.

My index and middle fingers prepared to attack with the death touch, but my body went numb, and I lost consciousness.

CHAPTER SIXTY-THREE

HUNG

"SU!" I shouted as a silhouette carried her away from me. "Ren!"

He didn't stop.

"If you touch her, I'll show you oblivion!" Rage flooded my veins, and my fists clenched with the desire to kill my former best friend.

I wanted to puncture his chest, rip out his heart, and burn it while I skinned him alive. I wanted him to feel all the pain he'd bestowed upon me and my family. And now the woman I love.

When Ren disappeared, so did the sooty fog. The soft glow from the hanging lanterns returned, and I saw the aftermath of the dead. Bones scattered on the ground like it was an animal farm. Too many innocent people died today. The thing with rage was that it didn't crumble you—it *propelled* you forward. Right now, I had things to do, things that would lead me to Ren. His death was my mission.

"You okay?" Tao approached with Keiya by his side.

"He has Su," I seethed, praying he wouldn't hurt her.

"I can't believe he's been playing us all these years!" Kai turned to me. "Don't worry. He's been in love with Su for a long time. He won't hurt her."

I prayed that was true. I hoped he wouldn't hurt her because of me. She was my weakness.

"Have the men clean up the mess. I need to brief Emperor Tang and meet with the council."

"Go." Tao waved me off.

The piles of bones and soot needed to be buried. A makeshift memorial should be erected to remember these possessed people. But I didn't have the mentality to think about that right now.

I turned to Keiya and the women and men who stood looking at what was left of the possessed. "Thank you for your help."

The warriors offered me a nod. "We want peace too."

"We have to head back to the river now, General," Keiya said. "I hope you'll return the favor if we need it in the future."

"Absolutely." I tapped a fist on my chest. "You have my word. I'm sure Tao will let me know."

Keiya walked over to Tao, and he embraced her. After exchanging some words with him, she left with her faction. Tao and Kai knew what they needed to do.

Tension strained my shoulders, but I ignored the discomfort as I stalked into the Imperial chamber. Emperor Tang and Three-Eyes were already seated at the table. I'd sent a letter to the Emperor notifying him of my suspicion before tonight's event.

"How did your plan go?" the Emperor asked, looking paler than I remembered.

"We eliminated most of the Soul Extractors. My men are cleaning up the soot and bones now. They'll be buried soon." I swallowed and confirmed, "Ru Malik is Ren, the poet and scholar. He's captured Su."

"General Zhou's heir?" Three-Eyes lifted his eyebrows. "He's the leader of the Bloodshade Bandits?

I nodded. "And apparently, the person who caused the possession of the Soul Extractors. He works at the Imperial Poetry School in the Market Square, and his home is just outside. You were sensing his dark energy."

Ren had somehow mastered masking his energy because my sword didn't thrum when I was near him.

"He fooled us," Three-Eyes said. "Does his father know about this?"

I looked over at the Emperor and the stacked documents beside him on the table.

"Why aren't the generals here at the meeting? Where's Gong?" Three-Eyes asked, looking at me and the Emperor.

When I encountered Moo the other day and walked him back to his home, he told me what had happened to him and his friends, Quack and Oink. Ren had located them a few years ago and killed them. Moo escaped because he feigned his death. Ren had held a grudge against anyone who bullied or looked down on him.

I didn't know he hated me all these years. Where had I gone wrong? Why hadn't I seen it? Betrayal from a close friend was like a serrated knife I couldn't yank out. It had cut me so deeply that I didn't know if the wound could be healed. It kept twisting inside me, killing me slowly over and over again.

"Hung asked me to review some documents." The Emperor tapped the pile. "Many of them were forged by General Zhou. He has been committing crimes for a long time. He's worked with members from the Deathcap Clan, Horned Rebels, Iron Resistance, and others."

You can rest in peace now, Mudpie.

He'd given his life so I could survive the battle with the Iron Resistance.

I'd learned the hard truth today, and it devastated me. The truth wasn't pure—it just *was*. Sometimes, it was covered in shit. Other times, it grew flowers. Despite that, I needed the truth. It showed me how to live unhindered by deception, which could lead to my demise.

Emperor Tang's lips thinned. "The Zhou family will be punished. Gong should have General Zhou apprehended right now." Sighing, he rose from his chair. "I never imagined one of my trusted generals would commit treason."

A knock sounded on the door. It was probably Gong.

"Come in," said the Emperor.

The Imperial guard entered, bowed, and walked over to hand Emperor Tang an envelope. "This just arrived for you, Emperor."

The Emperor ripped open the letter and read it as a ridge dug into his forehead.

His fist was clenched as he tossed the letter on the table. I grabbed the letter, looking at what had caused his rage.

"General Zhou has escaped," I said. "Gong is fighting the rebels that have broken through the security around the Central Border. There are Soul Extractors there." I looked at the Emperor. "It's easier to kill them with weapons laced in fish ink. I can have Kai and Tao organize the weapons now."

The Emperor nodded. "Do it."

Three-Eyes pinched the space between his eyebrows. "Something is in the palace. It's blocking my vision, giving me a headache."

Concern rose in me. With all that had happened, I wouldn't be surprised if Ren and his fucking father had placed something harmful in the palace.

"I'll take a walk around the palace."

Three-Eyes straightened his posture and moved his hands in a formation that conducted energy to harmonize himself.

"Go rest," said the Emperor. "I need my council members well and strong."

After Three-Eyes left, Emperor Tang and I reviewed a strategy to contain the rebels and the Soul Extractors.

"Gong will need more soldiers to help him."

"The soldiers can take the newly inked weapons with them. But first, we'll need extra help at the Military Pavilion to assist with the inking process. This will expedite everything."

He flicked a gaze at me, looking exhausted. "I need to cultivate my energy too."

"If the darkness is in the palace, you should move to a nondisclosed area." I scanned his features. "You're not looking well. Let's go *now*. I'll escort you and the Empress."

"The blue fulgurite increases my strength. Being away from it, I will take longer to recover."

"Whatever is here is probably masking its powers too. Is there a secluded place you can go?" Most of the places I knew, General Zhou would know as well. I needed a location he didn't know.

"There's a house in the woods. It's Yeeva's garden house. We can stay there for now."

"You need to disguise yourself and have your replacement in the palace. We don't want anyone to know you're not around. We need the Empress's lookalike here too."

I'd met their doubles a few times. The man and woman possessed features similar to those of the Emperor and the Empress. Their identities remained discreet to protect everyone involved.

Once Emperor Tang and Empress Jayaatu disguised themselves as commoners, wearing cotton tunics and pants with veiled hats that hid their faces, I escorted them to their destination. We took a supply of dry goods and clothing with us. After securing the small path in the woods, we arrived at the quaint cabin in the woods, surrounded by various trees and shrubbery. It had a well for water, an outdoor area for drying herbs, and a shed for storage.

After they settled, I told the Empress, "I'll have Kai and Yunxi stay with you. She's a healer and can watch over you and the baby."

"You and Wei have been friends for a long time. Consider me a friend too." She smiled as she placed a hand over her round belly. "When no one is around, please address me as Yeeva. I requested this of Su as well. Where is she?"

I flicked a glance at the Emperor.

"Tell her." He wrapped an arm around his wife, probably anticipating her reaction.

My initial thought was to tell her the truth, but I didn't know if he wanted to protect her because of her vulnerable state. However, she'd find out eventually.

"Su's been captured." I briefed her on the dire situation.

Yeeva gasped, her expression distressed. She paled and swayed on her feet. Emperor Tang tightened his grip on her.

"We have to find Su," Yeeva said.

"I promise I will," I said. "Don't worry. Focus on your baby and staying healthy. Yunxi will be here soon with all the prenatal things."

When Kai and Yunxi arrived, it was past midnight. I was dead tired, but adrenaline kept me moving. There was so much to do, organize, and see through. I needed a moment to catch my breath, but I wanted to ensure their safety first.

"You need to rest." Kai stared at me with concern.

"Soon," I said. "I need more fish ink so the soldiers can start preparing the weapons."

"Tao can assist with that."

"I'd need Keiya and her warriors to assist too."

"They are. Don't worry."

I didn't know the status of General Li or General Pao's territories. Had there been an influx of rebels or Soul Extractors? They could be attacked right now and might not have time to ask for help. They'd also need a shipment of inked weapons. Was there sufficient fish ink to make weapons? Did the river warriors harvest enough fish to help us?

It didn't take long for us to arrive at the Green Fog River. A few lanterns hung in the trees to shed enough light. Even though it was late in the night, people were still out on small boats with the oil lamps as they threw nets into the water.

A whistle sounded, and another whistle responded.

Seconds later, Tao emerged from the dark shrubbery. "Is everything okay? I was going to head back to the Military Pavilion once we got an extra supply of fish."

"Do you have ink for more weapons?" I asked.

"How many weapons?"

"A lot." I updated him on the news about General Zhou having escaped and how Gong was battling the rebels in his place, the relocation of the Emperor and the Empress, and the need for more weapons for General Li and General Pao.

"We're going to war," he muttered.

"It's like a civil war with Soul Extractors and rebels paid off by our people. How pathetic is that?"

As the weight of everything suffocated me, I sat down on a log to rest.

Sitting beside me, Tao placed a hand on my shoulder. "You look like hell."

I'd never experienced hell like this. Hopelessness had hobbled me.

I didn't know how to save the woman I loved. I was uncertain I could protect Lin Din Ni. My best friend was now my worst enemy. That was hard to accept. I blamed myself for not seeing it. Was there a moment when he genuinely considered me a friend?

In urgent situations during a war, I resorted to strategy and logic. I was trained in techniques that yielded results. Right now, I needed that skillset.

"They have a good supply, but they're catching more Inca fish. I don't know if that'll be enough ink for all the weapons."

"Do what you can. We'll improvise," I said. "Do you think Keiya and her warriors would help us?" I asked Tao. "I know it's a lot to ask. It could place them in danger, but we're out of options."

Lin Din Ni had always kept to itself. We remained neutral as much as possible. We didn't meddle in acquiring more lands like other empires. I didn't think the neighboring empires would send help if they knew what we were facing. The Soul Extractors could infect their men and therefore, their empire.

But it wouldn't hurt to ask. I'd deal with whatever came after.

"I'll ask the Emperor to draft a letter to the surrounding empires asking for assistance tomorrow morning."

"It's an option." He shrugged. "But I have a feeling they won't help."

"If they can help us destroy the Soul Extractors, then that will eliminate a threat for them too. We'll sell it that way."

"Keiya will help," Tao said. "Lin Din Ni is her home too."

Tao agreed to help deliver the inked weapons to Gong and the other military camps. As I made it back to my villa, I dropped into my office chair and scrubbed a hand over my face. Blowing out a heavy sigh, I leaned back in my chair, wondering if Su was safe. Where had he taken her?

Ren was right; I'd destroyed Su's chance at motherhood. I would've waited for another strategy if I hadn't been so determined to lure Ru Malik to Luklum. She'd forgiven me for poisoning her. But this was different.

Even if she forgave me, I couldn't forgive myself.

CHAPTER SIXTY-FOUR

SU

I WOKE to the sound of trickling water. My eyes scanned the dimly lit room and spotted a water fountain at the other end by a bamboo divider. Intricate wooden beams supported the spacious bedroom. Silk brocade fabrics draped from the beams and along the wide door that opened to somewhere. Candles sat on the counter and by the wall. An oil lantern illuminated a round table not too far from me. A window offered me a peek at the impending dawn.

I was lying in a comfortable bed with a beautifully embroidered pink silk blanket. I shifted my legs and arms, but soreness thrummed there. A flashback of last night replayed in my head.

Fear flooded me. Was Hung safe? Had Kai, Tao, and the others escaped unscathed? I had no idea what happened after I passed out.

Reaching down to my belt, I sighed with relief when I felt my dagger. I was afraid Ren would've noticed my small weapon and removed it.

Where was this place? What was Ren's plan? I still couldn't believe he was Ru Malik.

Was Ren nearby? Was he hiding somewhere, watching me? I closed my eyes, concentrating on the silence in the room. When I heard nothing, I pushed myself up to a sitting position. A wave of dizziness set in, so I remained still for a moment.

Don't rush it.

I took a deep breath, trying to harmonize my breathing. After a few more inhales, I channeled my energy around my body. A minute later, the tightness in my shoulders, arms, and legs relaxed. The strange spicy scent from yesterday had numbed and weakened my body. Was it another poison?

Trying my best not to make a sound, I walked to the window and looked outside. The early dawn cast a warm glow, and I could see a bamboo forest.

Could this be the same bamboo forest near the Jade Junction? Were we that close by? Or was this a different one?

Footsteps sounded, and I rushed back to the bed and pulled the blanket to my chin, pretending to sleep.

The door creaked open, and feet shuffled in.

"She's still out," Ren told someone. "She's not used to the sleep fern and purple tepal."

The purple tepal had a numbing property. I remembered Healer Churan saying it could alter a person's voice if used excessively. Then it dawned on me—Ren had used that berry to modify his voice. I'd wondered how I didn't recognize him talking when we fought in the Market Square.

"We'll use her against Hung," said General Zhou.

My heart raced, but I tried my best to remain calm. I slowed my breathing as much as my frayed nerves would allow. I couldn't let them hurt Hung. He was probably worried about me on top of dealing with the betrayal of his best friend. Not to mention, one of his generals had committed treason.

Regarding my infertility, I didn't know what to feel. A sense of loss, anger, and . . . surrender. I could do nothing to change it. But I didn't want to waste energy on that topic now. I'd think about it later. Right now, I had to survive.

These people needed to pay for all the lives they'd taken.

"I'll kill him," Ren said. "We don't need her as bait."

The way he talked about Hung—the best friend who had stood up for him when no one else had. Hung was like a big brother who protected him, and here he was talking about killing him as though he were a stranger.

How could a close friendship end like that? What had gone wrong?

"Think big, Ren," his father said. "Lin Din Ni will be ours. We'll make it our own. Anyone who doesn't side with us will have to die. Once we settle in, we can start expanding to other territories. The blue fulgurite will be ours. We'll use it to our advantage instead of keeping it hidden."

"You'll be a fantastic leader, Father. They should have respected you the way you deserved. You should've been Prime General."

"And you'll make an incredible prince."

I didn't know what to think about these two praising each other while their captive was asleep. Their narcissism needed applause and recognition.

"I've been waiting for this moment for too long." General Zhou grunted. "We've sacrificed too much already. I'd celebrate by using our enemies' heads as offerings to Lan."

Was she his wife? She shared the same first name as my mother. Had someone killed his wife, and he was now out to make them pay?

"I've given up a lot too," said Ren.

"Did the commanders from the Central Empire agree to help?" General Zhou asked.

"There's nothing gold can't buy." Ren chuckled.

"The soldiers at the border have been instructed not to let any letters enter or exit Lin Din Ni. They can't ask for help."

"Good. We both need to lie low for a few days," General Zhou said. "You need to rebuild your energy before you update the Dark Lorde. I don't like him, but he's been extremely supportive of us."

Who was the Dark Lorde?

"I'm grateful for his help. He knows my worth and respects me."

"He has his own agenda," General Zhou added. "And I have mine. We're using each other to get what we need."

"He promised us Lin Din Ni," Ren said. "I know he'll see it through to the end. We've delivered so many people for him to extract their souls. He's more powerful because of us."

"We've done everything he's asked. He even took you on as a disciple." His feet shifted, probably walking somewhere. I prayed it wasn't to the bed I was on. "Can you control the possession? I didn't like how he used you as a vessel to speak through you. Do you have that ability?"

"My powers are stronger now," Ren said. "So I'm able to drop into a possession and speak through it."

It was already difficult trying to defeat Ren and his warlord father. But now there was a third person.

"Excellent to hear."

When General Zhou left, Ren stayed in the room. I could feel his presence moving toward me. He sat down on the bed and touched my forehead. My hands were still under the blanket, and I pressed my nail into a finger to prevent my body from jerking or making any move to alert him I was awake.

"Why didn't you choose me?"

CHAPTER SIXTY-FIVE

HUNG

IT HAD BEEN two days since Su was captured, and I couldn't find any clues as to where Ren might have taken her. Had they left Lin Di Ni? Soldiers had combed through the Zhou mansion, but there were no signs of Ren or his father. Lina didn't know what had happened, and I didn't have time to explain anything to her. But I asked a guard to keep watch over her in case her brother or father reached out.

Where were they hiding?

A supply of inked weapons had been transported to Gong to assist him. Another supply was also sent to General Li and General Pao's territories. I strode through the Market Square and sensed the dread. My sword hissed a quiet sound, which confirmed the dark was all around us. But it wasn't the powerful darkness I was searching for.

Though people tried their best to resume their daily routines, the despair in their eyes showed hopelessness. Some of these people had loved ones who had been possessed. A group had volunteered to build a memorial gazebo for those who had died. I walked over to the men outside the Market Square laying bricks, cutting bamboo stalks, and hammering them to wooden poles.

My fingers clenched as rage stormed inside me. I'd tried not to think about Ren's betrayal, but the more I ignored it, the more it upset me. Where had I gone wrong? Why hadn't I seen any of the signs?

He completely fooled you. You trusted him like a brother.

My stomach growled, reminding me to eat something. I hadn't eaten anything since last night. I'd been helping my men ink the weapons. We had to wait a few hours for the fish to produce the ink before we could resume production.

If you don't eat, you won't have the energy to find Su.

Did she hate me for what I'd done? If I hadn't used the red thorn poison that day at the temple, she wouldn't have had to endure this pain. Giving birth was a sacred gift for women, and I took that away from her.

As I ambled back to the market for food, I noticed a man walking in front of me. He wore a brown cloak and held a bag of food in his hand. A ball rolled to his foot, and a little boy raced over, looking at him. The man bent, picked up the ball, and gave it to the boy. That was when I noticed his unique boots—custom-made for military generals. An arrogant man couldn't resist the materialistic things symbolizing power and respect. No matter what disguise General Zhou wore, there would always be pieces of his ego in them.

A thrill rushed through me as I kept my distance from him. I bought some pork buns and fed my stomach as my eyes trained on him. He strode through the market, buying more random things. I purchased a gray cloak with a hood and slipped it on. If he were to turn around, I'd just be a commoner in the street.

He headed into a pottery shop beside Heavenly Reflections, which Lina partially owned with other noblewomen. I made my way to the back courtyard through an alleyway.

Lina's voice sounded over the brick wall. "You can leave the new jewelry in the review room. I'll take a look soon. That's all for now."

Gathering my energy, I leaped onto the rooftop soundlessly

and crouched by a nook connecting the jewelry shop and another business.

General Zhou emerged in the courtyard, pushed back his hood, and sat in a chair at a table with a bonsai.

Lina stood facing him. "You shouldn't be here. Everyone is looking for you."

"They won't expect me to be so close to the palace." He reached for the shears and began snipping at the tree.

"Father, why are you doing this?" she asked, the distress in her voice clear. "Lin Din Ni is our home."

"It is still *our* home. I'm making it better."

"How can you say that?" Lina cried. "Ren is behind all those kidnappings. He possessed innocent people, and they all died."

"In war, sacrifices must be made."

"Hung won't forgive you or Ren!"

"You need to watch your mouth!" He shot out of his chair. "You're the daughter of the Zhou family. Think big, Lina." He walked over and placed a hand on each of her shoulders. "Prince Ying from the Central Empire will make a great husband. Your union with him will strengthen our empire."

"This isn't *your* empire." She stepped away from him.

He lifted a hand, preparing to hit her. Lina braced an arm, anticipating the threat. But he curled his fingers and lowered his arm.

"Kill me! I don't care!" she declared. "I'm not marrying a prince twelve years younger than me. He's practically a little boy! What is wrong with you? Have you ever considered *my* happiness?"

At twenty years old, Lina had more sense than her father, who had commanded an army of men. The Zhou family was colluding with the Central Empire to gain power. Had they struck a deal with Rebel Territory? It would explain the rise in attacks in recent years.

"I *am* considering your happiness. The Central Empire is a powerful country with a lot of territories. Sacrifice for your family, Lina." He grunted. "You cannot marry Hung. He will die."

"He's treated our family like his own." Tears streamed down her face. "You and Ren betrayed him! You've ruined our family." Her voice grew louder, and two servants appeared, asking her if everything was all right.

"I'm okay." She waved them away. "I don't understand, Father. Why?"

"This isn't something for a woman to understand," he replied. "I should have been Prime General. I should have received the accolades for winning battles, not the senior General Wen."

He'd hated my family for that long? I supposed when the autonomy of a man was threatened, he'd do anything to gain it back. The pressure in my chest increased as hatred for the Zhou family spread like wildfire.

"You were inconsolable when he and his wife died. Everything was a lie?"

"In life, you need to learn how to adjust to certain situations."

She stared at him for a moment. "Did you have something to do with their deaths?"

He let out a laugh as he walked back to the bonsai and snipped off a large section, ruining it. "A man with vision must eliminate all obstacles."

"But I thought it was the Deathcap Clan," Lina said.

"We worked with them and bought their poison. But they didn't kill the Wen family." He laughed. "I did. Blaming the Deathcap Clan made the most sense. We solved an issue and rid ourselves of a thorn. Keeping them around would only pose a problem."

The fire in me exploded. At that moment, I lost control. I wasn't a general anymore—I was a son wanting to kill the man responsible for my parents' deaths.

I leaped to the ground, tossed my cloak aside, and drew my sword, aiming it at General Zhou.

"They considered you as a friend!" I seethed as the wrath

coursed through my blood. "You slashed their throats! How could you?"

"Actually, I poisoned them first." He smirked. "Then I cut their throats to make it look like a bandit raid. I had Ren lure you away from the house. You were young and useless, so I gave you a pass."

Rage coursed through my veins, which throbbed on my neck, arms, and hands.

"Hung." Lina darted over to stand beside me, her expression distraught.

I wanted to shoo her away. She was part of the family who'd murdered my parents. I didn't want her close to me. I could kill her too. But the fear, shock, and confusion on her face showed me she was a victim too.

"I'm sorry for what happened." She wiped the tears away with her hands. "I didn't know."

"Shut up!" her father exclaimed. "Do not apologize to him. He's not worthy of you." General Zhou shucked off his cloak and drew out a sword.

"Father, please stop it!" Lina raced over to grab her father's arm. "Don't hurt him. You've done enough!"

He slapped her once and drew back his arm, preparing for another attack. I swung my sword down, chopping off the hand that had slapped her. It thudded to the floor as blood sprayed everywhere.

Lina screamed and rushed to her father's side. But he shoved her away. "Get away from me!"

Though bleeding, he stood glaring at me, unafraid that I could kill him. "If anything happens to me, Ren will annihilate you!"

"He can try," I said, pouring salt onto his family's wounds. "But like always, he will *never* measure up to me. You don't like your son always coming in second behind me. You've brainwashed him."

That didn't excuse Ren's evil deeds, but his father was the one who led him down the wrong path. Ren was a bullied child who became a vile bully himself.

I flicked the blood from my sword and pointed it at him. "You destroyed your children's lives for your own agenda. Your lineage will end when I behead him."

"Please, no!" Lina cried hysterically.

"You can't fight against the Dark Lorde or the Central Empire's army already on their way here." A sly smile slid onto his face. "If you surrender, we'll let Su live."

"Father! Ren loves Su!" Lina exclaimed. "You'll destroy him. Please stop the bloodshed."

"He cannot be with her!" Malevolence strained his face. "She's his half-sister!"

My mouth dropped open. Was he making false excuses to control his son? Or was this the truth?

"Does she know?" I asked.

"No. I loved Lan, Su's mother. But she didn't want to be my mistress, so she left me and married Rong. She was already pregnant with *my* child."

"Did *Me* know about this?" Lina yelled.

"When she found out, she threatened me." He sneered. "I had to stop her."

"You killed my mother . . ." Lina fell back and puked.

"Rong loved Su like his own. But I feared he would use that fact to threaten me one day, so I eliminated them. Su got lucky and escaped. Since she knew nothing, I let her live. But that won't happen to you!"

Though injured, he whipped a dart at me, but I dodged it. Growling like a crazed man, he charged at me with his sword, but Lina jumped in, blocking his sword from hurting me.

"Lina!" I shouted as the tip of his sword punctured her stomach, spearing through her back.

She fell against me, and I caught her limp body.

General Zhou widened his eyes as he stared at his wounded daughter.

Something dark washed over his face. "It's your fault she's hurt!" He reached for the shears on the table and rushed toward me.

With my empty hand, I flung my sword into his gut. The force sent the blade through his back, taking him with the sword as it pierced a wooden beam.

He glared at me, and even now, I could see he still blamed everyone else for all his wrongdoings.

"Please . . . t-t-take the sword out," Lina asked me with broken words. "I d-d-don't want that evil s-s-sword in me." Tears spilled from her eyes.

I fulfilled her request and yanked the sword, whipping it aside. Blood stained her stomach. There was nothing I could do for her. A sense of helplessness overcame me as I looked at the woman I'd always considered a sister. I'd never forget the little girl who always shared her candies with me when we were younger.

She wasn't responsible for her family's sins. Tears brimmed my eyes.

"I'm s-s-sorry for everything . . ." she breathed, reaching for my hand.

"It's not your fault." I squeezed her hand.

Two servants appeared and rushed over. I asked them to get Healer Churan and alert my guards.

"Healer Churan will be here to help you."

She smiled. "Don't l-l-lie to me, Hung. I know m-m-my s-s-situation." She met my gaze, and the spoiled girl had suddenly grown up. "Please f-f-forgive m-m-my family. Forgive m-m-me. I've been a thorn in y-y-your side."

"Save your energy. Don't talk." I squeezed her hand. "I forgive you, and I hope you'll forgive me."

Forgive me for not being able to return your love. I pray you'll meet someone who loves you in your next life.

She stared up at the sky and smiled. "I'm happy that Su is my big sister. No wonder I've always admired her. Please t-t-tell her I'm s-s-sorry . . ."

Lina's body jerked as she took her last breath. Her eyelids closed, and her body went lax and lifeless.

CHAPTER SIXTY-SIX

SU

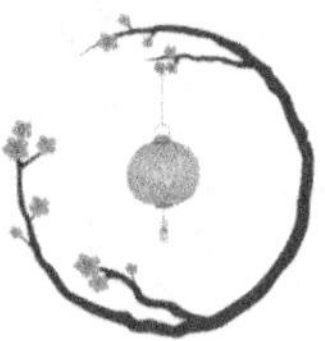

WEARING ALL BLACK, Ren sat on a chair across from me on his balcony, facing the bamboo forest. I didn't recognize this person before me. Though his features were the same, the energy emanating from him was cold.

I'd tried to escape this mansion for the past few days, but he had guards stationed at every corner. I didn't know if they were possessed. Plus, Ren hardly left me alone. He worked on the lower level, and his bedroom was next to mine.

At night, I could hear him talking to that eerie voice. I tried listening to them, but I couldn't make out what they were saying through the wall.

"Eat." He placed a dumpling on my plate with his chopsticks. "It's shrimp and pork—your favorite."

I didn't have an appetite, but I needed energy to escape.

"Why are you keeping me here?" I poked at the dumpling, wondering if he had dosed the food with something that could weaken me. So I reached for a peach instead and bit into it.

"To keep you safe, we're killing Hung. I don't want you around him."

"He's your *best* friend!" Anger and fear collided in me. "How can you do this to him?"

"Our friendship wasn't real." He looked at me. "I hated him more when he liked you."

"Hung felt guilty about it. But I told him I wasn't interested in you." I looked at him. "You *knew* that."

He shrugged. "A heart can change."

"No, it can't."

"You belong to me," he said firmly. "I've been in love with you since you saved me."

Saved him? I couldn't recall saving him from anything.

"When?" I asked, taking small bites from the peach. I didn't want to finish too soon and have him shove more food in my face.

How could I trust any of the food and drinks were safe? Maybe this peach was already tainted. I chewed as slowly as possible so I didn't have to finish it.

"Do you remember being at the Green Fog Lake a while ago?" He leaned back in his chair, studying me. "You and Healer Churan were helping a group of injured people. I was one of them."

"You were with the man from the Central Empire visiting his family? The ones who gave us the purple tepals?"

His expression warmed. "You remember."

"Everything was a lie." I'd been fooled. "What were you doing there?"

"Gathering people to deliver them to the Dark Lorde. A few of them fought back, and I got injured. I wasn't as powerful as I am now."

He'd looked different then, skinnier and probably in disguise, which was why I never made the connection. That had been a chaotic day with me trying to learn from Healer Churan and helping all the injured people.

"You used those tepal berries to change your voice."

"I've learned a few things here and there."

His skin had changed since I saw him yesterday. More scales appeared on his neck and hands. Dark veins crept up the side of his face. Whatever he was doing with that eerie voice had transformed him.

I finished the peach and dropped the pit onto my plate.

"Eat more," he said.

"I still don't have an appetite." Rubbing my stomach, I lied, "That toxic scent I inhaled did something to my body."

Ren furrowed his eyebrows. "I only used half of the standard dose." He got up from his chair and walked over to me, placing a hand on my forehead. I regretted saying anything to him. "You're warm." He looked at me. "Rest up some more so you'll have energy for the big day."

Fear spiked in me. "What big day?"

"We're getting married."

What?

My heart dropped into the pit of my stomach. His obsession with me had turned into something beyond sick. I wanted to tell him I didn't love him. But would that enrage him even more? To survive, I'd play it safe.

"Why are you obsessed with me?" I asked, believing the question was safe to ask. If I agreed to his demands too quickly, he would be suspicious.

"People say there's one love for each person in each lifetime. You're *it*. From the moment I met you. You were kind to me. You were nonjudgmental. I can't explain it, Su."

That was how I felt about Hung. We had a bond beyond time and space. I wanted to see Hung again, which was why I didn't grab the knife and stab Ren right now. Even if I did that, how far would I be able to go? His martial arts were better than mine, and this darkness in him—around him—was something I needed to be wary of. The negative vibration grew heavier every day. I felt it pulsing from next door.

"I didn't know how strong your feelings were for me," I said.

He placed an arm on my shoulder. "There's no other woman for me."

I couldn't help but think of my poor dead friend at that moment. "What about Beibei? She really liked you."

His jaw twitched as he got up and walked to the balcony railing. "She insulted me." He whirled to face me. "She said you and Hung made an admirable couple. That was an insult I couldn't accept. So I had to punish her."

What insanity was this? He was delusional and unhinged. How could he twist a simple, harmless statement into an insult?

I got up from the chair, walked to stand beside him at the railing, and glanced down. We were two stories up. I could probably use my energy to leap down and not break any bones. But how far could I run before he caught up to me? Would he send the darkness after me?

I could stab him with my dagger. But what if that one stab wouldn't affect him? Ren wasn't in his Soul Extractor form. Would the inked blade still work? I didn't want to risk failing and having him kill me.

"What if I accidentally insult you one day? Will you punish me like her?"

He brushed a finger down my cheek. "No. You're too perfect to make any mistakes."

I swallowed, testing his boundaries. "Who are you talking to at night? Sometimes I hear whispers." I tapped my head. "Or maybe I'm hallucinating."

His eyes bored into mine, and I saw something that twisted my gut. A face made of smoke formed in his irises. It moved across the whites of his eyes like a ghost.

I sucked in a breath, wanting to ask him. But I had a feeling the darkness was watching him, *controlling* him. He probably didn't even know it.

"I'm talking to my mentor," he said and winced, rubbing a spot on his arm. "You're going to be my wife, so there shouldn't be any secrets between us. When I was lost and didn't have anyone to talk to, the Dark Lorde appeared. He taught me how to punish bullies." His face brightened as he curled his fingers into a fist. "It felt good to break their bones and watch them die. If I want to be the best at anything, I must eliminate all obstacles around me. Anyone who mistreated me got what they deserved."

He'd been communicating with this darkness since he was a teen. It had seeped into his bones. This darkness had been feeding him vengeance, violence, betrayal—all the things that destroyed genuine relationships. All the things that turned a heart black.

"Hung was a good friend," he continued. "But he was also my biggest threat. He was so much better at everything than me." A crease deepened between his eyebrows. "When we're in a room, everyone respects him and dismisses me. I know he doesn't do it on purpose, but as long as he lives, I'll always be his shadow. His friendship has prolonged his life until now." His face turned bitter. "Until he took you away from me."

How could I respond in a way that didn't provoke him? I didn't want him to think I was trying to escape. So I focused on his relationship with his mentor.

"Does your mentor have other students? Is he from a different empire?"

Ren smiled. "I love your curious mind, Su." His eyes sparked. "He has other students, but they're not here. I think you'll make a great disciple."

An idea sparked, followed by an inner voice telling me to take things slow. But I wanted to see what was in his bedroom.

"Not right now," I said. "I need time to heal and recuperate my energy before I can consider learning martial arts or other forms of magic. But I'm curious what's in your room. Is your mentor staying there?"

"No, he's not in my bedroom." He laughed. "But I have access to him there."

A guard approached, bowed to him, and said, "Sorry to interrupt, Master Zhou. But we just received terrible news about General Zhou."

"What?" he barked.

"He's dead," he said. "His head is hanging in the Market

Square. People are chanting about treason and throwing food at him."

Ren released a series of curses as rage darkened his eyes. Dark veins grew there, like fat worms trying to wriggle free from his neck and face.

"There's one more thing," the soldier added, looking scared.

"What?"

"Lady Lina is also dead."

"What?" His eyes widened.

I gasped, wondering who had killed her.

"I'm going to fucking kill him!" Ren stalked up to the guard. "You and another guard stay here. Keep her safe. Don't let her leave this mansion. I'll be back as soon as I rip off his head." He turned to me. "I'll return soon."

Terror slid down my spine as his footsteps disappeared.

Had Hung killed his father and sister?

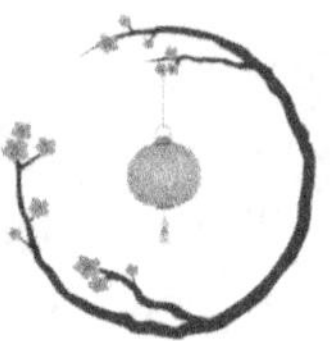

I STOOD inside my room with my heart thundering in my chest. This was my chance to escape. More importantly, I could use the opportunity to see what was in the room next to me. But a guard was standing outside my door.

I brought the food from the balcony back into the room, setting it on the table. Picking up a plate of dumplings, I smashed it on the floor. Shards scattered all over.

The guard rushed in. "Is everything okay?"

I crouched, held my hand, and winced. "I accidentally dropped it and cut myself. Can you please clean it up?"

While he was busy picking up the broken pieces, I pressed the death touch to a pressure point on his neck that would quickly knock him out. He wasn't an adept warrior, so my Dim Mak worked well on him.

I snuck to the door, opened it, and peeked out. The other guard was probably still guarding the lower level.

When it looked safe and I didn't hear anyone coming, I stepped out, closed the door quietly, and walked into Ren's room. Goosebumps rose on my arms and neck. The layout of the room resembled the one I was in, with intricate wooden beams and a door that opened to a balcony. A dark fabric draped over something on a stand. A chair sat in front of it.

A chill rushed through me as I neared it. Whispers came from whatever was under the fabric. The hem of the fabric fluttered as though a breeze were in the room. There wasn't.

How was Ren connecting with his mentor?

Gathering my nerve, I gripped the fabric, yanking it off. I leaped to the side, fearing something could hurt me. When nothing came out of the mirror, I studied the black surface.

"Kill everyone," said a gravelly voice.

The surface of the mirror shifted with the vibration of the voice.

Was he ordering Ren to kill?

"Hung isn't your friend. He's weakening your energy. He tricked your woman into leaving you, and he killed your father. *Kill him!*"

A wave of hatred and violence burst through the mirror, filling the room. I didn't know how I knew, but that emotion belonged to Ren. The darkness had contaminated his mind and his soul.

A thought popped into my head, and I reached for the dagger laced with ink that Hung had given me. I gripped the handle and stepped in front of the mirror. The mutable surface stopped shifting as it sensed my proximity. Before it could do anything, I punctured the surface with my blade, then dragged it down and up and around as though I were tearing into fabric.

An eerie cry erupted, chilling my bones. Cracks formed in the mirror where I had punctured it, and something from behind the mirror ripped the dagger from my hand like a magnet, swallowing it up. I rushed to the balcony, tugged at my energy, leaped to the ground, landed safely, and ran.

Something exploded behind me, but I didn't turn to look. I sped through the bamboo forest, unsure of the direction of the main road. My body shivered as the temperature dropped. Fear made my legs burn, but I didn't have time to be afraid.

The bamboo leaves around me shriveled.

"You can't run from me, Su. You cut me! Now I'm going to rip you to pieces!" The eerie voice echoed through the forest.

The bamboo stalks fell around me, and I dodged them as best I could. Dark mist rose from the ground, obscuring my vision.

Su. To your right.

A rift gleamed near me, and my heart leaped with hope.

"No!" the Dark Lorde shouted angrily, and the ground trembled.

Honing in on my energy, I jumped into the rift, trusting it would open wide.

CHAPTER SIXTY-EIGHT

SU

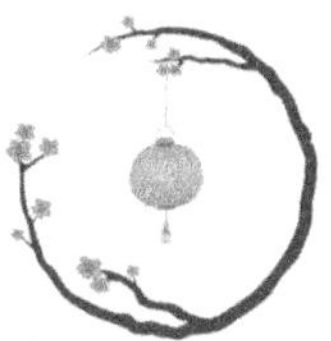

THE RIFT CLOSED AS SOON as I made it through the portal, separating me from that dangerous world.

I stood on a dirt path somewhere, catching my breath.

Something pushed at the space where the portal had closed, forcing me to jump away. Was the Dark Lorde trying to break through?

I stared at the pulsing energy, wishing I could do something to stop the darkness.

The veils thinned, and I gasped at the sight before me. A massive black serpent with a human face slithered around the area. Was he the Dark Lorde? A few scars crisscrossed his face. One slashed from his forehead down to his chin. Black blood dripped from the fresh wounds.

Had I done that with my inked dagger? Pride soared in me.

The snake whipped its body into the invisible wall again. The wall undulated as energy pulsed from it. Nerves bubbled as I feared the distorted serpent could break through.

Su.

I turned, and Roar of the Sky appeared. She swam close to me and swiped a claw at the invisible wall. The force shoved the serpent elsewhere for a moment, but it quickly reappeared, moving around us.

"You can't hurt me," he said to Roar of the Sky.

Ignoring him, she looked at me. "We have to go. Hung is in danger."

In an instant, the scenery changed, and the snake vanished. We were now in an open field with sloped hills. Pretty flowers grew nearby, giving me hope.

"Climb on," the dragon said.

"What?"

"Climb on my back." Her scales shifted, forming steps for me. "We have to hurry. They're attacking us from several angles."

I stepped on the iridescent scales, and they illuminated. When I reached the top of her neck, my stomach dropped as I glanced down and around me. The landscape looked different from this perspective. My body released a sigh as I breathed in the fresh air from high up. I wasn't afraid of heights, but I'd never stood on anything this elevated. It was like standing on top of a massive mountain.

"I made a throne for you, my friend."

Her scales shifted, twisted, and transformed between her horns, closer to her neck. They formed a seat for me. A small scale curved against my stomach as I sat, securing me in place. I couldn't believe I was sitting on a dragon. Two locks of hair spiraled in front of me as though waiting for me to grip them like reins.

When I clasped the reins, she said, "I need to show you something."

Roar of the Sky rose into the air with ease. Wind whipped my face as she swam across the sky. As her serpentine body moved, the seat shifted slightly. My stomach churned as I gripped the reins tightly. Despite the elevation and speed, I was secured in my seat.

The dragon swam up and up. A rift formed in the sky with golden light radiating through it. The wind increased, and I sensed a shift in energy. My body tingled as Roar of the Sky swam through the rift.

"Where are we?" I shouted, fearing the loud wind might swallow my voice.

"No need to shout. I can hear you fine." Her scales shifted, revealing two sets of ears.

How come I didn't see them before?

"We're in a place between realms," said the dragon.

I lifted my face to the golden light, loving its warmth. I inhaled the refreshing air that rejuvenated my lungs, giving me a much-needed boost of energy.

"The air is distinct here."

"You're breathing in the ether. Take in as much as you can before I return to the third-dimensional human realm."

"What is that serpent with the human face?" I asked. "Is that the Dark Lorde?"

"One of his many faces. That serpent is an aspect of him. He's in many places at once, creating chaos. But his true self is hiding in another place."

My stomach quivered as I realized what we were up against.

"He's an ancient darkness harnessing powers more quickly than I expected," said Roar of the Sky. "Beings from the other realms are also dealing with versions of him. The darkness plays with human emotions and feeds on the negative. Anyone with powerful dark thoughts is his ideal target."

We exited the rift and swam through a beautiful sky with colorful clouds floating in the distance. The soft colors created a gentle scenery that calmed me. I glanced to my right and saw three moons. At least, that was what they looked like to me. As I stared at them, many more appeared in shapes like oblongs and triangles, three-petal shapes, and other abstractions that blew my mind.

"Are those moons?" I squinted my eyes, staring at the impossible.

You're riding a dragon. Anything is possible.

"Yes," said the dragon. "The moons play an important role in all the realms."

"Where are we?"

"In one of the dimensional matrices outside of what you're used to. I'm taking you on a quick tour because I need you to know what's coming. There's a cosmic war, and we all have a part in it." She moved aside as a mesmerizing dragon swam by with her iridescent wings. I didn't know how I knew it was a female dragon.

The winged dragon looked at Roar of the Sky and nodded. Her green eyes darted to me, and she offered a nod before flying off. The massive wings almost brushed me. I should've felt a wind current, but the surrounding air remained calm.

"Who was that?" I asked.

"The Seventh Harmonic, my mate's ex."

Curious, I turned to get a better look at her rival, but she had disappeared.

"What's your mate's name?"

"Clash of Thunder."

"You're more beautiful than her," I said.

Roar of the Sky laughed. "We're friendly with each other. She's helping maintain harmony within the dragon realms. Her wings carry ancient codes that hold the secrets to our existence and evolution."

"What's your role?" I asked.

"To protect the womb of creation—the abyss where all things are born."

"You're like a protective mother." I could sense that.

She laughed, and I could hear the pride in her voice. "That's a practical way of seeing things."

"That's why you gave birth to six dragon eggs. Each one is from a different dimension." I paused, thinking. "You know, I don't understand all these things you're describing."

"I know," she said. "In time, your mind, soul, eyes, ears, and heart will automatically understand these things. For example, you just saw The Seventh Harmonic fly by. But she wasn't here with us in the same space. She was traveling across dimensions—or realms if that makes more sense to you."

"Oh." I recalled a slight difference in energy, but I couldn't pinpoint what it was. I remembered her talking to Hung and me about the dimensions, but I never got the chance to ask more questions. "How many dimensions are there?"

"At the present moment, there are forty-four dimensions. The energy is heavier and denser where you live. The higher you go, the more the frequency lightens. More dimensions are birthed when the Cosmos deems it appropriate."

"Wow," I muttered, still trying to grasp this surreal knowledge. Right now, it was beyond my scope of understanding. But somehow, a part of me understood it.

I needed her to confirm something for me. "Did your scale help me fight off the poisons?"

"Yes. My scale strengthened your body so it could defend itself naturally. But some things slipped through that couldn't be prevented."

I breathed a sigh of relief. "I'm human, so my body is prone to aches, pains, and exhaustion. Thanks to you and your scale, I'm healthy again."

"*You* did that by practicing your kung fu and cultivating your essa. The scale was merely a minor assistant that helped you remove the poisons."

"Regardless, thank you." I patted the whisker beside me.

"You're welcome."

We left the scenes of colorful clouds and entered a landscape with rolling mountains, creating a gorgeous backdrop for the river in front of us. I could tell this was a new realm because another series of tingles rushed through me.

She swam close to the river, and I glanced at the flowers growing beside the river's edge. People walked along the shore.

Some gathered around the river plants that bloomed with pretty flowers. The people in this realm had pointed ears, and their skin tones varied in color. When they spotted us, they paused and placed their hands over their hearts, nodding to us.

The dragon let out a roar, and the fish from the river jumped up and down as though cheering.

"Looks like they're happy to see you."

"They're worried about my mate and me. They also know we're fighting the darkness with their warriors, and they appreciate the help."

Geometric shapes floated away from the people and over to us.

"I see these floral shapes a lot. I've seen something similar in your eyes. What are they?"

"They're cosmic mandalas, patterns that create a specific shape. Within these shapes are ancient codes—sacred information." The dragon slowed her speed, lowering to the river, where I saw my reflection in the clear water. "Life is a series of patterns that repeat itself. You see patterns all around you. The petals on a flower. The insides of fruits when you cut them open. The scales on fish. On me." She dipped, and her belly touched the water. "All Infinara Dragons have a mandala given to them to carry out a mission, along with a dragonfly."

The imprint on her forehead gleamed.

"Dragonflies are so pretty," I said. My ears itched and popped, and a series of soft sounds echoed around me.

"They're sacred insects that can see so many things with their fractal eyes."

I appreciated all the wisdom Roar of the Sky was sharing with me, even though I might not understand everything.

"We all come from different dimensions to help *you* grow. Your survival is crucial to our survival."

"How?"

"Let me try to explain this better," said the dragon. "You understand the meridian lines in the human body. There are also meridian lines on the land. Those are called ley lines. Energy lines run all over the universe, intersecting with each other like the energy pathways crisscrossing on your bodies. Look at my eyes."

I glanced at the water's surface and saw the dragon's irises' reflection. A beautiful mandala emerged in each iris. It turned like a wheel that moved slowly while radiating a bright gold.

"That's my dragon mandala, unique to me. It's a key that allows me to move between realms efficiently."

I was going to ask more questions, but we left that realm and entered the night sky.

Something hopped around in the distance.

"Is that Tempo?" I missed the adorable rabbit.

"Yes." She soared over to him. He stood on an energy wave with a cluster of stars.

He saw me, hopped over, and jumped into my arms.

"I missed you," I said.

"Me too," he replied with his adorable voice as he nuzzled my face.

"I can hear you!" Excitement burst in me.

"Your frequency has changed because you've traveled through several dimensions," said Roar of the Sky.

Tempo's ear perked up, and he stiffened. "An egg just hatched. I have to go now."

"Go," the dragon replied. "Make sure my babies are safe."

"Be safe." Tempo placed a paw on my arm. "Thank you for all your help, Su." He had such wise eyes. Before I could say anything, he hopped onto the energy wave and disappeared.

"Do you need to be with your baby?" I asked.

"Tempo will be there with him."

"You know it's a male dragon?"

"Yes. I know each of their genders. Tempo has placed the eggs in specific places for their safety. When the egg resonates with an energy meant for it, it will trigger it to hatch. The dragon will locate that person when the time calls for it to do so."

"Like how your scale found me?" I asked.

"Yes. I'll visit my babies soon. Right now, I need to be here for something else."

She continued swimming through the night sky as floral designs burst and bloomed in the distance. I welcomed the silence that blanketed us.

"Su," Roar of the Sky broke the silence. "You have an unresolved issue that needs to be settled."

"What do you mean?"

"I want you to understand something." She dove, and my stomach flipped. "You're not flawed. Your inability to have children was fated. You're meant for something more. Some people make wonderful parents for children that aren't biologically theirs. Some love their pets like their children. Some people become mothers to groups of people because they love and want the best for them. You are perfect, just as you are."

I sucked in a breath, surprised that she could sense my sadness, confusion, and resentment. I didn't even know who I resented. Life? God? The Heavens?

Your inability to have children is fated.

With all that had gone on, I hadn't had time to truly process my emotions regarding my body. But in this quiet space with the dragon who understood me, I accepted my fate.

"Thank you," I said. "It was hard to accept it at first, but I'm okay with it now."

There was nothing I could do about it. Life often took you down shocking paths, and this was one of them.

"You're fated for another mission. You'll understand soon."

"I wanted to have a family with Hung one day. Give him a son or a daughter." I swallowed the lump that had formed in my throat. "I hope he'll be okay with that."

"He will," she confirmed. "You're both instrumental in this war between light and dark. The darkness wants to eliminate all light."

"It's targeting Lin Din Ni."

"Because that's where the seed of light is being born. This new baby will usher in a completely new energy. Your Empress can weave light. Your Emperor can manipulate time and space. Together, they create a powerful force. Their daughter will arrive soon, and the darkness wants to kill her."

CHAPTER SIXTY-NINE

SU

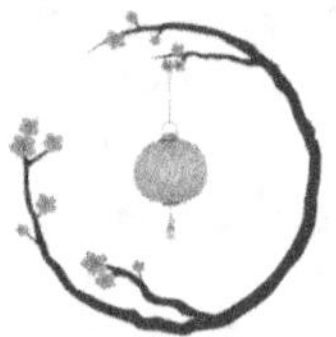

AN ENERGY SHIFT occurred as we entered a world where dark clouds loomed like a heaving blanket in the sky. The air thickened around me, and I gasped to breathe. Eerie wails echoed in the distance. People who looked half-human and half-monster wandered the barren land. A group of them attacked someone. When he was down, they all fed on him.

Trees stood in the distance, but they didn't look like normal trees. Something on the ground shifted. Heinous creatures hobbled up from the dirt, glaring at us with red eyes. More terrifying creatures crawled out of abandoned homes and turned toward us.

My gaze was fixed on a massive palace standing in the distance.

As we soared past a building, a group of fighters dressed in black stepped out and spotted us immediately. They wore hoods over masked faces. My eyes darted to a wagon dumping glowing balls into a flowing stream. The glowing balls were the only bright things in this dark world.

"Kill them!" One fighter grabbed a bow and arrow and shot at us, followed by his comrades.

Roar of the Sky dodged the arrows and swooped into a rift that opened for us.

"That was close." My heart thundered in my chest. "Who are they?"

"The Krix, the army of the Dark Lorde."

Icy dread settled in my stomach as I imagined the war we had to fight. "How does the portal know when to open?"

"I opened it." The dragon flew faster. "The Krix is coming to Luklum."

Terror gripped me. "What was that place?"

"A world taken over by the Dark Lorde. The growing famine and violence have morphed the people who used to live there. They are now half-human and half-beast. Those colorful balls are souls they've stolen from humans. The Dark Lorde absorbs them to empower himself."

"He was using Ren to capture people for him."

"He's using many people for himself," she said. "I wanted you to see what would become of Lin Din Ni and the other empires around you if the Dark Lorde wins. You've seen the peaceful worlds that differ from yours. But they are susceptible to the same destruction. Remember what you're fighting for. Don't let the darkness win."

"I'll do my best," I said.

"I know you will." Her scales shifted, making a lovely rhythm. "You may be a healer, but your warrior's spirit will help you survive. We're back in Luklum."

A shift in energy slammed into me when we entered Luklum. The heaviness weighed on my body, but it wasn't as heavy as the dark world.

"It's hard to breathe."

"Dark energy has swarmed Lin Din Ni. Look at the palace." The dragon soared toward the cloud of dark energy.

"It's coming from the ground too," I said, looking at the dark energy drifting up like mist.

As Roar of the Sky lowered her body, people from the streets glanced up, shouting and pointing. Some cheered in awe while others ran for cover. Dragons had graced books and art for so long. Depending on the dragon you believed in, people knew of the power, auspicious omen, wrath, and destruction. I was fated to meet a heavenly dragon who was here to help people. But I also knew there were unfriendly dragons that wanted to destroy us.

A dreadful roar sounded in the distance, and Roar of the Sky's scales went wild, creating an erratic sound like a warning.

"Su, another threat has arrived," said the dragon in her motherly calm voice. "I'm going to lower you to the rooftop. Leap off and go into the palace. Dark energy is breeding there. It's coming from a plant that's spreading its roots."

Another roar wailed, and I glanced over my shoulder to see a black dragon made of dense darkness. Its red eyes gleamed as it soared toward us.

Shit.

"What's that dragon?"

"A Despondo—a demonic dragon that snuck in from one tear in the Cosmos. I'll deal with the beast. You concentrate on the battle on the ground."

"Where did it come from?"

"A world you can't fathom right now. It's too complex to explain. Fight the battle here. Let me worry about the cosmic war."

I had so many questions, but this wasn't the right time for them. The people on the ground saw the Despondo and panicked.

"Is that snake with the human face going to appear?"

"I don't know. But you've injured him. Most likely, he'll possess a body to do what he needs to while conserving his energy."

Roar of the Sky swam to the Market Square, and I spotted Hung battling Ren.

"That rooftop over there!" I pointed. "I need to help Hung."

When she approached the roof of a three-story tavern, I jumped off. She lifted her body and soared toward the Despondo.

I raced across the roofs, jumping to a lower level until it was safe for me to leap onto the ground.

Chaos had consumed the Market Square. I didn't recognize my home anymore. People panicked, pushing each other out of the way. My heart raced as I refused to cede the thought that we could lose this battle.

I grabbed a sword from a fallen soldier and made my way toward Hung. Ren's body had increased in size. His shoulders, arms, and legs were somehow both bulkier and swifter.

"Die!" he shouted, pressing his weight onto the sword that screeched against Hung's. "You'll pay for killing my father!"

A light sparked, and Ren's sword broke. His face looked even more deformed than it did hours ago.

My eyes met Hung's, and he understood me.

"Ren!" I shouted from behind him.

CHAPTER SEVENTY

HUNG

WHEN REN TURNED TOWARD SU, I plunged my sword into his back, pulled it out, and stabbed him again. His improved fighting skills and increased strength had made it difficult to kill him until now. His love for my woman was rooted deeply inside him, right next to his hatred for me. Black blood poured from him, and his expression fluctuated between the Ren I knew and the man possessed by darkness and malice.

"Why did you kill Lina?" he asked, holding a hand to his wound. His face changed expressions.

"I didn't. Your father did."

Shock splashed onto his face as his body trembled, as though his heart had just exploded in his chest. Ren looked over at Su. Protectiveness surged in me, so I rushed over to her, surveying her quickly. Relief settled when I didn't see visible injuries.

"*Kill her!*" shouted the voice that came from Ren, but it didn't sound like him.

The possession had control of his mouth and body, but his eyes portrayed defiance. When Ren looked at Su, I could tell he was fighting the possession. A part of me felt sorry for my former friend. He'd betrayed my friendship and had done so many things to hurt me. He knew his father had planned on killing my parents and helped him with it.

I debated on telling him that his father had also killed his mother, but I chose not to. Perhaps I'd regret it one day, but at this moment, I wanted to give him a sliver of mercy.

Ren appeared to lose the internal battle as his eyes darkened, leaving no whites in his eyes. He charged at Su, but I swung my sword, chopping off an arm. An evil shriek erupted that sounded more animalistic than human.

"She's *my* wife!" Ren seethed.

"No." I inhaled a breath, preparing to deliver the blow that would destroy him. "She's your half-sister."

Su whipped a surprised look at me, probably wondering if I was lying.

Ren's body trembled, and the whites shone through again in only one of his eyes. "You're lying."

"I don't need to lie," I seethed. "You're dying. Consider the truth as my sendoff gift. Your father was an evil man. He manipulated you for his own greed. He confessed he killed Su's parents because he feared her stepfather would blackmail him. Su is your family. You can't marry her!"

Ren released a loud cry that rang out seemingly everywhere, sending a chill down my back. I could feel the pain in his voice. The truth broke him from the inside out. Holes appeared on his body as voices sounded from his open wounds.

"You lied to me!" Ren screamed in the air.

His body twitched, and when he opened his mouth, I knew it wasn't Ren speaking. "Sacrifices must be made to achieve great things. You are just *one* sacrifice."

Ren picked up a sword on the ground and began stabbing himself. "Die!"

He rushed over to a vendor stand with a wok, doused himself with the frying oil, ripped off a leg from a burning chair, and ignited his body.

"You can't use me anymore!" Flames erupted as he cried in

pain, sorrow, and resentment. When he looked at Su and me, I thought I saw regret. Or was that my mind wishing it were?

Despite what he'd done, a part of me felt sorry for him. I still remembered him as the younger brother who had needed my help. His weak heart had allowed the dark to seep in and destroy it. A man without a heart became a monster.

His body collapsed into a pile of soot. Unlike the other Soul Extractors, who had left bones in their deaths, Ren didn't leave any.

"I . . . I don't know what to do." Su wiped her eyes. "Should we bury him?"

The answer came for us when a gust of wind blew, dispersing his ashes.

I reached for the fulgurite dagger on my belt and gave it to Su. "The Empress said this is yours."

Su gripped the blue fulgurite dagger, and it glowed in response.

"We have to get to the Empress." I clasped Su's hand. "Yunxi said the baby is coming!"

Her expression switched, shoving personal feelings aside for now. "Roar of the Sky said there's a plant in the palace breeding dark energy."

"That's probably what's weakening the Emperor and Empress. You head to the Empress, and I'll check out the palace."

"No!" she exclaimed, looking into my eyes. "I don't want to lose you. No matter what happens, I want to be with you." She squeezed my hand. "It'll be more efficient if we work together."

I studied her, wondering how she took the news about Ren being her half-brother. "Are you okay?"

Her eyes glistened, but she didn't cry. "It's a lot to take in. When I have a moment, I want to know everything. Right now, we have things to do. I can't let my emotions become obstacles."

My warrior dahlia had more strength and courage than a lot of men I knew.

I kissed her forehead. "Let's go."

As we rushed toward the palace, she asked about everyone except her half-siblings. I told her what I knew. The last time I saw Healer Churan was when she took care of Lina's body. Tao and Keiya were fending off Soul Extractors at the Western Border with General Li's army. Kai was with Yunxi. We'd lost the battle at the Central Border because General Zhou had colluded with the Central Empire. Three-Eyes was probably protecting Blue Orchid somewhere. I prayed for their safety.

I didn't want to crush Su's hope by giving her my full analysis. I'd been in wars, so I knew the signs of an inevitable defeat. This war was incomparable to any I'd encountered. We weren't prepared for the swift attack from all angles by soldiers and possessed beings. Dark magic gave the enemies an advantage.

Lin Din Ni would fall today. But as long as we had each other, there was hope.

We entered the empty palace filled with dark mist. Bones scattered on the floor in the hallway showed the Soul Extractors had been here. Many bloodied soldiers' bodies had been piled nearby.

Waving the mist aside, we rushed through the hallway and came to a section filled with pots of flowers. All the plants had died except one with tiny flowers.

"This nascynth plant looks different." Su pointed to a pot. "Its colors are too dark, and it should be dead like the others."

I grabbed the pot and smashed it. Dark roots squirmed around like snakes, trying to penetrate the floor. I stabbed them with my sword, cutting them into pieces. I found an oil lantern in a room, brought it back, smashed it on the floor, and lit the roots.

When we arrived in the Empress's chamber, fog had covered every room.

"We need to hurry before the dark fog penetrates our minds," I said.

Su and I uprooted all the potted plants in the chamber. We rushed out to the Empress's garden and uprooted the plants that gave off a strange scent.

"There was no scent when I was here last."

"It probably masked itself until now," I said, connecting the dots. "The plants were polluting the air so delicately that no one knew. They were poisoning the Empress and the Emperor. They'd been breathing in toxic air night and day."

General Zhou could've placed a possessed plant in the palace with no one questioning him.

Fear sparked in Su's eyes. "I hope it didn't affect the baby."

I hoped so too.

I could only imagine what the Emperor was going through right now. My good friend's empire had fallen. Dead bodies were scattered in the streets. Homes and businesses were burned to the ground. The royal couple's safety was threatened, and his wife could deliver at any moment.

Su stomped a foot where we'd unearthed a plant. "What about the deeper roots under the ground?"

"There's nothing we can do about that right now."

The ground trembled, and noises sounded.

Su turned toward the sound. "It's the fulgurite stone! Something's happening to it."

My sword and her dagger glowed, thrumming loudly in the air. What else could go wrong? This stone had been the gem the other empires wanted. We ran toward the fulgurite stone.

When we arrived, the soil partially consumed the fulgurite that had once looked like a stunning blue hill. Dark roots surrounded it and hissed. A wall of powerful energy pulsed from the rock. The wall grew with blue flames that burned the roots. Shrieks erupted from the roots as the fulgurite dove deeper into the earth, with dirt covering it slowly.

"I think it senses the darkness trying to get it," I said.

"It's intelligent, and it's protecting itself."

It didn't take long for the fulgurite to disappear from the land. Dirt covered where it had been, and tiny grass sprouts slowly emerged.

"A sign of hope," Su said. "The stone gave birth when I was with Yeeva. She made this with it." She waved the dagger.

Thunder erupted in the sky, and I glanced up to see Roar of the Sky clawing at a black dragon.

"That's a Despondo," Su said. "It's an evil dragon."

The black dragon shrieked when Roar of the Sky severed one of its claws, sending it tumbling to the ground. It was like hate and love fighting each other.

"Truth is a mighty dragon. Set it free, and it will defend itself."

Su looked at me with gleaming eyes. "Love, peace, and joy are all truths that must be defended."

I nodded. "We need to get to the Empress now while it's distracted."

We grabbed two horses from the stable and galloped toward the cabin as quickly as possible.

CHAPTER SEVENTY-ONE

SU

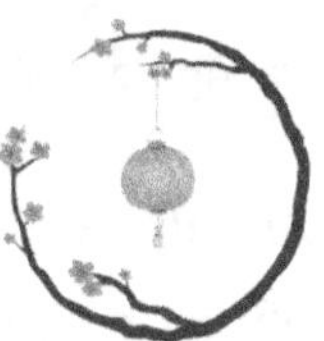

WHEN WE ARRIVED, I felt an air of peace. I rushed into the cabin and saw Gong standing at a table with Healer Churan. With the pestle, she crushed something in the mortar while he had his hand on her back, rubbing.

She glanced up, met my eyes, and rushed over. "You're safe!" She looked me up and down. "We've been so worried about you."

"Where's the Empress?" I asked.

"Safe and taking a nap in the room." Healer Churan gestured to the closed door.

I blew out a sigh of relief. "That's great to hear."

"Good to see you're all right," Gong told me and walked over to Hung.

While the two men talked, I studied Healer Churan, who appeared older. The growing danger had taken a toll on everyone. Seeing all the dead bodies of innocent people weighed on me, and I knew that also affected her.

There was no doubt we had to get out to Luklum. But how? Hung only had a small infantry force left.

Despite the fear, I gripped onto hope because I saw the same in my friends. "Are you okay? I was worried about you too. I can't believe what I'm seeing out there. Dead bodies, bones scattered everywhere."

She offered me a smile. "How we respond in dire times shows our character." She glanced over at Gong, who was talking with Hung. Both men wore strained expressions as they looked at the map on the table.

"Gong saved me from two Soul Extractors as we were transporting Lina's body to the crematory."

She told me about Lina's wound and how she had saved Hung. Lina was my half-sister, and my heart broke that things ended this way. I wondered if we could've been good friends. I needed to talk with Hung about my brother and sister later.

"He's still as stubborn and handsome as he was all those years ago." Healer Churan smiled as she scooped up the herbal paste and added it to a boiling pot. She put the rest in a jar with essential oil.

"Is Gong the man who broke your heart?" I asked.

Nodding, she pressed her lips into a thin line. "We were both very stubborn back then. It's the reason neither of us confronted each other. We let things spiral out of control based on assumptions." She sighed. "I assumed he chose his career over me, and he assumed I chose mine over him. We never told each other exactly what we wanted." She looked at me. "Communication is critical in a relationship. Be honest with each other. Don't be like me and waste all those years. Life is too short, and that fact is playing out before our eyes. Just look at our Luklum."

"Are you and Gong starting over?" I asked.

"I guess the stubborn man deserves a second chance."

I bumped shoulders with her. "Were *you* his student?"

"I wasn't an outstanding student, and he wasn't very patient with me . . . except when I showed him my dancing skills." Laughing, she snuck a glance at him. He probably sensed it because he looked at her and grinned.

My smile stretched as I imagined doing a special dance for

Hung to seduce him. "When you're ready to take on dancing students, let me know."

"When things settle, I can certainly show my favorite healers a few skills." Her eyes sparked. "I know that you and Yunxi are fans of my books, *The Art of Seduction* and *The Art of Intimacy*."

"What?" I exclaimed.

Gong and Hung stopped their conversation, turning toward us.

"Nothing important," we both said at once.

Hung arched an eyebrow at me before resuming his conversation.

"I can't believe this!" I gaped at her, and my cheeks warmed. Healer Churan was like my mother. I didn't know how to react to her knowing her books had taught me intimate skills in the bedroom. "How many other books do you have?"

"Just those two. I wanted to see if they'd sell, but I wanted my privacy so I could manage the apothecary appropriately."

"They're bestsellers amongst the secret women's club. I hear people whispering about them."

She beamed. "That's wonderful to hear."

"Did Gong inspire you to write those?"

She snorted. "He wishes. He doesn't know about them yet." She wiggled her eyebrows.

I laughed, enjoying this conversation and finally feeling a moment's reprieve from all the stress and sorrow.

Kai and Yunxi entered the cabin. Kai nodded at me and joined Hung and Gong while Yunxi walked over to us with her basket of clothing.

She placed the basket on the wooden bench and embraced me. "I'm so happy to see you."

"Me too." I tightened the embrace. "Where did you go?"

"Kai escorted me to a nearby stream to wash some clothing and towels to prepare for our new princess." She gestured to the basket of wet clothing that needed to be hung soon. "We ran into an injured Imperial guard who had rushed back from the Central

Border. He said an army of darkness is heading this way, wearing dark hooded armor."

My stomach clenched, and I glanced over at Hung. His expression told me that Kai had just described the situation to him.

"It's the Dark Lorde's army, The Krix."

"Who's that?" Yunxi asked.

It was time to tell them about the dragon. I met Hung's gaze, and he knew what I was thinking. He gestured for the men to follow him over to us.

"I know this sounds strange, and you might not believe us, but Hung and I encountered a dragon named Roar of the Sky."

The admission was met with shocked expressions and gasps, but no one interrupted us while we described our experience. They had questions, and we answered them.

"Is she going to help us?" Yunxi asked.

"She's already helping us. She's fighting a dark dragon right now," I said. "There's a cosmic war up there." I pointed to the sky. "That's even scarier because it affects us and other worlds. I know it doesn't make any sense, but she's patching up these dangerous holes in the Cosmos so the darkness can't come in."

"But some already made it through." Gong crossed his arms.

Hung nodded. "The Soul Extractor is an example of that darkness."

When the Emperor emerged from the room, Hung and the men went outside to discuss further. Healer Churan and Yunxi brought the wet clothes outside to hang. I knocked on the Empress's door.

"Come in," she said, sounding tired.

I pushed the door open, entered, and closed it.

"Su!" Tears brimmed in Yeeva's eyes. She tried to get out of the bed with her immense belly.

"Stay!" I demanded with my finger. "Don't move." I rushed over to sit on the edge of the bed, helping her sit up.

No one dared to speak to the Empress that way. But Yeeva

and I were best friends outside of her status. In this quaint cabin, she didn't wear her crown, jewels, or regal dresses. She was a natural beauty despite the obvious despair on her face. Being in the woods away from the chaos had boosted her energy.

She grabbed my hand as tears rolled down her face. "I've been praying for your safe return."

"I'm okay, and I'm here now. How are you feeling?" I pressed my fingers to her wrist, checking her pulse. Though I knew Healer Churan and Yunxi had done this several times, I wanted to check as well.

"Not bad. Tired, anxious, worried, sad, and angry." Her voice broke. "My beloved land is destroyed. We have to go into hiding soon."

"We can rebuild. As long as we stay alive, we can take back what belongs to us." I placed a hand on her belly, and the baby kicked. "She's strong."

Yeeva laughed. "She is indeed." Her smile faded. "I think she knows the dire situation and wants to come sooner rather than later. I can feel the contractions."

"Already?"

"Yes. Healer Churan has been monitoring me closely." She glanced at her protruding stomach. "I'm grateful for my baby, Su. Her birth and the birth of the fulgurite stone mean something to Lin Din Ni." Tears brimmed in her eyes. "I believe they're symbols of hope."

"Your princess is exactly that." I squeezed her hand and told her what the dragon told me. To my surprise, she wasn't as shocked about my encounter with Roar of the Sky as the others were.

"The dragon chose the perfect warrior to assist her," Yeeva said.

"Try not to worry," I reminded her. "You need the strength to give birth."

"My daughter comes from Wei and me. She'll have our abilities. Hopefully, she can take those abilities and improve on them.

Wei and I are weak now. But being here and practicing the Infinity Loop has helped me recuperate a portion of my energy and magic."

I told her about the poisonous plants in her palace. "Hung and I destroyed them."

"Thank you. The darkness had been planning this for a long time."

"It had help from those close to us," I said.

"It's true that those closest to you are the ones who can hurt you the most."

I nodded, thinking about my siblings. I didn't want to share that news with Yeeva right now. The stress on her was insurmountable.

Yeeva grabbed the cup of water on the table beside her, sipped, and placed it down. "When I was younger, my parents told me they'd encountered a dragon too. At the time, I thought they were joking with me. You know, tell a kid a fantasy story that stretches her imagination. But as I grew up and encountered fantastical beings, I believed in worlds beyond here."

"Oh, you know the little rabbit with four ears we both saw? His name is Tempo, and he's like the babysitter of baby dragons."

"We became friends because of Tempo." Her face lit up. "There's so much magic and so many synchronicities around us. Sometimes, we're chosen for specific tasks." Her expression warmed. "I'm grateful the dragon chose you."

A knock sounded on the door.

"Come in," Yeeva said, looking like she needed a nap.

"Time for some chicken porridge and herbal medicine." Healer Churan brought in a tray and placed it on the table.

"I'm getting so fat." She yawned. "All I do is eat and sleep."

"You need strength, and so does your baby." Healer Churan stirred the bowl with the spoon. "You look like you need a nap."

"I can nap better now that I know Su and Hung are safe."

"I'll check back on you soon," I said and headed out to look for Hung.

CHAPTER SEVENTY-TWO

WE HAD fish and vegetables from the small garden beside the cabin for dinner. Hung and I stayed in the shed in the garden because there wasn't enough room in the cabin. Yunxi and Kai were in the second bedroom. Healer Churan and Gong had erected a small military tent near the cabin to keep watch.

Everyone's priority was to protect the Emperor and the Empress.

I didn't mind the shed because I needed to talk to Hung. I needed his embrace more than I realized. Though I felt the urgency and danger in the air, I detached myself from those fears for now. Life was like practicing kung fu. I could only nurture my energy when my mind was calm. Disturbance became a distraction, a blockage. Plus, I desperately needed a good night's sleep.

Since I encountered Roar of the Sky, I believed certain things were meant to be. There was a cosmic order I couldn't change—couldn't stop. I had the power to change certain details within this macrocosmic plan, but there was a power beyond me.

Right now, I prayed for that power to bless those I loved. I glanced at my hands, studying my fingers. These were healing hands, but they also belonged to a warrior. I'd always wanted to fight for those who couldn't fight back. I could do that now. That awareness brought tears to my eyes. I could wield a dagger properly. I could use the death touch.

Ba *and* Mẹ, *I hope you're proud of me.*

Tears streamed down my face as I wondered what my mom felt, knowing her ex-lover had sent people to kill her and her family. I wanted to let my stepfather know he was the only father who mattered. He loved me even when I wasn't his biological daughter.

Following my heart had always been how I approached life. It was even more important now. My mind was cluttered with fear lately. It was difficult to see beyond the fear, and I couldn't let limitations be my demise. Hung pivoted whenever he encountered a problem. That ability made him an effective general. I'd learned so much from him, my warrior.

Truth was like a sunray that illuminated the shadows. I was grateful for all that I had learned.

I made myself comfortable on one side of the mat covered with a soft sheet. I got a large blanket from the cabin closet. This shed was a lot cleaner than the one we'd been in at Emerald Song Valley. Bags of beans, rice, and other dry goods were stacked against the wall. I could live quietly in this cabin, far away from the noise.

My heart and soul craved the quiet and peace right now.

Hung entered the shed, toweling his hair. He looked at me and smiled. "You look like you're ready to sleep—all tucked in."

I gripped the blanket to my chin, hiding the rest of my body.

"Are you cold?" he asked.

"No," I said, gazing at his body.

He only wore cotton pants, and my eyes raked over the muscles on his astounding chest and abdomen. The inner muscles of my thighs clenched, remembering how his body had felt on mine. It had been a while since he'd touched me like that. My fingers curled, wanting to touch him.

He lifted an eyebrow. "Are you waiting for me to sleep?" He slipped on a cotton tunic.

I should've told him to leave it off because I was going to remove it anyway. But I would let him discover what I had in mind. He needed something to take his mind off the danger. We could give each other that escape tonight.

What if something happened tomorrow or the next day? Would there be another time for me to show him how much I loved him? Was it wrong to take this moment for us tonight?

I watched my warrior take the oil lantern and bring it closer. After placing it on the floor, he sat on the mat but didn't slide under the blanket. He looked down at me, brushing a strand of hair from my face.

"Do you want to talk about Ren and Lina? How are you processing all that?"

I supposed I'd been processing it at my pace, thinking about it on and off.

"Doing better now," I admitted. "I have questions that won't ever be answered. But that's okay. They don't matter. What matters is that I know my parents *loved* me." I inhaled a breath, releasing the tension inside me with an exhale. "Maybe they planned on telling me the truth about my biological father when I got older. I don't know." I shifted under the blanket.

Hung probably assumed I was cold and threw the extra blanket over me.

"They were trying to protect you," he said.

I nodded. "How could I come from someone so evil? He's such a despicable man." My voice broke, and tears brimmed in my eyes.

"But you're not a bad person. The blood doesn't make a person evil, Su. I've met soldiers who came from orphanages. But they know they can carve out their own path despite where they came from. Don't be ashamed."

"I have so many what-ifs."

"Thinking of that will drive you mad. Let them go." He brushed a hand down my cheek, and I shivered. "The biggest victim here was Lina. She didn't know what her father and brother were doing. When she realized it, she wanted to correct their wrongdoings." He left his finger on my lips. "She wanted you to forgive her."

My chest tightened. "There's nothing to forgive. I don't blame her for anything." I wished things were different so I could have a sister to talk to. "My father used to say, 'Be like a bamboo, bending but never breaking. It bows to difficult situations with gratitude and bounces back with wisdom.' I feel like we all strive to be like a bamboo, but some of us break."

"You didn't, and you *won't*."

"I'm not making excuses for Ren, but he was also a victim," I said. "If he had known I was his sister, maybe he wouldn't have been so obsessed with me."

"If you're not mentally stable, the darkness can sneak in and turn a minor wound into a serious disease. I think Ren was a person who wanted to find his place in this world. But he lost his way." His finger trailed my jawline, and I quivered. "That cold? Are you getting sick?" He placed a hand over my forehead.

"I'm feeling unwell, *Sifu*." I smiled, feeling a lot better now we'd discussed my half-siblings. I'd sleep better tonight and move forward with my life. An evil father and brother didn't mean I would choose that path. "Only *you* can make me feel better."

He smirked. "Why do you have a mischievous look on your face?"

"Do I?" I fluttered my eyes. "I've been waiting for you under this blanket for a while."

A crease formed on his forehead as he lifted the blanket, and his mouth dropped open at my naked body. "So forward tonight. No *dudou* for me to strip off." He slipped under the covers, turned to the side, and propped on an elbow. He rested his head on his fist while his hand skimmed my body, making me melt.

"It's your fault," I breathed when his fingers captured a nipple, rolling it between his fingers. "You were taunting me, walking around the shed and showing off your body." His hand moved lower to cup my sex. I moaned as his palm pushed against me, creating a lovely friction. "Why are we always making out in a shed?" I asked, half-laughing and half-dazed with pleasure.

"I promise to fuck you even more when we have an actual bedroom to sleep in."

"I don't mind the shed." I placed a hand on his cheek. "It's our thing."

Laughing, his eyes darkened, watching me react to his touch. "I love seeing you like this: relaxed, seductive, malleable, and so responsive to me." He slipped a finger inside me and crooned. "You're so wet, my dahlia. He shoved the blanket away so I could see what he was doing to me.

"Oh, heavens," I moaned as I watched him thrust another finger into me. "So good."

He sat up, pumping me harder while his other hand squeezed my breast. "I've been wanting this for too long. You've read my mind for tonight."

Need darkened his eyes as he crushed his lips to mine, kissing me deeply. Sensations warred in me as our tongues mated.

I broke the kiss, sat up, and demanded. "Take off your clothes."

"As you wish, my warrior goddess." He stripped off his tunic, tossing it aside.

"Let me," I said, tugging at his pants and shoving them down his legs.

His glorious erection called to me, and I gripped it in my hand. His cock throbbed with heat as I slid my grip up and down his length. The image reminded me of *The Art of Seduction*, and I mimicked what I remembered from those pages.

"Su, you're driving me crazy."

Excellent. "I don't want you to think about anything but me tonight."

When I pressed my thumb on his crown, his stomach flexed. "Fuck." His hand gripped the blanket as though restraining himself. I loved seeing him on the edge like this.

My heart raced as I saw an image from the book I wanted to

do to him. I flicked him a wicked smile as I lowered my lips to his head, dropping kisses to it. He released a growl that turned me on.

I licked all over the crown, loving his taste and texture, before continuing to his magnificent stalk. The look on his face told me I held the power to make him lose control.

"Where did you learn this exceptional skill?" He placed a hand on my head, growling like a wild beast.

"From books—and a healthy imagination."

He laughed. "I have such a curious student."

I took him into my mouth.

"Su!" His face contorted, followed by a wicked smile. "Your mouth is a dangerous weapon."

I released him with a pop. He grabbed my face, kissed me, and nudged me down on the mat.

"My turn to devour you." He kissed my neck and shoulders, nibbling his way over to my breast.

He suckled a breast, drawing out my nipple, circling his tongue around it and sucking again. I felt the desperation in him. It reflected mine as heat soared in me. I arched into his mouth, offering him whatever he wanted. When he finished adoring one breast, he offered the other the same love.

Nudging my knees up, he positioned himself between them. He spread my thighs wider and gazed at me.

"I've been craving you for too long." He bent and kissed my mound.

I gasped as my thighs wanted to close.

"No, no, no." He shook his head. "I am not done with you, beautiful."

He pressed my knees into my body, making me feel wonderfully exposed and trapped. He continued to kiss me everywhere. My hands didn't know what to do, so I gripped his head, pulling at his hair. When the kissing turned to seductive licking, my body flew into another realm. The idea sounded inconceivable, but that was what it felt like. The bliss that rushed through me—this magnificent sensation I couldn't describe. My vision went black, and I was swimming in a starry night where flowers grew in the open space. I let my body, heart, and soul dwell in this magical world of being loved by a skilled man.

He groaned as his tongue slid in and out of me.

"You taste like heaven." He licked his lips. "So perfectly unique."

He feasted on me with a hunger that had my body thrashing for something it didn't understand. I wanted more, but I also wanted him to stop because the wave of sensation was too much. The clash between desire and the need to pause tore at me, creating this beautiful friction that trembled my thighs.

The swift flicking of his tongue, followed by the skillful sucking, pushed me close to the edge. "That's right, love. Come for me."

When he lifted my ass, fluttering at my bud, I fell off the cliff. My body quivered from the intense wave of pleasure.

He smiled as he watched me descend from my orgasm. "I love seeing your face overcome with pleasure."

Opening my thighs for him, I said, "I still need you."

The wolfish grin I loved appeared on his face as he rose and gripped his cock.

CHAPTER SEVENTY-THREE

HUNG

SHE MOANED as I teased her sweet center. Her taste still lingered on my lips. There would be no one else for me in this lifetime. Or the next. My soul would search for her, no matter where she was.

"Don't be evil and toy with me." She rose onto her elbows, looking adorably flushed.

"I love the desperation in you, my dahlia."

"I can't have kids," she said calmly. "I don't need to take anti-pregnancy herbs anymore, so we can have all the fun without worrying."

Even though I wasn't directly responsible for her infertility, I was partly responsible. What if I had never used that poison to lure Samo and his friends?

Stop thinking about it. Take your pleasure.

"Don't be sad, Hung. It's not your fault. It's something destined." She touched my cheek. "We have each other, and that's all that matters to me."

The sincerity and love in her eyes shoved the guilt aside.

"I want you to fuck me like the beastly warrior you are."

A laugh escaped me. I didn't realize I could love her more

than I did. But right now, my heart and soul swelled for her. She had opened me to possibilities I never knew existed.

I gripped her thighs and pummeled into her. "Is this beastly enough for you?"

"Yes!" She wrapped her legs around my waist and lifted her ass, allowing me to drive in even deeper. "More!"

I thrust into her, the tightness of her muscles clenching around me. I groaned, loving the connection of being inside her. No sensation could compare to this. My heart pounded in my chest as sweat streaked down my face.

She moaned as she sat up and gripped my face for a kiss. Then she broke free and breathed. "Want to try a new position?"

I quirked an eyebrow at the challenge in her voice. "What do you have in mind?"

"I want you to take me from behind."

"I'm a lucky man to have a woman who knows what she wants."

She got onto all fours and tossed a seductive look over her shoulder. Lowering herself, she stretched her arms out while her perky ass teased me.

I couldn't help myself and gave her buttocks a gentle slap. "You're misbehaving."

"Give me your punishment." She wiggled her ass. "You've turned me into a sex maniac."

She couldn't have said anything more fulfilling.

"This beautiful thing is mine." I placed both my hands on her ass, squeezing, claiming. "And so is this." I pressed my face into her, loving and licking her.

"Hung!" The way she squealed and squirmed under my grip proved she didn't expect it.

I didn't let her go and continued my delicious assault. I couldn't get enough of her. Heat scorched me as pleasure rose to the surface. I drove into her hard and fast. She met me with every thrust, moaning with pleasure.

"Hung . . ." she whimpered.

I loved every sound she made because of me.

Sensing my approaching climax, I lowered my body onto hers. With sweat dripping onto her back, I pummeled her with all my might.

Love filled my heart as I roared. "Su!"

As pleasure shot out of me, my vision blurred, and my ears rang. *Fuccck.* My body quaked over hers, and I *felt* her experience her second climax.

She turned her face to kiss me. After a few seconds to catch my breath, I pulled out. I cleaned myself with the towel from my bath earlier before cleaning her.

"Thank you." She patted my cheek. "We could do this every day."

My face warmed. "Once we're safe and settled, that's my plan. Take you in different positions. We'll create our own version of *The Art of Seduction* and *The Art of Intimacy.*"

She opened her mouth, about to say something, but closed it. She twisted her lips, then smiled. "We'll need pseudonyms to keep our true identities hidden. If one of our friends picks up the book, I'd rather they think it's someone else." She curled into my arms. "Certain things require discretion."

"Okay." I smiled and kissed the side of her head. "What names do you have in mind?"

She drew circles over my chest with her fingers. "How about—"

My sword glowed and hissed as a strange explosion boomed in the air nearby. The ground trembled as we shot to our feet.

"What was that?" Su asked, dressing quickly.

"I don't know," I said, pulling on my pants, tunic, and armor. Grabbing my sword, I cupped her chin. "You go into the cabin and stay with Yeeva, Yunxi, and Healer Churan. I'll check it out."

She kissed me. "Be careful."

As we headed out of the shed, Gong and Kai rushed toward me.

"Are you and Su hurt?" Kai asked.

"No. You?"

They shook their heads.

"The Emperor told us to go check out the explosion." Gong handed Kai and me an oblong-shaped berry. "Take it."

"What is it?" I asked, staring at the orange berry in my palm.

"Three-Eyes gave this to the Emperor a few days ago. He retrieved them from a place between places. Apparently, he saw strange birds eating them."

"That doesn't make me want to eat it," Kai said.

"He noticed that when the birds ate them, they disappeared. But then he opened his third eye and saw they were still there."

"Interesting. These could conceal us. Before we eat these, we need to divide up the area we're searching. If you're invisible, I won't be able to see you."

"I also don't know how long this invisibility will last," Gong said. "So let's be quick and efficient."

He also gave us each a crystal wand from the Imperial collection. It collected both sunlight and moonlight, offering a soft glow at nighttime. We couldn't bring a lantern into the woods, as our enemies would spot us easily.

Once we knew what area to survey, I popped the berry into my mouth and chewed. Sour juice spilled onto my tongue. I shuddered, wondering how those birds could eat this berry.

Kai made a face, and so did Gong.

Their bodies disappeared, but when Kai stepped on the wet soil, his footprints showed.

"Watch your tracks," I said, making a mental note to step onto grass or dry dirt.

In the distance, I saw the dawn glowing through the horizon. I entered the woods, using the crystal wand as my guiding light toward the stream where we'd bathed earlier. Kai took the outer edge of the woods, and Gong checked out the woods beyond the sloped hills.

Crickets chirped as I ambled ahead, trying not to step on any twigs. The forest had been eerily silent despite that strange noise earlier. Had it been an explosion?

Voices sounded in the distance, and I tucked the glowing crystal into the pocket of my armor and ambled my way toward the sounds. When I got to the edge of the stream, a campfire glowed in the distance. As I approached closer, I remained behind a big tree, listening.

"We have to relay the message and rush back," said a woman with a familiar voice.

"But we don't know where they've gone," said another woman.

"Tao told us to head into these woods, though."

I stepped out from behind the tree as I recognized two of the river warriors, Dayday and Chuluun.

"What did Tao want you to deliver?" I asked.

The two women jumped from the rocks they were sitting on, standing back-to-back as they gripped their daggers.

"Who's there?" asked Dayday.

Firehell. I'd forgotten I was invisible to them.

"It's General Wen. I'm invisible right now, and I'm standing in front of you by the fire." I bent down, reached for a pebble, and tossed it into the fire. "That was me."

The two women glanced at each other, clearly skeptical.

"You helped me fight the Soul Extractors, remember?" I tried to convince her. "How are Tao, Keiya, and everyone at the Green Fog River? I don't know when this invisibility will fade. I heard a noise, so I came here to see who it was."

Their suspicion softened, and Dayday said, "You probably heard us killing a giant snake earlier." They pointed to the immobile body of a snake by a tree. "The other part spiraled into the dirt. Tao saw an army that didn't belong to any empires by the Green Fog River, which means they're not far away. He's helping us escort the river villagers into the Misty Mountains."

"Thank you for the information," I said.

My sword thrummed against my back, radiating heat through my armor.

The ground under my feet shifted, and I looked down. The earth parted, and a giant snake slithered up.

"That's the snake just now."

It opened its mouth and released a loud sound that didn't belong to a snake. Fearing it was calling for backup, I drew my sword and beheaded it. It thrashed on the ground as blood spilled out of it. Chuluun brought over a branch with fire. To ensure there was no chance of revival, I sliced its head and body into several parts and we tossed it all into the fire.

"We can see you now, but you're translucent." Dayday studied me.

"Maybe the fire weakens the spell." I straightened and waved my hands around the fire, and my hands showed. I turned to Dayday and Chuluun. "Thank you for risking your lives to find me. You should head back and help your people."

"Are you okay with Tao staying with us?" Dayday asked, looking uncomfortable. "We'll need his help for a while."

"He's a great warrior, and I'm glad he's there to help you. You helped us when we needed you. I'm indebted to the river warriors." I placed a fist to my chest, offering my respect. "We have enough men here. Don't worry about us. When things settle, we'll find you."

I escorted them to the edge of the stream and headed back. Dawn approached as I walked back to the cabin, but a dark mist blanketed the ground.

A snake broke through the ground and sprang toward my face. Then two more snakes emerged.

CHAPTER SEVENTY-FOUR

SU

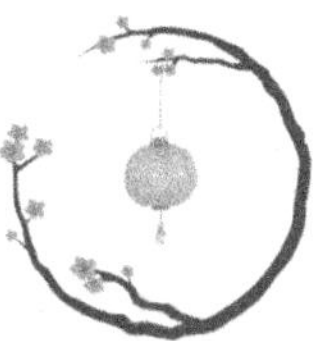

"I SHOULD BE OUT THERE with my men." The Emperor paced the kitchen area. He was dressed in armor, ready for battle.

"No, you should be here with the Empress." Healer Churan offered him a warm smile as she sorted herbs with me and Yunxi. "Your baby will be here at any moment."

Emperor Tang wasn't like other leaders, who preferred to sit on a throne while his men battled. He was a warrior himself, and I understood the conflict in him. The safety of his empire and the safety of his wife and unborn child weighed on him.

"Oh heavens!" Yeeva exclaimed.

The Emperor rushed into the bedroom, followed by me, Healer Churan, and Yunxi.

The Empress stood by the bed with a puddle at her feet. She met my eyes. "My water broke."

"What? Why?" The Emperor came up beside her. "Are you in pain?"

"Not yet." She smiled. "Our baby is coming soon."

Healer Churan, Yunxi, and I exchanged glances as we hurried to prepare the hot water, herbs, towels, and silk clothing for the new baby.

The Emperor stood by the bed, looking concerned and help-less. "Can I help with anything?"

"Wait outside." The Empress gripped his arm. "Your nerves won't help me, darling."

Looking resigned, he sighed. "Okay."

"We'll let you know when the baby arrives," I said.

"I want to be here in the room when she does." He looked at his wife for confirmation.

"I'd like that." Yeeva smiled at him and turned to me. "Please call him when the time comes."

From my previous experience in delivering babies, the nervous fathers usually stayed outside of the room. But I loved that Emperor Tang wanted to witness his daughter's birth.

As the Emperor left the room, I caught a glimpse of Hung and sighed with relief. I'd been worried about him and the others out in the woods. What had he discovered? I ensured Healer Churan and Yunxi were all set before I walked to the kitchen for Hung's update.

Gong and Kai entered the cabin with blood staining their uniforms.

"Are you all right?" I asked, raking a gaze over Hung's armor, which also had bloodstains.

"Not our blood." Kai grabbed a cloth from the basket and cleaned himself. "Those damn snakes."

"The Krix was spotted at the Green Fog River, heading here." Hung's lips thinned. "The snakes are traveling underground, searching for us. I believe their calls are signals to the army."

My eyes went wide. "The Empress's water just broke. It's too dangerous to move her. The baby is coming soon."

A moment of silence filled the cabin. The Emperor closed his eyes as if homing in on something.

When he opened his eyes, he said, "I've never encountered this kind of darkness before. It's powerful." He opened his palm, and essa flashed over it. "My energy is recovering, but my powers are still limited."

"They want your baby," I said, remembering the dragon's words. "The baby is the new light—a new essa."

"They want to eliminate all light. I won't let that happen." The Emperor's jaw tightened. "*We* won't let them." He walked over to the table with the map and pointed to a location. "The army was spotted here. We can meet them halfway. Attack them. Buy some time for the Empress to give birth safely."

Noises sounded outside the cabin, and Hung opened the window. "Four snakes are out there."

"I got them." Kai gripped his sword.

Hung reached for his sword. "It'll be quicker with more help."

"I'll join you." Gong followed them out.

The Emperor looked at me. "Keep the Empress and my daughter safe."

"I will."

Tears formed in my eyes, but I stopped them from coming. This wasn't the moment to cry. The men needed to see that I was okay. Hung needed to see that. I didn't want him to worry about me too.

The Emperor flexed his hand, and a swirl of energy formed on his palm. He muttered an invocation to heaven and earth, and the swirl of energy increased. It reminded me of the energy pattern I'd seen in the Cosmos when Roar of the Sky took me across several realms.

Emperor Tang dispersed the energy, filling the cabin. The house shuddered, and the snakes cried miserably. I looked through the window and saw a layer of energy pulsing around the house.

"The house is protected," the Emperor said as he walked over to the counter and attached more weapons to his belt and uniform. "It should keep the cabin hidden for a while."

I could tell he'd used a portion of his essa to protect the cabin. His face paled a shade. I prayed that the Emperor, Hung, Gong, and Kai could kill the dark army. The last thing I wanted to do was move the Empress and her daughter while they were vulnerable.

After destroying the snakes, Gong, Kai, and Hung returned and met with the Emperor. I went to Yeeva's room to give the women an update. The Emperor entered, probably to inform his wife he was going into battle.

Healer Churan, Yunxi, and I left the room to meet our significant others in the kitchen. Sorrow, fear, determination, and hope stirred in the room.

I knew Hung might not make it back from this battle. I couldn't hold back my tears any longer as I embraced him.

"Don't cry." He wiped the tears away. "I'll do my best to come back to you. I love you."

"Be careful," I said, running my hand down his arms as though wanting to remember every part of him. Emotions stormed through me, even though I knew he had to do this. He was a general, and he had to accompany his Emperor to battle this threat.

"I have this magical charm." He smiled and tapped the round talisman I'd given him. "That means I'm going to be okay." He leaned into my ear. "When I come back, I want you to show me all those new positions you want to try. And I want to know the pen names you've come up with for us."

My face flushed with embarrassment, even though I knew what he was trying to do. Even in a critical moment, Hung made me smile. Love for him overwhelmed me, and I threw my arms around him. I wanted to keep him safe. I wanted to start a life with him, grow old together, and write a hundred provocative books with him.

When the Emperor exited the bedroom, Hung drew back and kissed my forehead. "I've got to go now."

Kai was tasked with staying behind to guard the door as an extra layer of security.

Healer Churan remained strong when she returned to Yeeva's room, but I knew she was worried about Gong too.

I busied myself with crushing more herbs and folding and

refolding the same stack of towels repeatedly. Moments later, Yunxi shouted, "The baby is coming!"

CHAPTER SEVENTY-FIVE

HUNG

ON OUR HORSES, we galloped toward the Green Fog River. The sun rose, giving hope to the day. But despair stirred in the air. I knew Emperor Tang's energy had weakened from the spell he'd cast to protect the cabin. I wished he had more time to recover his energy. At his full force, he was extremely powerful. But now he probably only had a portion of his essa left. Even though he didn't admit it, I could see the weakness in his eyes and the dullness in his skin.

The orange berries that offered invisibility would have been useful now, but the Emperor had no more. We didn't know where Three-Eyes was. Even if we did, there wasn't time to reach him for more of those berries.

A wall of smoky mist appeared on the dirt path, and we yanked our horses' reins. The mist faded, revealing ten Krix soldiers dressed in hooded black attire and dark masks. They sat on their dark horses, staring at us. Eerie sounds emerged from the surrounding area. Dark clouds drifted in and blocked out the sunlight.

There were ten of them and three of us. They knew this, and I sensed their confidence. The Krix soldiers jumped off their horses and charged at us. We leaped off ours, and a battle erupted.

Swords screeched, and power sparked. I pierced a soldier with my blade, and black blood dripped out of him.

The ground shifted, and several snakes broke through the dirt as they traveled underneath, heading somewhere. Could they sense where we'd come from?

Fucking hell! I met the Emperor's eyes and understood his fear.

"Go!" I told him as I cut into another Krix soldier.

Gong beheaded one of them. "Hung, escort the Emperor back. I'll hold them off." He reached into his pouch and pulled out a round object the size of a rambutan. "My new toy. Wish I had more time to perfect it." He whipped it out at The Krix. An explosion bloomed, covering the space with smoke. "Go now! I'll catch up!"

Our eyes met, and we both knew he might die today. I leaped onto my horse and hurried toward the cabin with the Emperor. His face was paler than a moments ago. He'd exerted too much essa, but the determination in his eyes pushed him forward.

CHAPTER SEVENTY-SIX

SU

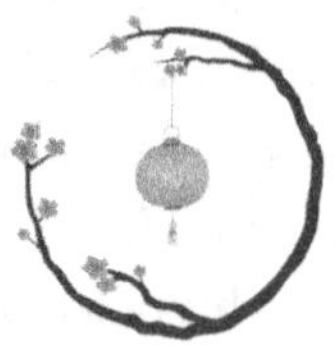

"THIS WILL HELP WITH THE PAIN." Healer Churan brought over a mug of herbal tonic.

I dabbed the sweat streaming down Yeeva's face. A beautiful aura radiated from her body, but its radiance fluctuated, reflecting her wavering energy level.

Yeeva drank the tonic and leaned against the headboard, taking a break from the contractions.

"I feel the darkness nearing." She gripped my arm as worry splashed onto her face. "They won't take my baby!"

"We won't let them," I said.

Healer Churan and Yunxi placed their hands over hers. "We'll protect her."

Another contraction came, and she gasped as agony strained her face.

The knots in my stomach tightened, but I pushed that anxiety aside to focus on delivering the baby safely. Yunxi and I positioned ourselves at the edge of the bed while Healer Churan gripped Yeeva's hand.

"Concentrate on your breathing," I said calmly.

When a person was under pressure, their breathing changed. They often held their breaths, which reduced the oxygen intake and hindered the flow of blood to all the muscles and organs. I needed Yeeva to be calm and healthy too. I could only imagine the pressure on her right now.

Her husband was fighting demons, her empire was in chaos, and the darkness wanted her baby dead.

When I realized I was also holding my breath, I exhaled slowly.

"Breathe like me." I demonstrated my inhale and exhale.

She met my eyes and nodded.

"Oh no," she cried as a wave of contractions rolled in.

"Who said having a kid was easy?" I smiled.

"No one!" Healer Churan and Yunxi chimed in.

Yeeva laughed and cried.

"Push!" I said. "You're doing wonderfully."

"He won't make it to see his daughter's birth," Yeeva breathed.

"He's making sure his wife and daughter are safe." Healer Churan reassured her.

"Breathe, push, breathe, push," I repeated.

Colorful lights sparkled around Yeeva's body. Was this the princess's essa? The brightness energized Yeeva's aura.

Excitement set in when I saw the baby's head crowning. "One more push!"

With a mighty push, the baby emerged, and her eyes opened, looking at me. I'd never seen a baby so aware at her first breath of life.

After I cut the umbilical cord, Healer Churan cleaned the baby, wrapped her in an embroidered red silk, and transferred the adorable bundle to her mother.

Yunxi brought over the pot of hot water so Yeeva could steam her body with healing herbs. The steam and herbs would prevent infections. The body needed to heal after that much trauma and blood loss.

Yeeva wept when she held her baby in her arms. A beautiful energy bloomed around them. A kaleidoscope of colors sparkled around the mother and daughter.

"There are gorgeous lights around you," Yunxi said. "So mesmerizing."

When the baby cried, the lights burst.

Yeeva calmed her baby girl. "Don't cry. Everything will be okay. You're a strong one, aren't you, my love?" She pressed her lips to the baby's cheek.

Tears spilled over my eyes to see the happy and healthy baby with her mother.

"Do you have a name for her?" Healer Churan asked.

"Not yet," she said, swaying a little, looking at her bundle of joy.

The baby opened her mouth and babbled, and a blanket of shock settled over the room.

"Wow . . . I've never seen a baby babble just minutes after birth," Yunxi said.

"Look at her eyes." Healer Churan smiled. "There's wisdom and responsibility in them."

The baby turned to look at me and offered a little smile.

The ground trembled, rattling the walls.

"They're here." Panic splashed onto Yeeva's face, followed by something I couldn't decipher.

As Yunxi ran out of the bedroom to check, she exclaimed, "The Emperor is back!"

I wrung my hands, wondering about Hung. I didn't have to wonder long as he entered the bedroom with the Emperor and Gong.

Gong stepped over to Healer Churan while the Emperor rushed to his family.

We all stepped out of the room to give the Emperor privacy with his wife and daughter.

"What's that noise?" I asked.

"Demonic snakes. They're burrowing underground." He looked toward the room. "I think they sensed the baby's birth."

Kai burst through the door and slammed it shut. "The Krix are here." He went out to survey the cabin after hearing several noises.

Yunxi rushed up to him, examining him closely.

Hung and Gong both cursed.

"Let's go kill them and give the Emperor time to escape with his family."

I looked out the crack in the window and saw the Krix soldiers using their dark magic to dispel the protective cloak the Emperor had cast. The shield throbbed, and the cabin shook.

Though the energy wall was still intact, I could sense its vulnerability.

"The snakes are likely trying to tunnel under to get to us." Hung glanced at the floor.

"I have something that might work."

Healer Churan walked over to the counter where she'd been crushing something into a paste. She lifted the lid of the porcelain jar and poured some round balls the size of berries into her palm. "These are made from the ignis plant."

I lifted a berry to my nose and sniffed. "Smells like oil."

The ignis plant was a rare wild plant that grew in forests. Its yang properties were too strong to treat the human body, but it could be an effective weapon to protect us.

Healer Churan nodded. "When I saw them in the backyard, I took it as a sign. I'm not sure if my idea will work, but look."

She placed one of the little balls on a metal plate. Gong got a match and lit it up. Fire burst from it, rising a few feet high. Healer Churan dumped a bucket of water onto it.

The height of the fire decreased, but it continued to burn.

"The oil from the plant is an accelerant." She lifted a stem with long, dry leaves.

"We'll need to ignite it while it's in the air," Hung said. "I can do that with my sword."

"We've got some bows and arrows," Kai added. "Light up the arrows first."

Yunxi walked over to him. "I feel helpless."

Healer Churan took out a big container from the storage room. "You can help me make more ignis balls." She pulled out a drawer full of small bags already prepared.

"I love how you're prepared. Excellent invention." Gong wrapped an arm around Healer Churan. "I'll harness my essa to ignite them." He took some bags, tucking them into his pocket. "I have smoke bombs, and you have fireballs. We're a match made in heaven."

Healer Churan rolled her eyes but smiled.

Hung shared the plan. He and I would escort the Emperor, the Empress, and their daughter to safety while the others would fight off The Krix and their demonic snakes.

"We'll fight with everything we have," Hung said. "If we make it out safely, we'll find each other."

Emotions surged in me as I grabbed the bow and arrow from the wall of weapons. The day my parents died flashed before my eyes, and the desire to protect them overwhelmed me. The threat to us today brought back those old hurts. But I wasn't a child anymore—I wasn't helpless. I was now a warrior who could protect those I love.

When I looked up, Hung's eyes warmed on me. I knew his thoughts reflected my own.

"Are you okay?" He placed a hand on each of my shoulders.

"Yeah. Just thinking about my parents."

"They're proud of you." He leaned in. "As your mentor, I'm proud of you too. I'm lucky to have a warrior like you fighting beside me."

I fell into his embrace, letting myself feel safe and warm again.

Drawing back, I intertwined my fingers with his.

"It's an honor to go into battle with you too, General Wen."

A blast of energy shook the cabin. The Emperor stepped out of the room, looking stern and exhausted. "Hung and Su, I need your help."

CHAPTER SEVENTY-SEVEN

SU

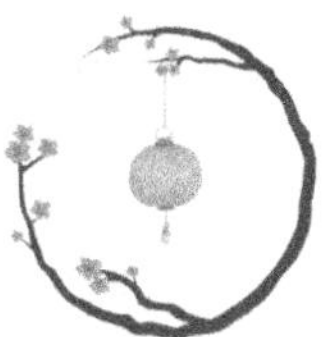

THE CABIN SHOOK AGAIN.

"We're out to kill them," Gong looked at the Emperor. "You need to escape with your family."

The Emperor walked up to Gong, Kai, Healer Churan, and Yunxi. "Thank you." He raised a fist and tapped it against his chest. "I appreciate what you've done for our land and my family."

Why did his words sound like a farewell?

"It is an honor to serve you," Gong said, offering the same fist to the chest.

Everyone else showed him respect, including Hung and me.

I embraced Healer Churan and Yunxi. "Stay safe. When we meet again, we'll do all the things we talked about. I want you to teach me how to dance."

With tears in our eyes, we nodded. Gong and Kai hurried outside to defend the cabin.

"Emperor," I said. "Look at Healer Churan's fireballs killing them."

From the window, we watched Gong and Kai step forward but remain within the protective barrier. The Krix soldiers continued whipping out dark magic, slamming the energy wall. Gong gathered his essa into his palms, and the ignis balls swirled above his hand. He pitched them into the air and sent another blast of his essa to ignite them. A massive ball of fire flew at The Krix. A few soldiers caught fire and tried to douse it by rolling on the ground. But it didn't help. When their masks fell off, demonic faces stared at us.

Three vicious panthers appeared seemingly out of nowhere, leaping against the protective barrier. The energy pulse threw them back, and they snarled, revealing large fangs. Holes grew from the ground, and demonic snakes slithered up.

Terror tightened my stomach as more Krix soldiers appeared. A glance told me we were fighting over a hundred soldiers. The dire situation looked impossible to defeat.

"Kill them all," the Emperor seethed as he stepped away from the window.

Hung tapped my shoulder, signifying me to follow the Emperor into the bedroom. What did the Emperor need our help with?

Worried about my friends, I looked over my shoulder and saw water spouting from the holes in the ground. Eerie sounds erupted, and I said a prayer for them.

I knew Roar of the Sky was fighting her own battle, but I said, "If you're available, please help us."

Was it selfish of me to ask when she was protecting the Cosmos? What if she came to help, and more evil took that opportunity to enter?

I shook my mind from the negative thought as Hung closed the door.

Yeeva approached me with her baby, now wrapped in a brown cotton fabric. "I want *you* to name her."

"What?" I asked, unsure of what to say.

"*You* should," I said. "You're her mother." The baby opened her eyes, cooing at me and Hung.

"She's perfect," he said.

"She is," the Emperor agreed and looked at his wife. When

she nodded, he said. "I would like to ask both of you for an important favor."

"Anything," Hung said.

"We have little time, and I need to get you, Su, and our princess to safety."

"What are you doing?" I asked, the ache in my stomach increasing.

"We'll be using our stored essa to ensure your safety."

Tears welled in my eyes when I realized what they were asking of Hung and me.

Yeeva placed her hand on my arm. "Please help us." Her lips trembled. "Please save our baby. Keep her safe. She's the light that will ensure the darkness will *never* win."

"You can come with us," I said, wanting my best friend to escape too.

She shook her head. "I'm too weak. I've given most of my essa to her." She smiled at her daughter. "Wei is also weak. He and I will combine what's left of our power to send you to safety. This is the only way."

The Emperor looked at Hung. "Will you help me?"

I'd never seen desperation on the Emperor's face before. I could understand the struggle within Hung because it reflected my own. We wanted to help our friends, but we also didn't want them to die.

When Hung didn't reply, the Emperor said, "If you say no, I'll force you with a decree."

A small smile lifted the corners of Hung's mouth. "You know I'll help." He looked at me for my confirmation. When I nodded, he said, "We'll do our best to keep your daughter safe."

Tears welled in my eyes as I embraced the Empress. "Oh, Yeeva."

The cabin shook again, and more eerie cries erupted.

"There's not enough time. We must hurry." The Empress transferred her daughter into my arms. "Love her as your own. Give her a name that has meaning."

I already knew what I wanted. "How about Luzi? Strong, courageous, and full of love and light." I looked at Hung, and he understood me.

"Isn't she the girl who saved you and Hung?"

I nodded. "Yes."

"Luzi," the Emperor repeated. "I love it."

"That's the perfect name for our princess." Yeeva pulled a strand of black hair from her head and placed it in her hand. She held it out for the Emperor, who clasped his hand over hers.

The husband and wife muttered a prayer. When they were finished, the Emperor lifted his hand, revealing the black strand had turned golden. With her finger, Yeeva directed the golden strand to wrap itself around the baby's wrist like a bracelet.

The golden strand embedded itself into her skin. "We've given her our powers we've cultivated over the years. It's up to Luzi to activate them and make them her own."

"Today, Lin Din Ni will be destroyed." The Emperor kissed his baby on the forehead. "But it will be reborn." He gripped his wife's hand, and light emanated from the couple.

They both waved a hand, and a bright swirl of energy opened. Sparkles of light burst from the portal.

Something smashed into the roof of the cabin, cracking wooden beams.

The darkness had penetrated the barrier. Nerves tumbled inside me as Hung secured the baby to my chest and tightened the ties over my back.

"You must go now! Our energy is focused on saving you and Luzi. We're using our last drop of essa to warp time and space. The speed of light will take you away from here."

Luzi cried, which made me and her mother cry.

I believed Luzi knew what was happening on some fundamental level. She could probably sense the energy—the danger and despair, the impending deaths of her parents.

"Where will we be?" I asked, trying to calm the cauldron of emotions roiling in me.

"That's up to the light," Yeeva said. "I trust it, and you should too."

Another blast of energy slammed into the roof, cracking it open. Dark energy slithered in but could only hover around the ceiling.

With a fist to his chest, Hung nodded to the Emperor and the Empress, grabbed my hand, and leaped into the portal. A rush of colorful essas surrounded us, along with fresh air that expanded my lungs. The portal closed too quickly for me to see Yeeva and her husband. Despair gripped me, but there wasn't time for that right now.

Hung and I stood inside a bubble of energy floating inside a forest. A translucent wall of energy pulsed around the bubble. I pressed my palm on the wall, and it fluctuated, moving faster or slower depending on where I placed my hand.

Hung and I exchanged a curious glance. He also placed his hand on the energy wall, maneuvering the bubble and adjusting its speed. "We could steer it."

"They used their last drop of life force to ensure our safety." I released a slow breath and looked down at Luzi, who was asleep. I bent down to kiss her head, loving her so much already. She represented my best friend, my savior, and my home.

Hung interlaced his fingers with mine, lifted my hand for a kiss, and studied Luzi. "She has us, so she'll be okay."

Eerie sounds approached, and the Dark Lorde appeared in his snake form with the human face. He slithered beside us, using his body to thwack the bubble. The bubble's mutable exterior swayed as Hung increased the speed, moving away from the demonic snake. It opened its mouth, trying to bite us, but the wall shifted shape and direction, and the snake missed.

A panther pounced and clawed at us. Reflex had me jumping away from the claw, even though it never penetrated the wall. It was as though the bubble was intelligent and knew how to shift itself to avoid the threat.

If I'd had more time to contemplate, I'd wonder about these

magical things before me. The bubble traveled faster out of the woods and into an open field I didn't recognize. Seconds later, the scene changed to a stream with flowers and mountains.

"It's not that far behind." Hung looked back at the demonic snake swimming through the air as it moaned and hissed. A storm of darkness grew behind it.

"We have to move faster," I said and heard a babble. Looking down at Luzi, I saw the light glow around her wrist. She smiled at me, and love filled my heart.

This beautiful little girl didn't know the responsibility she carried. She was the symbol of light for all of us. As I looked at her, a sense of calmness overcame me. Perhaps she sensed my fear and anxiety.

Somehow, the demonic snake appeared beside the bubble, looking even larger than it had earlier. "You will not get away! Give me that baby!"

"Go to hell!" I bellowed.

Hung tried his best to avoid the snake's bite by steering the bubble away. Even though the bubble shifted in several directions, somehow, we remained upright and stable instead of being tossed around. I knew that Yeeva and the Emperor's powers had ensured our safety in every way possible.

A familiar energy slid over me, and hope sparked.

Sorry I'm late.

Roar of the Sky's voice sounded in my head, making me feel like the sun had escaped from the dark clouds. But there was something off about her voice.

"Thank you for coming," I said, and Hung arched an eyebrow at me, probably wondering why I was seemingly talking to myself. "Roar of the Sky is here."

Like me, he glanced around.

"There!" Hung pointed behind to where Roar of the Sky blasted through the dark storm.

A demonic snake tried to stop her by wrapping around her with its dark stream of smoke. This snake looked different from the one she had fought before. She clawed at it and ripped off its head, but I saw the gash on her body.

"Are you okay?" I asked. "You're bleeding."

"It won't kill me. Are you, Hung, and the princess okay?"

"We're okay," Hung replied.

"We're doing our best to take Princess Luzi to safety."

I felt the dragon's heart swell.

"The perfect name. The fused magic of time, space, and light is protecting you. But it's not moving as fast as it should."

"Why?" I asked.

"Because it is intelligent. It knows my baby is searching for Luzi."

The Dark Lorde appeared, opened its mouth, and released a terrifying shriek that trembled the bubble. Demonic creatures with multiple eyes and wings flew out of its mouth. Some even grew from its body and flew toward us.

Roar of the Sky let out a massive roar that reverberated through my body. Hung and I looked at each other as we released a breath. The dark storm broke apart, dispersing. All the sounds from the demonic snake and its evil creatures became an irrelevant backdrop.

A blast of energy escaped the dragon's mouth, moving toward us like colorful waves of energy. I could tell she'd channeled a lot of energy into her call. As the dragon approached closer, the dragonfly imprint on her forehead shone. I looked into her fractal eyes, and more patterns appeared. Within the geometric shapes, images flashed, reminding me of the hallways where I had seen the past, the present, and the future all in one space. I saw Lin Din Ni burning, dead bodies covering the bloodied ground, and a seed of light growing from a mountain of soot.

Tears rolled down my face as I understood what had happened. So many people have died in Lin Din Ni. Rage, sorrow, and fear collided in me. My beloved home was now devoid of life and light. Did any of my friends survive? I prayed for their safety.

The colors sparkled everywhere as the geometric shapes on her scales lit up. Another form of energy rushed through me and pulsed within the bubble.

Luzi giggled as she glanced around.

The Dark Lorde shouted an eerie command, and his swarm of evil creatures charged at Roar of the Sky.

"Behind you!" I shouted as the evil creatures that had swarmed the dragon surrounded us, trying to break through the bubble's surface. But when their beaks and claws touched the exterior, the surface burned them to cinders.

This enraged the Dark Lorde even more. Roar of the Sky swiped at the demonic human-faced snake. The force of her energy skewered the creature, cutting it into pieces. But the gash in the dragon's belly grew, and more blood poured out.

"Oh my God, you're bleeding so much!" I covered my mouth with one hand.

"You need to patch up your wound," Hung said.

"Don't worry about me." Roar of the Sky looked toward a red stream of sparkling light swimming toward her. "There you are, my son."

The red stream didn't look like a dragon but more like a thread of light that swam around the dragon's face, eyes, nose, and ears. I could feel the love radiating from Roar of the Sky's heart.

"You are Spark of the Light, and you have your mission. I'll be around."

The red stream sparked and swam to the gash on its mother's belly and created a stitch-like pattern that stopped the bleeding.

Luzi giggled and babbled as the bracelet on her wrist sparked too. As the hair reacted, the red stream sparkled as though they were having a quiet conversation no one understood but them.

"I must go now. The cosmic rip is too wide. My mate and the other dragons need me."

"Thank you for your help," Hung said.

The dragon nodded. "Thank *you*, Su and Luzi. We must all work together to win this fight against the darkness."

"Will we see you again?" I asked, still worried about her wound.

"When the time is right." She opened her claw, and an oddly shaped fruit with a single leaf appeared on her palm. She gestured to me, and the fruit entered the bubble. "This is a cosmic fruit that will provide the nutrients for her to grow."

"You think of everything," I said with gratitude. I was afraid I couldn't produce milk for Luzi and she'd starve to death.

"I'm also a mother, so I know what's needed." She looked at me with warmth. "You're now a mother, and you a father." She turned to Hung. "Thank you for taking on this important responsibility. We—the Infinara Dragons—are indebted to you." She nodded at us, and her horns glowed, followed by her scales.

Hung placed a fist to his chest and bowed to the dragon. Then he wrapped an arm around me.

Roar of the Sky gestured to the red stream flowing around her. "It's time."

The red stream entered the bubble and swam to Luzi, who smiled at it. It emitted a tremendous bright light that blinded me. The bubble sped dizzyingly fast, as though whatever had held it back had broken free. A burst of energy erupted within the bubble, and I lost consciousness.

CHAPTER SEVENTY-EIGHT

HUNG

THE SOUND of birdsong woke me. I opened my eyes, and a loud chirp burst right beside my ear. I spied a small scarlet bird perched on a branch of a fallen tree, gawking at me. How could a small thing make such a racket? It cocked its head, chirped again, and flew down to land on a small rock beside me. A blue dragonfly flew by and landed on the bird's head before it landed on my arm, reminding me of Roar of the Sky, Su, and Luzi.

Fear made me shoot straight up off the grassy ground. I grabbed my sword, lying next to me, and secured it to my back. Glancing around, I searched for Su and Luzi. Relief settled when I spotted them leaning against a tree trunk a few feet away. We were in the woods, and the sun shone in the blue sky. I didn't hear or sense danger around us. My sword didn't react. I got up, but my legs wobbled. I waited a beat, inhaled, and exhaled to help my body to adjust to wherever I was. When I felt anchored, I hurried over to Su, who was still sleeping. Baby Luzi was also sound asleep.

I placed a gentle hand on Su's shoulder, slowly waking her. I had to ensure they weren't injured after the blast in the magical bubble. She cracked her eyes open, saw me, and smiled.

"Are you okay?" I asked.

"Yes. You?" She glanced down at her arm wrapped around Luzi.

"I'm okay." I pulled her to a standing position, still wary of our surroundings.

"Oh no!" she gasped and searched around. "The cosmic fruit. I need it."

I saw a bulge inside Luzi's wrap and reached in, pulling it out. "It's right here."

"We need to find a place to settle so I can prepare this fruit to feed Luzi. She'll be hungry."

Nodding, I embraced her, taking a moment to appreciate our survival. "We'll be okay."

"I know." She lifted her face to me. "Do you think the others made it to safety?"

I'd been in many battles, but none could compare to the one we just experienced. I knew in my heart that many people had died, but I prayed that Kai, Yunxi, Gong, Healer Churan, Tao, and Keiya and her warriors had survived.

"I hope so," I told Su.

Hope was the light that kept us going.

Hope was the magical thing with scales that swam into your soul.

It roared like a beast, sharing cosmic stories. It revealed the impossible with its all-seeing eyes. Most of all, it opened our hearts with an honest ferocity while taking us on an unforgettable journey. And all it asked was for us to protect that which gave hope—the light. Without light, there was no hope.

I looked at Luzi—our symbol of hope—who wore an adorable expression as though nothing in the world could disrupt her heavenly sleep. I thought about my good friends, Wei and Yeeva, who had sacrificed their lives for their daughter's safety, including Su's and mine.

As we walked out onto a deserted dirt path, Su turned to me. "What are you thinking about?"

"Vengeance," I admitted.

She paused on her feet and released a breath. "I'm glad you said that. It's what's echoing in my head too. The Dark Lorde still exists somewhere, which means he'll never stop searching for us. He's killed so many innocent people. My blood boils every time I think about him."

I rubbed her back. "He will pay. We're not the only ones fighting him." I looked up at the sky. "Roar of the Sky and others are fighting battles simultaneously somewhere. Right now, I'm only focusing on taking care of you and Luzi."

With her hand in mind, we ambled down the path.

"Where do you think we are right now?" Su asked.

"Not sure." I surveyed the woods on either side of the path. There was no signage and no travelers in sight.

Su walked over to the edge of the path and plucked a plant with red flowers. "This is the moonblood fern native to the Central Empire. Vendors often came to sell this to the apothecary. It helps reduce cramps during a woman's moon cycle."

"Oh," I said, understanding.

The Central Empire was about eight hundred miles away from Luklum. We'd traveled so far. I didn't dismiss the fact that their army had assisted General Zhou and the Rebel Territory in defeating Lin Din Ni. Was the Emperor of the Central Empire aware of his army's involvement? Or was this an act of a rogue general?

Laughter and water splashing echoed in the distance. Su glanced at my uniform. "I think you should strip out of that armor. We'll hide it somewhere. It's safer to blend in—be a commoner."

I agreed and removed my armor, leaving only the cotton tunic and pants. I tucked the armor into a crevice made from three boulders. "We'll retrieve it later." I also slid my sword into the hiding spot.

We walked toward the sounds and saw a river flowing down big rocks.

I slung an arm around Su. "We're a couple looking for a place to settle after bandits raided our village."

Su smiled. "I love your strategy."

My heart pulsed, wanting to say more, but I'd wait until later.

A woman with a friendly face and a basket on her hip made her way in our direction. She stopped when she spotted us.

Luzi woke and babbled. The woman with the basket looked at Luzi, and her cautious expression softened. She wore simple cotton clothing, revealing she wasn't part of a noble family. But then again, she could be a maid working for a prominent family.

"Are you looking for someone?" asked the woman. "I don't recognize you, and I've lived in this village for a long time." She peered over at Luzi, who smiled at her. "She's adorable. How many months old is she?"

I looked at Su to answer the question.

CHAPTER SEVENTY-NINE

SU

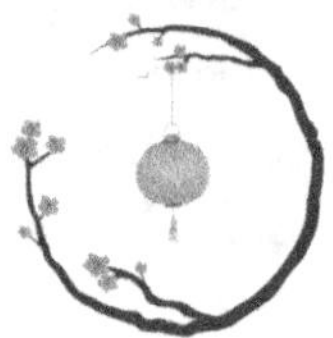

AS LUZI SQUIRMED in my arms, I bounced in place, trying to calm her. A bath and a change of clothes would comfort her.

I looked down at Luzi, who seemed so much more aware than a newborn barely an hour old. She looked more like a baby who was at least three months. I didn't want any questions about it. We had to be anonymous to ensure our safety.

"Luzi is only three months old. We're searching for a new home. Bandits destroyed our village. They killed everyone," I said as sadness naturally choked me up. I didn't need to pretend.

My home was destroyed, and vengeance rose like bile, burning my throat. It burrowed inside me like a terminal disease with no cure, poking and prodding at me. I acknowledged it and shoved it aside. Luzi needed love to grow and mature. Hate would ruin her.

"Do you know of a place we can stay?" I continued.

The woman placed a hand on her heart. "Oh, dear. That's awful. We heard about the tragedy in Lin Din Ni three months ago. I can only imagine the destruction and terror the people had to endure. Two others also escaped that horror and live in our village now."

Hope surged through me. "What are their names?"

"Kai and Yunxi. Do you know them?"

"We're friends." Hung placed a comforting hand on my lower back.

Joy rushed through me, and I couldn't stop myself from crying.

The woman placed a gentle hand on my arm. "Don't cry. We'll help you start over. Our Tenduk Village is small, and no one bothers us. We live simple but happy lives. There's plenty of room for your family. My name is Thu."

"I'm Su, and this is our baby girl, Luzi."

"I'm Hung, her husband." He met my gaze, smiled, and squeezed my hand. We had talked about this topic a while back. It seemed so long ago, the dreams of a wedding with friends and family. But now I just wanted to be with this man who loved me. A man who motivated me to chase my dreams and taught me the skills to defend myself and others.

I leaned into him, a yes to his indirect question. He kissed the top of my head.

Thu looked at us and giggled. "Let me introduce you to some new friends." She turned toward the river. "Ladies! Come over here!"

Three women approached and studied us. Each carried a basket of wet clothes. Thu briefed them on our situation.

"Hello. I'm Binh," said the woman with a side braid. "I'm sorry you had to experience that horror. I know what it feels like to lose a family member. My grandmother recently died."

"If you don't mind," said the woman with a big mole near her lip, "I have an extra room in my house. Stay as long as you need. All I ask is that you"—she pointed to Hung—"help my husband in his pottery shop. You look like you have skilled hands. I'm Yin, by the way."

"My name is Lei, and Tenduk is happy to have you," said the woman with a floral hairpin. "You can help Yunxi at her apothecary. She started it out of her home."

"I'm a healer too, so that's perfect," I said.

"What is Kai doing?" Hung asked.

"He's also helping my husband with his pottery shop," Yin said. "We often bring our goods to the markets to sell."

"I'm happy to help." Hung nodded.

The women surrounded me as we walked toward their village. Hung followed but stayed behind us, keeping watch.

"He's so handsome," Thu said. "The ladies in the village won't stop gawking. I hope you don't mind."

"I'm used to it."

They can gawk, but they can't touch, was what I wanted to say. But these women seemed harmless. I peered over my shoulder and met Hung's eyes. Love and relief splashed onto his face. We both couldn't wait to see Yunxi and Kai.

The women shared their romance stories with me, making me laugh. I needed the laughter more than I thought. Luzi had fallen back asleep, looking more adorable every time I stole a glance at her.

"If you ever need advice about things that happen in the bedroom, let me know," said Binh. "I've got books for you."

Yin slapped a playful hand on her arm. "Su is new here. Let her settle first. You're going to scare her."

"What do you mean? Every woman needs a copy of *The Art of Seduction* and *The Art of Intimacy.*"

Heat blossomed onto my cheeks, followed by sadness. Did Healer Churan and Gong make it out alive?

Not wanting to ruin the moment, I leaned in. "I had copies of both, but they were lost in the fire."

Binh stopped in her steps, propping a hand against her round hips. "Don't worry. I'll give you one of each!"

We arrived at the village, a quaint area thriving with life and love. The small business section reminded me of the Market Square. We met about ten families who welcomed us. When Yin led us to her pottery shop, I saw Kai and Yunxi eating lunch at an outside table.

"I'm going to hang these clothes to dry. Rest up. You're safe here." She smiled and walked to the house next to the pottery shop.

"Su!" Yunxi spotted me, placed her chopsticks down, and rushed over. "I was so worried about you!" She looked at me and then at Luzi. "We have so much to catch up on."

"We certainly do."

Kai and Hung exchanged their brothers-in-arms greetings and whispered on the side.

"Do you know if Healer Churan and Gong are safe?" I asked.

She shook her head. "After we settled here, Kai started searching for survivors and listening to any news. But nothing yet."

Hung walked up to Yunxi and placed a hand on her shoulder. "Glad you're safe."

Kai offered me a warm smile and looked at Luzi. "She's adorable. It's safe here, so you can rest up."

"How did you escape?" Hung asked as he helped me sit on the bench and sat beside me.

"Hold on a moment." Yunxi lifted a hand. "Let me get you some food first."

Yunxi got us each a bowl of noodle soup from an eatery down the road and placed them in front of us.

My stomach growled, and I looked at Luzi, who released a babbling sound. She hadn't been crying like I had expected. I peeked into her wrap and saw golden energy from the cosmic fruit encircling Luzi. It was transferring energy into her body. I had assumed I had to cut open the fruit to extract the juice to feed her, but I was wrong.

Yunxi sat beside Kai and bumped shoulders with him. "You want to start?"

"It was a miracle how we survived. The fireballs killed some of the Krix soldiers and the demonic snakes. But more kept coming up from the ground. We couldn't defend against so many. But water filled the holes, and we saw fish attacking the demonic snakes, biting into their scaly skin. It looked like the Inca fish from the Green Fog River."

"Interesting," Hung said. "Maybe Tao and Keiya helped us."

Kai nodded. "But I don't know where they are."

"We'll find them." Yunxi placed her hand over Kai's. "One of the holes sucked me into it, and Kai saw me and leaped to grab my hand. The water took us somewhere and spat us out in the woods at the border of Lin Din Ni and the Central Empire. We walked for a while and met some friendly villagers."

Yunxi and Kai continued to share their tale about how they'd settled in Tenduk.

Soon after, we gathered around a memorial that Kai and Yunxi had set up at the back of their home. Hung, Kai, Yunxi, and I offered food, wine, tea, and flowers to all those who had passed. We thought about Emperor Tang, Empress Yeeva, Gong, Healer Churan, Tao, Keiya and the river warriors, Three-Eyes, Blue Orchid, and all the innocent people of Lin Din Ni. We asked the heavens to bless those who had survived.

May they start over safely wherever they are.

My chest constricted, thinking about Roar of the Sky fighting the dark.

May the Cosmos bless her, her family, and Tempo wherever they are.

Maybe they wished the same for us somewhere out there. I had faith that we'd meet again someday.

Hung and I didn't discuss that it had been three months since the devastation. We'd been through yet another time warp. Exhaustion tugged at me, and I asked to take a bath. Yunxi offered to watch Luzi, who was still passed out. She was astounded by the cosmic fruit feeding the baby.

After my much-needed bath, I returned to see Yunxi wiping Luz's body with a wet cloth. Luzi looked around with curious eyes but didn't cry. A fresh baby wrap sat on the table.

"Did you see her red birthmark?" Yunxi gestured to the top of Luzi's right arm.

I studied the red flower mandala on Luzi and smiled. "It's a dragon blessing."

Was Spark of the Light dormant in Luzi's body? Or was he somewhere else? The baby dragon had connected with Luzi while we were inside the magic bubble, but I didn't know what happened after that. Had he come only to connect and return to wherever he was?

Or was he waiting for Luzi to be strong of mind, body, and energy before their connection could strengthen? It took a while for me to connect with Roar of the Sky. Perhaps it would be the same for Luzi.

"We're married now," Kai told us.

"Isn't he lucky?" Yunxi wrapped Luzi in her new cloth and swayed her.

I smiled, loving the joyful expression on my friend's face. Yunxi deserved all the happiness in the world.

"He's very lucky," Hung said, taking my hand and lifting it for a kiss. "And so am I."

That night, we stayed in the house Kai rented from Yin's family. They had an extra room for us. Yin didn't mind as Hung promised to help her husband Tuan and his pottery shop.

Yunxi offered to take Luzi for the night to give Hung and me a break. After Hung took his bath, he dressed in a cotton tunic and pants Kai gave him.

"I have something to show you." He offered his hand.

I stopped folding the clothes Yunxi had given me to use until I could buy my own.

I slid my hand into his.

"Feeling refreshed?" I asked.

"Feels good to wash off the dirt and death from the past."

"This is our new beginning," I said.

I couldn't forget the past. It became the painful threads that wove the fabric of our future.

Hung led me to the backyard, where a small garden sat in the corner. The crescent moon glowed in the sky.

He turned to me. "I know we've talked about this before. And I wish I could give you a better marriage proposal."

I pressed my finger to his lips. "You've already asked me two times. They were indirect, but I knew."

He brushed his knuckles down my cheek. "And you gave me an indirect yes."

I smiled. "If you want to hear it out loud, then yes, I'll marry you, my love."

He kissed me, drew back, and said, "Let's make it official. Let's get married under the moonlight. The heavens, earth, moon, sky, trees, and animals are our witnesses."

Tears filled my eyes as I dropped to my knees on the patch of grass alongside Hung. He held my hand as he looked up at the moon and promised to love and protect me forever.

I did the same, feeling so much love and warmth in my chest.

Ba, Mẹ, *I hope you approve of your son-in-law.* We loved each other in ways I could never explain. Hung reached into his pocket and took out a gold necklace with a pendant made from the fulgurite stone. He got up and assisted me to a standing position. Then he hooked it around my neck, and the gemstone glowed, resonating with my energy.

Stepping back, he studied me. "It's beautiful."

I looked down at the gorgeous necklace. "When did you get this?" I could wear this tonight but would have to put it away to avoid questions from the curious villagers.

"When I knew you were the only woman for me. Yeeva had an extra piece of the stone when she gave me your fulgurite dagger, so I asked the jeweler to make it."

"I don't have a gift for you," I said, feeling guilty.

"I don't need anything. All I need is *you.*" Hung kissed me and leaned into my ear. "I'll be happy with an unforgettable wedding night with my *wife.*"

I looked up at him, and desire darkened his eyes. "Then I have the perfect gift for you, my *husband.*"

He scooped me into his arms and whisked me into the bedroom, loving me the way a warrior husband knew how to love.

EPILOGUE

FIVE YEARS *later*

Su

I stood beside five-year-old Luzi and demonstrated the tiger claw stance.

"Look, *Mẹ*!" My adorable daughter, with her hair in the pigtails she'd desperately begged for, mimicked me with precision.

Her ability to see, learn, and process everything was indescribable. I shouldn't be surprised at her advancement. As a newborn, she'd been more aware than any baby I'd encountered.

As her mother, I wanted her to have a happy, peaceful, and safe life. But I knew Luzi's life demanded more from her. People always said that *with great power comes great responsibility*. But great responsibilities often came with mistakes, heartache, and pain. All I could do was prepare Luzi for all the things coming her way. I wanted her heart to be strong. A powerful heart could endure an avalanche of unexpected things. Even the best warriors crumbled sometimes.

"Show me how you would protect someone in need, my little egg custard," I said. Egg custard buns were her favorite pastries.

With her feet spread apart, her knees bent, and little fingers formed into claws, she struck at an invisible enemy with a swift swipe and a cute roar. My heart erupted with so much love as I saw Yeeva and Wei in her.

I smiled as I watched my daughter practice her kung fu techniques she'd learned from Hung, Uncle Kai, and me. Hung and I had started a martial arts school called Dynamic Martial Arts for anyone interested in learning how to defend themselves. We had students starting from five years old. It was important to teach young children—boys *and* girls—how to connect to their bodies and their energies. So far, we had ten children, five women, and twenty men.

Besides helping at the kung fu school, I also worked at the Tenduk Apothecary. The village had grown in size since we first settled here. The Central Empire didn't pay attention to a small village like us, which was exactly what we needed to keep Luzi safe.

Luzi's birthmark hadn't changed since she acquired it on that fateful day. Was Roar of the Sky still locked in battle? Had all her eggs hatched yet? Or were they waiting for the perfect match? How was Tempo?

I'd tried to connect to Roar of the Sky several times, but she'd never responded. I prayed she was safe. Her son, Spark of the Light, had remained quiet on Luzi's bicep, looking like another geometric floral shape. A part of me wanted to meet this dragon, but I knew that when it awakened, it would only mean change and danger. So I was at peace, letting it sleep so that my daughter could grow up undisturbed.

Whenever Luzi bathed and asked about the red birthmark, we told her it was a blessing from the heavens, and that she was meant for magnificent things. Birthmarks were artwork the heavens drew on us.

"They're symbols that the heavens are watching over you," I had told her.

Luzi didn't know about her real parents yet. I'd tell her when she got older. It was too dangerous to give her that information now. Children often told the unvarnished truth, not understanding the consequences. Who could be listening to her talking? For now, her safety was my priority.

Luzi ran from one end of the yard to the other, turned around, leaped, flipped, and landed with one hand on the floor. She rushed over to me, throwing her arms around me.

"What's that for?" I asked.

She drew back and looked at me. "Because I love you so much! *Ba* too! And Uncle Kai and Aunt Yunxi."

"We love you too." I brushed a hand over her hair.

Luzi darted off, performing the monkey formation and snake attack. "I saw Uncle Kai do this the other day. He looked funny." She swayed and performed the drunken kung fu style.

I laughed. "That's not for kids to learn yet."

Luzi tossed me a mischievous look that told me she would continue to practice the drunken move simply because it was forbidden. I saw myself in her—defiance and the need to carve her own path. Defiance wasn't always a bad thing. To defy that which was wrong was a good thing. To defy a law that promoted pain and suffering deserved my respect and admiration.

Luzi saw a pink butterfly and chased after it. My heart swelled, wondering if that was Luzi Shen's spirit coming to say hello. I thought of her whenever I looked at Luzi.

When the butterfly disappeared, she continued practicing her kung fu. I busied myself with sorting the dried herbs. From the corner of my eye, I saw Luzi practice the drunken move. She snuck a glance my way a few times, probably wondering if I could see her. I pretended not to. She needed to get it out of her system without me having to tell her.

As I sorted the lavender and yarrow, I wondered what had

become of Lin Din Ni—of Luklum. But I didn't want to jeopardize Luzi's safety. I'd visit it someday soon.

Hung opened the bamboo gate to the backyard of a home he and Kai had built. Kai and Yunxi lived down the path from us.

Beaming, Luzi ran to her father with open arms. "*Ba!* You're back!"

He scooped her up, kissing her on the cheek. She slung an arm around his neck, returning the kiss.

"How was your day? Did you practice your kung fu?" He tugged at her pigtail, and she giggled.

My heart melted at her bond with him.

"Uh-huh." She nodded and slid down from his arm. "I've got something amazing to show you later." Her eyes widened. "It's my new skill. *Me* thinks it's 'outstanding.'"

Luzi's ability to access her essa already was incredible. She wielded her own magic in no time. I knew the stored essa her parents had given her boosted her development.

"Oh really? I can't wait. I brought something back for you."

She gasped and looked at the bag in his hand. "Yum."

"How do you know what it is, my curious egg custard?" he asked.

"I can smell yum." She touched her nose and inhaled.

Hung laughed as he sat beside me. Luzi squeezed herself between us on the bench, her eyes fixed on the bag of yum.

Hung opened the bag and took out an egg custard bun for Luzi and one for me.

"I can eat ten of these!" Luzi exclaimed with a stuffed mouth.

I broke off a piece of the bun, offering it to my handsome husband. He opened his mouth for me to feed him.

"Any news?" I asked.

He shook his head. Whenever he made a trip into a big city in the Central Empire, he asked around for news of any survivors from Lin Din Ni. Yesterday, he accompanied Kai and Tuan to sell pottery in Blue Crane City. We held onto hope that someone we knew was still alive.

Luzi finished her two egg custards. "All done!" She took the napkin on the table and wiped her mouth, smearing some custard across her cheek. "Want to see my amazing skill now?"

Hung

"Show us," I said.

Smiling, Luzi rushed over to the edge of our yard and plucked a couple of blade-shaped leaves from a plant with her small fingers. She waved them back and forth with a mischievous look. Light radiated from the leaves and they hardened, seemingly turning to metal. She whipped one toward the tree in front of her, and it landed in the bark like a dart.

My mouth dropped as I looked at Su, who smiled with pride.

"When did you discover this?" I asked.

"Yesterday. Apparently, she's been doing this with fallen leaves." Su gestured to a basket filled with little metal leaves.

I couldn't believe my daughter could create weapons from leaves. I got up and walked over to Luzi. "May I see it?"

Beaming, Luzi dropped the leaf into my hand, sat at the table, reached into the pastry bag, and pulled out another custard bun.

I held the leaf-weapon by the stem and examined how the edges had curled, forming a dart while still keeping the "leaf" aspect.

"Phenomenal. This is her gift." I met Su's gaze.

"One of her gifts." Su looked at our daughter, who was busy eating her bun and looking at a dragonfly that had landed on the table.

"Hello," Luzi said to the little bug. "You're so pretty." When she touched the bug, it didn't fly off immediately.

Luzi dug into the bag of pastries and took out two buns. "I saved these for you." She looked at me and her mom.

"That's very thoughtful of you. Thank you." I took a bun and bit into it.

"Can you show me the death touch, *Ba*?" Luzi asked.

"No," Su said. "Wait until you're older."

A smirk slid onto my lips as I looked at Su. The last thing we needed was parents complaining that Luzi had frozen their kids in place at school or at the playground.

"I want you to focus on what we're teaching at school. The Dim Mak is for very few people."

"But I see you and *Mẹ* practicing it. I want to be a powerful warrior, like both of you."

"You'll be better than us," I said. "Besides, you don't need to know the death touch to be a powerful warrior." I tapped her heart. "A powerful warrior is someone with a warrior's heart. She's courageous, smart, kind, and listens to her parents."

"And she loves to eat egg custard buns."

Su and I laughed.

"Can I ask you for a favor?" I waved the leaf dart. "This is something you only do at home with us, okay? Don't show anyone else."

"Why?"

"Because it's going to make the other kids sad. They don't have your skills."

"Oh. Okay. I don't want my friends to be sad." She smiled. "They love doing the tiger stance."

The dragonfly returned and flew by Luzi. She chased after it with glee. Was that Roar of the Sky saying hello? Maybe this was her way of saying she was still around, busy doing dragon things.

Su laced her fingers in mine as we stood watching our daughter chase after a dragonfly. I reveled in this simple happiness. I had the best wife and the most talented daughter. What else could I ask for? I was a fulfilled man, even though I knew there would be a day when Luzi needed to know the truth about her past and reclaim her empire. For now, we were content with taking life one day at a time.

Thank you so much for reading! Don't miss the next book, **Spark of the Light**!

https://callazae.com/books/spark-of-the-light/

Here's a Roar of the Sky **bonus scene**!

Sign up for my **newsletter** to get the latest news on my books!

https://callazae.com/newsletter/

ACKNOWLEDGMENTS

Where do I begin? There are not enough words to express my appreciation and gratitude to all the incredible people who walked beside me on this amazing journey.

To my remarkable team, Anna, Lindsay, Violet, and Sharon, thank you for your insights, edits, suggestions, proofreads, and friendships. I am blessed to have you in my circle.

To my wonderful PA, Mindy, I'd be lost without you. Thank you for your friendship, laughter, and assistance with everything from behind the scenes.

To my remarkable Street Team, I'm sending you a massive hug! Thank you for reading and telling everyone about my book. Your support and enthusiasm motivate me daily.

To my Kickstarter supporters, thank you for believing in this book. You were the first to see my words and art. Your support allowed me to make the special edition of Roar of the Sky the best it could be. I'm truly grateful.

To my fabulous readers, thank you for reading my stories. I get to write stories I love because of you.

Like always, I'm saving the best for last. Thank you to my extraordinary husband and children. Your support means the world to me. Most of all, thank you for tolerating my creative and workaholic ways. I hope I've made you proud.

All my love,

Calla

ALSO BY CALLA ZAE

Soldiers of Saedo Series

An Alien Rescue (Soldiers of Saedo, #1)

An Alien Crush (Soldiers of Saedo, #2)

An Alien Dare (Soldiers of Saedo, #3)

An Alien Storm (Soldiers of Saedo, #4)

An Alien Lore (Soldiers of Saedo, #5)

An Alien Spark (Soldiers of Saedo, #6)

An Alien Future (Soldiers of Saedo, #7)

Norakian Warrior Series

The Alien's Allegiance (#1)

The Alien's Defiance (#2)

Seraphim Angel Order Series

Unlock the Angel

For a complete list of my books:

www.callazae.com/books

ABOUT THE AUTHOR
CALLA ZAE

Calla Zae writes otherworldly romance. She loves delving into fantastical worlds where her imagination roams wild. Calla is also an artist who enjoys playing with colors, textures, and patterns. She has a love for mysticism, astrology, astronomy, Kdramas, Cdramas, true crime TV shows, romantic suspense novels, cats, and nature.

Calla lives in Massachusetts with her husband who keeps her grounded to Earth and two creative children who think she has her own secret planet. They're onto something...